"You are that little girl, Rachel," the nun said, her eyes filling with tears. "You are Alyssa Dassante's daughter, Lillie."

"Why are you telling me this now?" Rachel asked after a moment. "Thirty-one years later."

"I wouldn't have told you at all, but yesterday a man came to see me. He seemed to know Alyssa hadn't died and he wanted information about her."

"Who is he?"

The nun reached into her habit again. This time her hand came out holding a business card, which she handed to Rachel.

Rachel glanced at it. And had yet another shock as she read the gold-embossed card: Gregory Shaw—Shaw and Associates. "Gregory," she murmured.

"Do you know him?" Sister Mary-Catherine asked.

Oh, yes, she knew him. But what was Gregory doing looking for her birth mother? From what she'd heard, he was no longer a struggling P.I. but the owner of a very successful agency. Why would he waste his time on such a small case? Unless he was doing someone a favor.

"Heggan weaves together several suspense plots into a satisfying whole...."
—*Publishers Weekly* on *Trust No One*

CHRISTIANE HEGGAN

ENEMY WITHIN

MIRA®

ISBN 1-55166-577-8

ENEMY WITHIN

Copyright © 2000 by Christiane Heggan.

Visit us at www.mirabooks.com

Printed in U.S.A.

**To Catherine Rieger
whose friendship I treasure**

ACKNOWLEDGMENT

I wish to extend a special thanks to Richard Hedrick
of Kornell Champagne Cellars, Calistoga, California,
for explaining, most convincingly, why American
champagne houses feel justified in calling
sparkling wine "champagne."

Equal thanks to Joan Allen of Sterling Vineyards,
Calistoga, California, for giving me the grand tour and for
introducing me to some of the country's greatest wines.

Thanks also to Darcy Barboza of Beaulieu Vineyard,
Rutherford, California, for graciously agreeing to give me
a firsthand view of what happens during the crush,
and for allowing me to taste BV's fabulous wines.

I would like to express my gratitude to winemaker
Bob Masyczek, also at Beaulieu Vineyard, for taking
time from his busy schedule to answer my numerous
questions. Any errors or liberties taken in the interest
of fiction are my own.

Many thanks also to Dianne Moggy, Amy Moore-Benson
and everyone at MIRA for their continued support.

And finally, thanks to my wonderful, ever-encouraging
agent, Maureen Walters.

Prologue

"She's alive."

At those words the man behind the desk tightened his grip on the phone. "Are you sure?" His voice, always so strong and steady, had become a hoarse whisper. "You've had false leads before."

"Not this time," the private investigator replied. "The information came from a very reliable source—a forger who made a passport for her."

The man's free hand reached for a pencil and squeezed it, hard. "You mean, she moved abroad?"

"Looks that way."

"Any idea where?"

"She didn't give my guy any information. She showed up at his place a week or so after the accident, told him what she wanted and paid cash."

Cash she had stolen from his house. "This forger... He came to you, just like that? After thirty-one years?"

"He didn't come to me. I tracked him down."

"How?" he asked suspiciously.

The investigator didn't seem to mind the third degree. He was used to it. "I'm doing some work for a local mobster, an old gizzard with friends in all the wrong places. When I told him I needed to find a woman who may have moved abroad under an alias more than thirty years ago, he put me in touch with the forger."

"What's this forger's name?"

The P.I. gave a short laugh. "Sorry. He'd rather remain anonymous. You understand." He paused. "He wouldn't talk, though. Not until I gave him five grand. I hope it's okay," he added, sounding a little uncertain. "You did say money was no object."

The man gave an impatient wave. "I don't give a rat's ass about the money. I just want to be sure he's not bullshitting you."

"He's not. He recognized the woman from a photograph the police circulated throughout the area at the time of the accident. She wore thick glasses and had a different hair color when she came to see him, but it was her. My friend stakes his reputation on it."

"What name did she use?"

"Virginia Potter."

In the darkened room, the man inhaled deeply, then slowly released his breath. It *was* her. Virginia had been her mother's name.

"She also gave him an address in Seattle," the P.I. continued. "I checked it out. It was phony."

Though the news he had just heard was a shock to his system, it didn't come as a surprise. He had been one of the few, then ultimately the only one who hadn't bought that ridiculous "accidental death" crap.

"Can't you see what she did?" he had bellowed at the police sergeant in charge of the investigation. "She faked her death by pushing her car over the cliff, then calmly walked away."

Doubtful, the authorities had nonetheless issued an all-points bulletin for the entire central California coast while divers searched the ocean floor. All they had recovered, besides the car, was a suitcase full of clothes—hers and the baby's.

At the end of the third day, the police had ordered an end to the search and had declared both woman and child dead by drowning.

He, on the other hand, had never stopped looking.

Because memories of that tragic night were never far from his mind, the hatred rose to his throat, swift and thick. That miserable slut. He had opened his home to her, treated her as a daughter. And how had she repaid him? By killing his most precious possession. His firstborn. His Mario.

But now, at last, his prayers had been answered. She was alive. And by God, he would find out where she was hiding. Not so she could be brought to justice—prison was too good for what she had done—but so *he* could punish her. He'd make the bitch suffer, nice and slow. When he was finished with her, death would be a blessing.

The thought of avenging his son's death in ways only he could imagine made him almost giddy with anticipation. Ah, yes, the long wait had been worth it, after all.

Slowly he squared his shoulders. This time when he spoke, his voice was once again strong. "Find her," he told his caller.

And snapped the pencil in two.

One

"Courtney!" In her hotel room high above Paris's right bank, Rachel Spaulding stared at her fingernails in mock horror. "What are you doing to me?"

Rachel's fifteen-year-old niece, a spunky, self-proclaimed fashion guru, gave Rachel's hand a light slap. "Adding a little oomph to your looks. And keep still, will you? Unless you want polish smeared all over your fingers."

"I agreed to a manicure," Rachel protested. "Not to have my fingernails painted harlot red."

Courtney chuckled but kept her head bent over Rachel's hand. "It's the latest shade, and it's not called harlot red. It's *Rouge de Passion*," she added in almost flawless French. "The saleswoman at the Lancôme counter said no man on earth would be able to resist it."

"Yes, well, I'm not here to inspire passion, but to win back Monsieur Fronsac's business."

"And you will." Courtney dipped her brush back into the small bottle and wiped the excess polish against the rim. "French men love women who aren't afraid of a little boldness every now and then."

Rachel couldn't quite hold back a smile. "Since when did you become such an authority on French men?"

Her brush held in midair, Courtney gave Rachel a knowing look. "I'm almost sixteen, Aunt Rachel. Not six."

"I see."

Rachel looked fondly at her niece. Only two months away from her sixteenth birthday, Courtney Aymes was what most people would define as the typical California girl. She had long, silky blond hair, blue eyes that were a trademark of all Spaulding women, and long, shapely legs that had not gone unnoticed with the customs inspectors at Charles de Gaulle Airport yesterday.

Rachel adored her niece. She was everything her mother, Rachel's sister, wasn't—warm, funny, caring and loyal to a fault. It was also no secret that Courtney had more in common with Rachel than she had with her own mother, something that never failed to aggravate Annie and fuelled her animosity toward her younger sister.

It was because of that animosity that Annie had flatly refused to let Courtney go to Paris with Rachel, even though classes hadn't yet started. Only when Grams had intervened, insisting the short trip would do Courtney good, had Annie finally given her permission.

"There." The teenager pulled back to admire her handiwork. "What do you think?"

"Well..." Rachel took a few seconds to study her perfectly laquered nails. "It's not a color I would have chosen for myself, but I have to admit, I don't hate it as much as I thought I would."

Courtney grinned. "Aren't you glad you brought me along?"

Rachel laughed. "Deliriously so. I don't know how I would have managed without you."

Leaning back in her chair, Courtney looked at Rachel from head to toe and gave a nod of approval. "You look hot."

Once again, Courtney's choice of words made Rachel

smile. The kid was definitely good for her ego. ''Thank you, sweetie.''

Holding her hands away from her so she wouldn't smudge the polish, Rachel walked to the large gilded mirror over the fireplace and inspected her reflection. At the last minute, and at Courtney's suggestion, she had opted for the understated but elegant black suit instead of the brown dress she had originally planned to wear. Never one to fuss with her looks, she had brushed her short brown hair back and had kept her makeup to a minimum—a dusting of blush on her cheeks and red gloss on her lips. It was a lot more than she wore at home in Calistoga where simplicity and comfort ruled. But, as Courtney never tired of reminding her, this *was* Paris.

Her gaze drifted to her left hand where the four-carat diamond solitaire Preston had given her for their engagement last month glowed brilliantly. When his mother's San Francisco jeweler had come to the Farley house for a private showing, Rachel had told the man she preferred simple, inconspicuous jewelery. But both Preston and his mother had been adamant. As the future wife of one of California's most promising attorneys, Rachel had to look the part—meaning, of course, she had to look affluent. She hadn't had the heart to disappoint them.

The thought of leaving the ring in the hotel safe came and went. She had to get used to the darn thing, and in a way, the expensive stone would make her feel as though Preston was right here, cheering her on. Lord knew she could do with a small dose of self-confidence right about now. This meeting with Monsieur Fronsac and his two associates had her in knots. According to Annie, the winery's marketing director, the man gave the word arrogance a new meaning, which was the reason Rachel had first turned down her grandmother's request to go to Paris to try to save the account.

"Annie is the one who insulted him," she had protested. "Let *her* go and apologize."

But Fronsac, the owner of France's largest chain of supermarkets, had wanted nothing more to do with Annie Spaulding or, for that matter, Spaulding Vineyards. In the end, Rachel had had no choice but to agree with her grandmother. If Spaulding Vineyards expected to earn a place in French markets, Monsieur Fronsac would have to be wooed back.

"You look as if you are about to face the guillotine," Courtney remarked with a giggle.

Rachel turned away from the mirror. "It shows, huh?"

"I'll say." Courtney tucked the bottle of nail polish in her makeup case. "But I don't know why you're so worried. I heard Grams and Preston talking the other day. They both agreed that if anyone can win back Old Goat Fronsac, it's you."

"Grams and Preston tend to overrate my abilities," Rachel replied. But deep down she was pleased at their faith in her. Especially Preston's. The son of a superior court judge and a San Francisco socialite, her handsome fiancé wasn't easily impressed. Needless to say, his compliments were few and far between.

Shaking off her apprehension, she waved her hands in the air. "Am I dry?"

Jumping from her chair, Courtney tested a nail with the tip of her finger and nodded. "Yes, ma'am."

Rachel walked over to the four-poster where her briefcase lay open and quickly checked the contents. Satisfied she had everything she needed for the meeting, she snapped the lid shut. "Wish me luck?" She gave Courtney a silly grin.

"Luck." Courtney gave her a quick hug. "And call me as soon as the meeting is over, okay? We'll celebrate your victory with a totally decadent lunch."

Rachel laughed. "You know something?" she said, wrapping her arm around her niece's waist as they both walked toward the door. "I *am* glad you came along."

It was ten minutes past eleven when Rachel emerged from the seventeenth-century building on rue Saint Jacques where Fronsac's office was located. Still feeling tense, she leaned against the facade and heaved a long sigh of relief.

After a grueling one-and-a-half hour meeting with Fronsac and his two associates, the businessman had agreed, for a price, to let bygones be bygones and to feature a select number of Spaulding wines in all of his five hundred stores.

It hadn't been easy. Or cheap. Annie's little blunder had cost the winery a whopping fifty percent case discount, five percent over what Fronsac had originally requested. She didn't know who she was more annoyed with, Annie or the Frenchman.

Her efforts, though, had been well rewarded. Not only had Fronsac signed on the dotted line, but he had insisted on announcing the deal between Supermarchés Fronsac and Spaulding Vineyards at a press conference.

Within twenty minutes, half a dozen reporters representing various newspapers and magazines had arrived, along with a television camera crew from France 2, and bombarded her with questions, in English, thank God.

Now that the excitement was over and the contracts signed, Rachel could finally feel herself relax. And Courtney's suggestion of a decadent lunch sounded even better than it had earlier.

Remembering her promise to call her niece, Rachel

scanned the busy street for a phone booth and spotted one only a few feet from La Sorbonne. Without missing a stride, she took her phone card from her purse and headed toward the famous university, inhaling the crisp autumn air as she walked.

Paris had always been one of her favorite places in the entire world. And nowhere did the City of Light look more appealing, or more French, than it did right here in the Latin Quarter.

Long known as a haven for Bohemian intellectualism, and once the home of such luminaries as Ernest Hemingway, Jean-Paul Sartre and Maurice Chevalier, this lively neighborhood was, for many, the heart and soul of Paris.

Rachel had no idea why she felt such an attachment to France. Like many Americans, her first trip to Europe had taken place during her high school junior year. Of all the countries she had visited in those twelve hectic days—Italy, Switzerland, Germany and France—it was the latter that had made the strongest impression on her.

She had come back often after that, for brief vacations she managed to squeeze in every now and then. Fascinated, she had absorbed the rich history like a sponge, traveling through the lush countryside, discovering charming little villages off the beaten track and learning the language as she went.

As she neared the phone booth, a lively rendition of "When the Saints Come Marching In" made her look up. A saxophonist, one of the many street musicians who performed throughout Paris, stood in the middle of the sidewalk, playing with great gusto while onlookers clapped their hands to the music.

By the time Rachel was able to make her way through the growing crowd, the phone booth was occupied. Rather than wait, she gave a careless shrug, dropped the token back into her purse and headed for the taxi stand.

Two

The sun was slowly rising above the Howell Mountains, its warm rays shimmering through the valley, turning the dew-covered grapes into tiny jewels.

Using a cane for support, Hannah Spaulding walked along a row of vines, something she had been doing every morning at this time of year for the past fifty-five years.

And what glorious years they had been, she reflected as her gaze swept over the sprawling five hundred acres that made up Spaulding Vineyards in the small town of Calistoga. It hadn't been easy, with Prohibition nearly destroying the Napa Valley's burgeoning wine industry, then the Great Depression and World War II soon after that. More than a hundred wineries in the Napa Valley alone had been forced to close operations during those difficult years. But Spaulding Vineyards, along with a handful of others, had managed to survive.

Then in 1968 something extraordinary happened. At a blind tasting in France, three Cabernet Sauvignons, one of which was produced by Spaulding, won major awards, beating vintage wines from Bordeaux and Burgundy. Suddenly the wines no one had wanted to take seriously were being talked about on both sides of the Atlantic, changing forever the way people perceived American winemaking.

Once again wineries began popping up like mushrooms, some growing so large they soon captured the world market. While Spaulding, with a production of five hundred thousand cases a year, was hardly a mom-and-pop operation, it had never been able to compete abroad. Until recently.

Hannah slowly resumed her walk. If Rachel was able to regain the Fronsac account—and Hannah felt certain she would—there would be no limit to what Spaulding could do. That's why she was still reluctant to give up control of the winery. Whatever lay ahead for Spaulding, Hannah wanted very much to be a part of it. But at seventy-six, and with two heart attacks behind her, her doctor's orders had been very strict. She was to avoid all stress and cut her work week from sixty hours to twenty. Hannah had scoffed at the ridiculous suggestion.

"Why, I'll die of inactivity within a week," she had told Dr. Warren. "You might as well bury me right now."

They had settled for thirty hours, with Hannah sneaking in a few more here and there.

Her girls, as she called her two granddaughters, had taken up the slack, each doing the job that suited her best. Annie's outgoing, exuberant personality had made her a shoe-in for marketing. Rachel, on the other hand, had shown an early fascination for winemaking and a love for the land that was just as strong as Hannah's.

A small smile played on Hannah's lips as she remembered the way Rachel, only a toddler at the time, used to cup the heavy grape clusters in her chubby little hands and bring them to her face to smell them. At age five she could name every grape Spaulding Vineyards grew and match them, correctly, with the wine produced. At ten, she was giving tours of the winery to her classmates and at sixteen, she worked in the cellars, hosing down the cement floors, scrubbing the tanks before harvest, doing whatever was required of her.

Now at thirty-one, she was well on her way to becoming one of the youngest and most talented winemakers in the valley. Hannah's only regret was that the girls had never learned to get along. Even now that they were grown up, the mere mention of Rachel's name made Annie bristle. Three years ago, tired of living under the same roof as Annie, Rachel had moved out of Hannah's home and bought her own house up on the Calistoga hills.

"Grams!"

At the sound of Annie's voice, Hannah turned in time to see her eldest granddaughter dismount Electra, the mare she had won as part of her fourth divorce settlement. With those snug riding pants, brown boots, and her fiery red hair glowing in the morning light, Annie looked nothing short of spectacular.

As usual when looking at Annie, Hannah was reminded of her late son Jack. He had possessed those same vibrant good looks, and for a while had been just as untamed and unpredictable as Annie. Marriage and a baby had changed him, thank God. But matrimony and motherhood hadn't changed Annie, who at thirty-nine and after four unsuccessful marriages, showed no sign of settling down. That was the reason Hannah had asked to speak to her this morning.

"Glad you could make it, dear," she said as her granddaughter kissed her cheek.

Annie wrapped the mare's bridle around her wrist and fell into step with Hannah. "I wouldn't pass up a chance to spend some quality time with you, Grams, you know that." She threw Hannah a mischievous grin. "Even if I have to get up at an ungodly hour to do so."

"You used to be an early riser, too."

"That was a long time ago." Annie raked back her hair,

made wild by the ride. "I'm a hardworking girl now. I need my eight hours' sleep."

"And you would have them," Hannah replied, "if you went to bed at a decent hour instead of closing every night-club in San Francisco."

As if she hadn't heard the comment, Annie bent over a ripe cluster, plucked a grape and popped it into her mouth. "Mmm. The cabernets are ready, aren't they?"

"Close."

"Careful." Annie looked west toward the Mayacamas, the mountain range that separated Napa Valley from the Pacific Ocean. "It may not look it right now, but rain is on the way."

Hannah followed her gaze. Even though the sky was a vibrant blue and the air was warm, she knew from experience how quickly the weather could turn at this time of year. "The trucks are standing by," she said with a nod. "Rachel is pretty certain we'll start picking on Friday."

"When did you hear from her?" Annie asked casually.

"This morning. She was a nervous wreck at the prospect of meeting Fronsac, though she has no reason to be. She'll do just fine."

Annie looked off into the distance. "Not like me, who always screws up."

"I didn't say that," Hannah protested.

"But that's what you were thinking."

"No, it's not."

"Oh, come on, Grams. Everyone knows you and Rachel have a special bond."

"If you're implying, *again*—" Hannah put added emphasis on the word "—that I love your sister more, then once again I'll have to tell you that you're wrong. That bond you mention does exists, that's true, but only because Rachel and I share the same passion for winemaking."

"And that passion makes her special."

"In a way, but it doesn't change the fact that I love you both the same, always have." Hannah studied the stubborn slant of Annie's chin, wondering if she would ever get through to her. "You two are the dearest people in my life, even though you're as different from one another as night and day."

"But it's Rachel you sent to Paris."

Hannah laughed. "Oh, darling, I could hardly have sent you, could I? If Monsieur Fronsac had any say on it, he'd have you banned from France forever."

"Fronsac is a jerk."

"Maybe so, but he is Spaulding's ticket to French markets." Her gaze settled on her beautiful, very outspoken granddaughter. "What could you have been thinking, darling? Insulting his Gallic pride by calling French wines inferior?"

"He made me mad." Annie kicked a stone and sent it flying. "He expected—no, correction, he *demanded* a forty-five percent case discount, and when I asked him if he would put Spaulding wines in a special display in return for my generosity, he just laughed at me and said that special displays were reserved for French wines. You should have heard him, Grams, acting as though he was doing us a *favor* by buying our wines." She turned to look at Hannah. "Is that why you called me here? To talk about that old grouch?"

"No." Their glances met briefly. "I wanted to talk to you about your new...conquest."

Annie raised a thin eyebrow, another gesture that reminded Hannah of her late son. "You mean, Rick Storm?"

"Yes. I understand you brought him back to the winery last night."

"How do you know?"

"It's hard to sleep through the roar of a Harley," Hannah said dryly.

"I'm sorry, Grams. I wasn't thinking. I should have asked him to leave the bike at the gate—"

Hannah made an impatient gesture. "I don't care about that. What does worry me, however, is that you're involved with him at all."

"Have you ever approved of any of the men I've dated?" Annie's tone was half teasing, half reproachful.

"Certainly. With the exception of that Argentinean gigolo who only wanted your money, I liked all your husbands. But this Rick Storm." She gave a disapproving shake of her head. "The man's a menace to society. Not a week goes by without him being involved in some bar brawl, or being arrested for assaulting a paparazzo, or for driving his bike at a hundred miles an hour through the streets of San Francisco."

"He's a rock star, Grams. Living on the edge is part of his image."

"And you're a Spaulding," Hannah snapped. "You, too, have an image to live up to." She heaved a helpless sigh. These intense conversations between her and Annie were getting more and more frequent lately, and although the girl always swore she would change, she never did. After four failed marriages, all because of her blatant infidelity, Annie was as wild as she had been in her college days.

"You don't have to worry anymore." Annie sent another spray of pebbles up in the air. "Rick and I are through."

"Oh." At last, good news. "How come?"

"He told me he was thinking of ordering some Spaulding wines for a party he's giving next week. Naturally, I agreed he should taste them first, which is why I brought him back here last night. When I realized all he really wanted was to get us both drunk, I kicked him out. I don't think I'll be hearing from him anytime soon.''

"Good.'' Hannah's voice softened. Maybe there was hope, after all. "I'm proud of you for standing up to him, Annie. You did the right—''

A sudden sharp pain shot through Hannah's chest, and she doubled over.

"Grams!'' Annie let go of her mare and wrapped her arm around her grandmother's waist. "What is it? What's wrong? Oh, my God,'' she cried as Hannah's knees slowly folded under her. "Is it a heart attack?''

Hannah tried to speak, but another pain, one that radiated through her entire chest, shot through her again. It *is* a heart attack, she thought, using all her willpower to stay conscious. And this one is bad.

Annie knelt beside her. "Don't die, Grams,'' she sobbed. "Please don't die.'' Then, as though realizing she had to do something, she lowered Hannah's head to the ground. "I'll go get help. You stay calm. I—''

But as Annie started to stand, Hannah's hand closed around her wrist. "No.''

"What do you mean, no? You're sick, Grams. You'll die if I don't get help.'' Another sob escaped from her granddaughter's throat. "What will become of me if you die?''

In spite of the excrutiating pain, Hannah wanted to laugh. How typical of Annie to think of herself at a time like this. "Too late for help, Annie. Need to…say…something.''

"Not now, Grams. I've got—''

"Listen to me.'' Hannah tried to take a breath and winced as the muscles in her chest constricted even more. She felt as if a big strong fist had taken hold of her heart and was slowly, mercilessly, squeezing the life out of it. "It's about Rachel…''

Annie's mouth tightened but she didn't say anything.

Hannah closed her eyes. Her breathing had turned shallow, and the sunlight, so bright and warm moments before, had begun to fade. Making a desperate effort, she squeezed Annie's hand again. "Tell Rachel...her mother...her *birth* mother, Alyssa, is alive."

Annie's mouth opened and her blue eyes grew huge with shock and disbelief. "But...she can't be. She died in childbirth."

"No, she didn't." Hannah licked her lips and took another short breath. "Rachel needs to know. Tell her...Sister Mary-Catherine...Our Lady of Good Counsel in Santa Rosa...will help."

As the light dimmed, Hannah struggled to keep her eyes open. She was running out of time. And there was still so much she needed to say. "Promise me... You'll...tell Rachel."

Waiting for a reply, Hannah tried to focus her gaze on Annie, but it was her late husband's face she saw instead. Dressed in the gray morning coat he had worn on their wedding day, Henry looked more handsome than ever, without a wrinkle on his face. The same beguiling smile that had turned her head so many years ago played on his lips. "Dear Hannah."

At the sound of his voice, the pain in her chest seemed to lessen and the anxiety she had experienced a moment before vanished. "Henry—"

"Grams! Grams!"

Annie's panicked cry brought her back and for a moment Hannah was filled with a great sadness at the thought of what her girls would have to go through. "Love you," she murmured.

She wanted to add "And Rachel," but Henry stepped closer. As he extended his hand, his gold wedding band caught the light and gleamed. "Come, Hannah," he said gently. "I've been waiting for you."

Hannah looked up at him, then with a small sigh she took his hand.

Three

"Aunt Rachel, come quick!" As Rachel walked into their hotel room, Courtney waved her over. "You're on TV!"

"Already?" Rachel glanced at the screen in time to see herself and Monsieur Fronsac smiling at the camera.

"Oh, darn," Courtney said as the shot disappeared and the broadcaster turned to other news. "It's over." Her disappointment short-lived, she turned to Rachel, her eyes glowing with excitement. "You did it, Aunt Rachel. Grams is going to be so proud of you."

Rachel tossed her briefcase onto a blue brocade sofa. "You can't imagine how relieved I am that it's all over. Your mother was right. Mr. Fronsac is an awesome negotiator. And those French reporters." She rolled her eyes. "They were relentless."

"Well, you must have done something right with them, too," Courtney said proudly. "Because they love you. They're calling you a modern day pioneer—the first American winemaker to have her wines distributed in Supermarchés Fronsac and, believe me, they made it sound like quite a coup." She snapped her fingers. "I know. Why don't we try to get a copy of that tape before we leave? Maybe Grams can talk one of our local TV stations into running it. Just think what such publicity would do for the winery."

Rachel laughed. It was one of the things she loved about Courtney. Even at her young age, she was already a born promoter, just like her mother.

"That's an excellent idea, Courtney. I'll call Mr. Fronsac after lunch to see if he can—"

She was interrupted by the ring of the telephone on the bedside table. Certain it was her grandmother calling about the meeting, she motioned to Courtney to turn down the volume on the television set before picking up the receiver. "Hello?"

"Rachel, it's Annie."

At the raw anguish in her sister's voice, Rachel's mouth went dry. "Annie, what's wrong?"

"It's Grams," Annie sobbed. "Oh, Rachel, she's dead. Grams is dead."

In the 767 taking her and Courtney back to the U.S., Rachel sat quietly, staring out the window, watching as white puffy clouds passed by. In the seat next to her, Courtney, exhausted from crying, slept.

Grams is dead.

Annie's words kept echoing in Rachel's head with a finality that brought a chill to her heart. The last time she had felt that same kind of grief had been fourteen years ago when the balloon her parents often used to fly VIPs over the vineyards had crashed, killing Jack and Helen Spaulding and their three guests.

Rachel had been devastated, certain that her own life had ended, as well. But thanks to Hannah, she had made it through that difficult year without major scars.

Wonderful memories of her grandmother rushed forth, bringing a lump to her throat. But one of them in particular stood out vividly. Her tenth birthday, the day her parents had told her, gently and lovingly, that she had been adopted.

Rachel could still remember the shock as if it were yesterday. Devastated, she had run to her room. She wasn't a Spaulding, she sobbed. She was a reject, a nobody someone had thrown away.

Refusing to listen to her parents, Rachel had later retreated to the only place she'd ever felt truly at peace—the vineyards. Grams had found her there, sitting on the ground, staring at the mountains and feeling sorry for herself. Hannah had sat beside her and, in that gentle voice of hers, had told her what Rachel's parents hadn't had a chance to explain.

"No one threw you away," she'd said, pushing Rachel's long brown hair from her damp face. "Your biological mother, barely seventeen, died in childbirth, and your father, not much older, was terrified at the thought of having to take care of a baby all by himself. So he left you in the care of loving nuns, women he knew would find you a good home. And they did," she'd added, bringing Rachel close. "Lord knows, we couldn't love you more if you had been born to us."

"Annie doesn't love me," Rachel had said stubbornly. "She hates me."

Grams had shaken her head. "Annie loves you in her own way. Someday you'll both realize that."

Rachel had never felt like a reject after that night. She had even learned to stand up to Annie, which hadn't been easy. But it wasn't until years later, when she had followed in Hannah's and Annie's footsteps and become an integral part of Spaulding Vineyards, that she had truly felt like a Spaulding.

What a team the three of them had made, Rachel recalled. Hannah with her incredible gift for winemaking,

Rachel with her vision for the future, and Annie with her flair for marketing Spaulding wines. A local newspaper, impressed by all that talent, had nicknamed them "Spaulding's Awesome Trio."

And now the Awesome Trio was minus one.

I should have paid more attention to her health, Rachel thought, suddenly torn with guilt. I should have forced her to cut down her hours at the winery even more. Instead I burdened her with insignificant little problems I should have been able to handle on my own.

Oh, Grams. Her heart aching with grief, Rachel pressed the back of her head against her seat and closed her eyes. I miss you already.

Alone in the big house where she had grown up, Annie sat in Grams's old rocker and stared at the fire Ming, the family housekeeper, had lit moments before. While October days could be blistering, the nights were often cool in the valley and Grams had always insisted on a fire.

Grams. She was gone now, Annie thought, feeling the prickle of fresh tears. Never again would she hear that warm, cascading laughter or the familiar click of Hannah's cane as she walked down the hall.

From the moment Annie was born, she had felt an inexplicable bond to Hannah. She wasn't just a beloved grandmother, but her best friend, the one person who had really understood her, who had loved her unconditionally. Oh, sure, they'd had their differences over the years. Grams could be so rigid at times, but no matter what stupid thing Annie did or said, Grams always forgave her.

Annie's damp gaze swept around the elegant parlor, remembering that it was in this very room that Grams had helped her through one of the most difficult periods of her life—the arrival of a new baby.

"Mama and Dad don't love me anymore," she had told Hannah only three days after Helen and Jack had brought Rachel home from the orphanage. Poker in hand, she had jabbed viciously at the burning logs. "All they care about is the baby."

Gently, Grams had taken the poker from Annie's hand and had sat her eight-year-old granddaughter on her lap. For the next half hour she had told her all about firstborns and the very special places they occupied in their parents' hearts. No one, she had told Annie, not even a new baby, could ever take that place away.

Hannah's words hadn't lessened Annie's resentment toward Rachel but it had made her feel important, and even a little superior, something she had never allowed herself to forget. And because she was so much smarter than her younger sister, she'd known exactly how to shift the blame onto Rachel for something she'd done, or, failing that, what theatrics to resort to so she wouldn't be punished.

"Oh, Annie," Hannah had often said. "I swear you should have been an actress."

It was Grams who had suggested Annie put her imagination to good use by joining Spaulding's marketing team. To her own surprise, Annie had loved the job instantly. She'd loved the day-to-day contacts with clients, the creation and development of new marketing techniques, the excitement a new campaign always generated.

In 1993, as the family celebrated Annie's thirty-second birthday, Hannah had announced that Spaulding's marketing director was retiring. Then, with a little flourish, she had handed Annie a contract and told her that as of that moment, *she* was to be Spaulding's new marketing director.

For the first time in her life Annie had been speechless. With tears in her eyes, she had read the contract, which had included a generous raise, bonuses and a five percent ownership of Spaulding Vineyards. No one had ever put that much faith in her before, and the thought that Hannah actually believed Annie could run an entire department had been absolutely incredible.

"I don't know what to say," Annie had murmured as everyone around the dining room table laughed.

"You don't have to say anything," Grams had replied. "Except that you'll do a good job."

And she had. For the most part. Unfortunately, Annie's fondness for handsome young men and her poor judgment regarding many of them had created havoc in her personal life and brought a great deal of friction between her and Grams.

The memory of the two of them walking through the vineyards yesterday morning, for the last time, was so painful that Annie bent forward in her chair, clutching her stomach. Then, as an awful thought came into her mind, she snapped back up. What if *she* had caused Grams's heart attack? All because of her involvement with that stupid, worthless rocker.

She shook her head. No. She mustn't think that. Grams had been sick for a long time. Old Doc Warren had said so.

"Hannah was on borrowed time," he had told Annie after Grams was pronounced dead. "And she knew it."

A small moan escaped Annie's throat. Why couldn't that borrowed time have lasted a few more years?

In the brick fireplace, blue and orange flames danced merrily. Sadness enveloped Annie as she realized the woman who had sat here two nights ago, watching similar flames, was gone forever.

Looking up at Hannah's portrait above the mantel, Annie wiped her tears. "You don't have to worry about the winery, Grams," she said, remembering her grandmother's promise that someday Annie would own Spaulding Vineyards. "I'll take good care of it. And I'll make you proud of me this time. That's a promise."

No longer able to hold back the flow of tears, she lowered her head into her hands and wept helplessly.

The first two people Rachel saw as she stepped out of the Cessna she had chartered to fly her and Courtney from San Francisco to Calistoga were Spaulding's head winemaker, Sam Hughes, and his wife Tina.

Sam had been a dear, devoted friend of the Spaulding family for close to thirty years. At sixty-five, he was a robust man with a full head of salt-and-pepper hair, a bushy mustache of the same color, and a warm smile.

Stopping on the plane's last step, Rachel looked around, disappointed not to see Preston. She was about to ask if he had been notified when Sam rushed toward her, arms extended. "I'm so sorry, honey."

"Oh, Sam." The tears Rachel had held back during the long flight home suddenly erupted. She threw herself into her old friend's arms and sobbed.

They remained embraced for some time before Rachel finally pulled away to hug Tina who had been comforting Courtney. Sam's wife was a petite, chubby woman with dark good looks she had inherited from her Italian ancestors and a sunny disposition. In spite of their difference in age, the two women had been best friends for years.

"Where is Preston?" Rachel asked when she was able to speak.

While Sam loaded the luggage into the trunk of his old Audi, Tina gently steered Rachel and Courtney toward the car. "He had a testimonial dinner he needed to attend. He said he'd see you tomorrow."

Rachel was quick to hear the disapproval in Tina's voice

and wasn't surprised. Brutally honest at times, Tina had never hidden the fact that she didn't like Preston. In her opinion, he was pompous, opportunistic and cold. The truth was, Tina simply didn't understand Preston. As with many people, she was unaware of his supportive nature, his quiet, resolute strength, and his unwavering determination.

"What about Mom?" Courtney asked as she settled into the back seat. "Where is she?"

"At home." Sam glanced in the mirror before backing out of the parking space. "Making preparations for Hannah's funeral."

"I hope she's not planning on some elaborate affair." Rachel searched inside her purse for a handkerchief. "Grams would hate that."

Sam turned left at the parking lot entrance and followed a sign pointing to Route 29, the two-lane highway that ran through Napa Valley. "I tried to tell her that," he said. "But you know your sister. If it ain't big, it ain't good."

Rachel didn't reply. She wondered how it would be now, working for Annie. It had never been a big secret that, as the oldest sibling, Annie would someday inherit the winery. And though Hannah had been explicit in her request that the structure of the company not be changed, there *would* be changes. Annie would see to that.

And then again, becoming head of Spaulding Vineyards might mellow Annie. It might even end that stupid jealousy of hers—a jealousy that had begun the very day their parents had brought Rachel home from the orphanage.

As if reading her mind, Sam glanced at her in the rearview mirror. "It's going to be all right, honey," he said gently. "Try not to worry, okay?"

"Okay." She gazed out the window at the familiar landscape that would never look quite the same again. "Tell me how Grams died."

"I thought Annie—"

"I want to hear it from you."

Sam nodded. "It was a massive heart attack. She died very quickly. Annie was with her, as you know, and though she went for help right away…" Sam let out a small sigh. "It was too late."

"Did you talk to Dr. Warren?"

"Yes. He said that considering the seriousness of the two previous attacks, it was a miracle Hannah lasted as long as she did."

"Dammit, Sam, why didn't he tell us that sooner? If he had we might have prevented…" Unable to continue, she pressed her handkerchief to her eyes.

"Hannah swore the doc to secrecy," Sam explained. "She didn't want you and Annie to worry."

That was Hannah. Always worrying about others, never about herself. Across the seat, Courtney's hand came to take Rachel's. Turning to look at her, Rachel managed a smile and took the offered hand. Both remained silent for the rest of the short trip home.

The next forty-eight hours were blissfully busy. While Annie made the necessary arrangements for what she considered an "appropriate" funeral, Rachel took calls from all over California and even Europe, as people whose lives Hannah had touched called to offer their condolences. Even crusty Monsieur Fronsac had sent a telegram to express his sorrow.

After the funeral, Ambrose Cavanaugh, Hannah's trusted attorney, had asked the family, along with Sam and Tina, to join him in Hannah's study for the reading of the will.

As expected, Hannah had generously provided for those who had served her so well all those years—two servants, long since retired, and Ming, the current and very efficient housekeeper who ran the Spaulding house better than Hannah herself.

To Sam, whose friendship she had cherished, she had left a Raoul Duffy painting her old friend had often admired. It was the artist's rendition of a Bordeaux vineyard where Sam had done his apprenticeship in the early fifties. "Along with this painting," she had specified, "I leave him the dubious honor of looking after my girls."

Rachel glanced at Sam and saw him wipe a tear with the back of his hand.

To Tina, she had left her antique Royal Doulton dinnerware set and thanked her for those wonderful Sunday meals and for always making her laugh.

A small but audible sigh made Rachel glance to her left, where Annie sat impatiently drumming her long, pearl-frosted nails on her lap.

As if he, too, had heard the sigh, Ambrose looked up and cleared his throat. "And now," he said quietly. "For the rest of Hannah's estate." He smiled at Courtney. "'To my dear, wonderful great-granddaughter, Courtney, I leave a trust fund of one million dollars, the distribution of which will begin on her twenty-first birthday. Along with that, I leave her my pearl necklace and matching earrings, which she has admired for so long. You won't have to borrow them anymore, darling. They're now yours.'"

As Courtney stifled a sob, Rachel gently patted her niece's hand. She couldn't think of a better person to show-case Grams's lovely pearls.

Ambrose waited a second or two before continuing. "'To my first and very dear granddaughter, Annie, I also leave the sum of one million dollars and the house where she was born. It is my most fervent wish that those familiar surroundings will be a constant reminder of how much I loved her.'

"'And to my other granddaughter, Rachel,'" he added after taking a short breath, "'who doesn't care about money and would kill me all over again if I tried to leave her as much as a cent, I leave what I know is dearest to her heart—Spaulding Vineyards.'"

As Rachel's mouth opened in shock, Annie sprang out of her chair. *"What?"* Her face ashen, she marched over to Ambrose's desk. "What did you say?"

The attorney removed his glasses. "Hannah left the winery to Rachel," he said with the look of one preparing for battle.

"She can't do that." Annie slammed her palms onto the desk, causing an antique inkwell to rattle. "The winery is mine! She told me it was. Everyone knows that."

"Hannah changed her will two years ago," Ambrose explained.

"Why would she change her will? She knew how much the winery meant to me."

"We can talk about the reasons later, in private—"

"Mom," Courtney interrupted. "Ambrose is right. You can discuss this later."

Annie stomped her foot. "I want to talk about it now, dammit. Why did she change her will?"

Ambrose glanced uneasily around him. "She was concerned about you, Annie, about your life-style and your unwillingness to settle down. She was afraid your wild streak, as she called it, would eventually affect the running of Spaulding Vineyards."

"So she gave it to *her?*" Without taking her eyes off Ambrose, she pointed her finger at Rachel.

"She felt your sister was better qualified."

"Bull. I'm the one best qualified to run this business. And I'm a Spaulding. A *legitimate* Spaulding," she added, her eyes deeply resentful as she glanced over her shoulder at Rachel. "Not some misfit abandoned on the steps of an orphanage."

"Mom!" Her face stricken, Courtney stood. "Don't talk about Aunt Rachel that way."

"Why not? It's the truth. She has no right to Spaulding Vineyards. I do. It's my birthright."

Rachel, who had remained silent during Annie's ranting, couldn't take it any longer. "For God's sake, Annie, must everything always be about you? Can't you show a little respect? Grams has been buried for only a few hours and already you're—"

"Oh, please," Annie sneered. "Spare me the moral indignation, will you? I'm not in the mood."

"Ladies, please." Sam, who had also stood, looked from Rachel to Annie, a deep scowl on his craggy face. "This isn't the time to argue. And it's certainly not what Hannah would have wanted you to do."

"Grams should have thought of that before she left my winery to...her," Annie said bitterly. Then, turning back to the attorney, she asked, "What do we have to do to break the will?"

"I beg your pardon?"

Annie put her fists on her hips. Whatever grief she had shown during Grams's funeral earlier had vanished. "Obviously Grams wasn't well when she wrote this version. Either that," she added, slanting another nasty look toward Rachel, "or someone forced her to do it."

"You can't break the will, Annie," Ambrose replied. "Hannah was perfectly sound of mind, as you well know. And no one forced her to do anything. I can vouch for that. And so can the two people who witnessed the signing— Sam and my secretary."

He glanced at his notes. "There's just one more thing I need to add. The only stipulation of the will is that should

Rachel bring disgrace to the Spaulding name in any way, ownership of Spaulding will go to Annie. I don't expect that to happen," he added, smiling briefly. "But since Hannah had included that stipulation in the first will, I wanted you both to know it still stands."

Rachel nodded to indicate she understood the terms. Ambrose glanced at Annie, who was still livid. "Any questions?"

For a moment Annie remained perfectly still. Only her eyes moved as she looked from Sam to Tina, as if seeking their support. When it was clear that no one was on her side, she threw one last hateful look at Rachel and stalked out of the room, leaving the door open behind her.

Four

Annie was still steaming when she returned to her office that afternoon. Slamming her car keys onto the desk, she let out a cry of pure undiluted rage. Rachel had done it again. The bitch had plotted and connived behind her back and somehow managed to convince Grams she and not Annie was best qualified to run Spaulding.

Ignoring her golden rule to never drink before six o'clock in the evening, she took a small flask from her desk drawer, splashed some Scotch into the silver cup and drank the liquor in one gulp, hoping it would calm her nerves. Then, still fuming, she walked over to the window that over-looked the vineyards and opened it wide.

Owning Spaulding Vineyards had been her lifelong ambition. Not because she had a special rapport with the land, as Rachel claimed to have, but because she wanted to do for Spaulding what Robert Mondavi had done for his winery—turn a small family business into a high-profile, prestigious, worldwide wine empire.

Unfortunately, with Hannah always accusing her older granddaughter of spending too much money, the expansion Annie dreamed of hadn't happened. As for Rachel, she wasn't against expansion, but believed in proceeding cautiously, which was just as bad. How could any business reach a high level of success if the people who ran it didn't take a few chances every now and then?

Rachel's red Cherokee suddenly turned onto the access road, followed by Sam's old Audi. Annie let out a short, sarcastic laugh. Sam and Tina had been so happy when Ambrose had announced that Rachel had inherited the winery, it was a wonder they hadn't stood up and cheered.

"Don't rejoice too soon, my friends," she said out loud. "And don't count me out just yet."

Arms folded across her chest, she watched Rachel step out of the Jeep and walk across the courtyard. When she had disappeared inside the cellars, Annie's thoughts drifted back to the day Grams died and the words she had whispered to Annie. *Rachel's birth mother is alive.*

Although at the time Annie had had every intention of relaying the message to Rachel, there had been no opportunity to do so. In fact, between coping with her grief, handling the stream of visitors, and taking care of the funeral arrangements, Annie had completely forgotten about Grams's confession. Until now.

What a startling revelation, Annie mused. And how puzzling that Grams had kept the woman's existence a secret for thirty-one years. Who was this mysterious Alyssa? What sinister reason could there be for the Spaulding family to have fabricated a story that Rachel's birth mother had died in childbirth?

Annie tapped a finger against her lip. Wouldn't it be wonderful if there was a juicy little scandal buried somewhere? One serious enough to make it necessary for Ambrose to enforce that clause in Hannah's will.

Suddenly filled with hope, Annie walked back to her desk and sat. There had to be a way for her to find out— without anyone knowing, of course.

You made a promise, Annie—to a dying woman.

Well...actually, she hadn't. She had been too upset that morning to say much of anything. And then, just as she was about to grant Hannah's last wish, her grandmother had died.

So, since no promise had been made, she was free to investigate this intriguing little matter all on her own.

But how was she going to do that when she didn't have Alyssa's last name? Maybe that nun Grams had mentioned would have the answer, provided she was alive and willing to talk.

Or, she reflected, her gaze resting on the phone, she could hire a private investigator, someone who specialized in missing persons. Yes, that was safer than going to Santa Rosa herself and running the risk of being recognized. Whoever she hired, however, would have to be very discreet. The last thing she needed was for Rachel or Ambrose to find out she had initiated the search for Alyssa.

After a while, a slow smile worked its way to her mouth. Of course. Gregory Shaw. Why hadn't she thought of him sooner? He was just the man she needed. He was smart, resourceful, experienced and, above all, discreet.

He also had principles, and convincing him to take the case might present a problem. It took Annie no more than a minute of deep thinking for her smile to widen.

She knew exactly how to get around that little difficulty.

"No, Mrs. Bigsbie," Gregory Shaw said patiently, "we don't provide bodyguards. Nor do we handle divorce cases. I'd be glad to recommend—"

The caller on the other end of the line interrupted him with a barrage of protests. What did he mean, he didn't handle divorce cases? And didn't provide bodyguards? What kind of detective agency was he running if he couldn't even protect her daughter from her abusive husband?

Sitting in his seventeenth-floor office, Gregory swiveled

around in his chair to gaze out the large window. The San Francisco skyline stretched out in front of him, shrouded in a light fog that gave the City by the Bay a unique, eerie quality.

The only reason he had agreed to talk to Kathryn Bigsbie at all was because she was an old friend of his aunt Willie's, something she had been quick to remind him the moment his secretary had put through the call.

"What you need is an investigator who specializes in matrimonial cases," he said when Mrs. Bigsbie finally stopped talking. "His name is Dylon Cross—"

"I thought *you* specialized in matrimonial cases," she said rather pointedly.

"Not anymore, Mrs. Bigsbie. I run a different kind of agency now. I investigate large companies and their CEOs."

"Oh." There was a slight pause. "Well...I certainly have no use for that."

He smiled. "No, you don't. You need someone like Dylon Cross. He's a good friend of mine and an excellent private investigator. Here's his number." He waited until she had located pen and paper before reciting the number. "Tell Dylon I sent you," he added. "He'll take good care of you."

He had barely hung up when his intercom buzzed again. "Mr. Shaw," his secretary said in her brisk tone. "There's a woman here who insists on seeing you even though she doesn't have an appointment. Her name is Annie Spaulding. She says you know her."

Gregory suppressed a chuckle. He hadn't seen Annie since her divorce from his friend Luke Aymes had become final in 1987. Never a big fan of Gregory, she had managed one parting shot that day, calling him a two-bit gumshoe whose only talent was to stick his nose where it didn't belong. She had even claimed that if it hadn't been for his snooping, she and Luke would still be married.

She had made no mention of the fact that Luke had hired Gregory to investigate her affair with a South American polo player, the same polo player she had later married and then divorced.

What could she possibly want with him now?

Curiosity got the better of him. "Show her in, Phyllis," he said as he rose from his chair and moved to stand in front of his desk.

Though the woman who entered his office was as beautiful as he remembered, the past twelve years had added a new maturity to her face. And a certain brittleness. "Hello, Annie."

Dressed in a snug red suit that accentuated every curve of her body, Annie smiled and crossed the room in an undulating walk not meant for the fainthearted. "It's been a long time, Gregory." Her voice was the same soft purr meant to convey a single message—sex.

"Yes, it has. How's Courtney?" he asked, remembering Luke's daughter had to be a young woman by now.

"She's fine, anxiously waiting to turn sixteen. Luke is still somewhere in Africa, photographing tigers or elephants or whatever it is he's obsessing over these days." Quickly dismissing her former husband, she gave Gregory a coy look. "I wasn't sure you'd see me."

He pointed to a chair in front of his desk. "You know me. I could never pass up a challenge."

She batted her long lashes. "Is that how you think of me? As a challenge?"

"Among other things."

She had the grace to blush. "I don't blame you for still being upset with me. I wasn't very nice to you the last time we ran into each other."

"You threatened to carve my heart out and feed it to your cat."

She chuckled. "Did I really?" She sat and crossed her shapely legs, making no effort to pull down her skirt. "I was a brat, Gregory. Say you forgive me."

"There's nothing to forgive." Gregory walked behind his desk and sat. "People are entitled to speak their mind."

"You ought to know. You were never one to mince words, either."

The light banter, though entertaining, was beginning to wear thin. Tilting back his chair, Gregory steepled his fingers. "What do you want, Annie?"

She was instantly businesslike. "I need your help in finding someone."

He shook his head. "Sorry," he said for the second time that day. "I don't do that kind of work anymore."

"I know." She looked around her, at the slick blue-upholstered teak furnishings, the antique Oriental carpet, the wraparound windows with the sweeping view. "You've come a long way since that hole-in-the-wall on Laguna Street."

Gregory was already reaching for a pad and a pen. "I'll be glad to refer you to another private investigator." Dylon, old boy, he thought as he started writing, you owe me a beer.

"I don't want another private investigator," Annie said flatly. "I want you, Gregory. No one else." She leaned forward, offering him an unobstructed view of her generous cleavage. "Say you'll do it. Please. For old times' sake?"

"I would if I could," he lied. "But I'm buried in work right now, with no relief in sight."

She looked crestfallen. "You won't help me?"

"I'm sorry."

To his surprise, she lowered her head into her hands and burst into tears.

For a few seconds all he could do was stare at her. As most men he knew, he was uncomfortable around crying women. Fortunately, his ex-wife hadn't been the crying type and neither was his twelve-year-old daughter, though the latter was beginning to learn that a few tears every now and then could go a long way to getting her what she wanted. "Annie, please don't cry," he said for lack of something better.

His plea went unnoticed.

Feeling like a heel, Gregory walked around his desk again and crouched in front of her. "Come on, Annie," he said, taking a crisp white handkerchief from his breast pocket and handing it to her. "It can't be that bad."

"It is." She took the handkerchief and pressed it against her eyes, instantly smearing her mascara. "My life is a complete mess."

At those words, he gave himself a mental kick for not having said something earlier. Hannah Spaulding. He had read about her death in the *Chronicle* last week. Annie had loved her grandmother very much, as had everyone who'd known her. No wonder Annie was so upset. "I'm sorry about your grandmother," he said gently. "I know how much she meant to you."

"She was everything to me." She sniffed, dabbed her eyes again, creating an even bigger mess, then added, "She left the winery to Rachel."

Gregory stood and leaned against the desk. So *that* was it. The inheritance Annie had expected had gone to some- one else. And not just anyone, but the sister she had re- sented all her life.

Although Gregory hadn't known Rachel very well, he remembered her vividly. A shy, rather gangly fifteen-year-old, she had been a bridesmaid at Annie and Luke's wedding and he had been the groom's best man. During the entire wedding ceremony, the teenager, obviously smitten, had stared at Gregory with adoring eyes. Later, at the reception, he and Luke had laughed about the girl's visible crush, unaware that Rachel had been standing behind them. Her cheeks blazing, Rachel had run out of the reception. Feeling awful, Gregory had run after her, begging her to accept his apologies. She had kept right on running.

He'd never seen her again after that, but he'd read somewhere that she had become a winemaker and was engaged to Preston Farley, a pedantic, moderately successful San Francisco attorney.

"I take it you didn't expect that," he said in reply to Annie's comment.

"No." Annie looked up, the smudged mascara giving her raccoon eyes. "You know how I love that winery, Gregory. I poured my heart and soul into it for the past twenty years, watching it grow, knowing that someday it would be mine. And it should have been, dammit."

She stared at the stained hankie in her hands and sighed. "I'm sorry, Gregory. I didn't mean to dump all my problems out on you. It's just that…now that Rachel is in charge, everyone is treating me like an outcast. Even Courtney, my own daughter, has turned away from me."

"I'm sure that's an exaggeration."

"No, it's not. In fact, if I were to die tomorrow, I'm convinced no one would miss me. On the contrary, they'd probably say good riddance." She dabbed at her eyes again. "Maybe I should make them all happy and kill myself."

Gregory had a difficult time keeping a straight face. Annie had always had a flair for theatrics, and apparently still did.

But if she was upset enough to put on such a performance, maybe he ought to at least listen to her problem. "Who is this person you want found?" he asked gently.

Annie met his gaze. "An old friend of my mother's. Her name is Alyssa. Mama never told me her last name but she did mention a nun, Sister Mary-Catherine, who used to work at a convent in Santa Rosa—Our Lady of Good Counsel."

"How does the nun fit in?"

"I'm not sure." She rolled the handkerchief into a tight ball. "From what I gathered, she—Alyssa—and my mother were friends."

"Have you ever seen this Alyssa?" Gregory asked. "In person? Or in a snapshot?"

Annie shook her head.

"Could she and your mother have been college roommates?"

"No." Annie kept her eyes downcast. "I think Mama met her in the late sixties. Nineteen sixty-eight, I believe. Yes, that's it. Nineteen sixty-eight."

Gregory rubbed his chin with his index finger. "She wasn't at your wedding? Any of them?" he added, remembering Annie had been married several times.

"No."

"What about your parents' funeral? Did she attend?"

Again, Annie shook her head. "No."

Gregory stared at her for a moment, not sure what to make of Annie, or of her bizarre story. What kind of friend had this Alyssa been if she hadn't even bothered to come to the Spauldings's funeral? Curious about Annie's true motive, he tried another question. "Why do you want to find this woman?"

"I told you. She was a friend of my mother's."

"But why now?" he insisted. "If this Alyssa means so much to you, why didn't you try to find her sooner?"

"Because I had Grams then!" Annie cried in exasperation. "And now that I'm all alone, with no one who cares, finding someone who knew Mama, who remembers her and can talk to me about her…would lift my spirits." She raised moist eyes at him. "Is that so hard to understand?"

"No," he admitted. "It isn't." Provided she was telling him the truth, which he seriously doubted. He waited a beat before adding, "Have you considered the possibility the woman may be dead?"

At those words Annie's expression turned so tragic he wished he hadn't said that. "No, I haven't," she mumbled, twisting the handkerchief again. "She can't be dead."

Gregory crossed his arms in front of him and continued to observe her. Something about this whole scenario didn't ring true. Maybe he was being overly suspicious, which wasn't surprising considering what he knew about Annie. And his earlier statement that he was busy was not an exaggeration. Between the ATC merger and his testimony at an insider's trading lawsuit next week, he hardly had any free time. And what he did have belonged to his daughter Noelle.

At the same time he couldn't help but feel sorry for Annie. Yes, she was cunning, and manipulative, and rude, and a liar to boot, but deep down he had always felt that she was a lost soul still in search of herself. What would it cost him to ask a few questions to find out at least if the mysterious Alyssa was alive? He didn't have to do any more than that. His aunt Willie might even cut his research time in half. As the former owner and publisher of the *Sacramento Ledger*, there wasn't much she didn't know.

Almost as if Annie had read his mind, she gave a little sniff. This time her voice held a heavy dose of melodrama. "I'm so alone, Gregory."

"You're not alone, Annie. You have a family, friends, a business."

She gave a short, bitter laugh. "My family is treating me like a leper. I have no friends. And as of yesterday, I no longer have a business, just a job." Her eyes filled with tears again. "Call me sentimental," she said, "but suddenly this woman has become terribly important to me."

"You haven't given me much information to go on," he reminded her, still looking for a diplomatic way out.

"I know. That's why I came to you." She gave him a sweet, trusting smile. "Luke always said you were the best. 'When all else has failed,' he used to say. 'Give the job to Gregory.'"

He allowed himself a small smile. Whatever happened to the "two-bit gumshoe"?

"I'm prepared to pay you whatever you want," she continued when he didn't answer. "Just name your retainer." She rummaged through her purse and pulled out a checkbook.

Before she had a chance to open it, Gregory stopped her. "Let's hold off on that for the moment, shall we? Let me see what I can find out first."

Her expression brightened instantly. "Then you'll do it? You'll find Alyssa for me?"

"I'll try," Gregory said, wondering if he was going to regret the decision. "That's all I can promise."

"That's all I ask." Her old self again, Annie rose from her chair, walked over to where he stood and kissed him on the cheek, pressing her body against his a little longer than necessary. "Thank you," she murmured in his ear.

Gregory gently uncoiled her arms. The last thing he wanted was to send her the wrong signals. "I'll call you in a couple of days to let you know what I found out."

"Good." She looked around her. "Do you have a powder room?" She smiled. "I think I need to clean up a bit."

He pointed to a door and watched her walk away in that same seductive swing. He chuckled. Annie may be distressed but she hadn't lost sight of her priorities.

She was back within moments. The raccoon eyes were gone and there was a fresh coat of shiny crimson lipstick on her lips. "I know you're discretion personified," she said, dropping a gold compact into her purse, "but I thought I'd say it anyway so there's no misunderstanding. I don't want anyone, and that includes the Spaulding family, to know about our little...arrangement."

Gregory inclined his head and took the business card she handed him.

"Call me at home rather than at the winery," she instructed. "Day or night. If I'm not there the machine will pick up."

At the door, which he held open for her, she paused. "Too bad I didn't have the good sense to marry you instead of Luke," she said with mind-boggling sincerity. "Something tells me we would have been good for each other."

This time the laugh came before he could stop it. Because of his profession, which she had deemed, at the time, far beneath her social status, Annie had hated him on sight. She had even resented Gregory's friendship with Luke, claiming he was a bad influence on her husband.

"I doubt that," he said.

She batted her eyelashes and walked out.

Our Lady of Good Counsel was a pink stucco structure reminiscent of the many missions the Spanish padres had built throughout the California coast in the eighteenth century. Located on the outskirts of Santa Rosa in Sonoma County, the convent was surrounded by a wrought-iron fence covered with English ivy. Beyond that fence, a shaded gravel path wound its way through a lush, shaded garden.

Before leaving his office, Gregory had contemplated calling the convent to make sure Sister Mary-Catherine was still there. Thirty-one years was a long time and, depending how old the nun had been in 1968, she could be retired by now or maybe even deceased. After careful consideration, however, he had opted to show up at the convent unannounced. Surprise, that old reliable element, often brought the best results. He hoped this would be one of those times.

After a moment he got out of his car and went to pull the chain of the old-fashioned bell. It only took a few seconds for a nun dressed in a black habit to appear.

"May I help you?" she asked pleasantly.

Up close, Gregory could see she was very young, no more than twenty-two or twenty-three. "Good morning, Sister," he said, bowing slightly. He had never addressed a nun before but figured a deferential attitude couldn't hurt. "My name is Gregory Shaw. I'm here to see Sister Mary-Catherine."

"Sister Mary-Catherine is in the chapel at the moment. She shouldn't be long, however." The nun took a key from a hook on the wall and unlocked the gate. "Would you care to wait in the garden?"

"Yes, I would, thank you."

She pulled open the gate. "As soon as Sister Mary-Catherine is free, I'll tell her you're here."

Gregory thanked her again and watched her walk away, her footsteps barely audible on the gravel path. Hands in his pockets, he looked around, absorbing the tranquillity of the place, the sense of total peace. He wondered what it was like living within these quiet walls twenty-four hours a day, three hundred and sixty-five days a year. Maybe the mysterious Alyssa had spent some time here. She could have been a nun herself.

"Good morning."

Startled, Gregory turned around. The nun who stood in front of him was much older than the previous one. Gregory estimated her to be in her mid-sixties. "Good morning." Feeling suddenly awkward, he removed his hands from his pockets and let them hang at his sides. "Sister Mary-Catherine?"

She inclined her head. "What can I do for you, Mr. Shaw?"

"I was hoping you could help me locate someone, Sister. A woman by the name of Alyssa. I'm afraid I don't have a last name, but she may have lived in this area in 1968."

Though the nun's facial expression didn't change, Gregory thought he saw a slight tensing of her shoulders. "I don't know anyone by that name." Her voice was calm and even, betraying none of the tension he thought he'd noticed.

"I see." Gregory was silent for a moment, not wanting to frighten her with a rush of questions. "What about Helen Spaulding?" he asked at last. "Does that name sound familiar to you? I was told she and Alyssa were friends and may have met right here in Santa Rosa."

Sister Mary-Catherine looked genuinely sorry. "I'm afraid I don't know her, either, Mr. Shaw."

"What about the other nuns? Do you suppose they may have known her?"

"Unfortunately the nuns who worked at Our Lady at that time have all passed away."

"I'm sorry to hear that." Again he waited until a sufficient, respectable amount of time had passed before speaking again. "If I may ask, Sister, what exactly do you do here?"

She gave him a serene smile. "We run a small orphanage."

"I see."

Sister Mary-Catherine tucked her hands into the front fold of her habit. "Would you mind telling me why you are looking for this woman, Mr. Shaw? Has she...done something wrong?"

She looked at him without flinching and yet that same feeling that she wasn't telling him all she knew kept nagging him. "I'm afraid I'm not at liberty to say." He gave her an apologetic smile. "I hope you understand."

"Of course. And I'm sorry I couldn't be of any help to you."

"So am I." He handed her his card. "Would you call me if you should remember anything?"

"Certainly."

She didn't accompany him to the gate, but remained standing on the gravel path. When he reached his car and turned around, she was still there, watching him.

Five

Gregory visited his aunt often, yet he never ceased to marvel at the beauty of Sausalito, the artsy little town across the Bay. A mecca for sophisticates, it stood on the north side of the Golden Gate Bridge, its pastel houses clinging to steep cliffs that rose gently above the sparkling harbor.

It was no surprise that Willie McBride had chosen to spend her retirement days in this posh community. A former artist, she had abandoned her vocation when she had inherited the *Sacramento Ledger* from her husband in 1970. From that moment on all her energy had been focused on the newspaper and on continuing the tradition of excellence established by her late husband. In 1997, after twenty-seven years in publishing and countless awards, she had sold the *Ledger* and returned to her first love, painting.

There was little she didn't know about people and events, and her recollection of those events, even those that had happened a half century ago, was astounding.

As always, Gregory found her in her sunny studio overlooking the harbor. She was a tall, heavyset woman with long gray hair she kept held back with a rubber band, and sturdy hands that moved across the canvas with strong, sure strokes. Wearing a paint-splattered smock over baggy chinos, she stood with her back to Gregory, totally absorbed in her current work, a colorful, rather modern rendition of the glittering bay below.

"I'll say it again," Gregory stated, one shoulder against the door frame. "Picasso had nothing over you."

A rich gurgling laugh escaped from his aunt's throat. "And that comment," she said as she applied one last splash of orange paint to her canvas, "could only come from my favorite nephew—the art critic."

"The last time I looked, I was your *only* nephew."

"And right you are." After dropping her brush into a coffee can, where it joined half a dozen others, she turned to him, her dark, intelligent eyes sparkling with humor. "Come here, you handsome devil," she said, opening her arms. "And give your old aunt a fat kiss."

Gregory quickly crossed the room and embraced her. "How are you, Aunt Willie?"

"Fit as a fiddle as you can see." She gave his arm a reproachful tap. "But why didn't you tell me you were coming? I would have made something special for lunch."

"That's exactly why I didn't tell you. You know how I hate it when you fuss. A sandwich and a beer will be just fine."

"Ah." She waved her hand in the air. "I can do better than that, even on short notice." She linked her arm through his. "But right now, a beer sounds like a wonderful idea."

Within moments Gregory was comfortably seated in Willie's parlor, a frosty bottle of Budweiser in his hand. This room, like the rest of the house, reminded him of an international bazaar. Spacious and as sunny as her studio, the room was crammed with furniture and artifacts Willie and her late husband, ace reporter Carl McBride, had brought back from their many travels—African masks, high-backed wicker chairs so deep a child could lose himself in one, tapestries depicting tribal ways of life, and the one item that had delighted him as a boy, a fifteen-foot kingfish his uncle had caught off the coast of Florida one winter.

"So." Willie leaned back in her chair and propped her feet on a table with lion's paw legs. "What kind of information do you need today?"

Gregory laughed. "You know me too well, Aunt Willie."

"And don't you forget it." She took a sip of her beer, which she also drank from the bottle. "Problems?"

"A puzzle. A tough one."

"Try me."

"I need to find a woman, but all I have is a first name, a town where she may or may not have lived, and a nun who should know her but claims not to."

"Why 'claims'?" Willie asked with a teasing smile. "You doubt the word of a nun?"

"In this case, yes. I'm almost certain she was holding back on me."

"Well…you have good instincts, so you could be right. What's the woman's name?"

"Alyssa. And the town is Santa Rosa."

Willie pursed her lips.

Always tuned to her reactions, Gregory was instantly alert. "Does the name ring a bell?"

"I think so." Willie gazed at her bottle for a moment. "But the Alyssa I'm thinking of lived in Winters, not Santa Rosa."

"Tell me about her."

"Her name was Alyssa Dassante. She—"

"Dassante as in the walnut growers?"

Willie nodded. "The very rich walnut growers, and not the nicest people you'd ever want to know."

"What's wrong with them?"

"Salvatore Dassante became rich by screwing people—his customers, whom he cheated shamelessly, his suppliers, whom he accused of overcharging, and his workers, whom he paid next to nothing and treated like animals. Anyone who lived within a hundred miles of the Dassante farm hated him with a passion."

"How did he get away with mistreating his workers?"

"Money. When a complaint was filed, the authorities would come, slap him with a small fine every now and then and shut down his farm for a day or two. But most of the time they looked the other way."

"He was paying them off."

Willie took another sip of her beer. "That's how Sal operates. He's more careful now, because of the new labor laws, but his reputation as a bastard still remains."

"How does Alyssa fit into this?"

"She was married to Mario Dassante, the eldest of Sal's boys. She wasn't from Santa Rosa, though, but from San Francisco." Her feet still on the table, Willie uncrossed and recrossed them. "She used to be a stripper in a downtown club."

"Is that where Mario met her?"

Willie nodded. "He walked into the Blue Parrot one night and fell for her—hard. Rumor has it Sal was not pleased. He wanted better for his golden boy, meaning of course, he wanted an Italian girl, preferably one who knew her place and would give him lots of grand bambinos. But Mario wanted Alyssa and Sal had no choice but to give his blessings. Their fairy-tale wedding made headlines from one end of California to the other. We covered it extensively in the *Ledger*."

"When was that?"

Willie was thoughtful for a moment. "Nineteen sixty-seven. Alyssa and Mario had been married less than twelve months when Alyssa killed him.''

Gregory lowered his beer. "You're kidding."

Willie shook her head. "The incident made headlines for weeks afterward. You don't remember any of this because you were just a little kid at the time, but the public couldn't get enough of that story. From what I recall, Alyssa and Mario had an argument late one night and during the course of that argument, she killed him."

"Was Alyssa arrested?"

"She was never found. She fled the Dassante farm, taking her two-week-old baby girl with her. Sal's youngest son, Nico, discovered his brother's body. Sal was beside himself with grief. And rage. The following morning, as the Winters police searched for Alyssa, a California state trooper reported a crash on Route 1. A car that fit the description of Alyssa's Mercedes had jumped off the embankment and tumbled into the Pacific Ocean just south of Bodega Bay."

"Did they find the bodies?"

"No." Willie stared into space. "Divers searched the ocean floor but only recovered a few personal effects that were later identified as Alyssa's and the baby's. Sal refused to believe they had drowned. He kept insisting Alyssa had faked her death so she could escape with the baby. Your uncle was so intrigued by the story that he covered it himself. He questioned a lot of people in the process, from Alyssa's former boss at the Blue Parrot—a man by the name of Jonsey Malone—to the deep-sea divers and of course, the police."

"What did Jonsey Malone say?"

Willie shrugged. "The same thing he told the police when they questioned him. He hadn't seen Alyssa since the day she'd left the Blue Parrot to get married."

"Did Uncle Carl believe him?"

"As a matter of fact, he didn't. He thought Jonsey's story was fishy, considering he and Alyssa were good friends, but Jonsey stuck to his story and there wasn't a damn thing anybody could do about it."

"So...the baby disappeared along with Alyssa?"

Willie's voice dropped. "The baby died. A couple of days after they dragged Alyssa's car from the ocean, your uncle found out Lillie Dassante had perished in a fire in a Santa Rosa orphanage."

Gregory sat up in his chair. Son of a gun. The nun had lied to him, after all.

"Alyssa had left her there for safekeeping before resuming her trip," Willie continued. "But never returned to claim her. After an extensive three-day search, the police declared Alyssa dead. Sal, certain she had faked her death, immediately hired a private detective to look for his daughter-in-law. He even put up a fifty-thousand-dollar reward for information leading to her capture."

"I take it no one came forward."

Willie laughed. "Oh, they came forward all right. Fifty thousand dollars has a way of getting people's attention, especially in those days, but there were no serious leads."

"Was a nun by the name of Sister Mary-Catherine ever mentioned?"

Willie pursed her lips. "I believe one of the nuns at the orphanage went to tell Sal the news about his granddaughter, but I don't remember her name."

"What about the name of the detective in charge of Mario Dassante's murder? Do you know who he was?"

"No, but we can find that out easily enough. I'll call Jimmy at the *Ledger*." As she talked, Willie picked up a cordless phone from the table next to her and dialed a number. When her former assistant came on the line, she told him what she needed and waited while he checked the archives on his computer. After a few moments, she thanked him and hung up.

"Detective's name is Harold Mertz," she said, looking back at Gregory. "He's probably retired by now, but I'm sure someone at the Winters police department knows how to get in touch with him." She drained the last of her beer in one gulp.

Gregory could tell by the sparkle of curiosity in her eyes that she was dying to know why he was interested in such an old story, but she knew better than to ask.

"If that's not enough, we can go to the paper and search through the archives ourselves," she suggested.

"Thanks, Aunt Willie, but what you told me is enough for now. I can do the legwork myself." He grinned. "And you're still the best newspaperwoman I know."

She laughed. "Don't let the new owner of the *Ledger* hear you say that. He'll ask me to come and work for him. He's already hinted once or twice, and frankly, becoming part of that rat race again is the last thing I want." She put her empty bottle on the table and kept her eyes on Gregory. "Seen your father lately?"

Gregory didn't flinch. It was a question she never failed to ask and, though his answer was always the same, he couldn't blame her for trying. A born mediator and fond of her brother, Willie had been trying for years to get her two favorite men to reconcile. "No," he said flatly. "I dropped Noelle off a couple of Sundays ago, but he didn't come out."

Willie bobbed her head a few times, looking thoughtful. Then, as if knowing there was nothing she could do about the situation, she rose from her chair and waved him toward the kitchen. "Come on. Let's go see what we can rustle up for lunch."

Six

A call to Information a little while later confirmed that the Blue Parrot was still in business. And after a call to the bar, Gregory confirmed it was still owned by Jonsey Malone, though he had long since delegated the running of his nightclub to his son.

Gregory drove directly from his aunt's to the Blue Parrot. After slipping the surly bartender a fifty-dollar bill to get a message to the boss, Gregory ordered a Pepsi and settled at the dim bar to wait for Jonsey to call him back on his cell phone. When he finally did, he told Gregory, in a rather curt tone, that he hadn't seen or heard from Alyssa since the day she had given her notice.

"The woman is dead, for Christ's sake," he mumbled as Gregory started to ask another question. "Can't you let her rest in peace?" Then, before Gregory had a chance to comment, he slammed down the phone.

Former detective Harold Mertz, whom Gregory had located with the help of the Winters police, was more forthcoming, if filled with self-importance. He was a heavyset man with droopy jowls, heavy bags under his eyes and a belly the size of a beach ball. He lived alone, in a small Cape Cod-style house on Anderson Avenue.

After Gregory introduced himself, Mertz led him to a screened-in porch overlooking a weed-infested backyard. Taking a pack of Malboros from his shirt pocket, he offered a cigarette to Gregory, who declined, then lit one for himself.

"What's your interest in Alyssa Dassante?" The man's tone was a little overbearing, as if he were the one with the questions.

"If you mean, who hired me," Gregory replied, "I'm not at liberty to say."

"But you did say you were a private detective."

"That's right."

"Well…" Mertz took a deep drag of his cigarette. "Mrs. Dassante is dead."

"So I've heard, but it's also my understanding that her body was never found."

Mertz leaned forward. "And it ain't never going to be found, son," he said as though he were talking to a child. "I'm tellin' you, the woman is dead." He squinted a little, his expression suddenly greedy. "This ain't a money matter, is it? An inheritance or somethin'? With a reward for whoever finds her?"

Gregory answered him with a question of his own. "Do you remember the incident, by any chance? And the circumstances of Mrs. Dassante's…death?"

"Hell, yes, I remember the incident." Mertz winced a little as he stretched what Gregory suspected was a bad leg in front of him. "It rocked this little town harder than a quake, let me tell you."

"I heard she and her husband were having problems. Is that true?"

Mertz chuckled. "She was a looker and Mario had a hot Italian temper, so yeah, I guess they had their problems." His snicker turned into a lewd laugh. "But nothing a little romp in the sack couldn't fix, if you know what I mean."

Gregory chose to ignore the crude comment. Years of interrogating had taught him that men such as Mertz, with inflated egos, were often a wealth of information and to get that information, a little patience was required.

"Did she have any friends?" he asked. "Anyone who might know where she went? Assuming she didn't die," he added as Mertz gave him another sharp look.

"Well..." The ex-cop took another slow, thoughtful drag. "There's that boss of hers in San Francisco. Forgot his name." Little puffs of smoke came out of his mouth as he spoke. "Alyssa was a stripper, you know." Eyes heavy with innuendo contemplated him through the smoky cloud.

Gregory nodded. "Jonsey Malone. I already talked to him. Anyone else besides him?"

"Nah, she didn't have nobody. The girl was a loner, kinda snooty, too, if you ask me. I mean, considerin' she was just a notch above a hooker when Mario met her, if you know what I mean."

Gregory wondered if the ex-cop had ever made a pass at Alyssa and had been turned down. That certainly would account for his insulting remarks about the woman. "She had no parents, either? No siblings?"

"Nope. Believe me, we looked, because we knew that in order for her to slip through that massive three-day manhunt, she would have had to have had help. We put notices everywhere and plastered her pretty face up and down the coast. Every damn newspaper in the state ran the story, day after day for weeks. She was never found."

"Yet Sal Dassante didn't believe she died."

Mertz's eyes narrowed. "How do you know that?"

"I read something about a reward he offered."

"Oh, that." He nodded. "Yeah, there was a reward. Fifty thousand big ones. But nothin' ever came of it."

Gregory leaned forward and forced a suggestion of respect in his voice. "What's your take on that, chief? You really think she died?"

The ex-detective's chest puffed up, as though he was pleased to have been asked his opinion. "At first I didn't think she had, but after we combed the entire central coast and didn't find her, I knew she was a goner. The gal may have been pretty, but she was too dammed dumb to cover up her tracks the way she did. Plus, we found her purse inside the car. It had eight thousand dollars in it." He shook his head. "No one would leave that kind of money behind."

Unless, Gregory reflected, that someone wasn't so dumb, after all, and wanted to leave proof that she had, indeed, died. "Any chance I could get a copy of the police report?" As he talked, Gregory took out several fifty-dollar bills from his pocket and peeled one off.

"Well now…" Mertz's greedy eyes went from the bill Gregory had laid on the small rusty table between them to the stack still in his hand. "I don't rightly know. I mean, it's been a long time. Reports disappear, if you know what I mean."

Gregory took another fifty and put it on top of the other.

This time the beady eyes lit up. "I'll make a call for you."

It took a while for the young rookie on duty to locate the thirty-one-year-old report on Alyssa Dassante, but he eventually did. Friendly and obliging, he shook the dust from the folder, made a copy of the contents and handed it to Gregory.

"Here you go, sir."

"Thank you, Officer."

Gregory read the six-page report in the parking lot, his back against the Jaguar. Except for exact times and locations, and an in-depth report from the deep-sea divers, there wasn't much in there Aunt Willie and Harold Mertz hadn't already told him.

As he headed back to San Francisco, he kept thinking about Alyssa Dassante. What had driven a woman, who seemingly had everything, to kill her husband? And where had she been going when her car plunged into the ocean? Bodega Bay was just north of San Francisco, where Jonsey Malone lived. Had the old guy lied to him, as well? And to the cops? Or had Alyssa found shelter elsewhere?

Gregory was processing these questions when another began to form in his mind. Why would a woman of Helen Spaulding's standing befriend a stripper?

Gregory wasn't sure what made him swing by the San Francisco courthouse on his way back from Winters and was even less sure why he went in. He hadn't done that in years, not since his college days, priming himself for a career in law, like his father.

The trial that had captured the attention of the entire country for the past three months was coming to an end, and the press had predicted high drama in the courtroom when the defense attorney—Milton Shaw—delivered his closing statements.

As always, when Gregory's father was defending a case, the gallery was packed, with standing room only. Slipping through the door quietly, Gregory positioned himself against the wall next to a young man, most likely a law student, taking notes.

Milton sat at the defense table, a broad-backed man with thinning gray hair that still had a touch of red in it. To his right was his assistant, a promising young woman by the name of Stella Doan, and to his left was Freddy Bloom, the defendant. Better known in the last two years as "The Slasher," Freddy had stabbed two women to death while having sex with them, and seriously wounded a third. His first words when he was finally apprehended were, "Get me Milton Shaw."

It was widely known that Milton Shaw wasn't big on pro bono cases. He did his share, but reluctantly, and made it no secret that he was in this business for the money. And money he'd made. Tons of it. The third child of a poor family, he had clawed his way to the top of his profession to become one of the most sought after criminal attorneys in the country.

Milton, Gregory had soon learned growing up, excelled in just about everything, including golf and tennis, which he still played regularly, cards, horse riding, even flying single-engine airplanes, a hobby he had taken up in the last year or so.

He had failed at only one thing—fatherhood.

From as far back as Gregory could remember, Milton had been an absentee father. As his reputation as a top attorney grew, he'd traveled from one end of the country to the other, leaving the boy in the care of nannies. When Milton was home, which was rarely, he was usually too busy to pay much attention to his son. On weekends Gregory was sent to his aunt Willie's in Sacramento.

It hadn't taken Gregory long to realize why his relationship with his father was so different from the ones his friends had with their own fathers. Gregory's mother had died in childbirth at the age of twenty-nine, and Milton, who had adored her, had blamed Gregory for her death.

"If it wasn't for him," he'd heard Milton say to Willie once, "Marjory would still be alive."

Only nine at the time, Gregory was deeply affected by those words. For years afterward, whenever he looked in the mirror, all he saw was a boy who had killed his mother. No wonder his father hated him. At times, he hated himself.

As the years went by, the abyss between the two men grew even wider, the resentment more bitter. Gregory's scholarship to Yale University might have changed the situation, but Gregory blew it when he chose to go to U.C.L.A. because they had a better football team. To redeem himself in the old man's eyes, Gregory took law as his major even though his heart wasn't in it.

Their relationship suffered another blow when, during Gregory's senior year at U.C.L.A., the San Francisco 49ers offered him a contract to play second-string quarterback the following season. His father had ranted and raved for a week, but nothing he could say or do changed Gregory's mind. Pro football was in, law school was out.

But professional ball wasn't in the cards, after all. On his last game for U.C.L.A., Gregory broke his right knee and had to undergo two operations. Then came the bad news. He'd never play football again.

Shortly after graduation, he moved out of his father's house in Pacific Heights and into a one-room apartment in North Beach. Angry at the whole world, with no plan for the future, no goal and an I-don't-give-a-damn attitude, Gregory began hitting the bars, drinking himself into oblivion every night until some good Samaritan would finally put him in a cab and send him home.

That's when his old high school buddy Dylon Cross found him. Feeling sorry for him, Dylon gave him a job in his private investigation agency where Gregory learned how to track down missing persons and tail cheating husbands.

The job was boring as hell and not terribly rewarding on the financial level, or on any level. But Gregory had taken it for two reasons. One, he needed the work; two, it had pissed his father off big-time.

Eventually he realized he needed more in his life than

sneaking in and out of dark alleys. In the fall of '85, he went back to graduate school, not to study law, as his father had hoped, but finance, which fascinated him. He met Lindsay, an advertising major, shortly after receiving his Master's. By Christmas of that year, he was married, and nine months later, he was the proud father of a baby girl. But by the time Noelle turned six, two major changes had occurred. Gregory had filed for divorce and he had traded his job as investment counsellor for an executive position in a Fortune 500 company. He was about to be promoted when he realized that his life needed a little spice, a little excitement, a little adventure.

In 1995, combining his knowledge of finance and investigative work, he opened his own agency, but this time, instead of handling divorce cases and missing persons, he branched into a new and fast-expanding field—evaluating companies and investigating the backgrounds of potential CEOs.

He had never regretted the decision. After a struggling couple of years, Shaw and Associates now ranked as one of the top five such agencies in the country.

His aunt Willie had hoped, as Gregory had, that his success would finally bring Milton around. It hadn't. Each time Willie tried to get both men to reach some sort of compromise, they'd start throwing accusations at each other and wouldn't stop until one of them, usually Gregory, stormed out of the house.

Gregory hadn't had a face-to-face encounter with his father in more than six months. His contact with the famous lawyer consisted of driving Noelle to the Pacific Heights house for Sunday dinner and picking her up a few hours later. Fortunately for Noelle, Milton was a better grandfather than he was a father, and she adored him.

A chair scraping against the floor jarred him out of his

thoughts. Focusing his gaze on the defense table, he saw his father rise and turn to face the jury.

One hand resting on Freddy's shoulder, Milton began his summation by depicting the boy's sad and lonely childhood. "Imagine this was your son," he said, looking at each of the twelve jurors. "And *you* had turned your back on him, *you* had beaten him mercilessly night after night, *you* had exposed him to street violence and drugs and drunken brawls. Wouldn't you have to take *some* of the responsibility for the way he turned out? Wouldn't you think, deep down, that perhaps this poor lost soul could be redeemed? And saved? *If* you gave him the chance?"

At those words, Gregory's mouth pulled into a cynical smile. Why was it that his father always felt so compassionate, so forgiving toward vermin such as Freddy but had never once held out a helping hand toward his own son?

Gregory listened to the entire summation, which, as usual, was brilliant and had every juror in that box leaning forward in their seats. As Milton returned to his chair, Gregory slipped out as discreetly as he had come in.

Seven

"**W**hy in the world should you feel guilty?" Preston asked. "You have a right to this winery as much as Annie does."

Rachel's fiancé had arrived moments earlier, surprising her with take-out from her favorite Chinese restaurant and a bouquet of daisies.

He was a tall, devastatingly handsome man, though at times she felt somewhat fickle for admiring his looks rather than his intellect. But she couldn't help it. With his blond hair always perfectly styled, his cool blue eyes and his expensive wardrobe, he looked more like a model for *GQ* than a criminal attorney.

She had met him a year ago at a posh San Francisco party she had reluctantly agreed to attend to promote Spaulding wines. Preston, who had just tried, and won, a high-profile arson case, was one of the guests, and very much the man of the moment. Suddenly, and much to her surprise, he had detached himself from the half dozen or so beautiful women surrounding him and had made his way across the room toward her. After introducing himself, he complimented her on her wines, which he and his family had been drinking for years, and invited her to dinner the following evening.

Two weeks later a San Francisco gossip columnist had dubbed them "the hottest couple in town." And just last month, tired of telling Preston she wasn't ready for marriage, Rachel had put an end to her indecision and finally accepted his proposal.

It wasn't that she didn't love Preston, or didn't want to marry him. On the contrary, she loved and admired him very much and knew without a doubt he'd make a caring husband and father. Sometimes, though, she wondered if he wasn't too perfect, too much of a Mr. Right, too…well, for lack of a better word, "packaged." It wasn't until Grams's death, when he had offered his unconditional support, that she had realized she had made the right decision in accepting his proposal.

"But I wasn't born into this family," she replied in answer to his comment. "I was adopted, which is why Annie was so distraught at the reading of the will."

Preston laughed. "I'm not sure distraught is the word. From what you told me about her behavior, enraged is more like it. But who cares how she felt? You work harder than anyone I know. And you have a great head for business. Your grandmother's decision makes perfect sense to me. Besides, Annie got the house, didn't she?"

Thank God for that, Rachel thought. Annie loved that big rambling house. During the first eight years of her life, prior to Rachel's arrival, she had reigned there like a little princess, adored by all. Then when Jack and Helen had brought the new baby home, her perfect world had, in Annie's own words, come crashing down. From that moment on, no matter how much her parents and Hannah told her they loved her as much as before, she hadn't believed them.

Still pensive, Rachel picked up their wineglasses from the kitchen counter and took them out to the terrace of her hillside bungalow, Preston behind her.

She had moved out of the Spaulding main house three years earlier when she had realized, sadly, that living under the same roof as Annie had become intolerable. Not a day went by without her older sister baiting her into an argument by making some sort of disparaging remark, though she'd been careful to never attack in front of Grams.

When Rachel had heard the Dunbars's bungalow up on Silverado Trail was for sale, she had bought it outright. She had filled the house with the kind of furniture she loved—big oak tables and bookcases, cheery chintzes, Navajo rugs, and pottery in a variety of shapes and colors.

The terrace was her favorite place. High enough to have a sweeping view of the entire valley, it also treated her to one of California's most spectacular attractions—the recurring eruptions of Old Faithful, the thousands-year-old geyser that shot steaming hot water sixty feet into the air every forty minutes.

Preston's arms encircled her from behind. "Forget about Annie," he whispered in her ear.

"I can't." She took a sip of her wine. "Something is going on with her. She's acting strange."

"She *is* strange."

"I'm serious. Except for that outbreak during the reading of the will the other day, she's been very subdued. There've been no wisecracks from her, no insults, not even a dirty look."

She felt Preston shrug. "My guess is that she finally resigned herself to the fact that there's nothing she can do about the will but accept it."

"It's more than that, Preston. Playing the silent victim isn't Annie's style. She's up to something."

"What makes you think that?"

"On Tuesday, she was gone for the entire morning and told the rest of the marketing staff she'd be at the beauty salon. But when I called there at about eleven to ask about a contract with one of our distributors, the people at the beauty salon said they hadn't seen her."

"Did you ask her where she went?"

Rachel let out a small chuckle. "What? And have her tell me it's none of my business? No thanks. I've taken enough grief from her as it is."

"It's your right to ask, you know." He squeezed her a little tighter. "You're the boss now." He chuckled. "I like the sound of that—Rachel, the boss lady."

He would, she thought, amused. Born to wealthy, influential parents, Preston was a firm believer that money and power ruled the world. Sometimes she wondered, again not without a certain amount of guilt, if he would have singled her out had she been a lowly employee instead of one of the heirs to Spaulding Vineyards.

"How's the harvest coming?" he asked, smoothly changing the subject. "Are you still planning on picking the cabernet grapes this week?"

"Friday if all goes well. As of this morning, the grapes registered twenty-one Brix," she added, referring to the way in which the sugar content in the fruit was measured. "Another couple of days should bring the reading to twenty-two, not as high as I would have liked, but as high as it'll get this year."

"I know you're going to be busy for the next few days," he said, sounding mildly apologetic, "but you didn't forget about my alumni dinner next week, did you?"

Damn, she thought, briefly closing her eyes. She *had* forgotten.

"Rachel?"

Hearing the concern in his voice, she patted his hand. "No, I didn't," she lied.

She was tempted to beg off. With Grams dead only a few days, she just didn't feel like being social right now.

But this was an important reunion for Preston. He had already told her how anxious he was to show her off, and bowing out at such a late date would be unfair. "You said eight o'clock, didn't you?" she asked.

"Seven."

"Oh." Before he could offer to pick her up, she added, "I'll meet you at the Fairmont a few minutes before seven then."

"Good." He kissed the top of her head. "Wear your blue suit—the one with the embroidered lapels?"

Accustomed to Preston telling her what to wear and knowing she probably would have picked something totally inappropriate, she nodded. "All right." Draining the last of her Chardonnay, she turned to him and gave him a big smile. "Now, why don't we demolish that wonderful dinner you brought before it gets cold?"

Even though Rachel had given herself a few days to grieve, getting back to work was difficult. Every nook and cranny of the winery was filled with memories of Hannah and the special place she had occupied at Spaulding and in Rachel's heart.

There were the cellars themselves where Rachel and Hannah had worked side by side. In each one was a glass-enclosed cabinet where Spaulding's older vintages and large format bottles were proudly displayed. And there was the catwalk from which Rachel and Hannah had observed the crush year after year.

And of course, there were the vineyards themselves, five hundred acres of rich, fertile soil planted with chardonnay grapes, sauvignon blanc, pinot noir, merlot and the pride of Napa Valley, cabernet sauvignon.

There was so much history here, Rachel thought as she stood in Hannah's cluttered office, so many dreams, some realized, others still in their infancy. How would she be able to see them all through now that she no longer had Hannah's support and constant encouragement?

The steady honking of horns announcing the arrival of the first truckloads of cabernet grapes chased her memories away. Wiping her tears, Rachel walked out of Hannah's office and onto the sunny courtyard where Father Bertolucci was being greeted by some of the workers. The well-known priest had come to deliver his annual Blessing of the Grapes, a time-honored tradition no vintner, Catholic or otherwise, dared to violate.

"How are you, my dear?" he said, coming to meet her, his hands extended. He was a small man with kind eyes and a soothing voice.

"Not too well today, I'm afraid, Father. This will be my first crush without Grams."

He squeezed her hands. "Be strong, my dear. I know this is a trying period for you and your sister, but I have faith in both of you." He smiled. "Almost as much as your grandmother did."

"Thank you, Father." She returned the smile. "I'll try not to disappoint either of you."

Just as he took his position in front of the first truckload, Sam came up behind her and touched her arm. "You have a phone call," he said in a hushed voice. "It's a woman. She wouldn't say who she was, but claims it's important."

"Ask her to wait, will you, Sam? Father Bertolucci is about to start his benediction."

Rachel waited until the parish priest had issued his blessing and driven away before reentering the cellars. In her office, she picked up her extension. "This is Rachel Spaulding."

The voice at the other end was hushed. "Miss Spaulding,

you don't know me," the woman said. "My name is Sister Mary-Catherine."

Rachel's first thought was that the church to which the nun was affiliated had been the recipient of Hannah's endless generosity and the sister was calling to offer her condolences.

"It's extremely important that I talk to you," the nun went on in an urgent tone.

"If it's about a contribution, Sister, I'll be glad to continue my grandmother's—"

"It's not about a contribution."

Outside, a cellar worker barked an order and an overflowing gondola lifted from the truck, paused above the crusher for a moment before tilting and dumping its load into the machine. "Then what is it?" she asked, trying not to sound impatient.

"I work at Our Lady of Good Counsel in Santa Rosa," Sister Mary-Catherine replied.

Rachel frowned. Our Lady of Good Counsel was the convent from which she had been adopted. "Why do you want to see me?" she asked.

"I can't discuss it on the phone, Miss Spaulding. I need to see you in person. I promise I'll explain everything when I see you."

There was an edge of desperation in the nun's voice Rachel couldn't ignore. She made a quick calculation. Santa Rosa was in Sonoma, across the Mayacamas and a mere twenty minutes from Calistoga. She wouldn't be able to go today, but if she left early tomorrow morning, she could be back at the winery by eight-thirty. She would make up for the lost time by working through the dinner hour. Now that Grams was gone, the evening meal, which she and her grandmother had often shared, no longer had the same appeal.

"I can be there tomorrow morning at seven-thirty. Would that be all right?"

At the other end of the line, Rachel heard a small sigh of relief. "Yes, yes, it is. Thank you, Miss Spaulding. We're located three miles north of town, just off Route 12."

Eight

"**M**iss Spaulding!"

The receiver still in her hand, Rachel turned around and recognized Joe Brock. A cellar master at Spaulding Vineyards for more than ten years, he had been fired six months before when Hannah had caught him loading cases of Spaulding Pinot Noir into his pickup. She had later found out he was selling the wine at a discount to a San Francisco restaurateur.

Hannah had fired him on the spot, but because he had a wife and four daughters, one of whom was a friend of Courtney's, she hadn't pressed charges against him.

Unable to find a job elsewhere, Joe had come back to Spaulding twice in the past six months, swearing he had learned his lesson and vowing he would never steal as much as a paper clip. Hannah, however, had stood firm on her decision to never rehire anyone who had stolen from her.

This was Joe's first visit to Spaulding since Grams's death, and Rachel wasn't looking forward to dealing with the belligerent ex-employee.

"How are you, Joe?" she asked, placing the receiver down.

"Lousy." He gave her a look that was long on remorse. "I need a job, Miss Spaulding. The debts are piling up and my wife is threatening to give me the boot if I don't start earning some decent money."

Rachel contemplated him for a moment. She hated thieves as much as Hannah had, especially those she had treated well. Joe had enjoyed a generous salary, frequent raises, large bonuses and, equally important, he'd had Rachel's and Hannah's absolute trust. "I'm sorry, Joe," she said. "I can't help you."

"Sure you can," he said, his voice rising a notch. "You're in charge now. You can do whatever you want."

"That's impossible, Joe," she said diplomatically. "The new cellar master is doing an excellent job and laying him off at this point would be unfair."

"Unfair?" Joe looked as if he were ready to explode. "What about me? I gave ten years of my life to this winery."

"The last two of which you spent stealing from us."

"I said I was sorry, didn't I?" He came to stand in front of her, and the whiff from his breath told her he had been drinking. "How many times do I have to apologize? And how many times are you going to kick a man when he's down?"

His close proximity made her uncomfortable but she refused to let him see that. "You're out of line, Joe," she said, holding the man's hot, angry gaze. "So why don't you leave right now and let me get back to work."

"I thought you'd be different," he said, his words slurring a little. "But you're not. You're just as coldhearted as your grandmother."

"Goodbye, Joe."

He pointed a warning finger at her. "You'll regret this. I swear you will."

"What the hell are you doing here?" Sam demanded

from the doorway. "I thought I told you to leave Rachel alone." He glanced at Rachel. "You okay?"

"I'm fine." She looked at her former cellar master. "Joe was just leaving."

Sister Mary-Catherine was waiting by the front gate when Rachel arrived at Our Lady of Good Counsel the following morning. She was a petite woman with wrinkled cheeks and light blue eyes that, at the moment, regarded her with great interest.

"Thank you for coming," she said in a quiet voice. "Would you mind if we walked as we talked?"

"Not at all."

"I know you have questions," the nun said as they started down the gravel path, "so I'll try to get to the point right away." Her fingers closed around the gold cross that hung from her neck. "A long time ago," she began, "as I was taking a late evening stroll in this same garden, a very frightened young woman ran to the gate and called out for help. I didn't know her but she told me her name was Virginia Potter and that she was running from a dangerous husband."

Not at all sure why she was being told this story, Rachel nonetheless nodded.

"She had a baby with her," Sister Mary-Catherine continued. "A little infant girl by the name of Sarah."

"Her baby?" Rachel asked.

"Yes. She begged me to keep Sarah safe until she came back for her, and not tell anyone she was here. The woman was terribly upset," Sister Mary-Catherine went on. "And so frightened for her baby that I had no choice but to give her my word I wouldn't tell a soul, except, of course, the other sisters."

"Did she come back for Sarah?" Rachel asked.

The nun looked off into the distance. "No. The following morning, we learned that Virginia's name was really Alyssa Dassante and that the baby's name wasn't Sarah but Lillie. Lillie Dassante."

"Dassante." Rachel pursed her lips in concentration. "I know that name from somewhere."

"The Dassantes were, and still are, the largest walnut growers in California. They live in Winters, an hour or so east of here."

Rachel nodded, remembering seeing their product in local stores and advertised on billboards.

"We also learned," Sister Mary-Catherine said, lowering her head, "that Alyssa was wanted by the police."

"Wanted by the police?" The nun's story was getting more bizarre by the minute. "For what?"

"For killing her husband, Mario Dassante," she said in a whisper. "The following day, we heard more bad news. Alyssa had been traveling on Route 1 when her car plunged into the Pacific."

Rachel came to an abrupt halt. "Oh, how awful."

"Yes." The nun paused for a couple of seconds. "After the other sisters and I discussed the situation, we decided we had no choice but return the child to the Dassantes."

In spite of herself, Rachel felt caught up in the story. "Of course."

"We never did." Sister Mary-Catherine resumed walking. "That night another tragedy struck, this time right here at the convent. While everyone slept, our heater, an old dinosaur we had been meaning to replace, caught fire. Within moments, the entire lower floor was engulfed in flames. By the time the firemen had put out the fire, two nuns had died. And one child." The older woman crossed herself. "Little Lillie."

Rachel's eyes widened in horror. "Oh, no."

Sister Mary-Catherine nodded. "It was a terrible time for us, but especially for me. I kept thinking that if I hadn't been so impulsive, if I had asked more questions about Alyssa's reason for leaving her family, I might have been able to counsel her, maybe even convince her to return home and talk things over with her husband. And the baby," she added in a voice filled with sorrow, "would have lived."

"You were only trying to help." Rachel waited until the nun had composed herself once again before asking, "Were you the one who told the Dassantes the baby had died?"

Sister Mary-Catherine nodded. "Sal Dassante, the baby's grandfather, took the news very badly. He had just lost his son and here I was, the bearer of more bad news."

"I'm so sorry, Sister. It's a sad, tragic story, but I don't understand why—"

"The day after the fire," the nun interrupted, "we received a frantic call. It was Alyssa. She hadn't died, after all, but had heard about the fire and wanted to make sure Lillie was all right.

"Telling her the baby who had died was her little girl was the most difficult thing I've ever had to do in my entire thirty-nine years as a servant of God," she said in a choked voice. "I'll never forget the heart-wrenching cry at the other end of the line. Before I could find out where Alyssa was, so I could go and comfort her, she hung up. We never heard from her after that."

"And you never called the police to tell them she was alive?"

"Oh, no." The nun gave a vehement shake of her head. "I couldn't do that, not after the grief I'd already caused her." She was silent for a moment. "In time, the part of the convent that was destroyed was rebuilt and most of the children in our care were adopted by area families, including another infant girl who was left with us only two days before Lillie Dassante arrived. She was the same age as Lillie—two weeks.

"I never made the connection between those two infants until sixteen years later, when I saw a picture of that little girl in a newspaper and noticed her extraordinary resemblance to Alyssa Dassante. That's when I realized the terrible mistake I and the other sisters had made on the night of the fire."

"Mistake?" Though she tried to stay calm, Rachel's mouth had gone dry. The nun wouldn't be telling her this story unless Rachel was somehow involved.

"Yes. It wasn't Lillie who had died in that blaze, you see, but that other little girl."

The convent's three bells suddenly began ringing, signaling the hour. Sister Mary-Catherine waited until they had stopped before continuing. "The other nuns and I were filled with remorse at the unnecessary pain we had caused Alyssa, and since I had, in fact, started this whole mess, I was elected to approach the little girl's adoptive family and explain the situation to them.

"I knew they had the means to search for Lillie's birth mother, and I was hoping that's what they'd do so Alyssa could be told her little girl was alive. At first they didn't believe me, so I showed them a picture of Alyssa, one I had cut from a newspaper. I could tell by their expression that this time, they did believe me."

"Did the girl's parents find Alyssa?" Rachel asked.

"No. They refused to look for her. They were afraid she would want her child back and they loved their daughter too much to give her up."

"You didn't pursue the matter? Notify the Dassantes?"

Sister Mary-Catherine looked down at the cross she had been holding all this time. "I thought about it. And I thought about the consequences my telling the Dassantes would have on that young girl. She was so happy, you see, so well adjusted. What would be accomplished by telling her she was the daughter of a woman suspected of murder?'' She pressed the cross against her chest. ''So we didn't say anything, and we never talked about it after that day. I and the other nuns lived with our secret all these years.'' She looked up. ''Until now.''

Rachel's mouth went dry. She was filled with a sudden premonition, a certainty that from this moment on her life would never be the same again. ''What are you trying to tell me, Sister?'' she asked in a trembling voice.

Sister Mary-Catherine's limpid blue eyes filled with tears. ''You are that little girl, Rachel. *You* are Lillie Dassante.''

Nine

Even though Rachel had already guessed the answer, her heart lunged in her chest in one powerful thump. Standing very still, she stared at the nun as a wave of emotions, ranging from shock to disbelief to anger, washed over her.

It was too much to absorb, to comprehend. She had always believed her birth mother had died in childbirth. Why should she believe any different now?

"It can't be," Rachel murmured at last. "You must be mistaken."

From the folds of her black habit, Sister Mary-Catherine pulled out a small, folded piece of paper. As she began to unfold it, Rachel realized it was a newspaper clipping, yellowed by time. "This is an old photo," she said, handling it carefully. "But I think you'll be able to see enough to know that I'm telling the truth, just as your parents did."

Rachel's fingers shook as she reached for the clipping. Lowering her gaze, she took a sharp intake of breath. The woman staring back at her could have been Rachel's twin sister. She had the same thick dark hair, the same large dark eyes, tilting up slightly at the outer corners, the same generous mouth and long neck. There was even a small mole above her right lip.

In an involuntary gesture, Rachel's fingertips went to touch her own birthmark, positioned at exactly the same place. She raised stricken eyes to Sister Mary-Catherine. "Alyssa?"

The nun nodded. "That picture ran in the *Winters Journal* when it was announced Alyssa and Mario would be married. Given the Dassantes's prominence in the community, that was big news back then, not only in Winters where they lived, but throughout California."

A door suddenly opened and children, laughing and shoving each other, spilled into the playground. They ranged in age from about two to early teens. Still in a state of shock, Rachel watched a little girl with dark curls head for the swing. A little girl who belonged to no one, Rachel thought with an ache in her heart. Just as she had belonged to no one, for a while.

"Why are you telling me this now?" Rachel asked, returning her gaze to the nun sitting beside her. "Thirty-one years later."

"I wouldn't have told you at all, but yesterday a man came to see me. He seemed to know Alyssa hadn't died and he wanted information about her."

"Who is he?"

The nun reached into her habit again. This time her hand came out holding a business card, which she handed to Rachel.

Rachel glanced at it. And had yet another shock as she read the gold-embossed card: Gregory Shaw—Shaw and Associates. "Gregory," she murmured.

"Do you know him?" Sister Mary Catherine asked.

Oh, yes, she knew him. A wave of embarrassment made her look away as she recalled Annie's wedding to Luke Aymes, sixteen years before, and Rachel's crush on the groom's handsome best man. Later, she had heard the two men talking about her and laughing at the way she had stared at Gregory during the entire wedding ceremony.

Mortified, Rachel had run back into the house, refusing to accept Gregory's apologies. "I never want to see you again," she had shouted as she slammed her bedroom door in his face.

Thanks to Annie's short-lived marriage to Luke, Rachel's wish was granted, but it had taken her weeks to get over that humiliating afternoon and be able to face people again.

So what was Gregory doing looking for her birth mother? From what she'd heard, he was no longer a struggling P.I. but the owner of a very successful agency. Why would he waste his time on such a small case? Unless he was doing someone a favor.

Rachel tapped the business card on the back of her hand. If Annie hadn't hated him so much, Rachel might have suspected her of having hired him. That kind of sneaky act was right up Annie's alley. But her dislike for Luke's best friend was almost as fierce as Rachel's. Annie had once claimed, rather convincingly, that she wouldn't lend Gregory a hand if he lay bleeding to death on a sidewalk.

"Yes, I know him," she said in answer to the nun's question. She looked up, suddenly concerned Gregory may have persuaded the nun to give him information. "Did you tell Mr. Shaw I was alive?" she asked.

"No. It wasn't my place to tell him anything. And since I'm the only one left who knows what happened that night, he'll never find out the truth here." She gripped her cross again, as if holding it gave her the strength to bear the weight of her lie. "I'm concerned, however, that he might be working for Sal Dassante."

"Why? Did he mention Sal's name?"

"No, but when your mother disappeared, Sal was the only person who didn't believe she had died. He kept insisting she had staged the accident so she could escape. He was so determined to find her that he offered a fifty-thousand-dollar reward for her capture. Eventually, he gave up, but now the search seems to be active again, otherwise why would this Mr. Shaw be here, looking for Alyssa?''

Why, indeed? Rachel mused. And even more important, what would happen if he found out Rachel was Alyssa Dassante's daughter? Would he expose her? Report his findings to whoever had hired him?

At the thought of the damage such a scandal could do, not only to her personally but to Spaulding Vineyards, Rachel was filled with panic. What if she lost the winery because of this?

Once again the possibility that Annie was behind this scheme crossed her mind, and once again Rachel rejected it. Annie couldn't possibly know about Alyssa. And if she did, she'd never go to Gregory for help, partly because she hated him and partly because she knew he'd never agree to do anything so deceitful. He just hadn't seemed that kind of man.

Sister Mary-Catherine was the first to break the silence. "You understand why I had to warn you, don't you, Rachel? Whatever happens, I couldn't let you hear the truth from anyone but me."

"I appreciate that, Sister." Rachel kept staring at the clipping in her hand. Questions rushed through her head, demanding answers. If Alyssa Dassante was alive, where was she? Would she come out of hiding if she knew her daughter was alive? Then came the question she wasn't yet ready to answer. Did she want to find this woman?

"You're a good person, Sister Mary-Catherine," she said, meaning every word. "I think I understand why…Alyssa trusted you with her child." She'd almost said "my mother" but caught herself in time. How odd, she mused, that the word should have entered her mind at all; this was a woman she didn't know and probably never would.

Feeling she ought to do something more to thank the nun, Rachel opened her purse and took out her checkbook.

Sister Mary-Catherine stopped her. "That's not necessary, my child."

"Please, let me do this." Rachel glanced toward the playground again. The little girl with the black curls was on the swing now, laughing happily as an older girl pushed her. "For the children."

Sister Mary-Catherine withdrew her hand. "Thank you," she said simply.

During the short trip home, Alyssa remained on Rachel's mind. Surely there was no worse tragedy than the loss of a child—no matter what Alyssa had done, she hadn't deserved that. And her little baby hadn't deserved to be left without a mother.

Another part of her didn't see it that way. Forget about Alyssa Dassante, a fierce voice whispered. She's nothing to you. You're Rachel Spaulding. You were raised by loving, devoted parents who made you who you are today.

Yet Rachel couldn't dismiss this knowledge of the person who had given birth to her and who had tried desperately to protect her from a family she apparently feared. Somewhere out there was a woman who was part of her, a woman whose blood ran in her veins, a woman whose looks, flaws and qualities Rachel had inherited.

As she drove back through the winding mountain pass, she thought of Alyssa driving down another treacherous road thirty-one years before. What thoughts had gone through her mind on that dark, frightening night as she tried to outrun the police?

When the sign for Route 29 came into view, Rachel

flicked on her directionals. "Where are you, Alyssa?" she murmured.

Fifteen minutes later, Rachel was back at the winery. After signing a work order her assistant, Ryan Cummings, handed her, Rachel hurried toward Sam's office. Sam had been her father's best friend, and if anyone could shed some light on this puzzling mystery, it was him.

She found the winemaker in front of his computer, studying a printout. "Sam, you got a minute?"

Sam looked up and started to smile, then, as Rachel closed the door behind her, his thick eyebrows drew into a worried line. "What's wrong, honey? Are you upset about something?"

"You could say that." She walked across the small office and perched a hip on the corner of his desk. "That call I had yesterday," she said, closely watching his reaction, "was from a nun in Santa Rosa. Sister Mary-Catherine?"

Sam turned pale.

"You know her, don't you?"

Sam watched her for a few seconds, his expression troubled. Then, with a sigh, he dropped the computer printout onto the desk. "What did she tell you?"

"Everything, from the night Alyssa Dassante rang the convent's bell to her frantic call the morning after the fire." She waited a few seconds before asking, "It's true, then? I'm Alyssa Dassante's daughter."

"It's true." Sam raked his thick gray hair back. "Why did she tell you now? She had agreed not to—"

"Because Gregory Shaw went to see her. Yes," she added when she saw the startled look on his face. "*That* Gregory Shaw. Somehow that jerk found out Alyssa was alive and now he's going around asking questions. That's why Sister Mary-Catherine called me. She wanted me to hear the truth from her first in case this thing blows wide open.''

''But that doesn't make sense. Gregory doesn't handle those kinds of cases anymore.''

''Maybe he did it as a favor to someone.'' She pursed her lips. ''Guess whose name popped into my mind?''

Sam shook his head. ''Not Annie, no way.''

''Dammit, Sam, someone had to hire him.''

''Yes, but not Annie. She despises the man. To this day she's convinced he's responsible for Luke divorcing her. And how would she know about your birth mother? She was living in Rutherford with Luke when Sister Mary-Catherine came to see your parents, and no one except them, Tina, Hannah and myself knew Alyssa Dassante was your—''

''Grams knew?''

Sam's expression was instantly regretful, as though he wished he hadn't spoken so quickly. ''Don't be upset with Hannah, Rachel. She was only trying to protect you.''

''Did she know the Dassantes?''

''No, but after that visit from Sister Mary-Catherine, she had them investigated.''

''Why?''

''She was afraid Sal might find out who you were and try to claim you. She wanted to have as much ammunition to fight them as possible.''

''What did she find out?''

''That Alyssa was a stripper before she married Mario, and Sal, your grandfather, was despised by all who knew him, but especially by his employees.''

''Why is that?''

''Lousy work conditions at the farm, low wages, poor treatment of migrant workers—you name it, he did it. But

Sal had deep pockets, so he never got in trouble, nothing serious, anyway.''

Trying to digest all she had heard in the space of a couple of hours, Rachel looked down at her fingernails and realized one was broken. Suddenly she remembered that morning in Paris when Courtney had turned her into a fashion plate. How simple things had been back then, with nothing more to worry about than an irascible Frenchman. "Do you know what happened on the night Alyssa ran away?" she asked.

Sam nodded. "It was one of the most talked about stories of that decade. Apparently Mario and Alyssa were heard arguing in the middle of the night. The Dassantes went down to investigate and found Mario dead. He had been pushed, and in the fall, he hit his head on a heavy piece of equipment.''

"And Alyssa?"

"She, her car, and the baby were gone. The following morning, a California state trooper reported a crash on Route 1. The car they pulled out of the ocean was Alyssa's Mercedes, the clothes inside the car, hers and the baby's. The police immediately initiated a state-wide search. Sal even offered a large reward, but she never turned up.''

"And now someone whose identity we don't know wants her found." Rachel looked up. "Why, Sam? So she can be arrested? Hasn't she suffered enough?''

Sam looked at her in surprise. "Do you have feelings for that woman?" he asked gently.

"No, of course not," she said, averting her eyes.

"Would you like to find her?" he pressed.

"I didn't say that." Still unable to look at him, she played with the crease on her gray slacks. She didn't know what she wanted.

"I see." Sam was silent for a moment. "I could talk to

Gregory," he offered. "Find out how much he knows. He and I always got along all right."

Rachel shook her head. "That would tip him off that we're involved somehow. It's better not to say anything."

"What about the Dassantes?"

This time she met his gaze. "What about them?"

"Do you intend to approach them? Tell them who you are?"

"Absolutely not." That was one thing she was sure of. "I don't know those people and have no desire to know them." Then, still worried the story might come out, she asked the question she'd been burning to ask. "Sam, if this scandal were to surface, if it became public that Alyssa Dassante was my mother, could I...lose the winery?"

"Absolutely not," Sam replied, sounding outraged. "None of this is your fault, and Ambrose would have to be crazy to even bring up that possibility."

Not entirely reassured, Rachel gave him a weak smile. "I suppose you're right."

"Good, now come on." Wrapping an arm around her shoulders, he led her out of his office. "I want your opinion on my latest Sauvignon Blanc."

The woman ran. Holding her precious bundle against her chest, she weaved through the forest, running faster and faster. From time to time, as the sounds of footsteps grew closer, she turned around to check her pursuers's progress. Fear was etched on her face and her heart beat painfully against her ribs.

Please, God, she prayed. Don't let them catch me. Not until my baby is safe.

Behind her, the enemy was gaining.

"Alyssa! No sense in running anymore."

"Give us the baby, Alyssa! She's ours, not yours."

"You're a murderer, Alyssa! You don't deserve Lillie!"

No! She wouldn't give them her baby. Never. Tears ran down her face as she tightened her hold around Lillie. "Don't cry, my little darling," she murmured as the baby began to whimper. "And don't be afraid. You're safe. No one will ever take you away from me. We'll make a new life for ourselves. Just you and me."

As she ran, she looked frantically around her. Where was that convent? She had been running for hours. She should have reached it by now. What if she was lost? What if she got caught?

That thought sent another wave of panic through her. She couldn't get caught. She couldn't let those horrible people raise her baby, turn her into one of them.

She was panting now, from fatigue and from fear. Then, like a beacon, she saw the clearing. And at the end of that clearing was the pink stucco building she remembered, its distinctive three bells on top. The convent! Thank you, God, thank you.

She had almost reached the gate when a hand closed over her shoulder—

Rachel awoke with a start. Drenched in perspiration and trembling, she sat up but didn't turn on the light. The taste of fear, Alyssa's fear, was in her mouth. The dream had been so vivid, she could still hear the pounding of footsteps behind her, feel the viselike hand closing over Alyssa's shoulder.

Taking big gulps of air, Rachel pushed the covers aside and climbed out of bed, not bothering to pull a robe around her.

On the terrace, the cool breeze turned her damp skin icy, but she paid no attention to it. All that mattered at the moment was that dream. Oh, God, it had been so real, the woman so alive, so much...a part of her. And so had the

baby. Rachel had actually felt the warmth of Alyssa's body
through the blanket, the pounding of her heart as she ran,
the gentle, musical sound of her voice as she talked to her
child, telling her not to be afraid.

"Mom."

The word no longer sounded foreign to her. She felt a
connection to Alyssa now, a bond no one would ever be
able to break. And with that realization came another one.

She had to find Alyssa Dassante.

She had to find her mother.

Ten

"**M**r. Dassante, this is Harold Mertz."

Sal Dassante, who had been sitting in his living room, enjoying a midafternoon sherry he wasn't supposed to have, was instantly alert. He hadn't seen or heard from the ex-Winters P.D. detective in—what, fifteen years? Twenty? "How are you, Harold?"

"Oh, I can't complain. I'm retired now, you know."

"No, I didn't know." And didn't really care. "I hope you're enjoying your free time."

"You bet I am. I do a little fishing every now and then, play ball with my grandkids, baby-sit." He chuckled. "You know how it is."

No, Harold, I don't know, Sal wanted to say. My only grandchild was taken away from me thirty-one years ago. But before the hatred could surface again, he pushed it aside and concentrated on Harold. The fact that the former homicide detective was calling so soon after the call from his private investigator gave him hope that Joe Kelsey had been right, after all. Alyssa *was* alive. And Harold Mertz had called to confirm it.

"The reason I called," Mertz continued, "is because I had a visitor today. A man by the name of Gregory Shaw."

Sal pursed his lips and searched his memory. "Never heard of him."

"He's a P.I. Owns a fancy agency that investigates companies' CEOs."

"He told you all that?"

"Hell, no. He didn't say nothin' about himself. I ran a check on him through the department," Harold added proudly.

Sal took another sip of his sherry. Well, what do you know, old Mertz wasn't as stupid as he looked. "What did he want?"

"Information." Mertz paused slightly, no doubt for effect. He had always been a little on the dramatic side. "On Alyssa."

Sal had trouble drawing his next breath. In thirty-one years, no one had ever shown the slightest interest in finding Alyssa, except him, of course. Now, all of a sudden, everyone seemed fascinated with the past. "How did he know to come to you?"

"He'd read some old newspaper articles dating back to the time of the investigation."

"What did you tell him?"

"The truth, that Alyssa was dead and he was wasting his time."

Yeah, that's what they all thought, Sal thought smugly, and they were wrong. "Did he tell you who he's working for?"

"I asked him but he was mum about that, too."

Sal put his glass on the table next to him and began twirling it slowly. So someone else was looking for Alyssa. How interesting. For a moment he debated whether to ask Mertz to find out more about this Gregory Shaw. After all, he'd paid that dumb cop a small fortune at the time of Mario's murder so he'd keep looking for Alyssa. Sal figured since Mertz hadn't found a damn thing, he still owed him. After a second or two, though, he changed his mind.

The job required someone with more sophistication and greater mobility. Someone like Joe Kelsey.

"Why don't you give me Shaw's address and phone number?" Sal said, reaching for a pad and pencil on the table near him.

"Sure thing, Mr. Dassante."

After he'd written down the information, Sal tucked the small square piece of paper in his pocket and made a mental note to call Kelsey later. "You keep your eyes and ears open, okay, Harold? You hear anything, you report to me."

"I will." There was another pause. "What's this all about, Mr. Dassante? Why is this Shaw character looking for your daughter-in-law?"

There was no harm in telling him what he had learned from Kelsey, Sal thought. The whole damn town would know soon enough. "My private investigator found out she's alive."

"Holy shit." Mertz's voice had risen a couple of octaves. "That's unbelievable. Where the hell is she?"

"Don't know that yet."

"You're goin' to tell the chief, aren't you?"

"Of course I'm gonna tell the chief. I'm gonna rub his goddamned nose in it. In the meantime, let me know if Shaw turns up again, okay?" He paused. "I'll make it worth your while." He already had, but what the hell. It never hurt to keep a cop, even an ex-cop, on your side.

"Thank you, Mr. Dassante. You can count on me."

"I know I can." After hanging up, Sal walked over to the window and watched the migrant workers walk slowly, too dammed slowly, toward the walnut grove that spread over his huge property.

Just as his retirement two years ago hadn't affected Sal's body clock—he still got up at the crack of dawn—it hadn't diminished his pleasure at watching the pickers harvest the walnuts that had made him a rich man.

As always that thought brought him immense satisfaction. Who would have thought that Salvatore Pietro Dassante, the scrawny, uneducated, dirt-poor kid from Pozzuoli would someday end up being so fucking rich?

The son of Italian parents who made a living selling rags, Sal hadn't let poverty stand in the way of his dream—to go to America someday and make lots of money. But no matter how hard he worked, picking olives, cleaning fish, and even washing his father's rags, he never seemed to make enough to buy himself a ticket on one of those fancy ships that docked in the Bay of Naples a couple of times a year.

At fifteen, afraid he'd end up being called "Ragman" like his father for the rest of his life, and knowing he'd never be able to afford the trip to America, Sal decided to stow away. When he made the announcement to his parents, they didn't even bat an eye. With ten other siblings at the dinner table every night, one less kid meant one less mouth to feed.

On September 1, 1939, as World War II ceased to be a threat and became a reality, Sal stowed away aboard a merchant marine ship bound for New York City. After a dozen stops along the way and an influenza epidemic that killed half the crew, the ship finally sailed into New York Harbor, where the sight of the Statue of Liberty had brought tears to Sal's eyes.

But after one month in the city where a handful of expatriates from the old country had made their fortune, Sal decided he didn't like it there. The weather was brutal and Italian immigrants still faced a lot of prejudice, making it hard to earn a living.

With five dollars in his pocket and all his worldly possessions packed in a single bag, he hitched a ride, then another and again another, until he reached Sacramento, where the sun and the work were plentiful. He found a job in a snack bar, washing dishes, sweeping floors and doing just about anything the boss wanted him to do. By the time he turned sixteen, he moved to Winters, a farming community west of Sacramento, where he found work picking walnuts.

The hours were long, the pay low, and the people mean. They made fun of his Italian accent and his scrawny looks. But in the end, he was the one who had the last laugh because the scrawny kid from Pozzuoli could climb a tree like a monkey and pick walnuts faster than anyone else. And since they were paid by the bushel, he was able to double his pay, day after day.

Soon, he was lending money to the other workers, who no longer called him names, and collecting interest. He may not have been educated, but he wasn't stupid.

When the field supervisor, a shrewd man by the name of Ben Marcione, realized Sal's potential, he introduced him to his daughter. After one look at the homely, not too bright girl, Sal told Ben, "I'll take her off your hands. For a hundred dollars."

Ben had been only too happy to pay.

It took Sal fourteen years to save enough money to buy a walnut farm of his own and another three years until he could purchase the property next door and expand.

That's when all the shit had started. Jealous of the little wop who had made it big, his neighbors had accused him of putting unfair pressure on the old property owner, offering him a fraction of what the land was worth. But what those morons called unethical, Sal called good business.

Later, those same flaming liberals had claimed he was taking advantage of his workers. He had put a stop to that rumor real quick, the only way he knew how—with cash in the right pockets.

Okay, so he was paying his workers below minimum wage, and maybe his farm wasn't the Ritz. But the men he employed still made three times what they made in their own country, didn't they? And they kept coming back at harvest time, didn't they? Year after year. Of their own free will. What did that tell you?

His mouth tightened into a thin, bitter line. Alyssa had been one of those flaming liberals. And she had been ballsy enough to call him a tyrant to his face, in front of the entire family. That's when Sal had realized she'd never be a true Dassante. But Mario, who thought with his crotch when it came to women, wouldn't listen.

"Give her time, Pop," he always said. "She'll come around."

But she hadn't come around, and when Mario finally realized Alyssa was a troublemaker, it was too late.

The thought of that night, of his son's body lying in the driveway, the back of his head bashed in and bloody, brought a small groan from Sal's throat. It was a night Sal would never forget. He had retired early and was sound asleep when he heard the pounding on his bedroom door.

"Come down quick, Pop!" his younger son had called. "Something happened to Mario."

Sal had run down the stairs and out the front door in his pajamas and found Nico kneeling on the ground, cradling his dead brother in his arms.

"She killed him, Pop," Nico sobbed as he turned to Sal. "That bitch killed my brother."

At that moment a piece of Sal had died with Mario. It was then that he had vowed to avenge his son's death. He would find Alyssa, and when he did, he would kill her.

But despite his efforts and all the money he had spent,

Alyssa had outsmarted them all—the authorities, Detective Mertz, even the two private investigators Sal had hired before teaming up with Joe Kelsey two years ago.

Kelsey, an ex-FBI man who'd had to take early retirement because of a drinking problem, had come through for him, and he would come through again. He would find Alyssa. Maybe with a little luck, Gregory Shaw would lead him right to her.

Lowering his gaze, Sal looked at his strong hands clasped in front of him. Little Salvatore wasn't so scrawny anymore, he thought with a silent chuckle. Even now, at seventy-four, Sal prided himself on being strong as an ox. He got up every morning at five, did twenty push-ups and swam laps in the backyard pool for ten uninterrupted minutes, three hundred and sixty-five days a year.

He didn't even look seventy-four, he thought, turning to catch his reflection in the open window. He still had a full head of hair, mostly gray, which he kept slicked back with pomade, the way he liked it, and sharp old eyes that missed nothing.

And now, thanks to the news from Kelsey and from Harold Mertz, he felt even better—invigorated, raring to go, the way he did after a cold shower. Alyssa was alive. The words kept dancing in his head like a tarantella, gaining momentum and filling him with an excitement he hadn't felt since he was seventeen.

The time had come to share the good news with the rest of the family and to tell them of his intention to talk to Chief Vernon about reopening the case. Not that he needed their permission for anything, but for the sake of harmony, he would call a family meeting.

They arrived promptly—his son Nico and his daughter-in-law, Erica, who still lived with him. "Pop." Moving quickly, Nico crossed the room and came to kiss his father on the cheek. "I thought you were playing bocce with your friends."

Dark-haired and a head taller than Sal, Nico had inherited his late mother's plain looks and her stupidity, while Mario had been more like Sal, sharp and rough on the edges.

"I didn't feel like playing bocce today," Sal said.

"Why not?" Erica, an attractive brunette with motherly instincts, came to sit next to him on the sofa, her expression worried. "Aren't you feeling well?"

Sal looked fondly at his daughter-in-law. Now, there was a true Dassante woman—quiet, caring, respectful and a good wife to Nico. Too bad the big jerk was sterile and hadn't been able to fulfill his wife's deepest desire—to have a child.

He looked at his son and waited until he, too, had taken a seat. Then, with slow, calculated movements, he opened an inlaid box next to him and selected a cigar.

"Pop," Nico said reproachfully. "You know what the doctor said. Only one cigar a day, after dinner."

"And you know what *I* say? Screw the doctor." He took a cheap Zippo lighter from the table, flicked it open and held the flame to the tip of the cigar, puffing quickly a few times. At the fourth puff, he held the smoke in his mouth for several seconds then released it slowly. Satisfied he had dragged the suspense long enough, he leaned back in his chair. "Alyssa is alive." He said the words slowly, relishing every syllable.

The announcement had exactly the effect he had expected. Erica gasped and covered her mouth with her hands and Nico fell back against his chair, his expression one of utter disbelief. "It can't be," he said at last.

"It's true." Sal took another puff. He was rather enjoying their shock. Both had been so damned quick to accept the police's version that Alyssa had died. It pleased him to no end that he had finally proven them wrong.

"How do you know?" Erica lowered her hands from her mouth and pressed them against her chest. "I thought you had abandoned the search years ago, after that last private detective told you he was giving up."

Holding the cigar between cupped fingers, Sal turned it around as though he were inspecting it. "But I didn't give up, *Cara*. I just got another private eye."

Nico frowned. "You never told us that."

"That's because I'm sick of you telling me I'm wasting my money."

Nico's expression grew sullen. "So, where is she?"

"That, I don't know." Sal repeated his conversation with Kelsey and Mertz.

As Nico started to say something, Erica raised her hand and Nico shut his mouth. "Sal," she said gently, "how can you be sure that woman is Alyssa?"

"My gut feeling tells me it's Alyssa." He looked from her to Nico, who stared at him with a blank look on his face. "Didn't you hear a word I said?" he asked, irritated they were both so thick. "She used the name Virginia Potter. *Virginia,*" he repeated. "Her mother's name. And according to that forger, she had a wad of cash with her. That alone is a dead giveaway. I always did wonder what happened to the rest of the money she stole from us. That bitch had more brains than we gave her credit for. She left eight thousand in the car for the cops to find and kept the other two thousand."

When Nico's expression remained doubtful, Sal added, "And now, less than a week after Kelsey called, this fancy private investigator shows up right here in Winters and starts asking questions about her." He pinched the fingers of his left hand together and shook them at Nico. "Don't you see the connection here?"

Nico glanced at his wife, who gave a helpless shrug. "Who's Gregory Shaw working for?" he asked.

"What's with all the questions?" Sal exploded. "What am I? A frigging psychic? I don't know who he's working for, but I know one thing. I'm gonna find Alyssa before he does."

"Aw, Pop!" Nico jumped out of his chair. "Not again."

"What you mean not again?" Sal said angrily. "The woman killed my son. Or you forgot that, maybe."

"I didn't forget anything, but dammit, Pop, Mario died thirty-one years ago. It's history. Let it go."

"Like hell I will." Sal banged his fist on the armrest. "She took my son. My firstborn. And if that wasn't enough, she took my granddaughter and left her in a convent to die." He shook his head. "No one gets away with that."

"Is that all that matters to you?" Nico's voice shook as he walked over to a well-stocked liquor cart and splashed bourbon into a glass. "Avenging Mario's death? Can't you be happy with what you have—me, Erica, a thriving business?"

Sal took a deep breath and tried to stay calm. Nico's reaction didn't surprise him. His younger son had never understood how men in the old country dealt with the likes of Alyssa. Only three years younger than Mario, Nico had nonetheless adopted the typical American mentality of forgive and forget, and had always scoffed at the Old World traditions Sal had tried to instill in the boys. Mario had been different, a true Italian son, with a strong sense of pride, the kind of pride the Dassante family was known for. And he'd had brass balls, just like his father.

"She killed my son," Sal repeated stubbornly.

Nico turned around, glass in hand, his dark eyes heavy

with resentment. "Would you rather *I* had died, Pop? Would that have made you happy?"

"Nico!" Erica stared at her husband in shock. "What a terrible thing to say."

"Can you blame me?" he asked his wife, keeping his eyes on Sal. "Thirty-one years and we're still at square one, still talking about Mario and how to avenge his death, as if that was the only thing that mattered. Not one day has passed since that night without my brother's name being mentioned. Do you know how that makes me feel, Pop?" he asked, stopping in front of Sal. "Knowing that I'm still second fiddle around here, that you don't appreciate a damn thing I do."

"Of course, I appreciate what you do," Sal said irritably. "Would I let you run my company if I didn't?"

"I don't know, Pop." Nico's tone turned sarcastic. "Maybe you're letting me run your company because there's no one else."

"That's garbage."

"Is it?" Nico's eyes narrowed. "Just tell me this. Let's say Alyssa *is* alive and you do find her. What will you do then? Escort her to the nearest police station and let justice run its course? Or will you take the law into your own hands and kill her yourself, as you threatened to do thirty-one years ago?"

Sal kept puffing on his cigar, watching Nico through the curling smoke.

"You can't answer me, can you? That's because we both know what the answer is. You'll never be happy until you've killed her with your own two hands. You don't care that you'll tear this family apart, or that you'll spend the rest of your life behind bars. All that matters is avenging Mario. It's always been Mario."

"Are you finished?" Sal asked coldly.

Nico took one last gulp of his drink. "Yeah, I'm finished."

Sal slowly put out his cigar in the big pewter ashtray next to him. "I thought you'd be happy for me," he said, looking at his son. "I thought you'd understand how it's been for me all these years." He shook his head. *"Ma capite niente."*

"You're wrong, Pop. I understand everything, but I'm not going to stand here and pretend to be happy that Alyssa is alive, because I'm not."

"You want her to get away with what she did?"

"I want peace in this family, Pop. That's what I want." In a quieter voice, he added, "I grieved for my brother, too. But I got past it. I didn't let it consume me the way it continues to consume you."

Erica, who seldom spoke against Sal, lay her hand on his arm. "He is right, you know," she said softly. "Your need to avenge Mario's death *has* consumed you. Look at you. You should be out with your friends every day, enjoying the sunshine, going for long walks. Instead you spend most of your time in this house, growing old and bitter. I tell you what," she added with a pretty smile. "Why don't you come to mass with me on Sunday? I'll introduce you to widow Cartelana." She gave his elbow a little nudge. "I think she's sweet on you."

Turning to look at his daughter-in-law, Sal was tempted to remind her that her place was to listen, not to lecture. But today, he was in too good a mood to get pissed off. So, he would take the sermon and shut up.

"Widow Cartelana has warts on her nose. And Sunday mass puts me to sleep." Seeing the look of disappointment on Erica's face, he patted her cheek. "But I'll take your advice about getting out more. In fact, I'm going for a drive right now." He stood. "Nico, bring the car around."

"Where are you going?"

He held his son's gaze. "To see Chief Vernon. I want to tell him Alyssa is alive. Once he hears I have proof, he'll reopen the case."

"Aw, Pop, don't do that," Nico said, sounding like a whiny five-year-old. "If you do, the press is going to be on our doorstep night and day, like they were before. Our lives will never be the same."

"And *I'll* never be the same until I find the woman who killed my son," Sal snapped. *"Capece?"* With the back of his hand, he tapped Nico's stomach, hard. "I'll get the car myself. Get out of my way."

Eleven

Rachel took a sip of the estate Merlot that had been aging for the past eighteen months, swished it around her mouth for a few seconds then spit it in the bucket at her feet.

Next to her, her assistant, Ryan Cummings, watched intently. "So what do you think?" He was a handsome young man with startling blue eyes, blond hair and a pouty mouth that made him look like Brad Pitt.

Because of the camaraderie that had always existed between them, Rachel made a face. "Hmm, I don't know, Ryan. I know this is your first wine and you were hoping for rave reviews, but…"

At the shattered expression on his face, she broke into laughter. "I was just teasing. It's excellent, Ryan." She sniffed the Merlot again. "The cherry aroma is very concentrated, very full. And blending this particular Merlot with a small amount of Cabernet Franc was a wonderful idea. A couple more years of cellaring and it'll be perfect."

Ryan beamed. "Thank you, Rachel."

She was about to move on to the next barrel when she saw Sam walking toward her, his face grim. "Ryan," she said quickly, sensing another disaster, "why don't we continue this a little later?"

"Sure thing, boss."

Sam watched him leave before he turned to Rachel. "You're not going to like this."

Rachel felt her shoulders sag. "What now?"

He pulled her into a quiet corner. "I went to Murphy's to get the *St. Helena Star* and right next to it was the *Winters Journal.* This was on the front page." He handed her a newspaper.

With a groan, Rachel read the blaring headline: New Spin On Search For Alyssa Dassante.

The article, under the byline of Stanley Fox, was a re-count of the Dassante tragedy thirty-one years ago, the loss of Sal's son and granddaughter, and his appeal for the good citizens of California to rally to help him bring Alyssa to justice. As an incentive, he had raised the reward from fifty thousand to one hundred thousand dollars.

Gregory Shaw had also made the news. According to the article, it was the P.I.'s visit to a retired Winters P.D. detective that had prompted Sal to go to the chief of police and to the newspapers.

Thanks a lot, Gregory. Because of you the noose around my neck just got a little tighter.

"It's all going to come out, isn't it?" Rachel set her wineglass on top of a barrel. "That hundred-thousand-dollar reward will have everyone in the state hunting Alyssa down like a dog, and in the process they'll find out about me."

"There's no reason why they should," Sam said, trying to sound reassuring. "You've read the article. That reporter has no idea you're Alyssa Dassante's daughter. And neither does Sal Dassante."

"What?"

At the shocked exclamation, Rachel and Sam spun around simultaneously. Preston stood there, stock-still, his mouth open, his face turning gray.

Rachel groaned. He had heard everything. "Preston." She took a tentative step toward him. "Darling—"

He backed away as though she had a contagious disease. "Tell me it's not true." He looked from Sam to Rachel.

"Tell me I misunderstood, or that it's some kind of sick joke."

"Let's go into my office, where we can talk." Rachel started to turn around, assuming Preston would follow her. He didn't move.

"We'll talk here," he said harshly.

"Preston, come on." Sam laid a hand on Preston's shoulder. "Let's not air family laundry in public, shall we?"

Preston's expression turned condescending. "This is between Rachel and me, Sam, so if you don't mind…"

Sam pulled his hand away and looked at Rachel, who nodded. "It'll be all right," she said.

Sam quietly walked away.

Rachel waited until the winemaker had disappeared deeper into the cellar before returning her gaze to Preston. Though he had regained his famous composure, his face was still pale. This wouldn't be easy, she thought in dismay. Preston had always been a proud man—proud of his accomplishments, his social standing in the San Francisco community, and above all, he was proud of his heritage.

"I know what a shock this must be," she began lamely. "It was to me, too."

"It's true, then? You're Alyssa Dassante's daughter?"

The way he spoke the words with shock and disgust made her wince. "Yes, it's true."

"Oh, my God." Sinking his fingers in his hair, he turned away from her and walked around in a small circle before facing her again. "How can that be? You told me your mother had died in childbirth."

"That's what I thought," she said, glad they were, at least, talking. "That's what I was told."

"When did you find out?"

She looked down at her hands. "A few days ago."

"*A few days ago?* And you didn't tell me?"

"I didn't know how," she said miserably. "I was in a state of shock."

"When were you going to do it?" His voice had turned accusing. "Or were you going to keep it hidden from me forever?"

"I don't know." Suddenly she couldn't look at him. "Part of me wanted to tell you and the other..." A sob rose in her throat and she let the sentence go unfinished.

"Dear God, Rachel. You found out you're the daughter of a murderer and you weren't going to tell me?" He took a step forward but made sure he didn't come within touching distance. "Didn't you think I had a right to know?"

"I didn't want to hurt you, or embarrass you. I thought... If no one found out, the whole thing would...go away."

"I see. And you had no qualms whatsoever about starting our married life together on a foundation of lies?"

"I didn't lie, Preston. I was trying to think this whole mess through. I didn't know what to do. That's why I didn't tell anyone—"

"You told Sam."

"Because he's an old friend of the family. And because," she added in a small voice, "I was hoping he'd tell me it wasn't true."

"But he didn't, did he?"

Rachel shook his head. "No. He confirmed it."

"How did *you* find out?"

She told him everything in a few rapid, breathless sentences while she still had enough courage to do so. When she was finished, she waited for words of comfort and understanding, and more than anything, she waited for his arms to open so she could rush into them and release the flow of tears she was trying so desperately to hold back.

He remained standing there, like a statue, his arms at his sides. "You're the daughter of a murderer," he said again, as if he would never be able to get past that fact.

"We don't know Alyssa is a murderer." In the midst of such drama, her feeble attempt to defend a woman she didn't even know sounded hollow. "I mean...no one ever heard her side of the story."

"Because she ran! I'm familiar with that story. Sal's right. She faked the accident so she could escape. She's a murderer *and* a fugitive."

"Preston," she begged. "Please calm down. We can get through this."

"How?" He turned and froze her with a scornful look. "I'm a Farley. And you're a...Dassante. You can't possibly imagine what this is going to do to my parents, to my father's career. And mine," he added grimly.

"We don't have to tell your parents. We don't have to tell anyone." No sooner had she spoken those words that she realized she had said the wrong thing.

"Lie to my parents? Is that what you're asking me to do?"

"Not lie," she protested, suddenly angry that her words kept being twisted. "I just don't see the need to broadcast the news, that's all."

"They would find out," he stated flatly. "And they'd never forgive me for keeping such news from them."

"Then let's tell them together. They'll understand I had nothing to do with this." Did she really believe that? she wondered. Or was she being overly optimistic?

Her silent question was quickly, and categorically, answered. "No, they won't. They were upset enough when they found out you were adopted and born of parents unknown. Don't you remember how I had to fight them for days before they finally accepted you?"

She did remember, and because of that reluctance on their part, she had delayed meeting the Farleys for weeks. "Nothing has changed, Preston," she reminded him gently. "I'm still the same person."

"Everything has changed."

The words were spoken with a finality that left her little hope they could ride out this storm. Why was he doing this to her? Why was he being so unfair, so unbending? This was a side of him that was totally foreign to her.

He didn't seem to notice her anguish, and even if he had she wasn't sure it would have changed anything. He was too wrapped up in his own feelings to be concerned about hers.

"I'll need some time to think." His eyes were flat. "To sort things out."

He was already alienating her, she thought, shutting her out. But even as she recognized the signs, she did what she had been taught to do since an early age—fight for what she wanted. And right now what she wanted more than anything in the world was to keep the man she loved. "Why don't we go away for a couple of days?" she suggested, forcing a lightness into her tone. "It'll give us a chance to talk."

A sense of dread settled on her stomach as he shook his head. "I need to be alone."

She knew the conversation was over when he glanced at his watch. Whatever he had come to tell her was now forgotten, or no longer important. "Preston, don't go yet," she pleaded. "I love you. And God knows, I've never needed you more. We can get through this," she repeated, but with less conviction than she had a moment ago.

He gazed at her for a moment, and her heart started beating with hope. Then, with another shake of his head, he walked out, his strides long and fast, as if he couldn't get out of there fast enough.

Twelve

Sitting at his desk, microphone in hand, Gregory glanced at a figure in the twelve-page report before resuming his dictation.

"The company's revenues have grown from twenty-five point two million in 1994 to thirty-nine point seven million in 1998, a compound annual growth of nine point five percent. In addition, the company continues to strategically target high-margin service sales, increasing its 1997 service and repairs revenues to nineteen point six million or sixty-two percent of sales. In 1998—"

He was interrupted by a buzz on the intercom. "It's your ex-wife, Mr. Shaw." Phyllis sounded agitated. "She—"

Oh, Christ! He was supposed to take Noelle to her gymnastic class. "Tell Lindsay I—"

But Phyllis had already put the call through. At the other end of the line, Lindsay was, for the first time in her life, talking incoherently. All he could make out were the words "accident" and "Noelle." His blood went cold.

"What kind of accident?" he barked.

"She was hit by a car," Lindsay sobbed. "I'm in the ambulance with her. They're taking her to St. Francis."

"How bad is it?"

"They don't know yet. She was unconscious for a while."

"Is she conscious now?"

"Yes. There doesn't appear to be anything broken."

"I'm on my way."

It took him all of fifteen minutes to reach the hospital on Hyde Street. In the emergency wing, a nurse directed him to a curtained room.

Noelle, her left arm in a sling and a nasty scrape on her cheek, lay on a gurney, looking almost as white as the sheets. Except for her dark blue eyes, which she had inherited from him, she looked just like her mother, blond, slender, but with a warmer smile.

Lindsay sat at Noelle's bedside, holding her right hand. She was an attractive woman with green eyes and pale blond hair she always wore in an impeccable French twist. Somehow, the twist had started to come undone, making her look, for once, almost human.

The moment Gregory walked in, she threw him a scathing look. She had apparently recovered from the shock and was on the warpath.

"This is all your fault," she said, her voice dripping venom. "If you hadn't been late—"

"Mommy, please," Noelle said, taking her mother's arm and shaking it gently. "Don't blame Daddy, okay? I'm the one who ran across the street without looking. I should have known better." Then as Lindsay's face turned red, Noelle gave Gregory a mischievous smile. "And I should have run faster."

Her attempt at humor had Gregory sighing with relief. If she could joke, she couldn't be too badly hurt. "Yeah," he said, adopting her light tone. "What's the use of being a track star if you can't even outrun a car."

"Oh, that's right, Gregory," Lindsay retorted. "Turn this into a comedy routine, why don't you? I suppose jokes help relieve the guilt."

Six years of constant battles had taught Gregory that indifference was often the best defense. Ignoring Lindsay's remark, he bent over his daughter and kissed her forehead. "What's with the sling?" he asked. "I thought there were no broken bones."

"That's just a sprained wrist." His daughter lifted her arm to show its mobility. "The doctor said I can go home tomorrow."

"Good." Gregory glanced at Lindsay. Satisfied she had calmed down, he asked, "What happened?"

"You were late," she said, determined to drive her point across. "And Noelle decided to wait for you outside. She thought she saw your car coming and she ran to meet you, unaware that another car was coming from the other direction. The driver jammed on his brakes, skidded to a stop but couldn't avoid hitting her."

"How long was she unconscious?"

"Only a few seconds, but it felt like an eternity. She just laid there and for a horrible moment I thought..." Instead of finishing the sentence, she brought Noelle's hand to her mouth. Gregory knew the worried look on his ex-wife's face was no act. Lindsay may not be the best mother in the world, but she loved her daughter.

"Mommy thought I had checked out," Noelle said with brutal accuracy.

"Noelle," Lindsay protested, letting go of her daughter's hand. "I won't have you talk like that."

She shrugged. "It's the truth, isn't it? You thought I was dead."

"But you're not dead, so stop being so morbid." Gregory brushed her blond hair from her forehead. "I'm sorry, pumpkin," he added, using the nickname he had given her long ago. "Your mother is right. If I had been there in time, none of this would have happened."

As if already sensing her advantage, Noelle gave him a sly smile. "Well...I suppose I *could* forgive you."

"Oh, really?" He played along. "Just what do I have to do to earn that forgiveness?"

"Take me and Zoe to the Spice Girls concert next month?"

Gregory groaned inwardly. The last time he had taken Noelle and her best friend to a concert, he was almost trampled by eighteen thousand screaming fans and it had taken two hours for his hearing to return to normal. "We'll see," he said, half hoping the show was already sold out. "In the meantime, I'd like to talk to your doctor. What's his name?"

"Dr. Muldor." Noelle giggled. "But all the nurses call him Dr. Dreamboat. Behind his back, of course."

A familiar feeling tugged at his heart. His little girl was growing up in leaps and bounds. And he wasn't sure how he felt about it.

Before he had a chance to comment on Noelle's remark, she gave his sleeve a pull. "Daddy? Will you stay with me tonight? Dr. Muldor said you could—"

"But, Noelle, darling," Lindsay cut in. "I thought... I mean, I assumed *I* would be spending the night here."

"You can't, Mommy, remember? You're having dinner with a client. That's why Dad was taking me to my gymnastic class."

"I can cancel."

Now he knew his ex-wife was badly shaken, Gregory thought. To his recollection, Lindsay, a successful advertising executive, had never canceled a business appointment. During their stormy six-year marriage, she had gone out almost every night, leaving Gregory and Noelle to fend for themselves.

"There's no need for you to do that," he said. "I'll be

glad to stay." As Lindsay shot him another murderous look, he motioned her toward the door, then rose. "Excuse us a moment, pumpkin. I need to talk to your mother."

Outside Noelle's room, Gregory turned to her. "What's your problem now?" he asked, trying to keep his voice down and not succeeding very well.

"My problem," she said in a furious whisper, "is that you keep butting heads with me in front of my daughter. Why is that, Gregory? So you can look like the wonderful daddy you're not? And undermine all my efforts?"

"For crying out loud, no one's trying to undermine you. You're doing a good job of that all by yourself."

"I wanted to stay with her."

"Then stay. We'll both stay. It's no big deal."

Her eyes filled with contempt. "I'd rather spend the night with a snake."

Gregory laughed. That human side she had showed a moment ago hadn't lasted long. "So would I, but for Noelle's sake, I'm willing to tolerate even your presence, so do your daughter a favor, will you? Stop being so selfish and think of what *she* wants for a change."

Her venom enveloped him like a bad aura. "Oh, you're a fine one to talk about selfishness. If it weren't for your misplaced sense of priorities, she wouldn't be lying in a hospital bed right now."

"At least I show up. And I'm there when it counts. That's more than I can say for you."

She moved to plant herself in front of him. "That's a cheap shot. I'm a working woman. And if I can't always be at her track and field events or at her gymnastic classes, that's because I'm busy earning a living."

Gregory sighed. He'd heard it all before but this time he wasn't going to turn the other cheek. "Don't give me that old excuse again. With the amount of support I'm paying you, you could afford to work part-time, but I guess that's too much to ask.''

"Would I ask *you* to work part-time? No," she said, not giving him a chance to reply. "Because I know your work is important to you, just as mine is to me. And for your information, I'm handling home and career just fine. You may not think so, but what do you know? You only have Noelle two weekends a month."

"I've told you before, anytime you want to change that arrangement, I'll be glad to take Noelle—permanently."

"You don't know the first thing about raising a twelve-year-old girl."

"And you do?" He shook his head. "Don't make me laugh."

"I'm an excellent mother."

"Really? When was the last time you spent quality time with her? Or cooked her a decent meal? Or took her to a movie?"

For a moment Lindsay just stood there, glaring at him with all the hatred she could muster. Then, jutting her chin in the air, she turned her back on him. As she did, what was left of her French twist came loose. With a cry of sheer frustration, she yanked the last pin out and walked back inside Noelle's room.

Gregory chuckled, glad that those occasional blowups no longer drained him, then he shrugged and went to look for Dr. Dreamboat.

Thirteen

Preston still hadn't called, and after a sleepless night, Rachel gave up on sleep and got up at seven-thirty. In her celestial-blue pajamas and her hair pointing in all directions, she padded to the kitchen to make coffee and turned on the under-the-counter TV set.

She was spooning hazelnut decaf into the filter cone when a familiar voice coming from the TV made her look up.

The voice belonged to Edwina Farley, Preston's mother. Judging from the picture on the screen, the news segment had been filmed the night before as Edwina, who had hosted an elegant preview dinner at the San Francisco Museum of Art, was just coming out of the building.

Rachel vaguely remembered Preston mentioning the gala and the fact that his mother, an important benefactor, was responsible for bringing a collection of Van Gogh's paintings to the museum.

As reporters clustered around her, Edwina, truly in her element, glowed and posed for photographs while graciously answering questions about the exhibition she had made possible.

Preston was wrong, Rachel thought as she continued to watch her future mother-in-law charm the press. Edwina was a kind, intelligent woman. She wouldn't blame Rachel for being Alyssa Dassante's daughter, and she certainly would not—

Rachel's thoughts stopped cold when a reporter asked an unexpected question.

"Mrs. Farley, is it true?" he asked as a camera closed in on Edwina's smiling face. "Your son broke his engagement to Rachel Spaulding?"

Stunned, Rachel stared at the screen. Where had that come from? Preston hadn't broken their engagement. The reporter was insane.

Edwina's expression turned regretful. She hesitated for a moment, as if not sure how to answer. Then, with a small sigh, she said, "Yes, he did."

The questions came all at once, a cacophony Rachel could barely understand.

"Ladies and gentlemen, please." Edwina raised a hand. "I know you're curious, and I'll be glad to answer your questions, but only if you speak one at a time."

"Why did they break up?" a voice in the back shouted.

Edwina let her gaze travel around the crowd. "Because," she said slowly, measuring each word, "only hours ago, my son learned that Rachel Spaulding was...Alyssa Dassante's daughter."

"Oh, my God!" Rachel sank into a chair.

For a moment there was no reaction from the crowd. One or two reporters looked at each other as if to ask "Who's Alyssa Dassante?" But the same reporter who had asked the first question, knew exactly who she was. "That's the woman who killed her husband thirty-one years ago, isn't it? Before she vanished?"

The statement hit the crowd like a bomb. Half the reporters immediately scrambled for their cell phones and began yelling into them while the rest pushed and shoved to get closer to Edwina.

In a state of utter shock, Rachel stared at the woman who, only a month earlier, had welcomed her into her family with a warmth and sincerity that had brought tears to Rachel's eyes.

"Paul and I are so delighted you're marrying our son, Rachel. We couldn't have chosen anyone better suited to Preston than you are."

And now, that same woman was publicly destroying her.

"No," Edwina said in reply to another question Rachel hadn't heard. "My son will not be available for comment at this time. As you can imagine, he is devastated."

"Are you certain Rachel Spaulding is Alyssa Dassante's daughter?" a skeptic asked. "Do you have proof?"

Edwina smiled her tolerant smile. "Would I be making such a serious accusation if I weren't sure?"

"But do you have proof, Mrs. Farley?"

"Yes. Miss Spaulding herself admitted who she was to my son."

Miss Spaulding. Not "my son's fiancée," which of course, according to Edwina, she no longer was, and not "Rachel," but Miss Spaulding. That alone said more about where Rachel stood with the Farleys than anything that had been said until now. The segment ended with Edwina thanking the reporters for their interest and hurrying toward a waiting limousine.

"Mrs. Farley was unable to make additional comment at that time," the news anchor said as his face once again filled the screen. "Stay tuned for further developments. In other news, San Francisco's mayor—"

Rachel shut off the television with a snap and stood back against the kitchen counter, wondering what had just hit her. Preston had broken their engagement? Without even discussing it with her? She shook her head. He wouldn't be that cruel. Nor could she believe he had leaked the story to the press. There had to be another explanation.

There was a soft knock at the door, and she threw a hopeful glance in that direction. "Please, dear God," she murmured as she ran across the foyer. "Let it be Preston."

Her heart sank when she realized it wasn't Preston, but Terrence, the Farleys's long-time butler. He stood on the threshold, a pained expression on his face. In his hands was an envelope.

"Good morning, Miss Spaulding. I..." As if looking at her was difficult, he lowered his gaze to the envelope. "Mr. Farley asked me to give you this." He handed her the envelope.

Knowing she must look frightful, she ran a hand through her hair. "Preston?"

He nodded. "He..." He cleared his throat. "He asked me to wait and said you'd understand after you read the letter."

Not sure she could trust her voice, Rachel nodded and walked back inside, aware that Terrence had followed her into the living room.

Her hand shaking, she tore open the envelope and pulled out the single sheet of cream paper with the embossed Farley crest at the top.

Rachel,
This is by far the most difficult thing I've ever had to do, but after a long and painful debate, I've decided that it would be best, for both of us, to terminate our relationship. I'm sorry to have to tell you this way. I know I should have come in person, but frankly, I'm much too upset to face you. I also want to apologize for the story being leaked to the press. I assure you I had nothing to do with that. A reporter who was at-

tending the gala dinner last night brought up the wedding and my mother had no choice but to tell her it was off. The news spread quickly after that. Kindly give the ring to Terrence. He'll come back at the end of the week to pick up my things. Thank you.

Preston

She stood there for a moment, unable to move, a little light-headed. Looking up, she stared at Terrence as if the butler could offer some magical explanation as to why this was happening to her.

He didn't. What could the man say? It was over. There would be no fairy-tale wedding, no honeymoon in a remote bungalow on Maui, no little Farleys running around the house, no Preston. With a few impersonal words, he had severed all ties, just like that, as if their love for each other had never existed.

Terrence's expression as he returned her gaze remained neutral, which was quite amazing considering she was falling apart in front of his very eyes. Was that the mark of a good butler? she wondered. Not to break in the face of disaster? It had to be. And, of course, Terrence was a good butler, a perfect butler, actually. Perfect Edwina would never have it any other way.

She pressed her fingers against her forehead and rubbed it absently. What was she doing? Why was she obsessing about the virtues of a servant instead of dealing with the contents of Preston's letter?

A polite harrumph, which Terrence covered with a curled index finger, snapped her out of her trance. The poor man was probably waiting for a reply, either written or spoken, anything that would relieve Preston of any guilt.

A string of insults came to mind, something crude and shocking that would shatter the butler's unflappable composure as well as Preston's. But somehow she couldn't think of anything. Her mind was a total blank.

Pulling herself as tall as her five-feet-six would permit, Rachel squared her shoulders in a brave if futile attempt to look dignified. "Thank you, Terrence. Please tell Mr. Farley that I understand perfectly."

Terrence bowed, another habit he had perfected over the years. When, after a moment, he continued to stand there, she reached for the door and opened it for him. What the hell. He had done it for her often enough.

He didn't move, but delivered another harrumph. This time he accompanied it with a quick telling glance at her left hand.

Oh, God, the ring. He had been waiting for it all along. The need to laugh was almost overwhelming. Did he think she wanted to keep it? That he might have to wrestle it off her finger?

Not wanting to give him a heart attack, she yanked the ring off and jammed it in his hand, which was already extended, palm out. "Here," she said. Then, hoping that, as the perfect butler, he would convey her exact message, she added, "Tell Preston I never liked it anyway."

Rachel stood in the middle of her living room after Terrence had left, lost and shattered. How could so many disasters happen in such rapid succession? First her grandmother's death, then the discovery she was Alyssa Dassante's daughter, and now the breakup with Preston.

Why did she always have to lose the people she loved? she thought as she looked helplessly around her. Was it a test of her own strength? Or some sinister conspiracy to make sure she ended up alone?

Her gaze stopped on the large wall-to-wall bookcase where old books, some she'd had since childhood, crammed the shelves. Here and there, pulling double duty as bookends, were little knickknacks and mementos. There was a porcelain sea lion Preston had bought her in Pebble Beach one weekend, a coffee mug with his face imprinted on it, a small Waterford clock he had given her on her birthday.

"To count the hours until our wedding," he had told her.

On a center shelf stood a framed photograph of her and Preston, staring into each other's eyes and looking blissfully happy. She let her fingers trace the contours of her fiancé's—ex-fiancé's—face. How could she have been so wrong about him? And how could he turn away from her at such a time as this?

As a sob rose to her throat, she yanked the picture from its cozy nook and hurled it against the wall. Then, with the sound of breaking glass filling her ears, Rachel fell to her knees, buried her face in her hands and wept hopelessly.

A few minutes later, her head throbbing but her hands steady, she rose, swept up and discarded the mess she had made and rearranged the bookcase shelf so she wouldn't be constantly reminded of what had once stood there.

She dragged an old suitcase from the attic, took it to her bedroom and began filling it with Preston's clothes—an Armani jacket, a Bill Blass suit, a couple of shirts, two pairs of pants and an assortment of neckties, T-shirts, belts and shoes. Preston had only spent one or two nights a week at the bungalow, but he liked to be prepared.

When there was nothing left of her ex-fiancé in the room, Rachel went back downstairs, checked a number in the phone book, picked up the receiver and dialed. "Good morning," she said when a woman at the other end answered. "I have some clothes I'd like to donate to the Goodwill. Could you please send someone to pick them up?"

She smiled. "Perfect. I'll leave the suitcase by the front door." She gave the woman her address. "Oh, and would you do me one more favor?" she asked sweetly. "Would you send the receipt for the tax deduction to Preston Farley?" She gave the Farleys's address, thanked the woman and hung up.

Then, feeling much better, she picked up the suitcase, set it outside by the front door, and went to get dressed.

"Joe." Sal greeted the private detective, who had made the trip from San Francisco to tell him something he probably could have said on the phone, and waved his housekeeper away. When she had closed the door, he motioned to a chair. "You came a long way. What's up?"

Kelsey sat, feet spread, and let his hands hang between his knees. He was a medium-framed, nondescript man in his fifties who, after fifteen years out of the FBI, still looked like a Fed. "I got news, Sal. Amazing news."

Sal moved forward in his chair, nerve ends tingling. "You found Alyssa."

"Better than that."

"What the hell could be better than finding Alyssa?"

Kelsey eyed him for a moment. "How about finding out your granddaughter is alive?"

Sal fell back in his chair as the wind went out of him. "You gotta be kidding."

"I'm not kidding. Your granddaughter is alive," Kelsey repeated. "I know this sounds incredible but it's the truth. I verified it before coming here. Her name is Rachel Spaulding. She was adopted by Helen and Jack Spaulding thirty-one years ago, and lives in Napa Valley. She's a winemaker."

"How...how do you know? Who told you?" Except for the night he had found Mario dead in the garage, Sal couldn't remember ever experiencing such a shock. The granddaughter he had thought dead for all these years was alive!

"You remember that contact I have at the *Chronicle?*" Kelsey leaned closer.

Sal nodded.

"He told me that Edwina Farley, the mother of the man Rachel Spaulding was engaged to marry, informed the press that Rachel Spaulding was Alyssa Dassante's daughter. According to Edwina, that's the reason her son broke his engagement."

"It's a lie. My granddaughter died in a fire. A nun told me. You know that."

"Lillie didn't die, Sal. It was a case of mistaken identity. The reason I didn't come here sooner was because I wanted to make sure my man at the *Chronicle* had all the facts. He did. Preston Farley later confirmed his mother's statement." Kelsey handed him a newspaper he had folded in two. "It's in all the papers, Sal. See for yourself."

Not convinced, Sal took the newspaper. When he saw the photograph, his hand began to shake. The young woman pictured was beautiful, with short brown hair, large eyes that looked directly at the camera, and a wide, friendly smile. Above her upper lip was a birthmark he knew only too well. "Alyssa," he murmured.

"No," Kelsey replied. "That's not Alyssa. It's Rachel Spaulding. The photograph was taken a month ago when she and Preston Farley became engaged."

Sal's fingers went to touch the photograph. "This is my granddaughter?"

"Yes, Sal."

He swallowed. He thought about pouring himself a drink to steady his nerves, but didn't think it would get past the knot in his throat. "How old is she?"

"Thirty-one. She was left at Our Lady of Good Counsel on August 14, 1968, and was adopted in September of that same year."

August fourteen, Sal thought. The day Mario died."

He closed his eyes. Lillie. Lillie was alive.

Long after Kelsey had left, Sal sat in the dark, all alone, the newspaper on his lap. The article had told him what he needed to know. But it was that picture of Lillie—of Rachel Spaulding—that had convinced him there was no mistake. This young woman was his granddaughter.

He hated it that she looked so much like her mother, but even with that striking resemblance, there was enough of Mario in those proud dark eyes to make his old heart beat a little faster.

That stupid nun, he thought, suddenly angry. If it hadn't been for her, he wouldn't have lost those thirty-one years. He wouldn't be sitting here right now, wondering how to approach his granddaughter, or whether she even wanted to see him.

Incensed, he stood and started pacing, forcing himself to stay calm. What did it matter what a nun did or didn't do? His granddaugther was alive. For that, he should kiss the ground.

"Rachel Spaulding." He made a face as he said the name out loud, trying to get used to it. Not a very Italian name, but so what? His first priority now was to meet her and get to know her. Maybe he'd invite her to the house for a big Sunday dinner. Or maybe he should wait until she called him. He shook his head. No, that was no good. What if she was shy or something?

He kept pacing, glancing at the phone from time to time, itching to pick it up. But what would he say? What did a grandfather say to a granddaughter he hadn't seen in thirty-one years?

Down the hall he heard the sounds of running footsteps. He smiled. That would be Nico. And the fact that the boy never ran, never hurried, could mean only one thing.

He had heard about Lillie.

Fourteen

Rachel had been too busy the rest of the day to dwell on Preston's betrayal and her disappointment with the way he had handled everything. Respecting her need for privacy, her co-workers hadn't said a word about the broken engagement, the news of which had traveled through the valley like brushfire. Only Sam, who cared too much to stay away, had stopped by her office to offer some much needed comfort.

At six o'clock that evening, she had turned down his invitation to have dinner with him and Tina and had worked right through, and well beyond, the dinner hour.

Now that she was back home and all alone on her terrace, however, her thoughts once again turned to her ex-fiancé. What had she ever seen in that man? she wondered as she sipped her Sauvignon Blanc and stared into the night. Once you took away his good looks and his easy charm, the rest of him was as phony as a three-dollar bill. Even that strength she had so often admired was a joke. Preston wasn't strong. He was a pawn in his mother's hands and was made of the same unsubstantial stock as she was.

And yet she had loved him. A part of her still did.

The phone rang just as she started to refill her glass. Glancing at her watch, she saw that it was a little after ten. At this hour, it could only be Sam or Tina. Or Preston. She wasn't sure how she felt about that, or if she could even talk to him without becoming irate.

Knowing there was only one way to find out, she set the bottle of Sauvignon on the table and reached for the cordless extension. "Hello?"

There was no reply, only silence.

"Preston, is that you?" she asked. But she already knew it wasn't. Preston had never been at a loss for words, even when he was wrong. "Look," she said curtly. "Whoever you are, if you're not going to talk, I'll—"

A soft click ended her sentence.

Rachel stared at the phone for a moment before pressing the off switch. If Preston hadn't made the call, then who had? As the question lingered on her mind, she glanced uneasily around her, suddenly aware of how vulnerable she was on this open terrace.

Peering into the night, she thought of Joe Brock and the threats the former cellar master had hurled at her a couple of days earlier. *You'll regret this. I swear you will.*

Because he had been intoxicated at the time, she hadn't taken him seriously. But what if he had been serious? And angry enough to want to frighten her. Or worse, harm her.

Irritated at this uncharacteristic anxiety on her part, she stood and tried to dismiss the thought. What was the matter with her? This wasn't the first crank call she'd ever had. And it wouldn't be the last. So why was she getting all bothered?

The pep talk seemed to work, but she was no longer in the mood for a quiet moment on her terrace. It was getting cold, anyway, and late. Picking up the wine bottle and the glass with one hand and the phone with the other, she carried them inside, locking the sliding doors behind her.

She started to take the phone off the hook then stopped herself. For God's sake, Rachel, she thought, laughing at her own fear. Go to bed before you turn into a paranoid mess.

Though she rarely took her own advice, she turned off the lights and walked down the hall to her bedroom, still chuckling.

Back home after a one-day marketing seminar in Dallas, Annie sat at the dining room table, flipping through the pages of the *St. Helena Star*. As she turned to page four, she let out a gasp. A photograph of Rachel and Preston was starring back at her. Above the photo the headline read Alyssa Dassante's Daughter Alive—Engagement Broken.

Her half grapefruit forgotten, Annie scanned the article in stunned disbelief. Rachel's birth mother was a murderer? Dear God.

After she had read about the thirty-one-year-old murder and Rachel's broken engagement, a sudden thought occurred to her. What if Rachel found out Annie was the one who had hired Gregory?

Groaning, Annie dropped her head between her hands. She had never dreamed the truth about Rachel's parentage would be so damaging, or that it would become public knowledge. All Annie had wanted was to get some leverage on Rachel so her sister would give up ownership of Spaulding Vineyards voluntarily.

She didn't even dare call Gregory, who must be furious with her by now. Oh, God, what a mess she had made.

"Mom? Are you okay?"

Annie looked up with a start. "Courtney." She forced a smile as her daughter walked into the room. "Yes, I'm fine. I just have a headache, that's all. Would you like some fruit, darling? Ming prepared—"

"I'm not hungry." Courtney sat at the opposite end of the table. "Did you know Preston broke up with Rachel?"

Annie averted her eyes. She couldn't let her daughter suspect anything. She couldn't let anyone suspect. "I just read about it. It's...awful."

"I just called the bungalow but there's no answer. I'm worried about her, Mom. She's not home, or at the winery, or at Tina's."

"I wouldn't worry, darling." Glad her hand didn't betray her nervousness, Annie picked up the silver pot and refilled her cup with Earl Grey tea. "She probably needs to be alone for a while, to get over the shock."

Courtney nodded. "I guess you're right." She shook her head. "I still can't believe any of it. Aunt Rachel is the daughter of a killer? Why didn't anyone tell us?"

Still unable to look at her daughter, Annie folded the paper in two and smoothed it down with the palm of her hand. "Probably because it's not the kind of information a family is anxious to spread around."

"And why is Daddy's best friend involved? Who is he working for?"

Annie let out a nervous laugh. "Darling, why ask me all those questions? I don't have the answers."

"But you know him. Gregory Shaw was best man at your wedding."

"I can't stand the man, Courtney. Everyone knows that."

"Aunt Rachel hates him, too."

Annie's head snapped up. "When did she tell you that?"

"A while back. You remember what happened. Gregory found out Aunt Rachel had a crush on him and he and Daddy made fun of her at your wedding reception." She glanced at the newspaper beside Annie's plate. "I wonder what she's going to do now that she knows he's responsible for this."

Cold sweat trickled between Annie's breasts. She knew

exactly what Rachel would do, which was the same thing Annie would do in her place—confront Gregory and badger him until he told her what she wanted to know.

And if Gregory was angry enough to tell Rachel the truth, Annie was, to put it crudely, in deep shit.

She barely felt Courtney's lips brush her cheek. "Here's my bus. 'Bye, Mom."

"'Bye, darling," Annie replied absently.

Rachel stood in the green-marbled lobby of San Francisco's Jackson Building on Montgomery Street as people hurried toward the bank of elevators in the back. Trying to stay out of the way, she let her gaze move down the list of law offices, brokerage firms and other related businesses until she came upon Shaw and Associates—seventeenth floor, Suite 1720.

She had made the decision to confront Gregory Shaw as she was getting ready for bed last night. But now that she was here, the thought of barging into his office and demanding he tell her who had hired him struck her as totally ridiculous. That was privileged information. What made her think he would share it with her? He may have been rude and crass and a number of other things, but he couldn't have achieved this level of success if he didn't have certain standards.

"Miss? May I help you with something?"

Turning, Rachel saw a smiling man in a guard's uniform. She returned the smile. "No, thank you. I found the person I was looking for."

Touching his hat, the guard walked back to his desk on the other side of the lobby.

Rachel kept looking at Gregory's name—white block letters on a black background. Who hired you, Gregory? she asked silently. Sister Mary-Catherine had suspected Sal

Dassante, but that didn't make sense. Why would Sal go to Gregory when he already had a private investigator?

The more she thought about it, the more she was convinced Gregory had taken the case as a favor to someone. And no matter how hard she tried to deny it, that someone kept taking the shape of her sister. Annie may hate Gregory, but she was quite capable of putting her feelings aside to get what she wanted—in this case, Spaulding Vineyards.

The question now was, would she ever be able to find out if Annie was the one who had betrayed her?

The answer came to her as she watched a man carrying a briefcase walk over to the pay phone near the guard's station.

Smiling, she took her cell phone out of her purse, checked Gregory's number from her book and dialed it.

"Shaw and Associates," a female voice answered.

"Good morning," Rachel said in what she hoped was a decent imitation of Annie's voice. "This is Annie Spaulding. I can't seem to find my briefcase anywhere and was wondering if I had left it up there when I came in last week."

"I don't believe so, Miss Spaulding, but let me check Mr. Shaw's office, just in case. I'll be right back." The secretary returned within a minute. "I'm sorry, Miss Spaulding, it isn't there. In fact, I'm almost certain you didn't have a briefcase when you came in, only a purse."

Rachel took a deep, sobering breath. If Annie had been standing in front of her at this very moment, she would have strangled her. Since she wasn't, Gregory would have to do. "Thank you," she said, struggling to keep her anger under control. "I must have left it somewhere else." She paused. "Is Gregory in, by any chance?"

"No, he's not."

"I see. When do you expect him?"

"Not until the latter part of the morning."

Frustrated, Rachel thanked the secretary and hung up. Gregory Shaw would have to wait.

It had been a long, restless night. Noelle had spent it tossing and turning while Gregory had watched over her, making sure she didn't harm her wrist. At eight o'clock this morning, Dr. Dreamboat had given her a clean bill of health and signed the discharge papers.

They had arrived home just as Lindsay, who had been persuaded to go home, was about to leave for the hospital. The realization that she had missed her daughter's discharge caused yet another flare-up, but Gregory was too tired to rise to the bait. After kissing his daughter goodbye and promising to call her later, he left.

As he drove off, he was tempted to go home and catch a couple hours of sleep. But a ten o'clock appointment with the head of ATC and the fact that his apartment was clear across town made that small luxury impossible. He'd have to settle for a quick shower and a change of clothes at the office before going to his meeting.

He was standing in front of his bathroom mirror with a towel around his hips and his face covered with lather, when his intercom rang.

Barefoot, he walked over to his desk and pressed a button. "Yes, Phyllis?"

"It's your aunt, Mr. Shaw."

Gregory picked up the phone right away. "Aunt Willie. Don't tell me you miss me already."

"I always miss you, kid." She paused, then asked, "Have you seen the papers?"

"Not yet. I just got back from the hospital—"

"Hospital?" There was sudden alarm in Willie's voice. "What happened?"

"Noelle was hit by a car, but she's fine," he hastened to say as Willie let out a small cry. "I just took her home." Knowing that under that crusty exterior, Willie was a softy at heart, he did his best to reassure her. "She even insisted on going to school," he added. "To show off her sling and to swoon over her young, handsome doctor."

"I swear that girl is as bad as you used to be at her age," Willie said with a sigh. "Accident prone as well as a daredevil. Not a very good combination. I used to worry sick about you."

"Why? Dad never did." Now why had he said that?

Willie laughed. "He worried more than you know. He just never showed it."

Rather than start another discussion about his father, Gregory returned to the reason for Willie's call. "Why did you want to know if I had seen the papers? Was there something there I should see?"

"Today's leading story, my dear nephew. You remember that woman you were looking for?"

"Alyssa Dassante. Sure."

"Her daughter has been found."

"Impossible." He picked up a paper from his desk, but it was yesterday's. "The baby died in a fire. You told me so yourself."

"That's what we had been told. But as it turns out, there was another infant girl at that convent. The nuns thought it was that baby who survived, when in fact it was the other way around."

"So Lillie Dassante was alive all along."

"Exactly. Except her name isn't Lillie anymore. It's Rachel." She paused. "Rachel Spaulding."

For a long second Gregory just stood still. "What did you say?" he asked when he could talk again.

"Rachel Spaulding. Your best friend's ex-sister-in-law is Alyssa Dassante's daughter."

Gregory ran his fingers through his damp hair. "Jesus Christ. Are you sure? I mean, who's the source?"

"According to Edwina Farley, Rachel herself. Get ahold of a paper, Gregory. It's quite a story." She chuckled. "Makes me wish I was still in publishing."

After hanging up, Gregory rang his secretary. "Phyllis, be a sweetheart and bring me this morning's *Chronicle*, will you?"

She came in within moments, stoically pretended not to notice he was half naked and placed a copy of the newspaper on his desk. The story was on page six and the first thing he saw was a photograph of Rachel, cheek to cheek with Preston Farley. It was the same photograph the social page had run at the time the couple announced their engagement.

As he had then, Gregory found himself lingering over the lovely features. There was nothing left of the shy, awkward teenager who had fled from him the night of Luke's wedding. She had cut her long hair short and brushed it back in a style that emphasized those great bones of hers. The braces were gone, but the eyes were the same, large, dark, and filled with laughter.

Above the photograph was the headline Salvatore Dassante's Granddaughter Alive.

"Son of a bitch," he muttered when he finished reading. His instincts about Annie had been right, after all. She *had* lied to him. Alyssa Dassante and Helen Spaulding hadn't been old friends. They never even knew each other. That was something Annie had fabricated to get him to take the case.

He slammed the paper down. So much for being a good guy. Steaming, he yanked the phone off the cradle and dialed Annie's number. "You conniving little bitch," he shouted when she answered. "You knew, didn't you? You knew all along Rachel was Alyssa's daughter."

"Gregory, let me explain—"

"Yes or no?"

"Yes, but—"

He slammed the phone down.

Fifteen

The tension in Ambrose Cavanaugh's office was high as Rachel and Annie sat facing the attorney's desk. After an awkward silence, during which Annie kept drumming her fingers, Ambrose's gaze settled on her.

"I'm disappointed in you, Annie," he said quietly. "And so would Hannah."

Annie was instantly on the defensive. "What have I done now?"

"You hired Gregory Shaw to find Alyssa Dassante, that's what you've done."

The fire in Annie's eyes died. She turned pale. "What are you talking about?" But the outrage, too, had lost its spark.

"Save the innocent act, Annie," Rachel said sharply. "I suspected you from the start, yet a part of me didn't want to believe you'd stoop that low, and neither did Sam, so I let it ride for a while. Then when the news of my parentage broke, I realized that only one person stood to gain from this scandal being made public. And that person was you, Annie."

"That's crazy."

"Is it? You weren't hoping that, under the terms of Grams's will, I would have to relinquish control of the winery?"

"No! That thought never entered my mind."

"Then why did you ask Gregory to find my birth mother?"

Annie's frightened gaze swung from Rachel to Ambrose and back to Rachel. "Did he tell you that?"

Unable to hold back a smug smile, Rachel shook her head. "No, I found out by myself. You see, Annie, you're not the only one in this family with acting talent."

"What the hell does that mean?"

"It means that I called Gregory's office earlier, pretending to be you, and asked his secretary to check if I had left my briefcase in the office when I was there last week. Do you know what she told me, Annie?"

Annie's expression turned hostile.

"She told me she hadn't found a briefcase and was almost certain you didn't have one with you when you came that day."

In the silence that followed, only the rhythmic ticking of Ambrose's grandfather clock could be heard.

Beaten, Annie seemed to shrink in her chair. "All right, so I asked Gregory to find Alyssa, but I swear I had nothing to do with the story getting out. I wasn't even here. All I wanted was to find out who Alyssa was, where she was, and why no one had ever mentioned her before."

"How did you know about Alyssa in the first place?" Rachel asked.

Annie licked her lip. "Grams told me," she whispered.

"*Grams?* When?"

There was another pause, a longer one this time. Then, after taking a breath, Annie met Rachel's gaze head-on. "She told me just before she died."

Ambrose threw his glasses on the desk. "For God's sake, Annie!"

Rachel gripped the arms of her chair and said nothing. When she had called to request this meeting earlier, she had promised Ambrose that no matter what Annie said, or what outrageous excuse she used to defend herself, she wouldn't lose her temper. At this moment Rachel was perilously close to breaking that promise. Counting to ten seemed like a good idea, so she did exactly that, slowly.

"What were Grams's exact words?" she asked when she was sure she could speak calmly.

Annie looked down at her hands, which were clenched in her lap. "She said, 'Tell Rachel her birth mother, Alyssa, is alive.' Then she told me that a Sister Mary-Catherine in Santa Rosa would help."

Rachel closed her eyes, imagining Grams in Annie's arms, dying and entrusting her beloved granddaughter with that last wish. "Why did you have to hire Gregory Shaw? Why didn't you go to Santa Rosa yourself?"

"I didn't want to get directly involved, and I knew I could trust Gregory to be discreet."

"And just like that he agreed to help you?"

"No, not just like that." Annie glanced from Rachel to Ambrose again. "I didn't tell him how I found out about Alyssa. I just told him she was an old friend of Mama's and now that Grams was gone and I was all alone, I wanted to find her."

"And he believed you?"

She looked down again. "I guess I was pretty convincing."

Yes, Rachel thought, remembering Annie's endless shenanigans when they were growing up. Being convincing was one of her sister's many talents. "So not only did you ignore Grams's dying request," she said coldly, "but you were planning to use the information for your own despicable purpose."

"No," she said stubbornly. "I told you I hadn't even thought about that."

"Then what were you going to do with the information?"

Annie fidgeted in her chair. "I...don't know. Nothing. I was just curious, that's all. I wanted to know why Grams and our parents had kept Alyssa's existence a secret all these years."

"You were hoping to unearth a scandal, preferably one juicy enough to make me resign from Spaulding Vineyards."

"Dammit, Rachel, that's not true." Annie managed to look outraged enough for Rachel to almost believe her. "I have known about Rachel's identity for days," she continued. "Ever since the article in the *Winters Journal* appeared. But did I say anything?" she asked, looking directly at Rachel. "Did I run to the newspapers and tell them Lillie Dassante wasn't dead but alive and living right here in Napa Valley? Or did I even come to you, Ambrose?"

"Why didn't you?" Rachel asked.

"Because I didn't want to hurt anyone, least of all the winery."

And that, Rachel thought, was Annie's only saving grace. She loved Spaulding Vinyards as much as Rachel did. Not for the same reasons, perhaps, but she loved it just the same.

Ambrose must have sensed that, too, because when he glanced at Rachel, all he could manage was a helpless shrug as if to say, "Annie will always be Annie."

When Rachel gave a slight nod, he picked up his glasses again and slipped them on. "All right then, let's get this matter settled. Rachel asked for this meeting because she had concerns about the terms of Hannah's will and how these recent developments might affect her ownership of Spaulding Vineyards. As Hannah's executor, it is my belief that there's been no breach of the will on Rachel's part, therefore the chain of command remains status quo.

"As for you, Annie." He looked at her over the rim of his glasses. "I find your behavior in this matter reprehensible." He sighed. "But since it's not for me to pass judgment, I'll let Rachel decide what course of action she should take."

"What?" Annie glared at Rachel. "You're going to fire me? Is that what this little powwow is all about?"

In spite of her anger, Rachel smiled. No matter what wrongful act Annie committed, she always saw herself as a victim. And more importantly she knew exactly how to make people see her in the same way.

The thought of firing her was tempting, but impractical. Annie was a superb marketing director, and replacing her at this critical period could be disastrous for the winery. If anyone could pull Spaulding out of this scandal unscarred, it was Annie.

"No, Annie, I'm not going to fire you. Unlike you, I don't allow my personal feelings to cloud my judgment. You're too valuable to replace."

Rachel hoped the compliment would make her sister at least remorseful, but Annie, in typical fashion, made no effort to apologize. Suddenly back in top form, she rose from her chair and walked over to the window. "What do we do with them?" she asked.

Both Ambrose and Rachel followed her gaze. Camera crews and reporters had gathered on the small lawn fronting the attorney's office. Though annoyed, Rachel wasn't surprised. Upon returning from San Francisco earlier, she had spotted the same group waiting in front of the winery and had managed to turn around without being seen, certain they'd eventually tire of the vigil, and of her.

Apparently she had underestimated them. The story of

Alyssa Dassante had been big news back in 1968, and this new, updated version threatened to become even bigger news.

Ambrose quickly clicked the miniblinds shut. "Someone must have tipped them off that you girls were here."

"Don't look at me," Annie said as Rachel threw her a suspicious glance. "I didn't even know we were coming here until Ambrose called."

"I could go out there," Ambrose offered. "And try to pacify them with a couple of statements while you two slip through the back but..." He shook his head as he looked at Rachel. "It would only postpone the inevitable."

"You want me to talk to them." It wasn't a question. Rachel had known for the last few hours that a confrontation with the press was, indeed, inevitable.

"I think you should. You don't have to answer all their questions, just those you feel comfortable discussing. Believe me, Rachel, it's the only way to get those guys off your back."

"He's right," Annie said, taking a gold compact from her purse and checking her makeup. "Might as well make nice to the press." She fingered a red curl in place. "You never know when you might need them."

Much as Rachel hated to admit it, both Annie and Ambrose had a point. The sooner she dealt with them the sooner she could resume her life.

Squaring her shoulders, she nodded at Ambrose who stood poised at the door, one hand on the knob. Together they walked out to meet the herd.

Annoyed that the press was ignoring her and focusing their attention on her sister, Annie stood aside and watched as reporters jostled her to get to Rachel.

At the same time, she couldn't help but admire her sister's poise. For someone who claimed to dislike dealing with the media, she was doing one hell of a job. She didn't even use that old ploy of asking the reporters to repeat the questions just to give herself a few more seconds to think of an answer. Pleasant and forthright, Rachel answered each query briefly but fully. She even managed to crack a joke every now and then, something that immediately endeared her to the group.

She was good, Annie admitted. And smart. But, thank God, not smart enough to realize Annie had lied to her. It had been touch and go there for a while. With Rachel and Ambrose scrutinizing her as though she was under a microscope, sounding properly outraged hadn't been easy.

Annie was still lost in thought when Rachel suddenly extended an arm toward her. "Actually," she said in answer to something a reporter had asked, "the Harvest Ball is more my sister's department, I'm sure she'd love to tell you what she has planned." She turned to Annie. "Annie? Do you mind?"

As every head suddenly turned to her, Annie gave a dazzling smile and stepped forward.

Sixteen

In the lab, where she spent several hours a day, Rachel held up a test tube and turned to Vince, Spaulding's head technician. "Let's add a little Merlot to this one," she suggested. "No more than two percent, and see what happens."

As Vince was jotting down the request, Rachel looked up and saw Courtney standing outside the window. In her faded jeans and pink twin set, and carrying her schoolbooks, she looked adorable. And a little flushed.

Setting the tube down in its rack beside several others, Rachel excused herself to Vince and walked out to meet her niece. "Courtney! What a pleasant surprise."

"Hi, Aunt Rachel. If you're too busy, I can come back later."

"Absolutely not. Vince can manage without me for a few minutes." She took the teenager's hand. "Come, let's go in my office. How are you doing?"

"I'm the one who should be asking that question." Rachel saw Courtney glance around her, as though she was looking for someone. "I tried to call you a couple of times," Courtney continued, "but I kept getting your machine."

Rachel led her into her office, leaving the door open. "I'm sorry about that. I've been pretty thoughtless lately." She assumed her favorite position, one hip perched on the edge of her desk. "The truth is, I was feeling a little sorry for myself those last couple of days, but I'm over it now, and I promise I won't ignore you anymore."

Courtney gave a quick shake of her head. "I didn't mean to imply you were ignoring me. It's just that...I wanted to help and didn't know how."

Rachel was touched by Courtney's thoughtfulness. "You're helping now, sweetie, just by being here."

"Oh, Aunt Rachel." Courtney's eyes filled with tears. "I'm so sorry about all that happened to you, especially with Preston. I can't believe he broke up with you. It was so cruel of him to do that."

"Actually, he did me a favor," Rachel said with a shrug. "He forced me to open my eyes and to see that he didn't love me at all. Can you imagine if I had found that out after we were married?"

"So..." Courtney frowned. "You're over him?"

"Not completely, but...I'm getting there."

"I'm glad." The teenager leaned forward. "Is it true you gave all his stuff to the Goodwill?"

"Yup."

Courtney choked back a laugh. "The Armani, too?"

"The Armani, the Bill Blass, the Bruno Maglis, everything."

"Gosh." Laughter shook Courtney's shoulders. "Does he know yet?"

"He just found out last night when he opened his mail and saw a note from the Goodwill thanking him for his generous donation."

"Did he call you? Was he furious?"

"He threatened to sue me," Rachel said, recalling last night's brief phone conversation. "So, yes, I'd say he was a little agitated. I listened to his ranting for about five seconds then I hung up."

"Did that make you feel better? To give his clothes away, I mean."

Rachel chuckled. "Actually, now that it's over, I feel pretty foolish, but at the time, yes, it did make me feel better."

As if a radar had suddenly gone up, Courtney's head whipped around, and she almost dropped her books. Following her gaze, Rachel saw Ryan Cummings standing outside her window, talking to the cellar master.

She smiled. In spite of Courtney's repeated efforts to act calm and cool whenever her handsome assistant was around, her niece's feelings for him were plainly evident. The girl was head over heels in love. And who could blame her? Ryan was gorgeous.

At the sound of Rachel's polite cough, Courtney blushed violently and quickly shifted her gaze back to her aunt.

"You like Ryan, don't you?" Rachel asked gently.

Courtney gave a careless shrug. "He's all right."

"He's also unattached, which means he probably doesn't have a date for the Harvest Ball. It's coming up, you know."

The Harvest Ball, which this year would be hosted by Spaulding Vineyards, was an annual charity event attended by area vintners and wine distributors from all over the world. A few days from now, preparations at Spaulding would be getting frantic, and Annie, as the principal organizer, would be even more impossible than ever.

"Are you saying I should go with him?" Courtney asked, her face turning even redder.

"Isn't that what you want?"

"Of course n-not," she said, stuttering a little. "What gave you that idea…" Then, because she had never been able to tell a lie, she slumped in her chair and sighed. "Yes, Aunt Rachel," Courtney admitted. "I would love to go to the ball with Ryan. The problem is, he doesn't even know I'm alive."

"Of course he does. It's just that he's been awfully busy these days, and because of that, a little forgetful. Why don't you march right out there and ask him if he has a date for the ball. If he doesn't—"

Courtney threw her aunt a horrified look. "You mean…I should ask *him?*" She shook her head. "No way, Aunt Rachel."

"Oh, come on." Rachel nudged Courtney's foot with the tip of her boot. "What happened to that warrior spirit of yours?"

Courtney slanted another quick glance in Ryan's direction. "It melts away when Ryan is around."

Realizing her assistant's conversation with the cellar master was almost over, Rachel pushed off from the desk and took her niece's hand. "Come with me."

"Why?" Courtney asked, clutching her books so they wouldn't fall. "What are you doing?"

"I need to ask Ryan something and you can use the excuse to bring up the ball." With a laugh, she gave Courtney's hand another tug and dragged her out of her office.

As the two women approached, Ryan looked up and grinned. "Hi, Courtney," he said, tucking a wine chart under his arm. "Playing hooky today?"

To Rachel's surprise, Courtney totally lost her nerve. Her face still red, she murmured a quick hello, said something about having a bus to catch and hurried away.

Ryan's friendly smile faded. "What did I do?"

"Nothing," Rachel said quickly. "Courtney has a lot on her mind these days, that's all." She gave Ryan's arm a brief, reassuring squeeze before running after Courtney.

But by the time she reached the courtyard, Courtney was already halfway down the access road where a school bus picked her up every morning. At the telephone pole, she turned around and gave a helpless shrug as if to say she was sorry.

Knowing exactly how she felt, Rachel nodded in understanding. The Harvest Ball was still three weeks away. There would be plenty of opportunities to get Courtney and Ryan together if only for that one magical evening.

As the yellow bus pulled up, Courtney turned to wave. Rachel waved back, wondering how such a warm, wonderful girl could be the product of someone such as Annie. Thank God, she didn't have to know her mother was behind this whole ugly mess with Gregory. For Courtney's sake, Rachel and Annie had both agreed to keep that little scheme between themselves and never talk about it again.

Her mind already on the blends she and Vince had been testing earlier, Rachel turned and headed back toward the lab.

The red light on her answering machine was blinking when Rachel got home that night. In an automatic gesture, she pressed the playback button and walked around the room, opening windows and turning on lights.

At the sound of the unfamiliar and slightly hesitant voice, she stopped. "Rachel, this is Sal Dassante...your grandfather."

She walked slowly back to the phone and stood staring at the machine. "I'm sure you have lots of questions," Sal continued. "And I want to answer them, Rachel, anytime you want." There was a pause. "Come and see me." He cleared his throat. "My number here at the farm is 555-6214. I—I'll be expecting your call." Then, clearly uncomfortable talking to an answering machine, he hung up abruptly.

Her teeth clamped on her bottom lip, Rachel rewound

the message and played it back, listening more attentively. Sal spoke in a low, gravelly voice that seemed like a perfect match for the photograph she had seen of him in the papers—rugged features, a strong jaw, piercing eyes.

So he wanted to see her. That didn't surprise her. In fact, she had been wondering how long it would be until he contacted her and what she would say when he did.

A little unsettled by the call, she went to stand by the window. There were no stars in the sky tonight and the air was too chilled to go out on the terrace.

Taking a deep breath, she remained at the window, not sure what to do. She had meant every word the other day when she had told Sam she had no intention of meeting the Dassantes. But that was before the news they were related leaked out. The circumstances were different now, and from what she'd heard about Sal, he wasn't the kind of man who would give up after just one call.

Her gaze drifted back toward the answering machine again. She could still hear the inflections in his voice, the unexpected hesitancy, as if he already suspected she wanted nothing to do with him.

While debating how to handle his phone call, she thought of all the things she had already learned about Sal in the past couple of days—the accusations he'd never bothered to deny, his undisguised hatred of her mother, his relentless pursuit and renewed efforts to find her. Rachel shivered. She had nothing in common with that man, except the blood that flowed in her veins, and even that wasn't enough to make her want to return his call.

Her mind made up, she walked back to the phone and with a push of her finger, erased Sal's message. She didn't have to do a thing. He'd realize soon enough she didn't want to meet him and once he did, he'd leave her alone. It was that simple.

Satisfied she had made the right decision, she went into the kitchen to make herself some dinner.

The silvery light of a crescent moon found its way between the closed blinds and came to rest on the green spread of the king-size bed. Annie giggled as her lover's hard body snuggled against hers.

"Stop that," she said when he cupped her breasts from behind.

"Why?" He nibbled her ear.

"Because I have to go home and get some sleep. I have an early day tomorrow."

She could already feel his erection, but didn't weaken. Now that she was getting older, these late hours took their toll on her face, as well as on her performance at work. "Come on," she said, trying to wiggle out of his grip. "Let me go."

"Not until we've made love again."

"God, you're insatiable."

He laughed. "What can I say? You bring out the beast in me."

She loved to hear that, loved the passion in his voice, and above all, she loved the power she had over him. At thirty-nine and getting closer to the big four-oh every day, having that kind of hold on a twenty-six-year-old stud like Ryan Cummings wasn't something too many middle-aged women could boast about.

But there was a slight drawback to this almost perfect relationship. Ryan was changing. She had barely noticed it at first and had found his sudden interest in her activities amusing, even flattering. Now she found it stifling. Then just a couple of days ago, he had told her he loved her.

That had scared the hell out of her. Love wasn't what

she wanted out of this relationship. A few laughs, yes. Good sex, certainly. But love? No way.

As he started caressing her back, she closed her eyes. She hated to let him go, though. For all his possessiveness, Ryan was a terrific lover. And, oh, Lord, what he could do with those hands of his.

Determined not to give in, she sat up, pulling the green bedspread over her bare breasts. "Later, Ryan."

"Okay." Unfazed, he propped himself up on one elbow and traced the contours of her mouth with his finger. "What are you doing tomorrow evening?"

"Catching up with my work," she said truthfully. "This mess with Rachel has put everyone behind schedule, including me. I have to work on the invitation list for the Harvest Ball and make a slew of phone calls."

"In the middle of the night?"

"Nighttime in the U.S. is morning in Europe, my dear."

"Hmm, I hadn't thought of that." His eyes shimmered with a new excitement. "I just had a brilliant idea. Let's go to the Harvest Ball together."

She gave him a startled look. "Are you crazy? That's all I need."

"What's wrong with going to the ball together? Aren't you allowed to have a date?"

"Somehow I don't think Rachel would approve of me dating her protégé. Knowing how paranoid she is these days, she'd see that as another form of betrayal."

"But that's dumb. There's nothing wrong in you and me having a relationship. We're not committing a crime."

"Believe me, it would raise eyebrows, and I don't want that to happen."

"We'll have to come out in the open eventually."

Annie stiffened. There it was again, that reference to

something much more serious than what she intended it to be. "Why?"

"Because," he said, lowering the bedspread and kissing the swell of her breast. "I'm planning to marry you and—"

"Whoa! Hold it a minute." Yanking the covers and holding them against her, she jumped out of bed. "Who said anything about marriage?"

Clearly hurt, Ryan gave her his sad puppy look. "We never actually discussed it, but...that's where we're heading, isn't it? I mean...I love you, Annie. You know that."

"How can you love me? We've only been together two weeks."

He laughed. "Oh, Annie, I've been crazy about you since I was a Boy Scout. *You* are the reason I came to work for Spaulding, baby, no one else. You don't know how many times I've wanted to tell you in the last two years. I wasn't sure if you felt the same way or not, so I kept my distance."

That was true. Ryan had never been anything but a perfect gentleman. It wasn't until the night of Grams's funeral that their relationship had taken a different turn. He had stopped by the house to make sure she was all right and he had found her alone in the gazebo, crying.

When she had told him Rachel had inherited the winery, he had been sweet and comforting, and one thing had led to another. They'd made love, right there under the stars, heedless of the fact that someone could walk out at any moment and find them in each other's arms. If anything, the fear of getting caught had brought an element of delicious danger to their lovemaking, an erotic kick that had made the act even more exciting.

Remembering how it had been that first night, and every night afterward, mellowed her a little. "You're a dear man,

Ryan," she said, hoping to soften the blow a little. "And a great lover, but I'm not ready for marriage."

"Why? Because of Rachel?"

"Because of a lot of things. One of them being that right now I'm on what you might call probation."

His attitude went from defensive to protective. "Why? What are they doing to you now?"

"Oh, it's just a little family matter my sister turned into something huge, as usual."

"What little family matter?"

"I can't tell you, but take my word for it. One infraction on my part, one hint of scandal, and I'm history."

"But that's unfair." His outrage was so genuine, she smiled. "You've done more for Spaulding Vineyards than Rachel, Sam and Hannah combined. Why, if it weren't for you, the company would have never grown at the rate it did in the last couple of years."

Annie stroked his cheek. Finally someone who appreciated her worth. How lovely. Maybe she'd keep him a little while longer. He was good for her ego. "Thank you for saying that, darling. Believe me, after today, I needed to hear it."

He caught her hand and brought it to his lips. "At least tell me that marriage is not out of the question."

She sighed. "Ryan, haven't you heard one word I said. I can't afford to antagonize my sister right now." She gave him a quick peck on the mouth. "Why don't you be a dear and drop this silly discussion? I have to get ready."

Ignoring his sulking pout, she walked into the bathroom for a quick shower.

Seventeen

Gregory had been in Napa Valley no more than a couple of times since Luke's wedding, once with Lindsay and another time with Noelle. Not surprisingly, Lindsay had hated the place. She had complained about everything—the heat, the lack of nightlife and the people whom she claimed could only talk about wine. Rather than listen to her ramblings, Gregory had cut their weekend short and had never brought her back.

Now, as he drove north on Route 29, toward Calistoga, he marveled at the miles after miles of lush vineyards, the quaint bed-and-breakfasts dotted along the country road, the pastoral calm of the area now that the crush was over.

The two majestic ponderosa pines that flanked Spaulding Vineyards were still there as was the hand-painted sign directing traffic in two directions—right for those who wanted to ride to the mountaintop winery on the sky gondola and to the left for those who preferred to stay on terra firma.

As Gregory drove his Jaguar up the winding road, he wondered what kind of reception was waiting for him. Although he could strangle Annie for her monumental lie, and still might if she was unlucky enough to cross his path, he took full responsibility for making such a mess of Rachel's life.

Yesterday, curious about the woman he had hurt once

again, he had gone to the library and caught up with the Spauldings, and Rachel in particular.

To say he had been impressed was an understatement. After graduating *summa cum laude* from Davis with a degree in enology, Rachel had spent the summer in Burgundy, honing her craft in a small but prestigious vineyard. In an article that was later reprinted in the *American Wine Journal,* the owner had told a reporter, "That girl has an incredible talent for winemaking. It's still a little raw, like a young wine, but it will mature beautifully and very quickly."

Within a few years, his predictions had come true. In 1996, in a national competition, Rachel's reserve Cabernet was awarded the Award of Excellence, making her the youngest winemaker in the country to receive such a high honor.

Gregory knew only too well how badly the publicity regarding her biological family had affected her personal life. But at least it hadn't damaged her career in the eye of the media. If anything, the press had been sympathetic toward her, and for the most part, had left her alone.

Now if he could only convince her to accept his apologies, he'd be even happier, though he wouldn't blame her if, after taking one look at him, she sent him rolling back down the mountain.

While the predicted rain had changed direction at the last moment and headed north, a cooler breeze had moved inland, chilling the air and making every vintner in the valley glad the harvest was over.

Crouched in front of a vine, Rachel inspected the section close to the root, scratching the old bark with her fingernail for signs of decay. That row of chardonnay grapes, along with dozens of others, had been planted more than three decades ago by her father, and though they were still giving decent fruit, the time had come to replace them.

Above her, a shrilling sound pierced the silence. Looking up, she saw a turkey buzzard skim by, heading for the nearby hills. She followed his flight for a moment, admiring the bird's majestic grace before returning to her task.

She was checking another vine when she heard the sound of footsteps behind her. Assuming it was the vineyard manager, she turned, a ready smile on her face. For a moment she had no idea who the handsome man smiling back at her was. He wore casual khaki pants, a red polo shirt with some kind of designer logo on the pocket, and comfortable loafers, standard attire for many valley vintners.

"Hello, Rachel."

Rising, she brushed the dirt off her jeans. His voice was low and rich. And vaguely familiar. "I'm afraid you have me at a disadvantage, Mr....?"

"Shaw. Gregory Shaw."

She felt the jolt and almost stumbled back from it. She wasn't sure how long she stood there, rooted to the ground, while he looked at her with that old familiar smile. Her heart tripped a little.

Annoyed he could still affect her that way, she gave herself a mental shake and took a long second look at him. Although he had barely aged since Annie's wedding sixteen years before, there were some notable differences. The Tom Selleck mustache was gone but his hair, cut shorter now, was just as black and thick as she remembered, the marine-blue eyes just as watchful. He looked broader somehow, more polished, even in casual clothes.

Her first impulse was to tell him this was private property and to get the hell out before she called security. The nerve of him sneaking up here unannounced. Maybe she wouldn't even bother with the warning. Maybe she'd call security right now and have him tossed out.

That alternative, as tempting as it was, had a major flaw, and that flaw was her own reaction to him. She hadn't been prepared for that smile of absolute delight on his part as he inspected her from head to toe, and she hadn't been prepared for her own rush of emotion as she returned his stare. What was the matter with her? She was acting as irrational as that naive fifteen-year-old who had fallen in love with him the day of Annie's wedding.

"What do you want, Gregory?" she asked, turning away from him and resuming her inspection.

"I came to see you. We need to talk."

"No, we don't. If you had called ahead of time I would have told you that."

"That's precisely why I didn't call. I knew you wouldn't want to see me."

She didn't bother to tell him that she had very much wanted to see him but he hadn't been available. And once she'd found out Annie had tricked him into helping her, much of her anger had dissipated.

Not quite ready to let him off the hook just yet, she gave him a challenging look. Now was the time to find out exactly what Gregory Shaw was made of. "All right, Gregory," she said with a nod, "if you want to talk, we'll talk. I'll start. Who hired you to find Alyssa?"

His face expressed instant regret. "I'm sorry, Rachel. I can't divulge that information."

Resentful or not, she couldn't help but admire the fact that he hadn't taken the easy way out by implicating Annie. He did have ethics, after all.

"Go ahead," he added when she continued to gaze at him. "Get it out of your system, including how rude and thoughtless I was the night of Luke's wedding. You were mad at me then, and you're mad at me now, and I don't blame you. I seem to come into your life for the sole purpose of hurting you, and for that I'm deeply sorry. I had no idea you were Alyssa Dassante's daughter when I first took this case.''

She moved to another vine and crouched again, putting it through the same rigorous examination she had the others. ''Would it have made a difference if you had?''

He squatted next to her, close enough for her to smell his aftershave. Sandalwood. ''Yes. Regardless of what you think of me, I'm not a heel. I may act like one sometimes, but I'm not.''

She fought back a laugh. A heel, an *insensitive* heel, actually, was how she had thought of him after Annie's wedding.

''I didn't mean to hurt you, Rachel,'' he said again. ''Or cause you any embarrassment. I need you to believe that.''

Standing, she jammed her hands into her pockets. ''Why?''

''Because it's important to me.''

Raising her head so she could look at him, she squinted against the morning sun. It was time to put him out of his misery but not until she'd had a little fun. ''Tell me something, then. If you're as smart as everyone says you are, how could you fall for that soapy story my sister fed you?''

She felt a certain degree of satisfaction at the look of surprise on his face. ''Your sister?'' he asked quietly.

''Yes. Dear Annie. I was testing your principles earlier. I already knew she was the one who asked you to find Alyssa.''

''She told you that?''

''No. I found out.''

For a second, his brows furrowed, as if trying to figure

out how she could have done that. Then a flicker of amusement danced in his eyes. "So it was you."

"What do you mean?" she asked innocently.

"The briefcase story. Annie didn't misplace it, did she? And she didn't call my secretary yesterday. That was you."

Rachel moved to another vine. "Very good, Sherlock."

A hearty laughter burst out of him. "Does Annie know?"

"Yes, although she didn't find my little ruse nearly as amusing as you seem to."

"No, I guess she wouldn't."

"You didn't answer my question."

She looked into those deep blue eyes and saw the spark of humor there. "I didn't fall for her story entirely," he replied. "Just enough to feel sorry for her, which obviously was a mistake."

And then again, Rachel thought as they held each other's gaze, maybe Sam was right, maybe Gregory was just a nice guy. But that, too, was a thought she wasn't ready to explore just yet.

She started walking along the row of vines, aware he was doing the same thing.

"I'm sorry about Hannah," he said gently. "She was quite a lady."

Once again his sincerity touched her. "The best." For a brief moment her eyes locked with his again before returning to the hills ahead of them. "She liked you. She thought you were a little wild, a little unsettled, but overall she thought you were one of the good guys."

"What about you?" he asked. "Have you changed your opinion of me yet?"

"The jury is still out on that one."

"Then let me do something to speed up the verdict."

His tone had turned playful. "Let me prove to you that your grandmother was right."

She stopped walking. "How do you propose to do that?"

He shrugged. "I don't know. Why don't you go out to dinner with me and we'll discuss it."

She smiled, remembering his latest, highly publicized liaison. "Won't Alexandra Bimmington object to you having dinner with another woman?" she asked.

His eyes twinkled with merriment and a touch of admiration. "Alexandra and I are no longer seeing each other. How do you know about her?"

"I do my homework. After finding out you were meddling into my life, I went to the library to see what I could learn about yours."

He laughed, that same hearty, contagious laugh.

"What's so funny?"

"I did the same thing, went to the library and read all about you." He paused. "Why don't we compare notes and see how much of what we learned is true and how much is journalistic fabrication. We could do that over dinner."

"And he's persistent, too."

"Is that a yes?"

The question drew another smile out of her. "Sorry. This is a busy time at the winery."

"You still have to eat."

"I usually do that alone, in the company of my computer."

"Then tell me what I can do to redeem myself."

That was kind of sweet, she thought. She wasn't used to men wanting to do things for her. With Preston it had been the other way around. "Well, let's see," she said, pretending to be thinking. "Can you get my fiancé back?"

This time his expression was mildly condescending. "No, and I wouldn't even if I could."

Rachel came to an abrupt halt. "You have something against Preston Farley?"

"You mean, other than the fact he's a jackass?"

She laughed. "You sound as though you know him."

"In a manner of speaking."

She wasn't interested enough in her former fiancé to ask Gregory how he had come to the conclusion that Preston was a jackass. "You don't have to worry. I wouldn't take him back if he came crawling on his knees."

"Good."

She glanced at her watch. "I'd better get back to the cellars before Sam sends out a search party. Goodbye, Gregory." She wanted to add, "It was good seeing you again," but didn't.

"Goodbye, Rachel." There was regret in his voice and a wistful expression in his eyes.

Ignoring both, Rachel walked away. She didn't like the warm signals her brain was sending her. After her bitter disappointment with Preston, the last thing she needed right now was another romantic entanglement.

As she walked, she kept listening for the sound of retreating footsteps, the slam of a car door, something to indicate he was leaving. When she didn't hear anything, she turned around. He was still standing where she had left him, hands in his pockets, that same regretful expression on his face. Then, as if he had been waiting for her to turn around, he waved and started toward his car, a sleek black Jaguar parked a few feet away.

It was better this way, she thought. They had finally settled things between them and now each could go back to their respective lives.

"Wait!" The single command was out before she could stop it.

He turned around.

She looked at him, wondering if she had lost her mind. "Can you help me find my mother?"

They sat at a picnic table, talking, and sipping orange soda, while around them, the activity began to slow as the lunch hour approached. Trying not to gawk at Rachel wasn't easy. Her face had a mobility and an expressiveness Gregory found riveting. Her hair, which he remembered as a forgettable brown, had darkened to a rich chestnut with threads of copper the sun managed to find every now and then and turn into fire.

Her body was even tougher to ignore. As she had led the way to this quiet, shady spot, the view from behind, a slender waist tapering down to rounded hips, had been enough to make him forget, for a moment, why he was here.

"So many people have tried to find Alyssa," she went on, obviously unaware of the direction his lusty thoughts had taken. "It's probably a hopeless quest."

He shook his head to get the fuzz out of his brain. "Maybe not as hopeless as you think." He watched her neck as she tilted her head back to take a swallow of her soda. "I've got a couple of ideas, especially now that I've seen her picture."

"What kind of ideas?"

"Your resemblance to your mother is astounding, as I'm sure you've heard. That resemblance could come in handy."

"How?"

He told her about Jonsey Malone's reluctance to talk to him, and his uncle's belief, some years ago, that the nightclub owner had lied.

Her expression turned hopeful. "Do you think he knows where Alyssa is?"

"He might. Although I thought he would have contacted me once he saw your picture in the papers."

"Maybe he hasn't seen the papers."

"I doubt it. I know you're not thrilled to hear that, but your story has been covered in every newspaper from Mendocino to San Diego. If he can read, he's seen it."

She gave a small shrug. "Then he's scared."

"That's why I'm going to call him back. If he agrees to see us and feels he can trust us, he might change his mind." He leaned forward and rested his elbows on the redwood table. "In the meantime, it wouldn't hurt to learn all we can about Alyssa Dassante."

"Haven't the newspapers and that police report you mentioned told us all we need to know?"

"Sometimes newspapers, and even cops, don't dig deep enough. I do."

"How?"

"By going to the source." He contemplated her for a second or two and realized he'd be perfectly content to do only that for the rest of the day. "Have you met the Dassantes yet?"

She stiffened visibly. "No. Why should I?"

"Sal didn't contact you?"

She looked away. "Four times. I didn't return the calls."

"I don't blame you. From what I heard, the Dassantes aren't exactly candidates for family of the year." He paused. "However, Sal isn't going to give up on his granddaughter." He dragged his can back and forth on the table. "There's another advantage to getting to know Sal."

"What's that?"

"You could learn valuable information about Alyssa, either from him, or from someone else in the family."

She gave a short nod. "I'll think about it."

"Good. Let me know what you decide."

"And you'll let me know about Jonsey?"

He smiled. She was focused. He liked that. Hell, he liked everything about her. "I will."

After getting into his car and starting to drive away, he kept her in his rearview mirror for as long as the twisting road allowed. When he could no longer see her, he thought of her all the way back to San Francisco.

Eighteen

Rachel sat in her Jeep Cherokee, staring at the imposing three-story stone house. Now that she knew this was where she was born, she waited for a stirring, a knot in her stomach, something that would signal to her she had a history here, that this was where her life had begun.

She felt nothing other than a deep anxiety and a desire to get this meeting over with. The phone conversation between her and Sal, when she had finally returned his call, had been brief and to the point, and nothing, not even the genuine emotion in the man's voice, had succeeded in changing her feelings toward him.

She had come here for only one reason—to learn more about Alyssa, and maybe, if she was lucky, to convince Sal to end this stupid vendetta against her mother.

In a downstairs window, a curtain moved. Rachel felt a shiver ripple over her skin as she realized she was being watched. Within moments, the front door opened and an old woman in an apron, and a net around her gray hair, came out and approached the Jeep.

"Miss Spaulding?" she asked.

Feeling stupid for having made an old woman come and get her, Rachel stepped out of the car. "Yes, I'm Rachel Spaulding."

"Follow me, please."

Rachel was led into a large foyer with hardwood floors

polished to a soft patina, down a hallway, and finally into
a large room furnished with massive, intricately carved furniture, well-worn rugs and sofas in a somber maroon color.
Cigar smoke had permeated the walls and mingled quite
nicely with the smell of lemon oil the old housekeeper
probably used to polish the woodwork.

"Hello, Lillie."

Startled, she turned and saw the man she assumed was
Sal Dassante. He sat in a deep chair, his hands on the arm-
rests. He was powerfully built, though he didn't appear very
tall. He had deep creases alongside his mouth and a full
head of gray hair greased back in an old-fashioned style.
His eyes were a light hazel, and at the moment they regarded her with an intensity that only added to her discom-
fort.

"Good afternoon." She didn't know what to call him.
He would have probably been insulted at "Mr. Dassante,"
"Sal" was too familiar and "Grandfather" was out of the
question. "If you don't mind," she added, feeling a need
to establish boundaries quickly, "I'd rather be called Rachel."

He stood and walked toward her. "Then Rachel it is. I
never liked Lillie, anyway. Your mother chose that name
just to irritate me." He looked boldly at her, inspecting
every feature of her face. "I guess you know you look like
her."

"So I've been told."

His lips parted in a humorless smile. "That's all right. I
won't hold it against you."

Touching her elbow, he led her toward one of the sofas.
On a low ebony table, a tray with a china pot and two
matching cups had been set up. "Let's have some coffee."
He said it in the tone of a man not accustomed to having
his wishes denied. "Maria makes it hot and strong."

"Thank you," Rachel said, glad she would have something to do with her hands.

They sat, Rachel on the sofa, Sal on the chair across from her. "You know," he said, as he poured coffee, "my son Nico thought you should take a blood test, to make sure you're who you say you are."

"I'm not the one who sought you out," she reminded him.

"I know that, but Nico is not too bright." He put the pot down. "So I spelled it out for him. I told him, 'Nico don't be stupid. I don't need no test to tell me that girl is my own flesh and blood.'" He tapped the left side of his chest with his index finger. "This tells me everything I need to know."

She smiled. "What did Nico say to that?"

"Who gives a damn what Nico said? I knew you were my granddaughter the moment I saw your picture in the paper, and that's all that counts." He handed her a cup. "Cream and sugar?"

"Just black, thank you."

Her answer seemed to please him. "Ah, you see? You're a Dassante already. We drink it black, too, except Erica, who uses tons of Sweet 'n Low in hers." He took a sip, slurping loudly. "Sometimes I wonder if the girl's really Italian or if she just told me that so she could marry Nico."

"Erica is your daughter-in-law?"

Sal inclined his head. "And your aunt. You'll like her. She drives me crazy with all her church stuff, but she's okay. And Nico is your uncle." He continued to scrutinize her. "Your father's younger brother."

Rachel took a sip of her coffee, which was very good. "Will Nico and Erica be joining us?"

"Later. I thought you and me should get to know each other first. I don't know much about you, except that you make wine." His lips pulled into what could pass for a smile. "Good wine?"

She smiled back. "The best."

"That's good. I like that. If you're gonna do something, do it well and make lots of money. That's a Dassante motto." He leaned back, holding his cup and saucer. "Go ahead, tell me about my granddaughter."

Rachel felt herself relax. His unexpected candor was moving the conversation along, making it less awkward. In between sips of coffee, she told him about her life at Spaulding, her early interest in winemaking, how much she had learned from her father and her grandmother.

He had many questions, which she answered as best as she could. She even laughed when he told her winemaking was a man's job.

"Nowadays women can do anything they want," she reminded him. "Sometime they even do it better than men."

He laughed, a short, awkward laugh that made her suspect he didn't do that very often. "Tell me about the guy who dumped you," he said abruptly. "Benson?"

"Preston. How do you know about him?"

"I know everything. You still love him?"

She shrugged. "It's rather hard to keep on loving someone who doesn't love you back, don't you think?"

"You didn't answer my question."

"No, I don't love him anymore." She took another sip. "And I don't really want to talk about him."

"Then we won't. And don't you worry..." he added, shaking his finger at her. "A pretty girl like you, you won't stay single long. We'll find you a nice Italian boy."

"I'm in no hurry to find another man."

He waved his hand as if to dismiss the suggestion. "You're right. Have a little fun first. And a little time for me," he added with twinkle in his eye. "I want you to come here often, Rachel. This house will always be open for you."

"That's very generous of you."

He threw a hand in the air. He didn't seem able to do much of anything without his hands being in constant motion. "What's with this generous stuff? You're my granddaughter. You think I'm gonna stand on formalities?"

Since he seemed to be in such a good mood, Rachel thought this was a perfect opportunity to bring up Alyssa. "Sal," she said, using his name for the first time and seeing the pleased expression on his face. "I wonder if I could ask you something."

"You can ask me anything."

"You might not like it. It's about Alyssa."

His expression cooled. "What about her?"

"I know you've started looking for her again, and that you've increased your previous reward to a hundred thousand dollars."

He continued to look at her but said nothing.

She cleared her throat. "I'd like you to give up that search. And cancel the reward."

"Why?" he asked bluntly.

"Because I want my life back. I don't want to come home after work and find reporters on my doorstep. And I don't want to turn on the six o'clock news at night and see my face on every channel and hear that some money-hungry individual spotted Alyssa somewhere. She's had enough, Sal. And *I*'ve had enough. Can you understand that?"

He was silent for a while, his eyes narrowed and watchful. "Sure, I can understand that." He put his cup down. "Can you understand how I felt when my son was taken from me? And my granddaughter? What it was like living without them all these years?"

"Yes." She moistened her lips. "I think I can."

He eyed her shrewdly. "Is that why you came?" he asked. "To ask me to leave Alyssa alone?"

He was sharp, too sharp to be told a lie. "Partly."

"What's the other part?"

She settled for a piece of the truth instead of the whole truth. "I felt I should."

A long silence fell between them. She could tell by his expression that her answer didn't please him, and she wouldn't have been a bit surprised if he had suddenly asked her to leave, but he didn't. Instead he asked her another question, and this time the sharpness was gone from his voice.

"And if I do what you ask, if I stop looking for your mother, that will make you happy?"

"Yes," she said, looking up and holding his gaze. "Very."

He gave a curt nod. "Okay, you got it."

"Really?" Shock almost made her stutter. She had expected a battle.

"Yes, really." He barked a laugh, as if pleased he had caught her off guard. "You see, Sal isn't such a bad guy, after all, is he?"

"I never said you were."

"No, but I know what you heard, what people are saying about me." As he talked, he picked up the phone and dialed a number. She heard him ask for Stanley Fox and remembered that was the name of the reporter who had written the initial story in the *Winters Journal*.

Sal waited a few moments then spoke briskly into the phone. "Stan, this is Sal Dassante. Yes, yes, I saw it. Good story, Stan, but I need you to do me a favor." He winked at her. "I'm not looking for Alyssa no more, Stan, and I want you to put that in your paper. That's right." He laughed. "What can I tell you, I'm an old man, I change my mind. And anyway," he added, glancing at Rachel again, "I found my granddaughter now, and she's all I need. No, no reward, not a penny. Will you print that, Stan?" He nodded. "Good. *Arrivederci.*"

He hung up. "How's that?"

"Thank you, Sal," Rachel said simply.

"You didn't think I was gonna do it, did you?"

"No. I mean...not so quickly."

Before she could say anything more, Sal slapped the arms of his chair. "Let's go find the rest of the family. They can't wait to meet you."

Rachel disliked Nico on sight and, judging from the dark look he gave her when Sal made the introductions, he felt exactly the same way. It was a different matter with Erica Dassante. Unlike Sal, who hadn't been thrilled with her resemblance to Alyssa, Erica loved it.

"You're every bit as beautiful as your mother," she said, greeting her with open arms.

"Thank you."

Rachel sat in that same austere living room for another half hour, with Nico sulking, Sal looking pleased, and Erica chatting happily and questioning Rachel about her work at the winery. From time to time Sal would throw Nico a nasty look and Nico would ask a question of his own before falling back into another sullen silence.

When a reasonable amount of time had passed, Rachel stood up, glad the ordeal was over. To Sal's obvious disappointment, she turned down his offer to tour the production plant.

"Another time then," he said, ignoring Nico's murderous look. "Dassante Farms is your heritage now. You remember that."

As she, Sal and Erica headed for the door, Nico started to walk in the other direction, but his father caught him by the sleeve and with an iron grip pulled him back. "We're walking Rachel out," he said in a thin voice.

Back in the Cherokee, Rachel glanced in her rearview mirror. The three of them were standing by the door, Sal and Erica waving, Nico rigid with barely concealed rage.

Brushing aside the sensation that something unpleasant was crawling all over her, she put the Jeep in gear, pressed on the gas and sped away.

Alone in his living room, Sal gazed at the chair Rachel had occupied earlier and felt an unexpected pinch in his stomach. She hadn't come here out of a desire to meet him, or even curiosity, but because she was concerned about Alyssa.

He was disappointed about that, but he was also glad she had told him the truth. He would have thought less of her if she had lied, which, for a moment, she had been ready to do.

All in all, the meeting had gone well, and he was glad he had persisted with his phone calls. He chuckled, remembering the first call he had made to her house the night he had learned she was his granddaughter. He had been so choked up at the sound of her voice, he hadn't been able to utter a single word and had hung up like some stupid crank caller. Maybe someday he'd tell her about that, but not now. She was still too stiff, too reserved, maybe even a little suspicious of him.

It was that suspicion that bothered him most. Hopefully, she'd come around. That call he had made to the *Journal* had earned him a few points already. Of course, he had no intention of honoring Rachel's request to drop the search for Alyssa. He liked the girl, sure, but nothing, not even his granddaughter, would stand in the way of what he had to do to avenge his son's death. That was priority number one.

"Sal?"

He turned around and saw Erica standing behind him.

"Maria said you wanted to see me."

"Where's Nico?"

"He had to meet with a client."

"That's okay. You're the one I really wanted to see." He folded his arms across his chest. "What do you think of my granddaughter?"

Erica smiled. "She's lovely, Sal. And very smart."

"I don't think she likes me."

"She doesn't know you, Sal. Give her time. Give her a chance to know you, to know all of us."

"She likes you."

Erica shrugged. "That's because I'm a woman. In a strange environment, a woman is always the first ally."

"It's more than that. I saw the way she looked at you, how you two laughed, like old friends. That's okay," he said when she started to protest. "I'm not upset. In fact, that's why I called you." He pointed to a chair. "Please, *Cara*, sit down."

"Sal?" Erica's tone turned suspicious. "I don't like that look. What is it now? What are you up to?"

In a gesture of total innocence, he spread his arms wide and let them fall back at his sides. "Why is everybody always thinking I'm up to something?"

Erica gave him a tolerant smile. "Why am I here, Sal?"

Sal opened his humidor and took his time selecting a cigar. "I want you to become Rachel's friend."

"What?"

"You heard me. I want you to become her friend. And I want you to put in a good word for me every now and then."

"Oh, Sal, I don't know. That sounds so deceitful."

He waived his cigar in the air. "Oh, don't give me that crap they fill your head with in church. We're family. And what I'm asking is for the good of the family, *capece?*" He came to stand in front of her. "What's the matter, don't you like the girl?"

"I told you I do. That's why—"

"Don't you want to know more about her, learn about her work, what she likes to do when she's not working? That kind of stuff."

"Yes, but…"

"So what's the problem?"

"The problem is, Sal, that we weren't going to crowd her, or pressure her in any way."

"Who said anything about pressuring her? All I'm asking is that you drop over for a visit, see how she's doing, see if she needs anything. Can you do that for me?"

"I don't know, Sal."

"If you do, I'll go to mass with you on Sunday."

That did it. There was nothing Erica liked better than saving souls.

"Oh, Sal," she said, shaking her head. "You do drive a hard bargain."

By the time Rachel reached the outskirts of St. Helena, dusk and a light fog had descended on the valley. As usual when she was coming from that direction, she decided to avoid busy Route 29 and take the less traveled Silverado Trail, which led directly to the back entrance of Spaulding Vineyards.

Approaching a series of treacherous curves, she slowed

the Cherokee, while at the same time glancing in the rear-view mirror. The pickup was still there. She had first noticed it on Route 128 just outside Winters, an old, dusty pickup that resembled dozens of others in that farming community.

The reason she had noticed it at all was because it seemed to be following her, slowing down when she slowed down, picking up speed when she did, but never passing, even when it could have easily done so.

At first she had wondered if it was Nico, though she had no idea why he would be following her. When the driver made no sign of stopping her, however, she had attributed her suspicions to her dislike for the man, and paid no more attention to the vehicle.

Now, with only the two of them on the road, the truck was once again in her sight and staying closer to the Cherokee than he had before. Rachel let out a sigh of irritation. What was the matter with this jerk? Couldn't he see the posted twenty-five mile-per-hour sign? And if he was in such a hurry, why the hell hadn't he passed her when he had the chance?

She tried to catch a glimpse of the driver, but except for a white baseball cap, which he wore low over his forehead, she couldn't see anything. As a signal to back off, she touched her brakes and glanced in the rearview mirror again. The pickup hadn't backed an inch.

"You, my friend, are getting reported," she muttered under her breath. Unfortunately, though, when she tried to read the license plate number, she saw that it was smeared with mud.

At any other time, she would have stopped to give the thrill-seeking driver a piece of her mind, but this stretch of road was too narrow and too winding to stop anywhere safely. Maybe she should call the police and—

The sharp and sudden impact took her completely by surprise.

With a jolt, she realized the pickup had struck her. As the Cherokee swerved dangerously, Rachel cursed and gave a sharp twist of the steering wheel. She didn't breathe a sigh of relief until she felt the tires grab the road again.

"What kind of stupid game are you playing?" she yelled, glaring once again in her mirror.

Before she could decide whether or not to stop, the driver gunned its engine as an even sharper curve loomed ahead. "Watch it, will you?"

But once again, her warning left the driver obviously indifferent. The truck roared closer and Rachel felt the first prickle of panic clutch at her stomach. That asshole wasn't out for a little fun and games. He was trying to push her off the road. Over the cliff.

This time the hit was vicious. At the impact, the Jeep shot forward, coming within inches of the precipitous edge. Rachel's head slammed back against the headrest.

Remembering everything her father, then Hannah, had taught her about mountain driving, she threw the gearshift into Low and pumped on the brakes while steering against the spin. Once again, through sheer determination, she managed to keep the Cherokee on the road.

As the truck began to pick up speed again, panic turned into plain, undiluted fear. The bastard wasn't going to quit until he had sent her tumbling into the abyss below.

Then, to her surprise, and great relief, he slowed down abruptly. She soon saw why. A car, and another one behind it, were climbing up the road, their fog lights visible through the mist.

Yanking the gearshift into Drive, she pressed on the gas, ignoring the speed limit, intent on only one thing—getting away from this maniac.

By the time he caught up with her again, she had reached Spaulding Vineyards. As the truck sped by, she spun the Cherokee onto the access road in a squeal of rubber and didn't slow down until she reached the courtyard parking lot.

Still shaken from the ordeal, she just sat there, chest heaving, her forehead resting on the steering wheel.

"Rachel?"

At the sound of Sam's concerned voice, she raised her head.

"What's wrong?" Sam asked, opening the driver's side door.

Holding his hand, Rachel climbed down and told him what had just happened.

His expression grim, Sam squinted toward the mountain road. "It's those punks again," he muttered.

"What punks?"

"Last weekend, two teenagers were arrested for pulling the same trick on the Oakville Grade. They scared an old man half to death. Then the parents brought in a couple of high-powered attorneys and the kids were released."

"I only saw one driver."

"What did he look like?"

She shook her head. "Couldn't tell. And the license plate was conveniently covered with mud."

She and Sam walked around the Jeep to check the damages. Not surprisingly, the rear fender was smashed in and both taillights were broken.

"We've got to report this," Sam said. "To the cops first, then to the insurance company." He started walking back toward the front of the car to use Rachel's car phone, but she stopped him.

"I don't want this to get out, Sam."

"Why the hell not? You could have been killed, for Christ's sake."

"I know, but I don't want to disrupt the operation of the winery any more than it already has been. Everything is finally starting to get back to normal, Sam. Let's keep it that way."

"Don't you want to throw the book at those kids?"

"If they did it, yes. But I want to do it quietly."

"How are you going to do that?"

"I'll call Rick."

Within minutes, a uniformed officer pulled up next to the Cherokee. Ricardo Torres, whom Rachel had known since third grade circled the Jeep, inspecting it briefly. "You're okay, Rach?" he asked, glancing at her.

"I'm fine."

He wrote down the information she gave him, but at Sam's suggestion that the perpetrators were the same teenagers who were arrested and released last weekend, Rick shook his head. "They may have been released, but their driving privileges were suspended and the pickup impounded. I doubt it's them."

"You'll still check, won't you?" Sam asked.

"Of course. I'll also scrape some of that gray paint off the Jeep and get the lab to analyze it to make sure it doesn't match any other vehicle the kids might have."

He pulled a pocketknife from his pocket then, crouching, took several paint samples and dropped them into a small plastic bag. "I'll call some of the body repair shops I know to see if a gray pickup with a banged-up front end was brought in, but I don't think anyone would be stupid enough to do that. And I'm afraid that without a license plate number, or a description of the man, we might never find this guy."

Rachel nodded. She had already thought of that. "Do what you can, Rick."

"I will." He kissed her on the cheek. "I'll let you know what I find. And I'll keep this thing under wraps as much as I can."

"I appreciate that."

After he left, Rachel turned down Sam's offer to drive her home, and took the Jeep back to the bungalow herself. From there, she called her insurance agent, an old friend of Hannah's, who promised to send an adjuster out right away.

While she waited for him to arrive, she wondered if this incident was the work of some show-off who enjoyed scaring people or someone else—someone with a personal vendetta against her.

The idea sounded totally absurd. The valley was a close-knit community, bound by friendly competition and a camaraderie unequaled anywhere in the country. She couldn't imagine anyone she knew wanting to harm her, and yet...

Once again, her thoughts turned to Joe Brock and the man's visible anger toward her, too visible, perhaps, which was the reason he seemed such a likely suspect.

Before she could give her suspicions further consideration, her front doorbell rang. The adjuster had arrived.

Nineteen

The early morning fog had burned off, revealing a cobalt-blue sky and a few whispy clouds. Walking rapidly, Rachel crossed the courtyard, heading for the sales office to check on an order a Sonoma restaurant owner claimed he hadn't received. She normally left such tasks to her office manager, but the client had called her personally and she had promised to look into the matter right away.

Earlier that morning, Rick Torres had called with the result from the police lab. The gray paint was a standard product used by several truck manufacturers in the seventies. He had suggested sending the samples to a San Francisco lab for more sophisticated tests to narrow down the year and the make, and Rachel had agreed, as long as the incident wasn't leaked to the press.

After what Rick had said the day before, she hadn't been surprised to hear that none of the body shops he had contacted had reported a gray pickup coming in for repairs. As for the teenagers Sam had suspected, neither one owned other cars.

On the positive side, Chuck Willard, the insurance adjuster, had perfectly understood her need to keep the incident quiet. He'd given her his word he wouldn't mention it to anyone outside the claims office, which, fortunately, was located in San Francisco. As for the Cherokee, thanks to Sam's connections, it would be ready in about a week. All she had to do now was arrange for a rental car.

She was almost at the door of the sales office when she saw a black BMW pull into the parking lot. Taking a closer look, she realized the woman behind the wheel was Erica Dassante.

"Rachel!" Erica gave the horn two quick beeps and waved through the open window.

Surprised, for she hadn't expected to see anyone in the Dassante family so soon after her visit, Rachel walked over to meet Erica, wondering what could possibly have brought the woman here.

"I hope you don't mind my dropping by unannounced," Erica said, getting out of her car. "I did it on the spur of the moment..." She sighed. "No, I didn't," she said, looking guilty. "The truth is, I'm here at Sal's request."

"I see." Touched by her candor, Rachel smiled. "Why don't you go sit down." She pointed at the same picnic table where she and Gregory had sat the day before. "I have to check on something, but I'll only be a couple of minutes."

"I've caught you at a bad time."

"No, not at all." She had, in fact. Post-harvest was every bit as hectic as pre-harvest, but Rachel didn't have the heart to tell her that. "How about if I bring us a couple of sodas? Ginger ale okay? I'm afraid that's all the machine has to offer today."

"That's fine, Rachel, thank you."

It took Rachel a little longer than expected to locate the twelve cases of Spaulding Merlot and have them rerouted. That settled, she took a handful of quarters from her jeans' pocket, fed them into the soda machine and walked over to the picnic table with two cans of ginger ale.

"It's so beautiful up here," Erica said, taking the can

Rachel handed her. "So peaceful." Her gaze swept over the valley below. "I was even tempted to come up on the cable car but at the last minute I chickened out and took the back road." She gave Rachel a sheepish grin. "I'm terrified of heights."

"Oh, there's nothing to be afraid of," Rachel replied. "It's only a three-minute ride and a lovely way to see the vineyards. Next time you visit, call me ahead of time and we'll ride up together. How's that?"

Erica didn't look convinced. "We'll see. I'm not promising anything."

Looking at her, Rachel felt an inexplicable connection with this woman, not as strong as she had with Alyssa after that dream the other night, but strong enough to make her feel glad she had come.

"So," Rachel said in a teasing tone, "what secret mission did Sal send you on?"

Erica brought a hand to her cheek. "I can't believe I betrayed him like that. He'd kill me if he knew."

"It'll be our secret."

Suddenly serious, Erica returned Rachel's gaze. "He's afraid you don't like him."

"I don't know him well enough to like him. Or dislike him."

"I told him that, but Sal's a man who expects instant gratification." She popped the tab on her ginger ale and took a deep swallow. "He's not all bad, you know. Oh, don't get me wrong, he has his faults. He's temperamental, demanding, even selfish at times. But he can also be tender, funny, and, you'll soon discover, he's totally devoted to his family."

Her voice softened and Rachel realized Erica was genuinely fond of the man. "Did you know his parents took him out of school when he was only nine years old so he could help support ten other siblings?'' she asked. ''Or that he stowed away on a New York-bound ship when he was fifteen? Or that he lost his wife when the boys were small?''

Rachel felt a pang of guilt. She hadn't cared enough to ask Sal anything about himself or his family. ''No, I didn't know that.''

''I'm not surprised. He's a very private man. That's why people don't like him very much. They don't know him.''

''He doesn't look like the type who would lose any sleep over it.''

''He never has.'' Erica brought the can to her mouth and took another sip. ''Until yesterday.''

Erica's gaze followed a pickup loaded with cases of wine as it started down the access road. ''He loved you very much, you know,'' she continued. ''During those two short weeks after you were born, he spent all his time looking at you and talking to you. Mario was his favorite son, and that made you very special.''

She lowered her gaze. ''Then Mario died and all that love turned to hate, hate for your mother for killing his son, hate for the police who couldn't find her. He was even angry with Nico and me, though Lord knows we did everything in our power to comfort him.''

Rachel felt sorry for the woman. It couldn't have been easy living in that house. ''Those first few weeks must have been difficult for you.''

''For all of us. But especially for Sal. He was only forty-two at the time, but almost overnight he aged twenty years. He lost interest in the business, in the few friends he had, and in the rest of his family. Without Mario, he had simply ceased to exist.''

''Is that when Nico took over the business?''

She laughed. ''Oh, heavens, no. Sal never had the faith

in Nico he had in Mario. He only took a leave of absence. Within a few months he was back at the helm. From that moment on, the farm was all that mattered.''

"And finding Alyssa," Rachel added. "I understand he never lost sight of that."

"No, he didn't. Nico and I desperately tried to make him forget Alyssa. I knew the only way to do that was to replace the grandchild he'd lost." She let out a long, sad sigh. "A few months later I found out we would never have children. Nico was sterile."

"Oh, Erica." Rachel was genuinely moved. "I'm sorry."

"So was I. Until Alyssa brought you home, I never realized how badly I wanted a child of my own."

Rachel thought about the adorable little girl she had seen at the convent. "Did you consider adopting?"

"Nico wouldn't hear of it. And neither would Sal. So, as the years passed, Sal's bitterness and hatred for Alyssa just kept on growing."

"I can't imagine living that way." Rachel shook her head. "With that kind of anger eating at me every minute of every day."

Erica rested her elbows on the picnic table and tucked a strand of ebony-black hair behind her ear. "That's how Sal is."

"But his search for Alyssa is over, right?" Rachel asked a little hesitantly. "I mean, he promised me he'd give it up."

"And he has. That's another thing about Sal not too many people are aware of. He keeps his word."

"I'm glad to hear that." Rachel hadn't been entirely convinced of his sincerity, especially with that phone call to the *Winters Journal,* which at first had seemed like a grandstand play, meant only to impress her. It was a relief to see that Erica trusted him so implicitly. "You like Sal very much, don't you," she said more as a remark than a question.

Erica nodded. "My father died when I was a teenager and when I married Nico, Sal became the father I had lost." She smiled. "And when Alyssa moved in, she became the sister I never had."

"I sensed your feelings for her right away," Rachel said, remembering Erica's warm welcome.

"It was impossible not to like Alyssa. She was beautiful, funny, and always kind, always ready to lend a helping hand. When she moved into that big old house she was like a breath of fresh air. She laughed all the time and she sang—bawdy songs she had learned in that strip club where she used to work." She laughed. "Sometimes, when we were alone, she would do one of her bump-and-grind routines for me. I loved it."

Erica's fingers moved across a splintered strip of redwood, tracing the ridges along its surface. "But the fun and games didn't last long."

Maybe here was her chance to learn more about Alyssa, Rachel thought. "I read in a newspaper she and Sal occasionally clashed."

"'Occasionally'?" Erica rolled her eyes. "They clashed all the time. Sal isn't a man who likes his decisions questioned, and Alyssa questioned them often. She didn't approve of the way he mistreated the migrant workers, and that made Sal furious."

"Was he mistreating the workers?"

Erica shrugged. "I don't know. I was only twenty-two at the time. I didn't pay much attention to what was going on at the farm. But your mother did. She was an idealist, you see, a champion of the underdog. The workers knew it and adored her. That made things even more tense at home."

"Did Sal ever try to change his ways?"

She laughed. "Are you kidding? Sal? Allow a woman to tell him what to do? How to run his business?" She gave an emphatic shake of her head. "No, he didn't. Instead, he told Mario to control his wife, but Alyssa wasn't someone you could control, not with threats, certainly."

A gust of wind blew her black hair into her face and she brushed it away again. "Eventually her life became so intolerable, she decided she'd had enough and asked Mario for a divorce. But Mario wouldn't hear of it."

Encouraged by Erica's candid revelations, Rachel asked the question that had been foremost on her mind. "Tell me about the night she...left." She was reluctant to say the words "killed Mario." The more she learned about Alyssa the less she believed the woman was a killer. "I've read several accounts in the papers, but I'd like to hear it from someone who was there."

Erica gazed at her for a moment. When she spoke again, her voice was subdued. "It was an awful night, dark and stormy, a night filled with premonitions of impending disaster. I couldn't sleep. Storms make me nervous. So I went to the little salon next to our bedroom and started to read. That's when I heard Alyssa and Mario arguing. Our room is right above the garage and when I went to the window, I could see Alyssa's Mercedes in the driveway. Lillie— you—" she corrected with a smile "—were in the passenger seat, snuggled in your little car bed.

"The fighting was getting worse, and I got scared because Mario had a violent temper and I was afraid he'd hurt Alyssa. I shook Nico awake and we ran downstairs."

She looked away again, wearily. "It was too late," she said in a low voice. "Mario was dead."

Rachel knew the rest, the escape in the Mercedes, the police hunt, the detour to Santa Rosa, the car plunging into the ocean.

"Do you think she killed him?" she asked in a whisper.

Erica sighed. "I honestly don't know, Rachel. I asked myself that question a hundred times. I know one thing, though. If she did kill him, it was an accident. I'm certain she was trying to get away and Mario wouldn't let her."

"Did you tell that to the police?"

"Of course. Sal was furious with me. He said I had betrayed the family. For a while, I thought he was going to throw me out of his house, but he didn't." Her expression softened again. "His bark is worse than his bite."

Erica opened a black tote bag and started rummaging through it. "I know you've seen pictures in the newspapers," she said. "But I thought...." Her hand came out holding a color photograph. "You might want this."

The snapshot she handed Rachel showed Alyssa in all her stunning beauty. Tanned and radiant, she stood aboard a sailboat, holding on to the mast, her long hair flying in the wind. She wore a white one-piece bathing suit with a plunging neckline and an embroidered anchor on the right hip. Next to her, a slender Erica smiled at the camera, one arm around Alyssa's shoulders.

A lump formed in Rachel's throat. She imagined that same beautiful woman holding Lillie, singing to her and murmuring soothing words the way she had in Rachel's dream. "She looks so happy," she said out loud.

"She was. That picture was taken shortly after she and Mario returned from their honeymoon."

Rachel looked up. "You look lovely."

Erica shook her head. "Your mother was the good-looking one. No one ever noticed me when she was around."

There was no animosity in her voice, Rachel noted, not one ounce of jealousy or resentment.

"After Mario died," Erica continued, "Sal burned all her pictures. I managed to salvage this one. Nico took it during a sailing trip to Tiburon across San Francisco Bay. No one even remembered I had it and I'm not even sure why I kept it." She handed it to Rachel. "Now, I do."

"Thank you." Rachel couldn't take her eyes off Alyssa.

After a long silence during which neither felt the need to talk, Erica leaned forward. "You want to find her, don't you?"

Rachel hesitated, wondering if Erica would go back and report her answer to Sal. What would he do if he knew she was trying to find her mother? Would he understand or would he be angry and take back his promise to end the search for Alyssa?

She decided to trust Erica, just as Erica had trusted her. "Yes," she said, watching for the woman's reaction. "I would like that very much."

"I thought so." Erica finished the last of her soda. "I'd help you, but I have no idea how to go about something like that."

"Neither do I. Fortunately, Gregory Shaw has agreed to help me."

"Gregory Shaw is a private investigator, isn't he?"

Rachel nodded. "Finding missing persons isn't exactly his line of work anymore, but he knows where and how to get information. It's been so long, though, the trails must be very cold by now." She gave Erica a hopeful smile. "I don't suppose you know of anyone who could provide information—a distant cousin, an aunt in a retirement home?"

"I'm afraid not. To my knowledge, Alyssa had no one.

GET 2

HOW TO GET YOUR
2 FREE BOOKS AND FREE GIFT!

1. Peel off the MIRA sticker on the front cover. Place it in the space provided at right. This automatically entitles you to receive two free books and an exciting mystery gift.

2. Send back this card and you'll get 2 "The Best of the Best™" novels. These books have a combined cover price of $11.00 or more in the U.S. and $13.00 or more in Canada, but they are yours to keep absolutely FREE!

3. There's <u>no</u> catch. You're under <u>no</u> obligation to buy anything. We charge nothing – ZERO – for your first shipment. And you don't have to make any minimum number of purchases – not even one!

4. We call this line "The Best of the Best" because each month you'll receive the best books by the world's hottest authors. These authors show up time and time again on all the major bestseller lists and their books sell out as soon as they hit the stores. You'll like the convenience of getting them delivered to your home at our special discount prices . . . and you'll love your subscriber newsletter featuring author news, horoscopes, recipes, book reviews and much more!

SPECIAL FREE GIFT!

We'll send you a fabulous surprise gift, absolutely FREE, simply for accepting our no-risk offer!

©1995 MIRA BOOKS

5. We hope that after receiving your free books you'll want to remain a subscriber. But the choice is yours – to continue or cancel, anytime at all! So why not take us up on our invitation, with no risk of any kind. You'll be glad you did!

6. And remember...we'll send you a mystery gift ABSOLUTELY FREE just for giving "The Best of the Best" a try.

Visit us at
www.mirabooks.com

® and TM are trademarks of Harlequin Enterprises Limited.

BOOKS FREE!

Hurry!

Return this card promptly to GET 2 FREE BOOKS & A FREE GIFT!

The Best of the Best™

YES! Please send me the 2 FREE "The Best of the Best" novels and FREE gift for which I qualify. I understand that I am under no obligation to purchase anything further, as explained on the opposite page.

Affix peel-off MIRA sticker here

385 MDL CY22

(BB3-00)
185 MDL CY23

NAME   (PLEASE PRINT CLEARLY)

ADDRESS

APT.#   CITY

STATE/PROV.   ZIP/POSTAL CODE

Offer limited to one per household and not valid to current subscribers of "The Best of the Best." All orders subject to approval. Books received may vary.

◄ DETACH AND MAIL CARD TODAY! ▼

The Best of the Best™ — Here's How it Works:

Accepting your 2 free books and gift places you under no obligation to buy anything. You may keep the books and gift and return the shipping statement marked "cancel." If you do not cancel, about a month later we will send you 4 additional novels and bill you just $4.24 each in the U.S., or $4.74 each in Canada, plus 25¢ delivery per book and applicable taxes if any.* That's the complete price and — compared to cover prices of $5.50 or more each in the U.S. and $6.50 or more each in Canada — it's quite a bargain! You may cancel at any time, but if you choose to continue, every month we'll send you 4 more books, which you may either purchase at the discount price or return to us and cancel your subscription.

*Terms and prices subject to change without notice. Sales tax applicable in N.Y. Canadian residents will be charged applicable provincial taxes and GST.

If offer card is missing write to: The Best of the Best, 3010 Walden Ave., P.O. Box 1867, Buffalo, NY 14240-1867

BUSINESS REPLY MAIL
FIRST-CLASS MAIL   PERMIT NO. 717   BUFFALO, NY

POSTAGE WILL BE PAID BY ADDRESSEE

THE BEST OF THE BEST
3010 WALDEN AVE
PO BOX 1867
BUFFALO NY 14240-9952

NO POSTAGE
NECESSARY
IF MAILED
IN THE
UNITED STATES

That's why the thought of a ready-made family appealed to her so much, at least it did at the beginning."

"Did she love Mario?"

Erica gazed into the distance again. "She did until he became abusive."

"Physically abusive?"

Erica nodded. "I wasn't going to tell you but you deserve to know the whole truth."

"Did Sal know?"

"Yes," she said with a sigh. "But he looked the other way. He always did when it came to Mario." As though realizing she had said more than she intended, she glanced at her watch. "Oh, my, where did the time go?"

"I'm glad you came," Rachel said, rising from the bench. "Next time, we'll go to lunch."

Erica beamed. "It's a date."

Twenty

"So," Sal said at dinner that night, "how did your visit with Rachel go?"

"Very well, but I have to warn you, Sal. I couldn't lie to her. I told her you sent me."

Irritated, Sal put his fork down. "Why did you do a dumb thing like that?"

"Because the girl is not stupid. She would have seen right through me."

"Okay, okay." He waved his fork in the air. "What did she say? She's coming back to see me?"

"Maybe, if we don't push her. She's a very independent young woman, Sal. She likes to make up her own mind."

"Did she ask about her mother?" Nico asked.

Sal saw Erica hesitate. "She asked questions."

Nico looked up from his plate of stuffed shells. "You see, Pop? She asked questions. What does that tell you?"

"Shut up, Nico. What kind of questions?"

Erica shrugged. "She wanted to know what Alyssa was like, what I thought of her, things like that."

"What did you say?"

"I told her what I knew. And don't look at me like that, Sal," she added in the same breath. "What was I supposed to do? Claim I didn't know anything about a woman whose roof I shared for more than a year?"

"I knew sending Erica there was a bad idea," Nico muttered.

Sal shot him an icy look. "Shut the fuck up, Nico." He looked at Erica. "Did she say anything about finding her mother?"

"No."

Erica didn't look at him when she said that, and he knew she was lying, but that was okay. It was enough that he knew.

"I was very impressed with her," Erica went on. "She runs quite an operation at Spaulding Vineyards. And she's a hard worker." She took a bite of her pasta. "She works almost every night, from seven in the morning until ten or eleven at night, sometimes later."

Sal was instantly concerned. "She's there all alone?"

"I guess so, but she didn't seem to mind." Erica broke a piece of crusty Italian bread and soaked it in the tomato sauce. "She says she gets more done at night when no one's around than she does during the day."

"I don't like it." Sal picked up a bottle of Spaulding Pinot Noir he had bought after Rachel's visit and filled his glass. "A woman alone at night, it's asking for trouble." He set the bottle down. "I'm gonna talk to her about that."

"For God's sake, Pop," Nico said, chewing as he talked. "She's a grown woman. What do you want to meddle in her life for? Or give her advice she won't take, anyway?"

"How do you know she won't take my advice? You're an expert in granddaughters all of a sudden?"

"I'm an expert in you, Pop, and I'm telling you you're making a fool of yourself where that girl is concerned. She's going to bring this family nothing but trouble. Just like her mother did."

"Watch your mouth, Nico."

"Why? You're afraid I'm telling the truth?"

"I'm afraid I'm gonna lose my temper and smack you."

Erica nudged her husband's arm discreetly but not discreetly enough for Sal to not notice.

Getting the message, Nico bent over his plate and finished the rest of his dinner in sullen silence.

"Well...is it wine yet?"

Recognizing Gregory's low baritone, Rachel turned, holding the glass from which she had been tasting. "It won't be wine—*great* wine, that is, for a few more years." She walked toward him, surprised his visit made her feel unexpectedly cheerful. "What brings you here?"

"I came to take you on a little ride."

"Don't you have a CEO to destroy?" She held the glass up to the light, inspecting the wine's deep purple color. "Or a company to bury?"

He laughed. "Is that what you think I do?"

"I've heard rumors. In financial circles, they call you the Bay Shark. You go after the wounded and eat them raw." She brought the glass to her nostrils and inhaled deeply, aware that Gregory was watching every movement.

He laughed. "You mustn't believe everything you hear. The truth is, I'm more of a guppy than a shark, once you get to know me."

Rachel sniffed the Cabernet again. "A ride where?"

"San Francisco. Jonsey Malone wants to see you."

Rachel's heart gave a little thump. "He does?"

"Uh-huh."

"When?"

"Right now, if you can get away."

She put the glass on a wooden shelf attached to the barrel. "Just give me a few minutes to wash up and talk to my assistant, and I'll be right with you."

Within moments Rachel was settled in the Jaguar, which

Gregory drove with a great deal of expertise. Grateful for the break and a chance to forget about the incident on the Silverado Trail, Rachel leaned back in her seat and told him what she had learned from Erica. "Alyssa had no family," she said with a sigh. "And except for Jonsey, no friends."

"Maybe Jonsey is all we need—" Gregory ended the sentence abruptly and reached over to turn up the volume on the car radio. Glancing at him, Rachel noticed his expression had cooled. "Earlier today," the announcer said, "Freddy Bloom, better known as The Slasher, was found guilty of first-degree murder in the death of two Marin County coeds. We switch to our correspondent outside the courthouse where Bloom's attorney, Milton Shaw, is expected to make a statement."

Just as abruptly as he had turned up the sound, Gregory shut it off. Startled, Rachel looked at him. "Why did you do that? Milton Shaw is your father, isn't he?"

"So?"

"So, he was about to speak. Why did you turn him off?"

"I'm not particularly interested in what he has to say. I was curious about the verdict, and now that I know Freddy got what he deserved, I really don't want to hear how my father is planning his appeal."

The way he said it, his words clipped and harsh, made her realize something was very wrong between him and his father. "I'm sorry. Did I say something I shouldn't have?"

"No."

Curiosity got the best of her. "You and your father don't get along?"

He swung the Jaguar around an 18-wheeler and sped past it before swinging back into the right lane. "Let's just say I was a major disappointment to him."

"In what way?"

"In every way—and from the moment I was born." A silence hung between them for a few seconds. "My mother died in childbirth."

"Oh, Gregory, I'm so sorry." She studied his hard profile. "Are you implying that he…blamed you for that?"

"I'm not implying anything. I know he blamed me for it. I heard him tell my aunt Willie when I was only a little kid."

She couldn't imagine a child growing up with that kind of guilt. "That's awful."

"I survived, but our relationship deteriorated quickly after that. It got even worse when I turned down a career in law to become a private investigator."

"Was that so terrible?"

He laughed. "My father thought so."

"But surely he's proud of you now, of what you've done with your life."

He kept his eyes on the road. "I doubt it. In his eyes I'll always be a quitter."

Beneath the bitterness Rachel sensed a much deeper emotion—sadness. "How often do you see him?" she asked gently.

"As little as possible. I drop my daughter off at his house once a month for Sunday dinner and I pick her up a few hours later. I never go in, though, and he never comes out." He shrugged. "It's easier that way."

"Maybe for you, but what about your daughter?"

Gregory's voice softened. "It's harder now that Noelle is older. She knows my father and I have differences and she says she understands, but I'm not sure she does."

Rachel smiled. "She sounds like a remarkable person."

A proud glow flickered through his eyes as he turned to look at her. "She is. You'd like her."

"I'm sure I would. How old is she?"

He passed another car. "Twelve going on thirty-five."
Coming from the opposite direction, a light-colored sedan
flashed its lights, signaling a patrol car in the area. Gregory
signaled back and brought the Jag down to the speed limit.
"She lives with her mother, but I have her every other
weekend. I try to do things with her during the week, as
well, little things Lindsay can't do, like take her to gymnastic class or to a friend's house."

His voice was warm and filled with fatherly pride as he
talked about Noelle. Rachel couldn't imagine a woman
having a man such as Gregory and ever letting him go.
"You and your ex-wife seem to have done a wonderful job
of raising Noelle," she said when he was finished.

"I like to think so." They had reached Oakland, and
Gregory smoothly swung the car onto the Bay bridge's
heavy traffic.

"I wish Courtney's father played a stronger role in her
life," Rachel said with a small sigh. "She misses him so
much, even though she's learned to adapt to his long ab-
sences." She pulled down the sun visor. "Do you ever hear
from Luke?"

"Not since last year when he came to the States to pick
up an additional film crew."

Rachel nodded. "That's when we saw him, too." She
laughed. "At first, I didn't even recognize him. With his
long hair, his beard, and those safari clothes he now wears,
he was a far cry from the sophisticated young man who
married my sister."

They were silent for a moment, then as they exited the
bridge, Gregory threw her a quick glance. "Rachel, about
that night...I never had a chance to apologize."

"Forget it," she said, feeling her cheeks turn red. "I
have."

He shook his head. "I can't forget it. I felt terrible when

I realized you were standing behind us. I have no excuse for some of the things we said that night except that we were just two stupid jerks with a lousy sense of humor and big egos.''

"I overreacted."

"I tried to catch up with you, but…" He chuckled. "You ran so dammed fast, and I kept slipping on the damp grass in my new shoes."

Rachel felt her mouth twitch. "Did you really?"

He nodded. "At one point I wasn't able to regain my balance and I fell right in front of the champagne fountain, with everyone staring at me, shaking their heads and saying, 'That's what you get for drinking too much, son.' A waiter felt sorry for me and helped me up. I tried to explain I wasn't drunk, but no one believed me."

Rachel laughed. "I'm sorry I missed that."

They were still laughing when they merged onto the Embarcadero Freeway.

Jonsey's house was near McLaren Park and high enough to afford an unobstructed view of Candlestick Park Stadium and beyond that, San Francisco Bay. A heavyset man with no neck and shoulders as wide as a mountain opened the gate. When Gregory told him his name, the man silently led them to the back of the house where a lush garden grew with a profusion of lemon trees, wildflowers and rosebushes of every hybrid imaginable.

A thin, round-shouldered man in baggy pants and a ragged straw hat was pruning a rambling bush, his movements short and precise.

"Mr. Malone," the surly man said. "Your guests are here."

Placing one hand on the small of his back, Jonsey Malone straightened and turned around. Eyes as blue as the distant Bay settled immediately on Rachel, regarding her with a mixture of interest and mild disbelief.

"Well, I'll be." Sheers still in his hand, he walked toward her. "That picture in the paper didn't lie, after all. You really do look like her. Right down to—" he pointed at her upper lip "—that little mole right there."

After a while he nodded toward Gregory. "He tells me you want to find Alyssa."

"That's right."

"Why?"

"Because she's my mother," Rachel said simply. "And because she would want to find me, too, if she knew I was alive."

Jonsey was silent for a long time, looking from Rachel to Gregory then back at Rachel. "Yes," he said at last, "I guess she would at that. She loved you very much."

"Is she alive, Mr. Malone?"

"Call me Jonsey." He nodded. "Yes, Alyssa is alive."

Rachel grasped Gregory's hand. "Do you know where she is?"

He shook his head. "No idea. We both agreed it would be safer if I didn't know."

Rachel's shoulders sagged. She should have known better than to allow her hopes to rest on just one person.

Gregory's arm circled her shoulders. "What *can* you tell us?" he asked. When the man remained silent, he lowered his voice. "I give you my word this conversation will go no further and that no harm will come to Alyssa."

Looking thoughtful, Jonsey stole another glance in Rachel's direction before nodding. "All right." He shook a finger. "But I'm holding you to your promise. Anything happens to that girl…"

He let the sentence hang between them for a second or two before he spoke again. "After Alyssa found out her baby had died in that fire, she went nuts on me. She didn't give a damn if she lived or died. It took me several days to convince her to leave the country before it was too late.''

"So she went abroad," Rachel said.

Jonsey nodded. "I introduced her to a man I knew and arranged for him to make her a counterfeit passport and other documents. When the papers were ready, she took a plane out of the country under the name of Virginia Potter. I never saw her again after that."

"Would the forger know where she went?"

"No way. I told her it was crucial that no one knew, and she was smart enough to know I was right."

Rachel felt all her hopes vanish. "She never called? Or wrote?"

"She calls me every Christmas." He smiled, showing small, yellow teeth. "She tells me she's fine. She's remarried now and happy. That's all I know. That's all I want to know."

"The police didn't wire your house?" Gregory asked. "In case she contacted you?"

"Sure they did, but once they were satisfied she had drowned, they took the bugs off and left me alone."

Christmas was a little more than two months away, Rachel reflected. And since it didn't look as if they would find Alyssa anytime soon, she had no choice but to wait until then. Gregory, on the other hand, wasn't ready to give up so quickly.

"Did she ever talk about a particular place?" he asked. "A country she had a yearn to visit?"

Jonsey smiled. "Tahiti. When she worked for me, she used to say that if she ever struck it rich, she would retire in Tahiti."

"What about relatives?" Gregory asked. "Or friends."

He shook his head. "She had no one. She left home when she was sixteen and never looked back. I'm the closest thing to a family she ever had."

Gregory shook the man's hand. "You were a big help, Jonsey. Thanks."

Rachel went to him and took his hand, as well. "If we don't find her and she should call before Christmas, would you tell her I'm looking for her?"

"You bet."

On impulse, Rachel kissed him on the cheek, a gesture that brought a quick smile to the old man's craggy face.

"Good luck, girl."

"Well," Rachel said when she and Gregory were back in the Jaguar, "what do you think our chances are now?"

"Not as hopeless as you might think. We know Alyssa's alive, and we know which name she assumed."

"And that's all we know. Jonsey gave us no lead whatsoever." She sighed. "We'll have to wait until Christmas."

"Maybe not."

His unwarranted optimism was beginning to irritate her. "How can you be so hopeful when all our leads are being shot down one by one?"

"Because I have a friend who works at Interpol. I left him a couple of messages already. If Alyssa Dassante, alias Virginia Potter, is anywhere in Europe, Todd will find her."

"Okay, Europe is covered. What about Tahiti?"

"I'll check that, too."

His amused tone made her realize what she was doing. "You think I'm a pain, don't you?" she asked.

Gregory flashed a lopsided grin. "Why? Because you're telling me how to do my job?"

"Is that what I'm doing?"

"Yeah, but don't worry. I'm used to pushy broads."

She nodded. "I guess I had that coming."

Sal had just finished talking to his attorney and was hanging up when Nico stormed in.

"Did I hear you right?" Nico barked. "You told your lawyer you're rewriting your will? Splitting everything right down the middle between Rachel and me?"

Nico's outburst didn't faze Sal. These days he had better things to do than to let his son rile him. "You got a problem with that?"

"Damm right I got a problem. You think I worked my ass off all these years to see half my inheritance go to a stranger?"

"She's not a stranger, she's your niece, and my flesh and blood."

"Oh, yeah? And how many times has your flesh and blood come to see you since she was here last? Or even called? None. Zip. And you know why? Because she doesn't give a damm about us, about being part of this family. She doesn't even like us, Pop. Couldn't you tell? Couldn't you see how she looked at us, like we weren't good enough for her?"

"You're full of shit. She just needs time, that's all."

"Bull. She wants nothing to do with us, and you know I'm right. You just don't want to admit it. You're letting yourself be blinded by the fact that she's Mario's daughter. And having her back is like having a part of Mario back. You still can't get away from that, can you? Mourning for your dead son?"

Sal had had it with Nico's whining. "Listen to me, you punk." Not the least bit intimidated by his son's size, Sal came to stand directly in front of Nico. "First of all, it's my goddamed money so I'll do what I damn please with it. And second, Rachel is part of this family, my heir. When I die, half of everything I own will be hers. It's her birthright. You got that?"

Nico's face turned so red that for a moment Sal thought he was going to pop a vein. Then, with a shake of his head and a low growl, his son stalked out of the room.

Twenty-One

Inside her farmhouse deep in the mountainous region of the Auvergne, Ginnie Laperousse tossed aside a circular advertising half-price sofas and continued to sort through the mail that had accumulated over the past three weeks.

That was the trouble with vacations, she thought as she kept tossing. Not only did it take days to get back into a routine, it took just as long to catch up with the mail.

From the stack still waiting to be read, she picked up a copy of the weekly newsmagazine, *Paris Match*, and began thumbing absently through it as memories of her recent trip played in her mind. What a wonderful time she and Hubert had had in Venice. They had walked through the streets of that magical city, hand in hand, like two young lovers, taking in the incredible sights, riding gondolas and eating in little unknown trattorias where Hubert, thank God, hadn't been recognized.

She laughed as she turned a page. They had even kissed as they'd passed under the Bridge of Sighs, prompting their gondolier to break into a powerful rendition of "'O Sole Mio.''

As she smiled at the recollection, a piano adaptation of Beethoven's Fifth Symphony flowed in from the music room, filling the salon with the rich and powerful sounds of Hubert's immense talent.

Ginnie laid the magazine down for a moment to listen.

At sixty-eight, and after thirty-five years as a concert pianist, her husband had never sounded better, never played with more fervor, or, as one critic had pointed out, with more heart. No wonder he kept getting requests to play Europe's greatest concert halls—and kept getting standing ovations night after night.

Flipping another page of the magazine, Ginnie glanced absently at the pictures. She was glad Hubert's next tour wouldn't begin until November. She rather enjoyed having him home, surprising him in the music room in the middle of the afternoon with a tea tray and their housekeeper's sinful little cream horns, an Auvergne specialty Ginnie had become addicted to.

She glanced at her watch and realized it was almost that time. Hubert must have noticed, too, for he had stopped playing. She was about to call Mme. Desforges to let her know they were ready when her gaze fell on the page open on her lap.

The blood seemed to drain from her entire body, leaving her suddenly cold as ice.

The face that stared back at her was that of a young woman, a beautiful young woman, who looked enough like Ginnie thirty years ago to have been her identical twin. "Oh, my God!"

Before Ginnie could call her husband, Hubert rushed out of the music room, his expression worried. He was a tall, handsome man with silver hair, a thin black mustache and elegant, aristocratic features.

"*Chérie,* what is it?" he asked in his lightly accented English. "I heard you cry out." Sitting beside her on the sofa, he took her hand. "Did you hurt yourself?"

She shook her head and handed him the magazine.

His eyes swept briefly over the photograph. "She looks just like you," he said, looking puzzled. "Or at least, the way you did when I met you." He glanced at the picture again. "Who is she?"

"I don't know."

Hubert was already reading the short article to the right of the picture. "Well, according to this, her name is Rachel Spaulding. She's an American winemaker, the first to sell her wines to Supermarchés Fronsac. That is why she is featured in *Paris Match*."

Ginnie felt herself tremble. "Where…does she live?" she asked, clamping her hands in front of her mouth.

He glanced at the magazine again. "Napa Valley."

Napa Valley. Ginnie's heart began to pound.

"*Chérie,* what's happening to you? You're trembling." Hubert lay the magazine on the coffee table and took her hands in his. "Why is the picture of this young woman upsetting you so?"

"Don't you know?"

He started to shake his head, then stopped as he looked at the photograph again then back at Ginnie. "*Mon Dieu,* you're not thinking…"

"Look at her, Hubert," she said, surprised she could speak at all. "Look at the color of her eyes, the shape of her mouth, of her jaw. And that mole above her upper lip." She touched the spot where her own mole had been before she'd had it removed.

"It could just be a coincidence," he said. "You know what they say, everyone has a double somewhere in the world."

"She's not my double," she whispered.

Hubert's eyes searched her face. "Oh, Ginnie, I don't think…"

Her voice turned fierce. "Don't you find it strange that a young woman who looks so much like me is living in

Napa Valley? Only a short distance from the Santa Rosa convent where I left my daughter thirty-one years ago?''

"Do you really think this young woman could be... Lillie?''

"Is that so inconceivable?'' Her eyes drifted back to the photograph. "Considering this girl is about the same age as Lillie would be?''

"But Lillie died in a fire. You told me so yourself.''

Unable to pull her gaze from the photograph, Ginnie picked up *Paris Match* again and studied the picture. A feeling she couldn't describe—longing, hope, fear—filled her. "Because that's what I was told. But what if she *didn't* die, Hubert. What if...something happened.''

"Like what?''

"I don't know!'' She sprung out of her seat, the magazine clutched against her chest. "A mix-up, a mistake, anything.''

Hubert let a long second pass. Then gently, evenly, he said, "Why don't you call the convent? That way, you will know.''

Suddenly hopeful, Ginnie stared at the phone as if it were a lifeline. "Oh, Hubert, do you think I could? Do you think Sister Mary-Catherine still works there? After all this time?''

"There's only one way to find out.''

"Yes, yes, of course. You're right.'' Her hand was trembling so badly, she had to redial the overseas information number twice before she did it correctly.

After a few moments the operator gave her the number of the convent in Santa Rosa. Ginnie glanced at her watch: 3:00 p.m. That would make it 6:00 a.m. on the West Coast. The sisters would be up. After another glance at Hubert, who gave her an encouraging nod, she said a quick silent prayer and dialed.

The nun who answered identified herself as Sister Carmela, and when Ginnie asked if Sister Mary-Catherine was still at the convent, the nun said yes, she was.

Ginnie's relief was so overwhelming, she almost cried out with joy. "May I speak to her, please?" she asked, making a desperate effort to keep her voice on an even keel.

"Certainly. May I ask who's calling?"

"An old friend." She hoped that would be enough. "Tell her I can't say any more than that."

Perhaps because nuns were accustomed to all sorts of strange requests, the sister didn't press her any further, but simply said, "Just a moment, please."

Several agonizing minutes passed before another voice came on the line, an older, cautious voice Ginnie recognized instantly. "Oh, Sister Mary-Catherine." Too shaken to say anything more, Ginnie bit her bottom lip.

"Yes," the nun replied quickly. "I'm Sister Mary-Catherine. Who is this? How can I help you?"

"Sister, I..."

Hubert came to stand beside her and wrapped his arm around her shoulders. That simple gesture gave Ginnie the strength to continue and to say the words she hadn't spoken in thirty-one years. "This is...Alyssa. Alyssa Dassante."

There was a startled, unmistakable gasp. Then, in a whisper Ginnie could barely hear, the nun asked, "Mrs. Dassante? Is that really you?"

"Yes." Tears ran freely down Ginnie's face now. The nun's voice brought back memories so powerful, no amount of self-control could hold back the flow of emotion. "It's me. I wasn't sure you'd still be there. I was afraid you might have been sent somewhere else."

"My dear child." There was emotion in the nun's voice, as well. "How wonderful to hear from you. I, too, had wondered if..." She didn't finish the sentence, but Ginnie knew what she was thinking.

Sister Mary-Catherine lowered her voice again, and this time Ginnie had to strain to hear her. "Lillie's alive," she said. "Your little girl is alive."

Her legs suddenly too weak to support her, Ginnie sank into a chair. "Oh, Sister, is she? Are you sure?"

"As sure as I'm standing on God's green earth. She came to see me only a few days ago, at my request."

Ginnie wiped her tears with her fingers and forced herself to talk calmly. "At your request? I don't understand."

For the next few minutes Ginnie listened to the most amazing story of how Sister Mary-Catherine and the other nuns had realized, sixteen years after the fire, that the surviving child was in fact Lillie Dassante, the little girl they had all thought had died.

"I couldn't make myself go to the authorities," Sister Mary-Catherine said when she was finished. "I left the Spauldings house that day, knowing Lillie was in a good home, with parents and a grandmother who adored her, a sister, and friends she loved. It would have been cruel to take her away from all that."

"I understand, Sister, really I do." Ginnie squeezed Hubert's hand. "Please tell me about her, Sister. Tell me everything."

Several more minutes went by, during which Ginnie cried and laughed and sighed with pride at Lillie's remarkable accomplishments, all of which Sister Mary-Catherine had learned from numerous newspaper articles.

"Has there been a lot of publicity since the truth came out?" Ginnie asked.

"Too much, in my opinion. But you don't have to worry. Rachel is handling it all remarkably well. She's a strong, wonderful young woman. You should be very proud of her.''

"Oh, I am, Sister, I am. What about you?'' she asked in a quieter tone. "Have the police questioned you? Are you in any kind of trouble?''

"Your daughter called me with the very same concerns. Fortunately, the church enjoys a certain amount of leniency when it comes to such matters, and though the police questioned me at length, they understood I intended no harm to anyone.''

"I'm glad.'' Then, as excitement began to build again, Ginnie added, "I want to see my daughter, Sister.'' The words came out in a rush, and even as she saw the flicker of worry in Hubert's eyes, she knew deep in her heart that she'd never have another moment's happiness until she saw her daughter again. "Where is Spaulding Vineyards located?''

"In Calistoga.'' There was a short pause. "You must be very careful, Alyssa. Sal Dassante is still looking for you.'' Her voice was once again low and urgent. "So are other people.''

Ginnie wasn't surprised to hear Sal hadn't given up on finding her. He was one of the most stubborn and vengeful men she knew. But why should anyone else be looking for her? "What other people?'' she asked.

"A man came to see me not too long ago. I don't know how he found out about me, or who he's working for, but he did ask if I knew you. I said I didn't and as soon as he left, I called Rachel.''

"I'm glad you're the one who told her, Sister.'' As soon as it was safe to do so, she would make a generous donation to the convent. "What's the man's name?''

"Gregory Shaw.''

Ginnie searched her memory but couldn't recall anyone

by that name. "Thank you, Sister," she said again. "For giving me such wonderful news and for not telling the authorities I was alive thirty-one years ago. I know you took a big risk in doing that."

The sister's voice was calm and serene when she answered. "You don't have to thank me. I did what I was put on this earth to do, help people in need. And you definitely needed help when you rang our bell that night."

"I'll never forget what you did for me."

"Goodbye, my child. May God be with you."

Ginnie hung up and had to hold on to the table for a moment.

"Come, *chérie*." Very gently, Hubert led her back to the sofa. "Would you like some water? Something stronger?"

She shook her head. "I'm fine." She looked up and felt her eyes fill with tears, tears of absolute joy. "Oh, Hubert, my baby is alive. My beautiful little girl is alive."

Hubert's eyes, too, were moist as he gazed at her tenderly. "I know, darling. It's wonderful news. Incredible news."

She met his gaze. "I want to see her, Hubert. I want to go to California."

Worry clouded Hubert's eyes again. "Is that wise?"

"I don't care if it's wise or not. I need to see my daughter. And I need your support on this, Hubert. Please tell me you understand and that you'll come with me."

"Of course, I'll come with you. It's just…"

"What?"

"Are people looking for you? Is that what the sister said?"

Ginnie nodded. "Sal Dassante is still looking for me, and one other man by the name of Gregory Shaw."

"Is he anyone we should worry about?"

"I don't know. I've never heard of him." He could be

working for Sal, she suddenly realized. She remembered Jonsey telling her during one of their more recent phone conversations that Sal had hired another private detective.

Hubert paced the room for a while, his arms folded against his chest, his index finger tapping against his mouth, the way he did when he was working on a musical arrangement. "All right," he said at last. "We'll go, but we won't stay in a hotel, or even in a bed-and-breakfast. We'll rent a house somewhere in Napa Valley and keep a low profile. I can't risk having someone recognize you. Or notice your resemblance to Rachel Spaulding."

Ginnie's taut nerves began to relax. Dear, wonderful Hubert. He had been such a positive, calming influence on her life all these years, and he would continue to do so, no matter what crisis lay ahead.

While Hubert was on the phone making travel arrangements, Ginnie stood at the window, the silver-framed photograph of her two-week-old baby clutched against her chest.

In the green, open pasture, half a dozen cows that had earlier been lazily grazing were beginning to gather close to each other, a sign that a storm was approaching. In the distance the Rocher St. Michel, topped by the small Moorish chapel of the same name, was visible through the mist. Farther still, across the Allier River, heavy rain clouds were forming and moving closer. Winter came early in the Auvergne and soon the Cantal Mountains would be covered with snow.

Ginnie had arrived in this rugged part of central France thirty-one years ago, still recovering from a devastating loss. To her surprise, she had found peace here, and happiness, both of which she owed to Hubert.

The approaching storm reminded her of that awful night

in Winters, a night she had played and replayed in her mind a thousand times, wishing she had done things differently.

She couldn't remember when she had realized she no longer loved Mario. Looking back, she wasn't sure she had truly loved him, the way she loved Hubert, though she certainly had been attracted to him. Who wouldn't be? He had such presence when he entered a room, such charisma. And he'd been so different from the loud, groping men who'd frequented the Blue Parrot on a nightly basis. Dazzled by his charm, she had let herself be swept off her feet. It wasn't until they'd returned from their honeymoon that she realized how different he was from the man she knew—thought she knew.

To her shock, the attentive, seductive man she had fallen in love with suddenly revealed himself as a mean, hot-tempered, demanding bully. Sal and Nico weren't much better. The only person she felt any closeness to was Nico's young wife Erica.

The situation between Alyssa and the Dassante men deteriorated rapidly when she began to notice the deplorable conditions migrant workers at Dassante Farms had to endure and she complained to Sal.

"Those people are being treated like animals by your own supervisors," she had told her father-in-law at dinner one night. "They get no breaks and are forced to work long hours in the hot sun without enough water to go around. It's inhuman."

At first no one paid much attention to her. Eventually, Mario told her the running of the farm was none of her business. But Alyssa was too passionate about her beliefs to abandon her crusade. One night, only a few days after Lillie was born, she brought up the subject again, explaining to Mario she couldn't allow their baby to grow up in such an environment.

Mario ended the dispute with a backhand that snapped her head from one side to the other.

At that moment whatever feelings she'd had for Mario, love, attraction, or just affection, vanished and she knew she had to leave him. But when she asked him for a divorce, he just laughed.

"Go ahead," he told her. "Divorce me all you want, but I warn you. Lillie stays here."

Knowing there was no use in even trying to fight him, she started making plans to secretly leave him—with Lillie.

On August fourteen, after everyone had gone to bed, Ginnie took ten thousand dollars from her husband's safe, packed a few belongings for her and Lillie, and tiptoed down to the garage.

She had rehearsed that moment a dozen times, had every detail, every mile of her journey carefully orchestrated. Then everything went sour. As she was loading her suitcase in the trunk of her Mercedes, Mario suddenly appeared. Furious, he started to take Lillie from the car, but Alyssa wouldn't let him. They fought, and in the struggle, Mario tripped, fell backward and hit his head on a tractor.

For a moment Alyssa feared she had killed him and didn't know what to do. Then, as he started to sit up, cursing and threatening to strangle her, she fled. Her plan was to drive to San Francisco and ask her friend, Jonsey Malone, to hide her and Lillie for a while, until she decided on a legal course of action.

An hour later, as she reached the outskirts of Vallejo, what she heard on the car radio changed her life forever. Mario Dassante had been found dead outside his home and the police were looking for his killer—Alyssa Dassante.

Alyssa was stunned. How could Mario be dead? He was fine and cursing up a storm when she left him. A little dazed, perhaps, but alive.

Terrified the police would never believe her, Alyssa quickly changed directions, heading for a small convent she knew in Santa Rosa. In spite of the late hour, the sister who answered the bell was kind and understanding. She asked no questions and promised to keep Alyssa's baby until Alyssa came back for her in a few days. To make sure Sal wouldn't find her, Alyssa told the nun the baby's name was Sarah.

She didn't stop driving until she reached an area south of Bodega Bay. There, she got out of the Mercedes, and in the pouring rain, pushed the car over the cliff, hoping the authorities would believe she and Lillie had died in the crash. To make the ruse even more believable, she had left most of the money she had taken from Mario, keeping only two thousand dollars.

Jonsey, whose connections spread far and wide, offered to take her to a man he knew, a forger who would make phony identity papers so she and Lillie could leave the country.

That's when she heard the convent had caught fire. Frantic, she called Sister Mary-Catherine to make sure Lillie was all right. To her horror, the nun began to cry. The blaze, Alyssa soon learned, had not only destroyed part of the convent, it had also claimed the lives of two nuns. And Alyssa's baby.

For days Alyssa walked the floor of Jonsey's house as though she were a zombie, blaming herself for Lillie's death and wishing she, too, could die. If it hadn't been for her old friend, she would have turned herself in and faced whatever punishment awaited her. It took Jonsey a week to convince her to leave the U.S. while she still could.

Two weeks after Mario's death Alyssa boarded an Air France flight for Paris under the name of Virginia Potter. Within days of landing in the French capital, she moved into a cheap rooming house on the Left Bank and found a job as an usherette at the Olympia, Paris's renowned concert hall.

It was there that she caught the eye of Hubert Laperousse, a concert pianist with a huge talent and an even bigger heart. Though he pursued her ardently, Alyssa didn't want to burden herself with a romance—not after all she had gone through with Mario. But Hubert was a persistent man, and eventually she agreed to marry him. Though not before telling him the truth about her past.

On a clear autumn afternoon, Virginia Potter left her Parisian garret and moved into Hubert's beautiful, peaceful country home on the outskirts of Le Puy, where he promised she would be safe.

She adapted slowly but steadily to the French country life and learned the language as well as the customs of this rugged area, which were vastly different from any others she had ever known.

She had everything her heart desired, yet as one near perfect day made room for another, the sadness inside her heart had never waned. Something was missing from her life.

Ginnie pulled the photograph away from her and gazed tenderly at the baby she had never stopped loving. Her Lillie. Not a day went by without Ginnie thinking of her, remembering her sweet baby smell, her petal-soft skin. If only she had kept on going that night, instead of stopping at the convent. If, if, if...

"Trés bien. Merci, Madame."

As Hubert thanked the travel agent, Ginnie turned around, watching her husband through tearful eyes. "Well?" she asked as he hung up.

"It's all set. We leave on Tuesday."

Twenty-Two

Rachel loved working in the quiet empty cellars late at night, with no phone ringing, no problem to solve, no one to interrupt her. Sitting at her computer, with the last of her ham-and-cheese sandwich beside her, she hit a key and waited for the current sales figures to come up on the screen.

She had caught up with most of her paperwork and was now free to see for herself if Sam's prediction that the Dassante scandal hadn't affected Spaulding business was true.

As the numbers appeared, she let out a sigh of dismay. Sales were down from the previous month by fifteen percent, and unless business picked up in the next few weeks, the holiday season would be a disaster. Which meant she and Annie had to put their heads together and come up with new ways to bring customers back.

Maybe they could revamp Spaulding Vineyards's ads in such trade magazines as the *Wine Spectator*. Or they could work on that special retail display Annie had suggested a few months ago. Grams had thought the idea too costly, but apparently the time had come for a more aggressive campaign.

Stifling a yawn, Rachel glanced at her watch. Eleven o'clock. She had been working nonstop since returning from Jonsey's house and should really call it a night.

An odd sound coming from the next room made her look up. Without moving from her chair, she peered into the dimly lit cellar, wondering if Sam, who thought she worked too hard, had noticed the light from his house and had come to shoo her home.

Pushing her chair back, she stood, stretched and walked out of her office. "Sam?"

In the eerie silence, the only sound was that of her boot heels clicking sharply against the concrete floor. Certain she hadn't imagined the noise, she passed through an archway and entered the smaller cellar. Rows of freshly scrubbed sixty-gallon barrels were stacked on top of each other, waiting to be filled with this year's Merlot, which was still fermenting. Against the wall, adjacent to another archway, was Hannah's glassed-in office. It, too, was in darkness.

"Sam?" she called again. "Ryan?"

Just as she flicked on the lights, she heard that same sound again, but couldn't identify it. The muscles in her stomach tightened into a ball. In all the years she had worked at Spaulding, she had never had a reason to be frightened. In fact, except for Joe Brock, who had made those threats after being fired, there had never been an incident at Spaulding Vineyards requiring police intervention.

Nervous nonetheless, she didn't go any farther. She would call the police and let them investigate the disturbance. It could be nothing more threatening than an animal that had found its way inside the cellar and couldn't get out, but after her terrifying encounter on the Silverado Trail, she was taking no chances.

She was about to return to her office when she heard the rumble. It came from behind her, the ominous, unmistakable sound of barrels tumbling down.

Reacting on sheer instinct, Rachel broke into a run just as a second row thundered toward her. Knees and elbows pumping hard, she kept her eyes focused on that second archway just beyond Hannah's office. Her breath was coming in fast ragged gasps as she tried desperately to outrun the flying barrels.

She took the corner in a slide and flattened herself against the wall as an avalanche of barrels crashed into Hannah's office.

The sound of exploding glass was deafening. Eyes closed, Rachel didn't move. She pressed her back and hands against the rough wall surface and waited for the last barrel to come to a stop.

When it finally did and the cellars were once again silent, she slid slowly to the floor. Her body was drenched in sweat and her lungs hurt as she tried to breathe. It was a long time until she felt steady enough to pull herself up.

Standing under the archway, she viewed the damage. The place looked as if it had been hit by an earthquake. More than two dozen barrels lay helter-skelter on top of each other, all of them crushed. One had shot through the window of Hannah's office and smashed into the wall, pulverizing the computer on Hannah's desk.

As her gaze swept over the disaster once more, she forced herself to take a deep, sobering breath. The cellars were deadly quiet now, yet there was no doubt in her mind. Someone had been here.

As the pounding in her heart receded and her head began to clear, a new fear worked its way into her thoughts.

Had someone just tried to kill her?

Sam and Tina, the first people Rachel called, arrived within moments. It took Sam only an instant to assess the situation.

"God Almighty!" Moving quickly, he sidestepped the

debris and gripped her shoulders, checking her over from head to toe. "Are you all right?"

Still shaky, Rachel nodded.

"Aunt Rachel!" Wearing nothing but pink-striped pajamas, Courtney rushed into Rachel's open arms. "Mom and I heard a terrible crash…"

"I'm all right, sweetie."

Behind Courtney, Annie, in a black silk negligée, stared in horror at the shambles around her. "My God, what happened?"

More sick than frightened now, Rachel kept her arm around Courtney. "I don't know. I was in my office, going over the sales figures for the month, when I heard a noise. I went out to investigate—"

"Why?" Sam asked, his gaze heavy with reproach. "Why didn't you get the hell out of here and come to get me? Or call the police right away?"

"I wasn't thinking, Sam. I thought it was you or Ryan. Then when I heard that sound again, I decided to call the police. Next thing I knew, a row of barrels was tumbling down, then another."

"You could have been killed," Tina said, looking around her.

Annie let out a short derisive laugh. "Who did you piss off now?"

Sam threw her a nasty look. "Don't start, Annie."

Outside, a car screeched to a halt. Within seconds Officer Ricardo Torres, on night duty, hurried in. After making sure Rachel and the others were all right, he looked around him and slowly took his little black book out of his back pocket. "Jesus. How did this happen?"

For Rick's benefit, Rachel told her story once more and answered his questions. Yes, she had left the cellar door open. They all did when they worked late because there had never been a reason not to. No, she hadn't seen or heard a car. She had been too involved in her work.

When she finished, Sam walked through the wreckage and stopped at the threshold to Hannah's office. His jaw set, he turned around. "This was no accident, Rick."

The young officer looked up from his notes. "What makes you say that?"

"The three of us," Sam said, carefully making his way back through the debris, "Rachel, Ryan and myself, spend the greater part of our workday right here in these cellars. If the barrels had been stacked improperly, one of us would have noticed."

Annie looked at Rachel. "I thought stacking barrels was the responsibility of the cellar master."

"It is," Sam replied. "But it's also everyone's responsibility to make sure safety procedures are followed. With me, as I know it is with Rachel and Ryan, checking how barrels are stacked is automatic. Most of the time we do it without even thinking. If something is off, anywhere in the cellars, we spot it right away. Besides," he added, "those barrels were brought in weeks ago. If they had been stacked incorrectly, they would have collapsed long before tonight. Someone did this intentionally. Someone tried to kill Rachel."

"Rachel?" Rick turned to look at her. "You agree with that? You think someone wanted to harm you?"

Once again, her mind rebelled at the possibility. What could she have done to provoke such rage? "I agree it was probably no accident, but I'm not sure I agree with Sam's theory that someone tried to kill me. That's a little too drastic."

"Even after what happened on the Silverado Trail?" Sam asked.

At those words, all eyes turned toward Rachel. "What happened on the Silverado Trail?" Annie asked sharply.

Oh, well, Rachel thought with a small sigh, there wasn't much point in hiding that incident any longer. Not after tonight. "Someone tried to run me off the road," she replied.

Courtney gasped. "Aunt Rachel! Why didn't you tell us?"

"I didn't want to upset anyone or to disrupt the workers."

Tina came to hug her. "Oh, honey. You must have been so frightened. Were you hurt?"

"No."

Tina turned to Rick. "I guess they didn't catch who did it."

Rick shook his head. "We're working on it." His concern evident, he looked at Rachel again. "Let's just assume, for now, that someone did try to kill you. Can you think of who that could be?"

She had been asking herself that same question. To her knowledge, she had no enemy—except maybe Annie, but even she was incapable of something like that. And, anyway, she couldn't have dislodged those barrels by herself. Only a man, a strong one at that, could have. "No," Rachel replied. "I can't."

"I can," Sam said. "Joe Brock."

"Oh, no," Courtney murmured. "Not Joe."

Remembering that Joe's eldest daughter was a friend of Courtney's, Rachel tightened her hold around her niece's waist. "Joe wouldn't do this," she said.

The officer was instantly alert. "Who's Joe Brock?"

"Our former cellar master."

"He doesn't work here anymore?"

"No. My grandmother fired him last July when she caught him stealing Spaulding wines one night."

Rick looked up. "Was he upset when she fired him?"

"He was spitting fire," Sam snapped. "And he was verbally abusive, to Hannah and to Rachel, who supported her grandmother's decision. He even came here last week and made a scene when Rachel wouldn't give him his job back."

"He was drunk," Rachel said in Joe's defense.

"Yeah." Sam's voice was tight with anger. "Drunk and mean and bent on revenge."

Rick snapped his book shut. "I'm going to have to call Detective Crowley on my radio. He's the one who should be handling this. In the meantime, stay right here and don't touch anything. He'll want the place dusted for fingerprints."

It took another ten minutes for Crowley, a thin, narrow-faced man in his forties, and a lab technician to arrive, and another ten for Rachel to bring the detective up to date on everything, including the Silverado Trail incident.

Crowley's questions were more specific than Rick's and he didn't spare the other four people there, even Courtney. Without a change in expression, he asked where they were at the time of the accident and if they had seen or heard anything suspicious. Except for Annie and Courtney, who had been awakened by the crash, no one had.

At twenty minutes past midnight, his interrogation finished, Crowley glanced at the technician, who nodded. "We're done here," the detective told Rachel. "I'll be back in the morning to talk to the staff."

At the thought of the disruption this would cause, not to mention the speculation it would arouse, Rachel groaned inwardly but didn't say anything. If a would-be killer was on the prowl, she was just as anxious as Detective Crowley to have him caught.

Gently but firmly, Tina led Rachel toward the door. "Come, honey, you'll sleep at our house tonight. Sam will lock up."

"We should clean up this mess—"

Tina didn't give her a chance to finish. "Tomorrow, Rachel. Right now you need to go to bed."

"Tina's right, Aunt Rachel." Courtney rubbed Rachel's back in a comforting up and down motion. "You look as if you're ready to drop."

"I'm perfectly capable of driving myself home."

"Oh, for crying out loud," Annie snapped as she, too, headed for the door. "For once in your life, Rachel, just once, do as you're told."

Then, her black negligée billowing behind her, she walked out.

Twenty-Three

The sound of voices mingling with the rattling of pots and pans brought Rachel out of a heavy sleep. Sinking deeper into the cocoony-like warmth of a lavender-scented duvet, she opened her eyes and tried to familiarize herself with the surroundings. Then, as the events of the previous night snapped through her sleepy brain, her eyes popped wide open.

She was in the Hughes's guest room. And last night, someone had tried to kill her.

Or at least, that's what everyone seemed to think.

A discreet knock at the door broke through her morbid speculations. "Yes?"

Tina, looking homey in a print dress and white apron, opened the door and stuck her head inside. "Slept well, honey?"

As the delicious aroma of freshly brewed coffee wafted in from the kitchen, Rachel inhaled deeply. "Shamelessly well, considering."

"Good, because you have a visitor."

Rachel glanced at the antique clock on the bedside table. "Detective Crowley?" she moaned. "At eight-thirty in the morning?"

"It's not Detective Crowley." Tina's eyes danced with mirth. "It's Gregory Shaw."

"Gregory? Here?" In a half-conscious gesture, Rachel fluffed up her hair. "What does he want?"

"To see you, of course. And make sure you're all right."

"Oh, Tina, you didn't call him."

"Of course not." Tina walked over to the window and pulled the heavy blue draperies open. Morning light spilled into the room. "Sam did."

"Why?"

"Because," Tina replied, turning around, "Sam thought Gregory should know what happened."

"And, of course, you agreed." Rachel tried to sound reproachful but fell somewhat short of her goal.

"Why wouldn't I? Gregory is a good man, and he feels guilty for making such a mess of your life."

"He told you that?"

"No, but Sam could tell that's just how he feels." Her hands on the railing at the foot of the bed, the older woman leaned forward and whispered, "So what do you say? Are you ready to take pity on the poor man?"

Rachel's hand went to her mouth to cover a yawn. "Tell him I'll be right out."

"Good." Tina nodded toward the bathroom. "You'll find everything you need in there—a toothbrush, a bathrobe, slippers." She grinned. "A comb in case you want to look a little more presentable."

"I don't. He'll have to take me just as I am."

Tina's look was laced with innuendo. "Oh, I'm sure he would, honey. In a heartbeat." She closed the door softly behind her.

Gregory stood looking out the Hughes's kitchen window, the mug of coffee Tina had given him in his hand. A van with the words We Clean It, We Bag It, We Haul It painted on its doors was parked outside the winery, while three men in overalls carried the debris of last night's mishap from the cellars to the truck.

Sam's call had caught him as he was about to step into the shower. At the news that someone had tried to kill Rachel, cold fear had washed over him like a tidal wave. Gregory had always had an aversion for men who preyed on women, and when the woman happened to be someone he was beginning to grow very fond of, that aversion turned into something infinitely more dangerous.

Now, standing in Tina's cozy kitchen with its gingham curtains and homey smells, rage gave way to another emotion—guilt. What if the attempt on Rachel's life had something to do with her connection to Sal Dassante? Sal was a despised man. Was it so far-fetched to think someone would want to hurt him through his granddaughter?

"Hi."

He whipped around, and when he saw Rachel standing there in a white terry bathrobe, unhurt and smiling, he had to call on every ounce of willpower not to rush to her and kiss her senseless.

"Hi, yourself." Rather than let her see he had been worried, he decided to hide the fear under a little humor. "I hear you've taken up a new hobby—juggling wine barrels."

She came right back at him. "And with a little more practice I might be able to join the circus." Looking around her, she asked, "Where's everybody?"

"Sam is at the winery, helping with the cleanup and Tina went to the market." He nodded toward the round maple table where a basket of blueberry muffins waited. "She said if we don't eat, there will be hell to pay."

Rachel walked over to the table. "I'm sure there would be. Tina's mission in life, besides being my friend, has always been to keep me well fed. She says food is good for the soul."

Following her, Gregory sat and watched as she picked up the coffeepot and topped up his mug before filling hers.

"You didn't have to come all this way to check on me, you know," she said as she put the pot down. "A phone call would have been sufficient."

"I wanted to see for myself that you were all right." He studied her closely. "Are you, Rachel? Sometimes a brush with death can produce some delayed reactions."

"Physically, I'm fine. Emotionally, I'm still a little shaken." She reached for a muffin and started to break it into small pieces, which she arranged neatly on her plate. "We've never had an accident like this at Spaulding."

"Sam doesn't call it an accident. Especially since this isn't the first." When she didn't comment he added, "Why didn't you tell me someone tried to run you off the road the other day?"

"Because," she replied with a small shrug, "I saw no point in it."

She was tough, he thought. But she was also frightened. "Tina thinks you should stay here for a while."

She shook her head. "I can't do that."

"She warned me you'd say that. According to her, you're the most stubborn person she knows."

Rachel smiled. "It takes one to know one."

Her dismissal of the danger she had faced—could still face—irritated him. "This is nothing to joke about, Rachel. You could have been killed. Twice."

"So everyone keeps reminding me. Look," she said when he continued to frown, "I don't mean to give the impression that I'm taking what happened last night lightly."

"That's exactly what you're doing."

"No, I'm simply convinced that whoever did this wanted to hurt Spaulding, not me."

"Hurt Spaulding by destroying a couple dozen empty barrels?"

"Maybe they didn't know they were empty. If they had been full, the damages would have amounted to the hundreds of thousand of dollars."

"What about that driver up on the Silverado Trail? Do you also think he only wanted to hurt Spaulding?"

"We're not even sure the two incidents are related."

His hunch said they were. "Sam thinks that ex-employee of yours is responsible for what happened last night."

Her gaze heated up. "He's wrong. Joe Brock would never do something like that. He has too much respect for the work we all do here."

"But he threatened you when he came to the winery last week."

She took another piece of muffin and chewed it slowly. "He wasn't himself that day. He had been drinking. People say a lot of things they don't mean when they're drunk."

"In that case, you don't mind if I check him out, do you?"

The sharp look she gave him told him she minded very much. "Why would you want to do that?"

"Because I'm not going to remain idle while some lunatic is out there waiting to take another shot at you."

"If you're trying to scare me, it's working." She watched him solemnly as she chewed another morsel. "But I'll still stay at my own house."

Damn but she was stubborn. "On one condition," he conceded. "No more late nights. From now on you go home at five, like the rest of your staff."

A smile edged the corners of her mouth. "You're getting to be a royal pain, you know that?"

"Get used to it." He finished the rest of his coffee. "Are you planning to go to work today?"

"Of course." She looked shocked that he could think otherwise.

"Good. I'll come with you. You can give me the grand tour and introduce me to the people who work with you."

She didn't look too happy about that. "You mean, you're going to question my staff?"

"How else am I going to find the guy who did this to you?"

"Detective Crowley isn't going to like having a private eye underfoot."

"Guess what?" He took a piece of muffin from her plate and fed it to her, watching her eyes narrow slightly as she took it into her mouth. "I don't give a rat's ass what Crowley likes or doesn't like."

She made a little huffing sound. "And they call me smug."

As he sat there looking at her, his long-standing maxim to never mix business with pleasure was shot to hell. Leaning across the table, he took her chin between two fingers and kissed her full on the mouth.

Before she could react, he let her go. "Go get ready. I have to be back in my office by ten."

Twenty-Four

Rachel was exhausted. In addition to her regular daily tasks, she'd had to meet with insurance people regarding last night's damages, contractors and, of course, with Detective Crowley, whose questioning of Joe Brock had produced little result. Joe had categorically denied being anywhere near Spaulding Vineyards the previous night. He had been in bed, sleeping, a claim his wife had confirmed. As for the incident on the Silverado Trail, he had owned a pickup at one time, but had traded it for a van a few months ago.

Her first task, in order to quiet speculation, had been to gather Spaulding employees in the courtyard and explain why the police needed to question them.

"No one at Spaulding is being regarded as a suspect," she told them as she saw the concern on their faces. "Detective Crowley only wants information, if you have any, and your cooperation, that's all."

Now, as she drove home in the white Jeep she had rented while hers was being repaired, her thoughts were on a cool glass of Chardonnay, a hot bubble bath and her comfortable bed. As much as she loved spending time at the Hughes's house, she was looking forward to some solitude.

But peace and quiet weren't on the agenda. As she turned the bend and the bungalow came into view, so did Erica's BMW. And this time she had brought company—Sal.

Rachel let out a groan of frustration. For a moment the thought of turning around, whether or not they'd seen her, was tempting. But even as she considered the idea, she tossed it aside. Rudeness wasn't her style. They must have heard about last night's incident and were concerned. And since they had come all this way, the least she could do was be hospitable.

Forcing a smile, she stepped out of the Jeep. "How are you, Sal?" she said as he came to meet her.

He gave her a long, reproachful look. "Very unhappy. I had to hear from the television news that my granddaughter was almost killed last night."

"I'm sorry, Sal, but I saw no reason to worry you." Rachel led the way to the front door. "I'm fine, see?" She turned around and spread her arms wide. "Not a scratch."

In spite of his obvious irritation, a little light danced in those shrewd old eyes. "You're a daredevil, just like your father."

"And you worry too much."

"Maybe. They got the moron who did this yet?"

She moved aside to let them in. "No. The police are investigating."

"They said something about an angry worker," Erica commented.

Rachel went to open the window. A cool coastal wind had shifted to the east, causing the temperature to drop a few more degrees. "He didn't do it. He was home last night. His wife confirmed it."

Sal clicked his tongue. "Wives lie."

Coming to stand beside her father-in-law, Erica lay a hand on his arm. "Sal, you said you wanted to see with your own eyes that she was all right. You did, now let's go. The girl is beat. Can't you see that? She needs to rest."

Sal ignored her. "You shouldn't be working late all by

yourself," he said, shaking a finger at Rachel. "It's asking for trouble. Didn't I tell you that, Erica?" he asked, keeping his gaze on Rachel. "Didn't I?"

Erica rolled her eyes. "You told me, Sal."

"You come to work at the farm," he continued, dead serious. "You won't have to work nights. What?" he asked as Rachel's mouth pulled at the corners. "You don't think I'm serious? I'm serious. Tell her I'm serious, Erica."

"Oh, he's serious. That's all he talked about during the trip here."

"Damned right." Sal gave a nod. "Running a farm is no different from running a winery. You take care of the land and the land takes care of you."

A simplistic approach, Rachel mused, but nonetheless true. "It's a generous offer, Sal, and I appreciate it—"

"But you're turning me down."

"I'm afraid so. My heart is here, Sal, at Spaulding, doing what I do best, what I've been doing most of my life."

"I know, I know, Erica told me you were good at your job." He looked around him. "Nice house you got. You own it?"

"Sal," Erica scolded. "That's none of your business."

"She's my granddaughter," Sal replied, a touch of exasperation in his voice. "You're telling me my granddaughter is none of my business? Okay, okay." He waved an impatient hand. "Don't answer that." His voice softened as he addressed Rachel again. "I like your house. It suits you."

"Thank you, Sal. I'll take that as a compliment."

"And now we'd better go," Erica said. "Nico gets upset when dinner is delayed." Sal didn't budge, so she gave him a little nudge. "Sal?" She dragged out his name a little, demanding an answer.

"I heard you, I'm not deaf. And you," he said, again

pointing his finger at Rachel. "You need something, you come to me, you hear? We're family. And families stick together." Then, with a wave that said he was finished, he turned and headed for the door. "So, you coming or what?" he said as he brushed past Erica.

Rolling her eyes again, Erica kissed Rachel. "Don't be mad at him," she said in a low voice, "or at me for bringing him. He was like a wounded lion when he heard what happened. I thought he was too upset to make the trip alone, so I offered to drive him."

"I'm not mad, Erica. In fact, I think it was kind of sweet of you to bring him."

Rachel stood on the porch until the BMW had disappeared. There had been no mention of Nico, whether he, too, had been concerned. Remembering the way he had looked at her, his expression full of unspoken resentment, she doubted he gave a damn about her safety.

She could feel that same creepy feeling coming back, but before it made her too uneasy, she shook it off and walked back inside.

Gregory stood in the kitchen of his high-rise condo, filled a bowl with corn flakes and poured milk over it. Then, in nothing more than green-striped boxer shorts, he leaned against the counter and studied the crime chart he had pinned on the wall.

He had learned early in his career that no matter how complex a case, he could always untangle it by laying it all out and taking a step back.

Spread across the chart were five squares. In each square the name of a possible suspect was written with an erasable grease pencil. As he found connections between those suspects, he dragged his pencil from one name to the other in a series of connecting lines. To an outsider, the chart might resemble a spider's web gone awry. To Gregory, it was the key to case-solving. As the investigation progressed, new names were added to the list while others were removed.

Chewing on a mouthful of cereal, he studied each name—Joe Brock, Nico Dassante, Erica Dassante, Annie, and his latest entry, Ryan Cummings.

Gregory liked Ryan. The young assistant had been helpful, and understood Gregory's need to question the winery staff, himself included. But years of investigating had taught him that in criminal cases, almost everyone questioned had something to hide, not necessarily something directly related to the case, just something they didn't want revealed.

After observing Ryan Cummings and listening to his answers, Gregory had come to the conclusion that Rachel's assistant was hiding something. And until he found out what it was, the young man would remain on his list of suspects.

As for Joe Brock, the former cellar master didn't interest him nearly as much as Nico Dassante, who stood to lose a considerable amount of money if Sal suddenly decided to make his newfound granddaughter a legal heir.

Annie was on the list for obvious reasons. She wanted Spaulding and would go to any length to get it, but she wasn't a murderer. As for Erica, he didn't have a motive for her. He had penciled her in simply because she was Nico's wife.

He scooped in the last spoonful of cereal and put the bowl in the dishwasher. Maybe he'd call Detective Crowley to find out if the lab had come up with any prints yet.

An hour later Gregory was in his office finishing a conference call with a prospective client when Ed Sumner, his

Senior V.P., ducked his head inside the room. "I've got those tickets you wanted."

Gregory hung up the phone and groaned. "You mean, that concert wasn't sold out, after all?"

Ed, a tall, lanky man with rimless glasses, laughed as he draped his long body into a chair. "Are you kidding? It's been sold out for weeks. But when you're the father of two teenagers, you learn to make connections in all the right places."

He took three tickets from his breast pocket and set them on Gregory's desk. "Those are compliments of ATC, for a job well done. Buzz Felman himself gave them to me."

"Wow, now I'm really impressed. Thanks, Ed. I'll make sure my daughter calls you to thank you in person." Tucking the tickets in his shirt pocket, he added, "How's the evaluation of Tyler Communications coming along?"

"I just finished it. It'll be on your desk before five."

"Results?"

Ed sighed. "Not good for Tyler Communications. Proposed government regulations will put a serious crimp on their expansion program and reduce their revenues by fifteen percent the first year alone. Consequently it's highly improbable that Brechner Technologies will go through with the purchase."

"You spoke with them?"

"Just got off the phone. They're disappointed but glad we were so thorough. They'll definitely hire us again."

"Good." Gregory opened another file. "About that background check on the chief financial officer of Prentis Enterprises. I'd like you to take a look at his file and review what I have so far. I may need you to take over for me."

"Sure. You're going somewhere?"

"No, but I'll be in and out of the office for the next

week or so. I'm investigating the incident at Spaulding Vineyards."

"I heard about that. Anything I can help you with there?"

Gregory shook his head. "I don't think so, but thanks for offering, Ed."

They spent the next hour going over new projects, time frames, which of Shaw's three other associates would be assigned to a particular job and the approximate man-hours required for each.

At eight o'clock that evening, Gregory's night line rang and the call he had been waiting for finally came through. Though it was 5:00 a.m. in Paris, his Interpol friend, Todd Stark, sounded wide awake. "You're a hard man to track down," Gregory said in reply to his greeting.

Todd laughed. "You'd be, too, if you did any real work instead of sitting in your fancy tower, crunching numbers all day long."

"And you call what you do real work? Prancing all over Europe, dating beautiful women, sipping expensive champagne, all in the name of God and country, of course."

There was a light chuckle at the other end of the line. "The last beautiful woman I dated shoved me out of a third-floor balcony window."

Gregory laughed. That's how it had been between them in college—good laughs and friendly banter.

"So," Todd said, "are you going to tell me why you've been leaving messages for me all over France?"

Suddenly serious, Gregory told him what he knew about Alyssa Dassante, alias Virginia Potter.

"Neither of those names is familiar to me," Todd said as Gregory heard the rapid click of computer keys. "And they're not showing up on my data sheet. How long did you say she's been missing?"

"Thirty-one years."

"Do you have a social security number for her? Or a birth date?"

"No, but I can get that information to you within the hour or so. Will you still be up?"

Todd let out an exaggerated yawn. "Barely, but for you I'll make an exception. Oh, and get me her mother's maiden name, as well, if you can."

Gregory found Jonsey at home and got the information he needed, except for Alyssa's social security number. The employment records she had filled out at the time of her hiring had been discarded long ago.

"That's all right," Todd said when Gregory called back. "I can get it from here. It might take me a couple of days. Is that all right?"

"That's fine. Thanks, Todd."

"This is going to cost you, my friend. And I don't mean a fajita dinner at your favorite Tex-Mex hangout."

"Not even if I spring for refried beans?"

Todd laughed. "Now you're talking. Give my regards to your lovely aunt."

"I'll do that. And stay away from high balcony windows."

"What should we order?" Noelle, who considered herself an authority on Chinese food, studied her menu with the practiced eye of the connoisseur. "Cantonese or Szechuan?"

"I don't care," Gregory said. "As long as it's chow mein."

She made a face. "Oh, Daddy, nobody eats chow mein anymore."

"It's on the menu, isn't it?"

That logic went totally over her head. "Chow mein is

what people ordered back in the fifties. Americans are much more sophisticated than they used to be.''

Amused, Gregory watched his daughter. She had recovered quickly from her accident and was back at the top of her form, which, with a daughter like Noelle, could be exhausting. ''How do you know Americans are more sophisticated than they used to be?''

''I heard it on the food channel.''

''Are you taking up gourmet cooking now?''

She made another face. ''No, Mom is. Since my accident, she's been cooking up a storm. It's not always good, and it never looks like it does on TV, but she's improving. Emeril Lagasse is her favorite chef.''

Well, what do you know, Gregory mused. Wonders would never cease. Maybe that little talk with Lindsay hadn't been a total waste of time, after all.

Noelle's gaze swept up and down the menu once again. ''Let's see... We'll have fried dumplings to start, then some Kung Pao shrimp and sesame chicken. That way we can share.'' She looked up. ''Okay?''

Gregory laughed. ''It sounds risky, but what the heck. We only live once.''

Noelle giggled. ''Oh, Daddy, you're so funny.''

''How's the wrist?''

''Good.'' Letting go of her menu, she moved her wrist up and down and around. ''I wanted to start cutting grass again, but Mom won't let me. She says it's too soon.''

''She's right. Wait another week or two.''

''But, Daddy,'' Noelle said with a look of sheer anguish on her expressive face, ''the grass-cutting season is almost over and I have to make some money before Christmas.''

''What about the ten-dollar-a-week allowance I give you?''

''I can't manage on ten dollars a week, Daddy. Everything is so expensive." She shrugged. "And, anyway, I like cutting grass. It gives me a chance to check out the new boy next door."

That gave Gregory pause. "The boy next door?"

Noelle gave him her most reassuring smile. "It's just healthy curiosity, Daddy. Nothing for you to worry about."

"I'm so relieved to hear you say that," he replied, not relieved at all. Then, afraid he'd start obsessing over the boy next door, he changed the subject. "You're planning to cut grass on the afternoon of November sixth?"

"November sixth. November sixth." Noelle tapped a finger against her mouth. "I might. Is that a Saturday?"

"Last time we talked, it was a very important Saturday, at least for you." Affecting a smug expression, he took the three concert tickets from his breast pocket and waved them in front of her nose. "But if you're busy..."

Her mouth opened in shock. *"You got tickets for the Spice Girls concert?* Oh, Daddy, you're the coolest dad in the world." Much to the amusement of the other diners, she jumped out of her seat and threw her arms around Gregory's neck. "Thank you, thank you, thank you."

"Thank Ed next time you see him. He's the one who pulled strings to get the tickets."

"I will, Daddy. And you got three," she added in total ecstasy. "So I can take Zoe, right?"

He grinned. "Unless you want to take the boy next door."

"Nah." She made a face. "He's more into Hanson than the Spice Girls."

After a waitress had come to take their order, Noelle brought Gregory up to date on all the events of her busy life, from her upcoming gymnastic tournament to her grades, which continued to be excellent.

"I still have problems with math, though." The way she

said it, watching him under lowered lashes, cued him that she was about to broach another delicate subject—that of moving in with him.

"Why don't you sit down with your mother and have her explain it to you? She's pretty good at it."

"Not like you, Daddy," she said sweetly as their waitress brought their food to the table. "You make it all sound so simple."

"Math is, once you understand the theory. Next time you come over, I'll show you how it works."

"But that's just it, Daddy." Her voice turned slightly melodramatic. "When I'm with you, I don't want to do math. I want to have fun."

She dipped a dry noodle into the wickedly hot mustard and popped it in her mouth without as much as a blink. "Now if I were living with you *permanently*," she added, slanting him another of her lethal looks, "we would have lots of time for math."

"I'd love to have you with me, pumpkin," he said sincerely. "You know that. But your mother would never go for it."

"My friend Clarisse used to live with her mother, then her mother started to bring boyfriends home and Clarisse's dad went back to court and now she's living with him."

"Does your mother bring boyfriends home?"

Noelle laughed. "No."

"Then what's the problem?"

"She's always working."

"I thought you said she was spending more time at home now, cooking you gourmet meals."

"She is. Yesterday she was home before I was." Her tone turned cajoling. "But she's not as much fun as you are, Daddy."

"Living with me wouldn't be as much fun as you think.

I work long hours, too. And sometimes I have to go out of town, which means I'd have to hire someone to watch you.''

"No, you wouldn't. I'll be thirteen in February. I can take care of myself. That's what I do most of the time now, anyway.''

And that, Gregory thought, would be his major argument if and when he ever decided to get serious about gaining custody of Noelle.

In the hour or so it took to get back from Calistoga, Sal had done a lot of thinking about Rachel. He wasn't mad at her anymore for wanting to look for her mother. Hell, the kid had a right. Just as he had a right to make the most of a situation he couldn't control. He just wished she had trusted him enough to tell him about it.

Once home, Sal thanked Erica for the ride and went directly to his living room to call Joe Kelsey. "Joe," he told his private investigator, "I got a job for you."

"Besides looking for Alyssa?"

"Yeah, besides that. I want you to put a tail on my granddaughter. I want to know where she goes, who she sees, all that stuff. Hire as many men as you need to, but do the job right."

"Are you trying to protect Rachel from whoever tried to kill her last night?" Kelsey asked. "Because if you are, I've got bodyguards who can—"

"That's not the reason. I want her followed because she's trying to find Alyssa, and if she does, she'll lead you right to her."

"I got you."

"She's sharp, Joe, so don't let her catch you, okay?"

"I'm not a novice," Joe said, sounding offended. "I've been doing this a long time, and I haven't been caught yet."

"Keep it that way," Sal said before hanging up.

He stood by the phone for a moment, smiling, feeling good. He didn't really give a damn who found Alyssa first—Kelsey or Rachel—just as long as they found her.

Then he would take over.

And God help anyone who stood in his way.

Twenty-Five

Rachel was fresh out of her bath and heating up a can of tomato soup on the stove when the phone rang.

"Well, I'm glad to see you're a woman of your word," Gregory said when she answered.

The sound of his voice stirred warm memories. "Did you doubt it?"

"When it comes to you quitting work at five, yes, I did have my doubts."

Chuckling, Rachel turned the burner to low, picked up her glass of Chardonnay and leaned against the kitchen counter. "As a matter of fact, I did try to sneak in an extra hour. Sam wouldn't let me. He said if I didn't go home with the rest of the workers, he'd carry me out and toss away my keys."

"Sam's a good man."

"You would say that. The two of you are cut from the same cloth."

"That's because we care. What are you doing now?"

"Cooking dinner."

"Which is?"

"Campbell's tomato soup."

"Yummy."

She laughed. "Look who's talking. The king of take-outs."

"Not tonight. Tonight I had dinner with my daughter."

"How is she doing?"

"Much better, especially now that I came through with Spice Girls concert tickets."

"You're a good dad, Gregory."

"Thank you, but I didn't call to brag." His voice turned serious. "I talked to my friend at Interpol. He should know something in a couple of days. Joe Brock, on the other hand, was no help at all. Or rather, his wife wasn't."

"Teresa has been under a lot of stress."

"Maybe. The fact is, she wouldn't let me talk to him."

"It doesn't matter, Gregory. Joe is no longer a prime suspect. Not only was he in bed that night, but the police didn't come up with his fingerprints, or Nico's for that matter."

"I know," he said, sounding disappointed. "I talked to Crowley."

Knowing what a grouch the detective was, that statement surprised her. "You mean, he volunteered the information?"

"Are you kidding? I had to pull every word out of his mouth. I've met some tough cops in my time, but this one beats them all."

"I tried to warn you."

There was another pause before he asked, "How long has Ryan Cummings been working for you?"

The question startled her. "Two years, why?"

"I think he's hiding something."

"Oh, Gregory, you can't possibly suspect him. I've known Ryan since we were teenagers. He's totally devoted to me, and to Spaulding."

"I'm not saying he's the one who tried to kill you, but he was definitely uncomfortable when I questioned him, especially when I asked where he had been the night of the accident."

"Wasn't he home?"

"He says he was, but he was cagey about it."

Rachel sighed. "I may know why," she said reluctantly. She hated to gossip about her people, but at the same time she couldn't let Ryan be suspected of something he didn't do.

"I'm listening," Gregory said.

"Courtney has a crush on Ryan and for the last several weeks, she's been hoping he would ask her to the Harvest Ball. When it became obvious he wouldn't, I took it upon myself to find out if he had a girlfriend, someone I knew nothing about."

"I didn't know matchmaking was another of your talents."

"It's not, and believe me after this fiasco, I'll never butt into someone's romantic life ever again."

"What happened?"

"I asked Ryan point blank if he was involved. He turned beet red, told me no, then said something about being busy, and walked away."

"You didn't believe him?"

"No." She took a sip of her wine. "I think he's involved with a married woman."

"And if he was with that woman the night of the incident at Spaulding," Gregory said after a short pause, "he wouldn't want to have to produce her as an alibi. Why didn't I think of that?"

"Because men often overlook the obvious."

She heard him laugh. "And women don't?"

"I just proved that, didn't I? But all joking aside, this little suspicion of mine leaves me with a big problem."

"What's that?"

"Do I tell Courtney or do I keep quiet?"

"The latter, definitely," Gregory replied. "First, because

you don't know if your suspicions are correct, and second, because it really isn't your place to tell her. The worst that can happen is that he won't ask her to the dance, which is something she probably suspects already.''

He wasn't just a good dad, Rachel thought with a smile, he was also an intuitive dad. "I guess you're right.''

They chatted for a few more minutes, long enough for Rachel to tell him that Spauldings's regular tour guide, JoAnn, was down with the flu and Rachel had volunteered to fill in for her until she returned. "I'm petrified,'' she admitted with a nervous laugh. "I haven't given a tour since I was ten.''

"You'll knock them dead, Spaulding.''

"Thanks.''

She went to bed that night with the sound of his voice lulling her to sleep.

"Good morning, my name is Rachel Spaulding.'' The young woman smiled broadly as she gazed at the small assembled crowd waiting to take the first morning tour. "I'm one of the winemakers here, and since our regular tour guide has the flu today, I'll be filling in for her.''

Her mouth suddenly dry, Ginnie gripped Hubert's hand and squeezed it hard. Finding herself face-to-face with her daughter was the last thing she had expected when she and Hubert had signed up for a tour of Spaulding Vineyards. When Rachel had walked into the front room minutes earlier, the shock had been so powerful, Ginnie had experienced a brief moment of dizziness.

Once again in control, thanks to Hubert's arm around her, she looked at her daughter from behind her tinted glasses and felt her chest swell with pride. What a beautiful young woman she had become. And so gracious. One smile from her, one kind word, and strangers felt instantly at ease.

"Easy, *chérie*," Hubert murmured in her ear as she continued to squeeze his hand. "Don't give yourself away."

Rachel was already talking and pointing as she led the small group toward a large courtyard filled with heavy machinery. "As you can see, the crush is over," she said, turning to look at her guests and walking backward. "But this is where it takes place. The grapes are brought in from the vineyards by trucks and the contents are dumped into this crusher, which doubles up as a de-stemmer."

As Rachel patted the large metal container, Ginnie gave a small tug to the scarf on her head, making sure it was still in place. In the sunlight, Rachel's chestnut hair had the same red highlights as Ginnie's, and while that little detail pleased her, it also frightened her. How difficult would it be for an overzealous reporter to notice the resemblance? And start to speculate. Relax, she thought, trying to concentrate on what Rachel was saying. There are no reporters here.

Letting go of Hubert's hand, Ginnie followed the group, trying to keep a comfortable distance between herself and Rachel. It wasn't easy. She couldn't take her eyes off her daughter couldn't get enough of her voice, her laughter, the way she looked directly at each person when she talked.

"Don't mind the dust," Rachel said as they passed a small construction crew inside the second cellar. "We're doing some remodeling."

Ginnie felt a quick burst of anger. It was more than remodeling. According to the newspapers, someone had tried to kill Rachel a couple of nights ago, and though the police had launched an extensive investigation, the culprit was still at large.

"Any questions, so far?" Rachel turned and looked directly at Ginnie.

Ginnie swallowed past the lump in her throat and shook

her head, grateful that a man in the front row raised his hand and asked a question she didn't catch.

"No." Rachel splayed her hand on a huge redwood barrel. "We no longer store wine in those giant barrels. Nowadays their function is purely ornamental. And perhaps a little sentimental," she added with another enchanting smile. "My great-grandfather had them built at the turn of the century before anyone realized that wines age much better in oak barrels."

Recovered from the shock of having Rachel look directly at her, Ginnie relaxed again. The girl was a delight. Not only was she intelligent, informative and funny, she was also proud of her work and of the place Spaulding Vineyards occupied in the wine industry.

"We produce a total of five hundred thousand cases a year," Rachel continued as they passed through yet another cellar. "And since we've just begun distributing our wines abroad, our production is expected to double in the next five years."

As the group walked through an archway, Rachel stood back. Ginnie realized, not without another twist of alarm, that she was waiting for her and Hubert to catch up.

"It's a lot to absorb in just one visit, isn't it?" she asked, smiling at both of them.

Worried she would look suspicious if she didn't answer, Ginnie returned Rachel's friendly smile. "Not when you explain it."

"I agree," Hubert replied. "You make winemaking sound both easy and exciting. Most tours are not that comprehensive."

"Then this isn't your first visit to a winery?" Rachel looked from one to the other.

"We've visited wineries abroad," Ginnie replied, adding, "my husband and I are from France."

"France?" Excitement bubbled in Rachel's eyes. "How wonderful. I love France. We have a new client there. His name is Anatole Fronsac. Perhaps you know him?"

"The owner of Supermarchés Fronsac." Hubert gave an approving nod. "Certainly. And congratulations, *mademoiselle*. You must have impressed him very much. I don't believe I have ever seen a California wine in any of Monsieur Fronsac's stores."

She laughed. "I know. He told me that repeatedly during our negotiations."

"We'll make a point to look for your wines when we get back home."

Rachel seemed delighted and immediately asked Ginnie another question. "What part of France are you from?"

"The central region."

"Your English is flawless."

"Thank you." Ginnie thought it safer to not let on she wasn't French.

"Will you be staying in the valley long?"

Nervous, yet pleased at the same time to have been singled out from all the other visitors, Ginnie cast her husband a quick look.

"A couple of weeks," Hubert said, looking completely at ease. "And I intend to sample as many California wines as I can while I'm here."

"In that case, I'm anxious for you to taste ours first and to hear your impressions."

Ginnie's compliment came from the heart. "We've already tasted one of your wines, Miss Spaulding—a wonderful Cabernet that was every bit as good as the Margaux we normally drink at home. Don't you agree, darling?" she added, turning once again to Hubert.

"My wife is right. That Cabernet was superb."

Rachel's cheeks colored with pride. "Thank you. That's no small compliment coming from French visitors."

Her eyes misting behind the glasses, Ginnie watched her daughter make her way back to the head of the group.

In the salesroom that doubled as tasting room, Rachel slipped behind the counter and began pouring the wines she had selected for today's visitors. From time to time, as she described the particular varietal she was pouring, she kept glancing at the French couple, but especially at the woman.

Other than the fact that she was French, she had seemed reluctant to say anything too specific about herself. Not that her background was any of Rachel's business. People were entitled to their privacy. In the past three weeks no one had come to appreciate that more than Rachel.

Half an hour later, as she and the salesroom manager took orders from their visitors, Rachel suddenly looked up from an order form and found the French woman staring at her. Behind the dark glasses, her eyes were inscrutable, yet, somehow, Rachel knew the woman's stare was as intense as her own.

With no warning, that same premonition she had experienced at the convent a few days ago skittered through her, as if something terribly significant was about to happen.

After a second or two Rachel shook off the strange feeling and returned her attention to the order form. She was being silly, spooked over the incident in the cellars the other night. Despite the fact that she didn't scare easily, knowing that someone who may have wanted her harmed was still out there, possibly preparing for a third attempt, had her glancing over her shoulder every five minutes.

When she looked up again, the French couple was gone.

Twenty-Six

"Oh, Hubert." Back at the little yellow cottage Hubert had rented through their travel agency, Ginnie tossed her sunglasses onto a table and collapsed on the sofa. She felt emotionally drained. "Isn't she absolutely wonderful? Isn't she the warmest, most intelligent, most beautiful woman you've ever seen?"

"Hmm, I don't know about that." Walking over to a cabinet, Hubert took out two glasses and filled them with mineral water. "I remember another equally beautiful young woman I met some years ago."

Ginnie took the glass he handed her and removed her scarf from her head, allowing her hair to tumble to her shoulders. "Not like her, Hubert," she said, feeling the same motherly pride she had experienced over the phone when she had talked to Sister Mary-Catherine. "It took all my willpower not to take her in my arms and tell her everything."

"I could tell, and I must say, for a moment I was worried you would give our little secret away."

"I was tempted."

"Promise me you will not do anything foolish, Ginnie." Hubert sat next to her. "We have no idea how Rachel would react, or what her feelings about you are now that she knows the truth. She could be angry. She could go to the police. Or to Sal."

"No." Ginnie shook her head. "I don't believe that for a minute. The young woman we met today would never do something so cruel. I know you didn't notice, Hubert, but earlier, as she was writing up an order, she looked up and caught me staring at her. Something happened in that instant, Hubert. I felt it the moment our gazes crossed, and so did she."

She touched her husband's face, her finger stroking his cheek. "Don't frown, darling. As much as I'd love to tell her who I am, I won't. Not yet, anyway."

She took a sip of her water. "To tell you the truth, I'm a little nervous myself. I feel so...vulnerable all of a sudden. Wherever we go, I keep expecting someone to point at me and shout, 'Here she is! Here's Mario Dassante's murderer!'"

Hubert gave a firm shake of his head. "That won't happen. Not as long as we keep to ourselves."

She played with a corner of her scarf, twisting it. "That's not always easy to do. Everyone here is so friendly, so genuinely interested." She smiled. "Whenever someone asks me a question and I don't answer it, I feel as though I'm contributing to the impression Americans have that the French aren't friendly."

"In that case," Hubert replied philosophically, "they won't think our attitude odd at all, will they?" He patted her hand. "Stop worrying. This is not Dassante territory. No one here has any interest in Sal's ex-daughter-in-law."

"Reporters might. Catching me would be a big story, Hubert. Possibly the biggest story of their careers. You saw that article in last night's local paper. Now that the press knows Lillie is alive, my whereabouts are once again front-page news. One reporter even hinted the police should use Rachel to trap Alyssa into coming out in the open." She let out a small, dry chuckle. "Little do they know Alyssa already has."

"That's why I insisted we rent this house instead of going to one of those charming bed-and-breakfasts," Hubert replied. "As far as anyone is concerned, we are just an ordinary French couple on a vacation to the wine country."

He was right. The little cottage Hubert had rented was tucked into a hillside on the northern end of the valley, away from the main road and about a hundred feet from their nearest neighbor.

Ginnie looked around her at the small but comfortable living room with its Early American furniture upholstered in brown-and-yellow plaid and its old-fashioned hooked rugs. She could live here forever, she thought, in perfect, blissful comfort, but she knew that couldn't be.

"Do you think we bought enough wine?" she asked suddenly as her thoughts returned to Rachel.

Hubert laughed. "We bought six cases, *chérie*. Six times as much as anyone there."

"But still, I think we should order another case or two—to give away to our friends."

"Are you sure you are not looking for an excuse to return to Spaulding Vineyards?"

Ginnie smiled. "Am I that transparent?"

Hubert held up his glass and looked through it. "As transparent as this water." He put the glass down and took her hand. "We will go back," he said gently. "In a couple of days. That way we won't arouse any suspicion. Is that all right?"

"Yes, it's perfect." Ginnie leaned her head against the cushion and closed her eyes. "Everything is perfect."

Rachel was back in the cellars by 1:00 p.m. and was surprised to find Detective Crowley waiting for her.

"You have news?" she asked, praying he wasn't here to ask more questions. The routine at Spaulding had finally returned to normal, and she didn't think she and her staff could take another disruption.

"I do have news," he replied, his expression grim. "Just not the kind you might expect."

"Why? What happened?"

"Joe Brock is missing."

In spite of her reluctance to believe Joe was guilty, she felt a twinge of apprehension. "What do you mean, missing?"

"His wife called the station earlier and reported him missing. Apparently, he took off sometime during the night. She never heard him get out of bed. When she looked in the closet this morning, she found some of his clothes gone. He also withdrew six hundred dollars from an ATM in the last two days, suggesting he had been planning to leave town."

"Oh, Joe," she murmured, not realizing she had spoken out loud.

"It gets worse." The detective paused to let a worker walk by. "He took his gun with him."

She wasn't sure whether it was nerves or the slight melodrama of the situation that made her laugh. "Are you implying he's going to use that gun on me? That he didn't succeed in killing me the first two times so he's now going to shoot me? Like in some bad Western?"

Crowley wasn't amused. "Whatever you believe or don't believe about Brock, there's no doubt in my mind he skipped town because he was scared."

"Wouldn't you be if the police suddenly showed up on your doorstep and started questioning you about your possible involvement in an attempted murder?"

"I wouldn't get too complacent about this if I were

you," Crowley said sourly. "We don't know what Brock is thinking right now. Or what he plans to do. He might turn the gun on himself, then again, he could be angry enough to come after you."

"I find that hard to believe." She still couldn't bring herself to think of the barrel incident as an attempt on her life. The whole thing was just too bizarre.

"Believe it. As far as Joe Brock is concerned, you could be the reason he's in such a mess."

Rachel glanced nervously beyond his shoulder, toward the courtyard where someone could easily hide without being detected.

"I wouldn't worry too much about the daytime hours," Crowley said, catching her glance. "He wouldn't be stupid enough to show up here with half a dozen eyewitnesses around. It's after hours I'm worried about. You live alone, don't you?"

"Yes."

"I'd move in with the Hughes if I were you. I already talked to Sam about that and he agrees."

"How long will it take you to find Joe?" she asked.

He shrugged. "Hard to say. If his intention was to flee, he could be hundreds of miles from here by now. But if he decided to stick around, he could be anywhere."

And come after her.

Brennan's, on Calistoga's main street, was already packed when Gregory and Rachel arrived for dinner. As usual, the conversation among patrons centered around wine matters—the rising price of oak, how much pruning to do in the spring, new marketing strategies. At any other time, Rachel would have enjoyed a little eavesdropping since it never hurt to know what the competition was doing. Tonight, however, her mind was elsewhere.

"Crowley came to see me earlier," she said as soon as a waiter had taken their drink orders. "Joe Brock left town."

Gregory stiffened perceptibly. "Left town?"

She nodded. "During the night. He took his clothes, his car, money and just...left." She licked her dry lips. "He also took his gun." She told him about Crowley's suggestion she move in with the Hughes.

"And that's exactly what you're going to do," Gregory said. "If I have to take you there myself and tie you down."

The visual image made her want to put his threat to the test. "I already have. Sam wouldn't even let me think about it. He took me home to pack a few things then took me back to his house." She stared at the bar where a couple of vintners she knew were laughing loudly. "I feel like such a coward."

Gregory took her hand. "You're not a coward, Rachel." His tone was so convincing she almost believed him. "You're simply taking preventive measures. Crowley is right. We don't know what's in Brock's mind. He could be a desperate man right now, and desperate men are dangerous men."

"If he wants to kill me he'll do it regardless of where I am."

"Maybe, but why make it easy for him? From now on, you don't go anywhere alone—"

"Now just a minute." She waited until the waiter had set the two beers in front of them and walked away before finishing her thought. "I'm not going to turn paranoid, or start walking around with an entourage. I have a business to run, people to supervise."

"I won't let you be a target again."

"We don't even know if I was a target in the first place,"

she protested, but secretly she was pleased that he worried about her.

"Right, and whoever sneaked into the cellars that night waited until you were conveniently in the way to release those barrels. And that old pickup that almost drove you off the edge just happened to be there." He shook his head. "That's a little too coincidental for me, Rachel."

When he put it that way, there wasn't much she could say.

His voice softened as he leaned forward. "I know how protective you are of your people," he said. "Even those who no longer work for you. It's an admirable quality, but this is serious stuff, Rachel. Your life could be at stake."

She nodded. "I promise I'll be careful." And she meant it.

He straightened, apparently satisfied. "Good."

She took a sip of her beer and put it down almost right away. Since meeting that French couple this morning, her stomach was in such knots that nothing tasted good. She probably wouldn't be able to eat a thing. "There's another reason I wanted to see you tonight," she said, staring into her glass.

"More bad news?"

"No." Rachel looked up. "You know that I filled in for JoAnn this morning."

He nodded. "The tour guide with the flu. I remember. How did it go?"

"Fine. I had a foreign couple in the group—a man and a woman from France."

"Don't tell me." His smile was teasing. "They trashed American wines."

"No, far from it. They bought six cases." She hesitated, wondering if she was going to sound like a lunatic. "There was something about the woman. Something…oddly familiar.''

Gregory frowned. "Familiar? How?"

"I don't know. I felt a sense of déjà vu, a connection."

"Perhaps because she lives in France?" he asked. "You did tell me you have a strong attachment to that country, didn't you?"

"Yes, but…it was more than that. And the woman felt it, too. I caught her looking at me with an intensity I can't even begin to describe. Or explain, unless…" She stared into Gregory's eyes. "I felt as if…she was Alyssa."

He watched her for a long second. "Did she look like you?"

Rachel shook her head. "No. I mean…I couldn't tell. A scarf covered most of her hair and she wore dark glasses."

"Dark glasses? Inside a dark cellar? That's odd."

"They weren't dark dark, just…tinted enough so I couldn't see her eyes. But I really felt as if I had seen her before."

"Can you describe her?"

"She was in her mid- to late-fifties, I guess, very attractive from what I could see, well-dressed. There was no mole above her upper lip."

"Moles can be surgically removed. Did she have a French accent?"

"Not a trace. At the time I thought her English was simply flawless. In fact, I told her so."

"What did she say?"

"She thanked me."

Gregory set his glass down and stared at it. "Hmm. Attractive women don't normally hide their features unless they don't want to be recognized. And the age fits."

Rachel clasped her hands in front of her. "Oh, Gregory,

you don't think I'm crazy to think this woman could be Alyssa? Or obsessed?''

"No. I believe in instincts. And I believe that when the situation warrants, people should act on those instincts.''

"But why would she come here after all this time? Risk everything? Sister Mary-Catherine told her I had died in a fire.''

"I can't answer that," he said, looking thoughtful. "Unless Sister Mary-Catherine knew where she was all along and called her.''

"Maybe I should go back to Santa Rosa.''

"No, don't go there alone. Call her, instead. What's the couple's name?''

"Laperousse. Our salesroom manager took their order, but I checked it out after they left. They gave the address of the house where they're staying and the phone number.'' She looked out the window. "It's right here in Calistoga, just a few minutes away.''

"I'll call Todd as soon as I return to San Francisco," he said. "It'll be easier for him to get information now that we have a name.''

The waiter had come back to take their dinner order. And not a moment too soon, Rachel thought. She was suddenly famished.

"Sister Mary-Catherine," Rachel said when the nun picked up the phone. "This is Rachel Spaulding.''

The woman's tone was immediately softer. "Hello, Rachel. How are you, my dear?''

"Sister, I—I need to ask you something very important. Can you talk?''

"Yes.''

"Have you heard from my mother since the last time we spoke?''

There was a slight pause at the end of the line. "Why do you ask?"

Rachel threw a cautious glance around her. "Because," she said when she was certain no one was within earshot, "a woman toured the winery yesterday. I couldn't tell much about her features because she wore dark glasses and a scarf, but I'm almost certain it was Alyssa."

"Oh."

That single, breathless exclamation was all Rachel needed to hear. "Please tell me, Sister. Did she contact you?"

"Yes," Sister Mary-Catherine said at last. "She did contact me. I don't know where she called from or why. We never got to that part because as soon as I knew who she was, I told her you were alive. I can't tell you what that did to her, Rachel. She was so happy, laughing and crying at the same time, asking a million questions about you."

"Did she say she wanted to see me? That she might come to Napa Valley?"

"Oh, she very much wanted to see you. She even asked me where Spaulding Vineyards was located. I told her to be careful because Sal Dassante was still looking for her, but she didn't seem to care about that."

Rachel's mouth had gone dry again. It was her. It had to be. "Thank you, Sister. You're a true miracle worker."

Rachel and Sam were in her office, studying a local artist's sketch for the label Spaulding would be putting on their soon-to-be-bottled Sauvignon Blanc, when her phone rang. It was Gregory.

"Madame Laperousse's name before marrying her husband," he said as she discreetly excused herself and moved out of earshot, "was Virginia Potter."

Rachel gripped the phone a little tighter. "Are you sure?"

"Positive. Hubert Laperousse is a concert pianist, known all over Europe. He's even toured in the United States, though never in California. According to a report my Interpol friend received earlier, Hubert met Alyssa in Paris in August of 1968. She had only been there for a couple of weeks."

Rachel blinked away tears. The pieces of the puzzle were slowly falling into place. "I learned something, too," she said, her voice trembling with emotion. "Alyssa did contact Sister Mary-Catherine and found out from her that I was alive."

"All right, listen to me," Gregory said in that nononsense tone of voice she was beginning to know so well. "Don't do anything on your own and don't tell anyone about this, not even Sam and Tina."

"I won't."

"I'll be there first thing in the morning and I'll take you to the Laperousses's house. Do not go there alone. Is that understood?"

"I don't normally take orders from bullies, but yes." She smiled. "I understand."

Twenty-Seven

"Where are you going?" Rachel asked as Gregory headed south on Route 29. "The Laperousses's house is in the other direction."

"I want to make sure we're not being followed."

"Who would want to follow us?"

"Maybe the same person who tried to kill you. Maybe someone else. Maybe no one. I'm taking no chances."

She suppressed a smile. "Are you going to tell me where we're going or is that a military secret?"

He drove just under the speed limit, probably not by choice, Rachel thought, knowing his driving habits, but because at this time of the morning, the commuting traffic on Route 29 was excruciatingly slow.

"We're going to The Diner for breakfast."

The Diner, where the portions were huge and the prices low, was a fifties-type restaurant and one of Napa Valley's most popular eateries. "That's an excellent choice if you want to get lost in the crowd, but if you want a table, be prepared for a long wait."

"Hmm." His expression was smug. "We'll see."

As predicted, there was already a long line of hungry tourists waiting to be seated when they arrived. But an attractive waitress mysteriously appeared, greeted Gregory as if he were a long-lost friend and quickly escorted them to a small booth in the back.

"Will this be all right, Mr. Shaw?"

"Perfect, Thelma. Thank you."

Rachel waited until the waitress had gone before leaning across the table. "Mr. Shaw? Thelma? What's going on here?"

Gregory picked up his menu. "In private investigative circles it's called reconnaissance work. I came, I saw, I booked."

"How could you book? They don't take reservations."

"They do if you're charming, which obviously I am, and if you give a fat tip, which obviously I did." He laughed, clearly pleased with himself. "Close your mouth, Spaulding. Your admiration is showing."

Rachel snapped her mouth shut. "Don't let it go to your head."

"I won't. Order some food."

Rachel scanned her menu. "If you had told me we were going out for breakfast, I wouldn't have pigged out on Tina's English scones."

He threw a discreet look around. "We won't be eating."

"But you said—"

The waitress had returned. With another smile at Gregory, she pulled a pencil from behind her beehive hairdo. "So, folks, what will it be?"

"*Huevos rancheros* for me." Gregory raised a brow. "Rachel? Did you say you wanted the German pancakes?"

"Uh..." Totally confused, she gave the waitress a vacuous smile before glancing once again at the menu. "Yes...that will be fine."

"*Huevos rancheros* and German pancakes coming up."

Her eyes on the retreating waitress, Rachel leaned across the table again. "I thought you said we weren't eating."

"We're not. We're just going through the motions, should someone be watching us."

"Aren't you being a little paranoid? First you thought we were being followed, now you think we're being watched. What will it be next?"

"In private investigative circles—"

She laughed. "Let me guess, it's called taking preventive measures."

He grinned at her. "You're a fast learner."

"I'll remember that, if I ever become bored with wine-making or—"

She never had a chance to finish. Gregory suddenly grabbed her hand and pulled her out of the booth. "Come on, let's go."

Speechless, she let herself be dragged through a door marked Employees Only. Inside, the frantic activity of the busy kitchen hardly slowed as they entered. Thelma, who was clipping an order to an overhanging rack, winked when she saw them.

"Thanks, sweetheart," Gregory said, stuffing what was probably another generous tip into her pocket.

"How do you propose we get back to Calistoga?" Rachel asked as they ran toward a back door. "Since I assume we won't be taking the Jaguar. Oh, don't tell me. Part of your training as a private detective included hot-wiring cars."

"It did, but we won't need that talent today." He pushed the door open. In the smaller parking lot were several cars of every make and size. Her rented Jeep was also there, nestled between a station wagon and a delivery van.

She couldn't help it. Her mouth dropped open again. "How did you manage that?"

"With Sam's help. I asked him to bring the Jeep here and he did. I've got to hand it to the guy. He must have been dying of curiosity but he never asked a single question." Gregory opened the passenger door. "Hurry up, get in."

Her heart beating a little faster from all the intrigue, she did as she was told. She even took a shot at a little humor of her own when he slid behind the wheel. "How do you want me to handle a possible high-speed chase?" she asked. "Do I blow the tires? Or do I just put a bullet between the eyes of our pursuer?"

In the morning light, Gregory's eyes gleamed with laughter. "Whatever turns you on, baby."

Once back on Route 29, he glanced in the rearview mirror from time to time, and Rachel found herself doing the same with her side mirror. No one seemed to be following them. The ruse, well thought out and perfectly executed, had either worked or had been a complete waste of time.

Ten minutes later, as they approached Calistoga, Rachel lost her nerve. What if Alyssa, or Virginia, as she ought to call her now, wasn't ready to reveal who she was? What if, in spite of all those precautions, someone *had* followed them?

She had no sooner asked herself that last question than Gregory turned onto Pickett Road. At the sight of the little yellow cottage, Rachel's heart began beating even faster.

"You go in," Gregory said as he stopped the Jeep. "I'll wait out here."

"I don't see a car. Maybe they're not home."

"Why don't you go ring the bell and find out?"

Still uncertain, Rachel got out of the Cherokee and stared at the house. What now? she wondered. Did she just walk up to the front door, ring the bell and announce, "I'm your long-lost daughter"? Or should she make up some sort of excuse for being here, and wait for Virginia Laperousse to say something?

Her speculations were brought to an end when the front

door suddenly opened and Mrs. Laperousse walked out, holding a straw basket and a pair of garden clippers. The scarf was gone and her long brown hair fell to her shoulders in soft waves. As she reached the last step, she suddenly looked up.

The clippers fell to the ground and Virginia's hand went to her chest. It was several seconds before she could speak. "Miss Spaulding." Her eyes, dark and luminous, stared at Rachel with a mixture of joy and fear.

Rachel couldn't move. Or utter a single word. All the clever phrases she had rehearsed half the night and on the way here seemed to have been wiped out of her memory.

The woman who now called herself Virginia approached slowly. Up close, Rachel could see that she, too, had gone pale. "Is there something wrong with our order?" she asked at last.

Her eyes never leaving the woman's face, Rachel shook her head.

Virginia gestured toward the house. "Would you care to come in?" She glanced beyond Rachel's shoulder, toward Gregory's car. "Is that gentleman a friend of yours?"

"Yes." There, that was better. Her voice was a little unsteady, but at least her vocal cords were functioning.

"Would he like to come in, too?"

"No. He'll... He wants to wait in the car." Her legs felt stiff and her hands clammy as she walked up the few steps to the porch.

The first thing that struck Rachel as she entered the house were the flowers. There were fresh bouquets everywhere, on the windowsill, on the coffee table, in a large urn near the front door. She loves flowers, too, Rachel thought. Just like I do.

"May I offer you something to drink?" the woman asked. "Some tea, perhaps? Or coffee?"

Rachel's throat was so tight, air barely passed through. "Nothing right now, Madame Laperousse."

"Oh, please call me Ginnie." They stood staring awkwardly at each other.

"Are you alone?" Rachel asked, throwing a quick glance around.

"Yes. My husband went down to the local bakery." She smiled. "I'm afraid I've become addicted to your doughnuts."

She was still pretending to be French, Rachel thought, or maybe she was waiting for Rachel to make the first move.

The next question put an end to her speculations. "You know, don't you?" Ginnie's voice was barely audible. "That's why you're here."

Rachel's heart thumped painfully against her rib cage. "Yes," she said in a strangled voice. "I think I knew the moment I first saw you. I just...didn't recognize the signs right away."

"Oh, Lillie!" Her eyes brimming with tears, Ginnie pressed her hands to her mouth as if to stop from crying. "My darling, beautiful little girl. You're here. You're really here."

Rachel wasn't sure who went to whom first, but suddenly they were in each other's arms, embracing and crying softly.

"I never thought I'd ever see you again," Ginnie whispered, holding her fiercely.

Emotions choking her, Rachel returned the embrace, burying her head into her mother's soft, scented hair. "And I never thought I'd find you."

Smiling through her tears, Ginnie pulled away and cupped Rachel's face between her hands. "Let me look at you. Really look at you." Her eyes swept over each feature.

"That picture didn't do you justice," she said. "You are so much more beautiful in person."

Rachel let herself be led to the sofa. "What picture?"

"The one in *Paris Match*. A photographer took it following your deal with Supermarchés Fronsac."

"Oh."

"That's how I found you. Hubert and I had just returned from vacation and I was catching up with my mail, leafing through the pages of the magazine, when I saw your picture. The resemblance was so striking...I didn't dare hope...and yet, I knew... I just knew it was you. And when I heard you lived in Napa Valley, so close to Santa Rosa, I no longer had any doubts."

"You took a great risk in coming here."

Ginnie's mouth curved into a lovely smile. "I would do it again, my darling, even if all we had was this moment." She took Rachel's hand. "But what about you? How did you know?"

"I told Gregory about you, about the way I felt drawn to you the other day when you took the tour."

"Gregory is the young man I saw outside?"

"Yes. He's a private investigator and has contacts all over the world. I gave him your name, which I took from the order form, and he called a friend of his at Interpol. A very discreet friend," she added as a look of alarm shadowed Ginnie's face. "He confirmed you were the former Virginia Potter."

Rachel wiped a tear. "I've been to France many times," she said. "And I could never explain why I felt such a strong attachment to that country, why I kept going back, time after time." She smiled. "Now I can. A part of me must have known you were there. I think Gregory sensed that before I did."

Ginnie's eyes twinkled. "You seem to be very fond of this Gregory," she remarked.

Rachel felt her cheeks heat up. At the same time she felt no qualms about opening up to this woman, or revealing her innermost thoughts, the way she had with Grams. "I guess I do," she said quietly. "Now."

"Do you trust him?"

"Totally," Rachel replied without a moment's hesitation.

"That's good." Ginnie smiled. "Trust is important in a relationship."

"I didn't say we were having a relationship." She felt the color in her cheeks intensify. "We're just friends." Then, before talk about Gregory got to be more than she could handle, she added, "Tell me about—"

The door was suddenly flung open and Mr. Laperousse, a small paper bag in his hands, stood on the threshold, looking worried as he glanced from his wife to Rachel.

"Qui est cet homme dehors?" he asked, probably unaware that Rachel understood French.

"It's all right, Hubert." Ginnie smiled. "Mr. Shaw is a friend of Rachel's." At the silent question in his eyes, she gave a slight nod. "Rachel knows, darling. She knows I'm her mother."

"Oh."

"There's nothing to worry about," she added reassuringly.

"Are you sure?"

"Yes."

"All right." He looked at Rachel again, then at his wife. There was relief in his eyes now. "In that case, I'll leave you two alone and go talk to that lonely young man out there. And I'll take this," he added, shaking the paper bag. "I don't think your mind is on doughnuts right now."

Rachel watched him leave. "You have a very nice husband," she said. "And he seems to love you very much."

Ginnie laughed, a soft, bubbly laugh that sounded totally free of worry, though that was probably not true. "I love him, too. Through the last thirty-one years, he's been my tower of strength, loving, dependable, solid. I don't know what I would have done without him, especially those first few months after I thought...you had died."

"Tell me about you." Rachel leaned forward. "Tell me everything."

Ginnie nodded. And began her incredible story.

"She didn't do it, Gregory." Back in the Jeep after her visit with her mother, Rachel snapped her seat belt on. "Alyssa, I mean...Ginnie didn't kill Mario. He was alive when she left that night."

At the end of the driveway, Gregory turned south on Route 29. "Then why did she run?"

"Because she was scared. She knew the police wouldn't believe her. She had very little time to make a decision and she made it, not knowing she'd come to regret it later." She repeated what Ginnie had told her up to the moment she had walked into the winery and had found herself face-to-face with her daughter.

"And there's something else," Rachel said when she was finished. "A month before Mario died, he told Ginnie that Nico, who was the company's treasurer at the time, might be embezzling money from the farm. He was going to look into it, but never mentioned it again. After a while, Ginnie forgot all about it."

Gregory nodded thoughtfully. "If Nico *was* embezzling money and he knew his brother suspected him, it would have given him one hell of a motive to kill Mario."

"Exactly." Tears stung her eyes. "Oh, Gregory, is there any way we can find out if that's true?"

Without taking his eyes off the road, Gregory put his hand on Rachel's and gripped it in a gentle squeeze. "I'm sure there is. Just let me think about it for a while, okay?"

While Sal hadn't expected to hear from Kelsey so soon, he was thrilled to get a call from his private investigator on Thursday morning. "Joe." He opened the humidor on the table and fingered a cigar. "You got something already?"

"Sort of. I've been following your granddaughter as you asked."

"Yes. And?"

"She's been spending a lot of time with Gregory Shaw, the man you asked me to check out last week."

Well, well, Sal mused. Rachel had enlisted the services of that private investigator. How clever of her. "What are they up to?"

"Well…" Kelsey's tone turned humble. "That's the part you're not going to like, Sal. A couple of hours ago, I took over the watch from one of my operatives." He sighed. "I lost them, Sal. That son of a bitch gave me the slip."

"What do you mean, you lost them?" Sal bellowed. "You're a private dick, for Christ's sake. Tailing people is your business. How the hell could you lose them?"

"Shaw tricked me. I followed them all the way to The Diner. It's a place in Yountville where a lot of tourists go for breakfast. When they went in, I went in, too, and had a cup of coffee at the counter, you know, in case they were planning to go in one way and out the other. When they ordered their food, I figured they'd be there for a while, so I went back to my car and waited for them to come out."

"Don't tell me," Sal said dryly. "They never did."

"No." Kelsey mumbled something Sal couldn't hear. "I talked to their waitress but she couldn't remember them because the place was so damned busy. They must have slipped through the back."

"What did they use for transportation?"

"They must have had another car waiting, because Shaw's Jaguar was still in the front lot."

"You stupid ass," Sal said disgustedly. "Shaw pulled the oldest trick in the book and you fell for it." He took a deep breath, then let it out.

"I'm sorry, Sal. I really am. It won't happen again, I swear."

"See that it doesn't. And find out where the fuck they went, you hear?" Enraged, Sal slammed down the phone.

Twenty-Eight

"So," Sam said as they were finishing dinner that night. "Gregory got the Jaguar back from The Diner okay?" Though he made a point of sounding matter-of-fact, Rachel could tell he was peeved to not have been included in their little intrigue.

She felt awful. In all the years she had known Sam and Tina, she had never lied to them. If it had been up to her, she would have told them everything right here and now, but Hubert and Ginnie had been adamant about that. No one must know they were here.

"Yes, he did." To avoid looking at him, she poured herself another cup of coffee. "And thanks for helping us, Sam. I appreciate it."

"No problem. Let me know if you need me to do that again."

She smiled at his not-so-subtle attempt to learn more. "I will." Then, finding that lying was much too stressful, she stood and started clearing the table.

Within moments Sam was in his favorite chair, reading the evening paper while Tina chatted about the upcoming Harvest Ball. "Are you planning to invite Gregory?" Tina asked as she stacked the dishes into the dishwasher.

Rachel shrugged. "I hadn't thought about it. To tell you the truth, I'm not even sure I'll be going this year. Without Grams there, I'd feel too sad."

"Oh, honey, your grandmother would be so upset if she knew you weren't going on account of her. This will be a wonderful opportunity for you to promote your wines."

"Promoting Spaulding wines is Annie's specialty. And she does it better than anyone I know."

Tina wrapped her arm around Rachel's shoulders and gave her an affectionate shake. "No one, not even Annie, has your passion for wines, honey, and conveys that passion better than you do. Think about that." Tina bent over the dishwasher and turned a knob. "And think about inviting Gregory. I bet he'd love escorting you to a fancy ball like that."

"Hmm. And I bet you've already mentioned it to him."

Tina gave her an innocent look. "And what's wrong with that?"

"What's wrong is that I've imposed on Gregory too much as it is, and asking him to come to the ball with me would be just one more imposition."

"Oh, nonsense. The man is crazy about you. You'd have to be blind not to see that."

"He's not," Rachel protested halfheartedly. "So don't you start getting ideas in that stubborn head of yours, do you hear?"

"Me?" Tina said. "Why would I be getting ideas?"

"Because you think Gregory and I are made for each other. Don't deny it," she added, catching Tina's quick smile. "I heard you and Sam talking the other night. You practically have me married to the man."

"I just want you to be happy, honey."

I'm happy, Rachel thought, wishing she could tell her friend why. More than you know.

It was ten-fifteen when Rachel said good-night to the Hughes and went back to her room. Lips pursed, she looked at the clock and wondered if it was too late to call Gregory. Taking a chance it wasn't, she picked up her cell phone and dialed his number.

"Hi," she said when he answered.

"Well, hello. I was just thinking about you. You've had quite a day."

"And I owe it all to you."

"I didn't do that much."

That was another side of him she was beginning to like very much. He was modest to a fault. "You were there for me, holding my hand, keeping my spirits up when they were sinking, giving me that last burst of courage when I needed it."

"I'm glad it all worked out for you and Ginnie."

"I'll never be able to repay you."

"Oh, I don't know. We might come up with something." His tone had turned playful. "What are you doing this weekend?"

"Well, let's see, on Saturday I've been invited to have lunch with Ginnie and Hubert. Beyond that, I have no plans. What about you? What are you doing?"

"I'm taking Noelle to a figure skating exhibition on Saturday afternoon, but I'm free on Sunday, so perhaps we could do something together."

"What did you have in mind?"

"How about dinner at my aunt's house in Sausalito?"

"Your aunt?"

He laughed. "You make her sound like a nuclear threat."

"Maybe that's because I've heard a lot about her and I'm a little intimidated."

"You don't have to be. She's a sweetheart. And very anxious to meet you."

"Why?"

"Oh, I don't know. I guess her journalistic nose couldn't take the suspense any longer. Don't worry, she doesn't know anything about Ginnie. That secret is safe."

"Good."

"So what do you say, Spaulding? I could use a bit of R and R myself."

The offer was tempting. "Well..."

"I'll come and get you."

"No, that would be too much driving for you."

"Then meet me at my apartment."

She wrote down the address and the directions to his condo. "About noon?" she asked.

"Perfect. Good night, Spaulding."

"Good night, Sherlock."

After hanging up, Rachel undressed, but instead of putting on a nightgown and going to bed, she slipped into a two-piece bathing suit and grabbed a thick towel from the stack in the bathroom.

Swimming always did wonders for her nerves, and she had fallen into the habit of going for a swim in the Hughes's pool every night after Sam and Tina went to bed. She loved it there, with the stars above her, the dark mountains in the distance, and the blissful silence broken only by the sound of the cicadas. Afraid the pool lights would shine into Sam and Tina's bedroom and wake them, she didn't turn them on.

The air was brisk when she stepped out onto the pool deck, but she knew the water would be warm in contrast. Shivering a little, she walked to the edge of the diving board, took a deep breath and dived in, headfirst.

She resurfaced within seconds and began swimming with long, powerful strokes. Back in high school, she had been on the swim team, and good enough to be considered Olympic potential. But when her parents were killed in that devastating balloon accident, Rachel had lost her zest for competitive swimming and quit the team.

At the shallow end, she touched the wall and started on her second lap, slicing the water even faster, enjoying the punishing physical effort, just as she had all those years ago.

You still have it, old girl. As if to prove it, she finished a third lap then dove deep and swam underwater, holding her breath for half the length of the pool before coming up for air.

Flipping onto her back, she swam the rest of the way in a lazy backstroke, remembering that in her days as a life-guard, she could hold her breath for a lot longer than—

Suddenly a hand grabbed her ankle in a steel grip.

Startled, Rachel's mouth opened but she never had a chance to scream. Whoever held her gave a vicious pull and she was yanked underwater and dragged to the bottom.

She wasn't sure where the fear ended and the need to survive took over. With that thought in mind, she started fighting her attacker furiously, kicking at his face, his stomach, every part of his body she could make contact with. Though she tried, she couldn't see his face, but she was certain it was a man.

The blows hardly seemed to affect him. With his right hand, he took a handful of her hair, swam back up and held her down, just below the surface. Even with her training, she was no match for him.

In a move she hadn't tried since a water rescue course years before, she pulled her knees to her chest and did a flip, kicking her assailant in the chest. As his grip loosened, she pushed away from him and shot out of the water like a rocket, choking and gasping for breath.

"Sam!" she cried. "Tina! Help!" She raced toward the edge, praying she'd have enough time to reach the ladder.

She never made it. In two fast strokes, the attacker was on her again. Holding the diving board with one hand, he gripped the back of her neck with the other and forced her down.

This time she knew it was hopeless, yet she fought him with every ounce of strength she had left. It just wasn't enough.

Her vision blurred, her lungs felt as though they were about to burst.

She was going to die.

Suddenly, a tremendous force broke through the water and the grip on her neck was released. Rachel wasted no time wondering how or why. Willing her legs to move, she gave a feeble kick, then another, and rose slowly to the surface.

Coughing and spitting water, she grabbed the pool's edge. A few feet from her, the water churned wildly as her assailant fought with Sam. Oh, God, she had to help him. She couldn't let Sam die because of her.

She started to swim in his direction just as Tina, a long-handled net in her hand, came running like a Viking warrior toward the pool.

"Get your hands off my husband, you bastard!"

As the first blow caught him on the back of the head, the attacker lifted himself out of the pool and took off at a dead run, scooping up his clothes in one quick motion.

Tina dropped the net and knelt on the concrete. "Sam, honey, are you all right?"

"I'm okay." He turned to Rachel, who could barely tread water. "Rachel?"

Too weak to talk, Rachel just nodded, and let herself be pulled out of the water. She would have gladly collapsed on the concrete deck but didn't want to alarm Tina, so she just sat there, arms braced behind her, eyes closed, breathing hard.

She heard Tina's anxious voice. "Sam, is she okay? Should we call a doctor?"

"I'm fine," Rachel heard herself murmur. "Just need…a moment…"

"My poor baby." Kneeling beside her, Tina wrapped her in a thick towel and held her tightly.

When Rachel opened her eyes again, the pool area was brilliantly lit and Sam, his pajamas dripping, was staring toward a grove of thick eucalyptus trees into which the attacker had disappeared.

"Did you see who it was?" he asked.

Rachel shook her head. "It happened so fast. All my concentration went into holding my breath and staying alive. I know he was tall, broad-shouldered, and quick on his feet. That's about all I can tell you."

Once again, she thought of Nico. He had the same build, and Sal had said something about him being a good swimmer. "Almost as good as the old man," he had told Rachel with a grin.

But how could Nico have known she was staying with the Hughes when she hadn't told anyone except Gregory, Annie, and Courtney? And even if he had managed to find out, how would he know she always swam at this time of night?

"Detective Crowley is here," Tina said as a set of headlights came up the driveway.

"How did he…?"

"I called him."

Rachel nodded. Here we go again, she thought. Then, exhausted, she leaned against the lounge chair and waited for the detective.

* * *

"I found out where they went, Sal." This time Kelsey's voice was so excited, the words blurted through the phone like a geyser. "No wonder they gave me the slip."

"Out with it, Joe," Sal said impatiently.

"Alyssa is here. In Napa Valley. She rented a house in Calistoga. That's where Rachel and Shaw went the other day."

The old heart started beating so fast, Sal thought it would explode. He sat. Thirty-one years of not knowing where she was, of wondering if he'd ever find her, if he'd ever have the chance to avenge his son's death. There was a God, after all. And he had heard him.

"How can you be sure it's her?"

"Rachel went back to see her. This time she went alone. She took a few detours, too, but she wasn't able to give me the slip the way Shaw did. She drove me straight to a small house Alyssa and her husband—a Frenchman, I learned—are renting."

"And you're sure the woman is Alyssa."

"No mistake about it, Sal. I had my binoculars on her when she opened the door. She's Rachel's spitting image."

"The kid stayed there long?"

"Only a few minutes, then she went to the winery."

"You got an address?" Sal asked.

"And a phone number." This time Kelsey's tone was smug. "I found out her new name is Virginia Laperousse."

With a hand he tried to keep steady, Sal wrote down the information. "You did good, Joe," he said, figuring Kelsey was due for a little praise. "I won't forget." He dropped his pen back onto the desk. "Alyssa's old man ever go out of the house?"

"I don't know."

"Find out and call me back," he said before hanging up.

He had her. He was finally going to be face-to-face with the slut who had killed his son.

Too excited to stand still, he began pacing the room, his mind already working. Before he could do anything he had to convince Alyssa to meet him somewhere. What good was knowing where she was if he couldn't get to her? His mind was a blank right now, but he'd think of something.

His step quicker than usual, he walked down the hall to his office. Since his retirement, he seldom went there anymore, but Maria knew better than to ignore this room in her daily cleaning.

Once there, he closed the door, locked it and went straight to the far wall where a large safe was hidden behind an oil painting of his native Pozzuoli.

He worked the combination lock quickly, his fingers spinning and stopping on the numbers he knew by heart. Inside the safe were a handful of documents that had been there for years—his birth certificate, his naturalization papers and a passport that he kept current though he didn't know why. He hadn't gone back to Italy in more than a decade.

Behind those documents, and occupying the rest of the space, were stacks and stacks of hundred-dollar bills in neat bundles, money the IRS knew nothing about. Reaching under one stack, he felt the .45-caliber Colt he had stolen from one of his workers thirty-one years ago, when he'd first started looking for Alyssa. He had kept it in perfect condition all this time, taking it out once or twice a year to clean it, waiting for the moment he could use it.

The moment had come.

Alongside the Colt was a box of ammunition. He took that, too. Then after closing the safe, he went to sit at his desk and set the gun and the box of ammo down.

A smile on his lips and a glint in his eyes, he began to load the clip.

Twenty-Nine

"What's the matter, Spaulding?" Gregory asked as he walked onto Sam's deck where Rachel was sitting. "You're going for a record here?"

Rachel smiled. She preferred humor over concern. She'd had enough of the latter from Sam and Tina to last her a lifetime. Humor kept her grounded. And it kept the fear at bay.

Breaking her own rules, she had called Gregory early that morning and told him about last night's attack, knowing he'd be furious if she didn't. She had tried to tell him it wasn't necessary for him to come over, she was fine, unharmed, in good spirits, but as usual, he hadn't listened.

"What's Crowley saying?" he asked, sitting and helping himself to a cup of coffee from the pot on the redwood table.

"Nothing encouraging, but then I didn't give him much to work with. All I know is that the man who attacked me last night and the one who tried to run me off the road last week *could* have been one and the same, but other than that...."

She cursed herself for not having been more observant. At one time, as she and her attacker had struggled in the water, she could have tried to make out a few details—the length of his hair or the width of his shoulders. But the fear had blocked everything, except that basic instinct to survive.

"Have you told the rest of your family? Or Ginnie?"

"No," she said quickly. "And I won't. Detective Crowley agrees it's not necessary. I also asked him not to question my staff anymore. It's not an inside job, Gregory," she added when she saw irritation flare in his eyes. "And I'd be insulting everyone who works at Spaulding Vineyards if I kept them under this constant cloud of suspicion."

She stood and moved to the railing, her muscles aching from last night's exertion. "We've already lost a couple of big clients. If the news of what happened last night gets out, either through the police or through unhappy employees, we could lose even more."

Gregory came to stand beside her. "You're not responsible for what some maniac is doing to you."

"People don't care whether or not I'm responsible. Too often in business, your success is based not on your performance but on how people perceive you. Image is everything. That's why Grams was so adamant about not tarnishing the Spaulding name."

Taking her shoulders, he turned her around. The gesture was so tender, she wanted to lean her head on his shoulder and wait for all her troubles to go away.

"It's going to be all right, Rachel," he said quietly. "We're going to find this bozo. I don't care how clever he thinks he is, sooner or later he's going to make a mistake."

"I hope so." She looked up. "How are you making out in the case against my mother?"

"I've got a couple of leads. I'll tell you about them later, when I know more." He let go of her shoulders. "Are we still on for Sunday?"

At the thought of spending an afternoon in a beautiful

and totally different setting, her spirits lifted considerably. "I wouldn't miss it for the world."

Her straw basket hooked over her arm, Ginnie walked to the daisy patch behind the cottage. Yesterday, when Rachel had stopped by for a few minutes on her way to work, Ginnie had learned that daisies were her favorite flowers. So, tomorrow, when she came for lunch, the house would be filled with them. And there would be a huge bouquet for her to take home later.

The thought of having her daughter over for a meal, something mothers around the world did routinely, filled her with an overwhelming joy. And a certain apprehension. She wanted everything to be perfect, right down to the smallest detail.

She would set the table in the garden, under that lovely old oak, and, of course, they would serve Spaulding wines—a crisp Chardonnay for the first course and Rachel's prize-winning Cabernet to go with the roasted leg of lamb. Since Spaulding Vineyards didn't make champagne, Rachel had recommended an excellent one from Kornell Champagne Cellars, right here in Calistoga. Hubert, who loved sparkling wine, had ordered two cases.

"We'll celebrate your reunion with your daughter every day of our stay in Napa Valley," he had told Ginnie.

The daisy patch stretched all the way from the clothesline to the start of the wooded area, forming a blanket of white flowers that looked as spectacular inside as they did outside.

Humming an old nursery rhyme she used to sing to Lillie, Ginnie began clipping, filling her basket and wishing it were already tomorrow.

As she circled the water well, she heard a snapping sound in the woods, as if someone or something had stepped on a dry branch. Thinking a wild animal had probably strayed too far from home, Ginnie looked up, half expecting to see a frightened deer scurry away, as they did back in the Auvergne.

But there was no deer, just tall trees and thick bushes—and a sudden silence as the birds stopped chirping.

Ginnie had just returned her attention to her flower cutting when she heard the shot.

She jumped back, dropping her basket and looking wildly around her, not sure where the shot had come from, or if it even was a gunshot. Had hunting season already started? If so, she would have to talk to Hubert to see if the rental agency would place a No Hunting sign on the property.

Hubert, she knew, would laugh at her fears. A born hunter, he filled their freezer every winter with all sorts of game. Ginnie, on the other hand, hated guns and saw no justification, not even hunting, for normal citizens to own them.

Crouching down, she picked up the flowers that had fallen and put them back in the basket.

A second shot rang out, this one louder and much closer.

Ginnie let out a cry of alarm. Angry, as well as frightened, she clutched her basket and took a step back. This was no stray gunfire. Whoever had fired that last shot was much too close. Though accidents happened all too often, a hunter would have a hard time convincing her he had made a mistake. In her white slacks and bright orange top, she could hardly be mistaken for a deer.

So if it wasn't a careless hunter, who was it? Her mouth dry, she licked her lips and slowly backed away. No, she thought, shaking her head. It couldn't be. Not Sal.

She continued to walk backward, too frightened to turn her back on the dense forest where someone could so easily be hiding. When nothing happened, she scolded herself. This was silly. What would Sal be doing here? He was miles away, holed up in his big, lonely house, probably counting his millions. And no one, except Gregory and Rachel, knew that the Frenchwoman in the yellow cottage was in reality Alyssa Dassante.

A light honk told her Hubert was back from the doughnut shop. After a last worried glance toward the wooded area, she turned and ran to meet him.

Sal chuckled as he watched Alyssa run like a scared rabbit. Standing behind an evergreen, he lifted the Colt to his mouth and kissed it. This baby wasn't the most accurate gun in the world, but it sure could make a racket. The look on Alyssa's face when she had heard that second shot was worth all the trouble he had gone to getting here and finding this hiding place.

His first intention had been to simply kill her on the spot.

"She spends a lot of time in the garden," Kelsey had told him. "And in the morning, her husband goes out for the paper and doughnuts."

One shot, two at the most, and his nightmare would be over, his duty toward his son accomplished. After a while, he had decided against the idea. A quick death was not what he wanted for that bitch. He wanted her to suffer, to beg. He wanted her to be scared shitless and to know, not only that she was going to die, but exactly who had killed her.

So today, he had played with her. And he had been well rewarded. For a moment he had been tempted to fire a third shot, just to see that trapped look on Alyssa's face again. Too bad her husband had come back so soon.

He tucked the gun into his belt and buttoned his jacket.

The weapon made the garment bulge, but that was all right. He didn't have far to walk.

Whistling happily, he turned and followed the same narrow path down the hillside he'd traveled up earlier, and headed for his car, parked below, behind an old abandoned paper mill.

Suspicious of Nico from the start, Gregory had already learned a few interesting facts about the younger Dassante son. The first was that, contrary to what many believed, Nico didn't own Dassante Farms. He simply ran it.

The second was equally enlightening. At twenty-one, while serving in the army, Nico had been caught stealing money from the N.C.O. club where he moonlighted as a bartender. He was court-martialed, found guilty and kicked out of the army with a dishonorable discharge.

It may not sound like much, Gregory thought as he drove south on Route 29, but it proved one thing—Nico had larceny in his heart. And if Mario's suspicions about his brother turned out to be true, Nico could be much more than an embezzler. He could be a murderer.

Gregory's first stop was Rio Vista, a small town twenty miles or so south of Winters. The police report on Mario Dassante's death had mentioned an employee, an eighteen-year-old by the name of Luis Ventura who claimed to have witnessed several violent arguments between Mario and Alyssa thirty-one years ago.

Luis was a man now and the owner of a small grocery store in the center of town.

Standing out of the way, Gregory watched the stocky, dark-haired man in the white apron cut neatly and forcefully through a wheel of Parmesan cheese.

"Here you go, Mrs. Delanco," he said, tossing the wedge on the digital scale. "Half a pound exactly."

The customer shook her head in wonder. "I don't know how you do it, Luis." She handed him a bill. "You're never an ounce over, or under."

Smiling affably, Luis made change for her and said goodbye before turning to Gregory. "And for you, sir?"

Pulling away from the ice-cream freezer, Gregory came forward, hand extended. "How are you, Mr. Ventura? My name is Gregory Shaw."

Looking puzzled, Luis nevertheless wiped his hands on his apron and shook Gregory's hand. "Pleased to meet you, Mr. Shaw."

"I'm here for some information."

"About what?"

"Something that happened a long time ago." As the man's friendly smile cooled a little, Gregory added, "I understand you were employed at Dassante Farms at the time Mario Dassante was killed."

This time the smile faded completely. "That's right."

"And, according to the police report, you used to work at the processing plant, is that right? Close to Mario's office?"

Shrewd dark eyes surveyed him. "What exactly do you do, Mr. Shaw?"

"I'm a private investigator. I'm looking into the death of Mario Dassante."

"His father hired you?"

Gregory smiled. "Hardly."

"Then who?"

"Someone interested in uncovering the truth. That's all I can say at the moment."

Luis shrugged. "Okay. But if you read the police report, what do you want with me?"

The man was smart and he was quick. "I like to get my information firsthand."

Taking a cloth from under the counter, Luis began wiping the already gleaming glass case under which an assortment of cheeses and meats were displayed. "You came to the wrong guy, mister. All I know about Mario Dassante's death is what's in that report and what I read in the newspapers. My answers aren't going to change."

"Perhaps," Gregory suggested gently, "you weren't asked the right questions."

"And what kind of questions would *you* be asking?"

"Oh, I'd be asking if you had ever heard Mario and Alyssa argue about someone in particular. Like a jealous admirer, maybe? Someone who could have had a reason for wanting Mario dead?"

Luis gave a hearty laugh. "A better question would be who did *not* have a reason to kill him."

"People hated him that much?"

"Yep." He kept wiping the display case.

Luis was a man of few words. Maybe a more direct approach would have better results. "Can you tell me what Mario and Alyssa argued about?"

"Always the same thing. She wanted better conditions for the field workers and he didn't want her butting in."

"Is that why the workers liked her?"

"That's right."

"Did you like her, too?"

"Sure, I did."

"Then why did you mention those arguments to the police? You had to know your statement would make their case against her that much stronger."

Luis's face remained impassive. "The cops scared the hell out of me, that's why. They said if I didn't tell them what I knew, they'd have me and my family deported. I couldn't afford that. I already had a wife, and a baby on the way, and I needed the work. I didn't mean Mrs. Dassante any harm. I just had no choice.''

"So, no one coached you on what to say to the police?''

"No, no one coached me. Why would you think that?''

"Because Sal Dassante was very anxious to pin this murder on his daughter-in-law.''

Luis shrugged. "I wouldn't know about that.''

"What about Nico?" Gregory pressed. "Did you ever hear him and Mario argue?''

Luis kept his eyes on his task. "No, they got along okay.''

Gregory kept watching Luis as he tossed his cloth under the counter before moving to a small sink to wash his hands. He liked the man, but something about him, about his body language and the way he kept averting his eyes, made him wonder if Luis was telling him all he knew.

"Did you ever hear anyone talking, either the workers or the bosses, about any embezzling going on at the farms?''

"Can't say I did.''

Behind Gregory a bell tinkled and a new customer walked in.

Luis looked up. "How you're doing today, Mr. Finch?'' He raised an eyebrow in Gregory's direction. "Anything else you wanted to know?''

Gregory shook his head. "No, Mr. Ventura. Thanks for your time.''

Luis remained on Gregory's mind for much of the trip back to San Francisco. He had been hopeful that Dassante's former employee would have recalled something important, but that hadn't happened.

Unless Luis was lying.

Willie McBride's house was a charming two-story Victorian painted candy pink and as pretty on the inside as it was on the outside. Her studio, which was drenched in sunshine when Rachel and Gregory arrived shortly after noon on Sunday, was an explosion of colors. Paintings of people and places were everywhere—hung on the walls, stacked against them and propped up on easels.

Willie herself was a dynamo of a woman, friendly, down to earth and a fabulous cook. Almost as good as Ginnie, Rachel thought with fond memories of yesterday's wonderful lunch.

"I can only do two things," Willie told Rachel as she carved a roasted chicken that smelled like Provence. "Run a newspaper and cook, but I'm damned good at both."

After dinner Willie turned down their offer to help with the cleanup and sent them out to the porch to watch a regatta race already in progress.

"So, what do you think of Willie so far?" Gregory asked as they stood at the railing.

"You were right, she's wonderful. And I love the relationship between the two of you. You're more like two best friends than aunt and nephew."

"Willie can be everything, your best friend, your big sister, the mother you never had. When I was growing up I spent all my weekends with her even though she lived in Sacramento. My father would put me on a plane Friday afternoon after school and I'd come back on Sunday evening. The visits got less frequent when I started college, but from the moment Noelle was born, I made it a point to take her there every chance I had."

"Does Noelle love your aunt as much as you do?"

"She adores her. And, of course, Willie spoils her rotten. Lindsay, however, was another story."

"She didn't like Willie?"

"She didn't have anything against Willie. It was the trek

to Sacramento she objected to. She hates anything outside the city limits.''

Rachel gazed into the distance where a lovely red-and-white sailboat was beginning to pull away from the others. ''Your ex-wife reminds me a lot of Preston,'' she said. ''He's a city boy through and through, and the mere thought he might have to live in the valley after we were married gave him chills.''

''Couldn't you have found something halfway?''

She remembered the long, tedious discussions, Preston's refusal to compromise, her own frustration. ''I suggested that, but for Preston it was San Francisco or nothing. Arguing was too exhausting, so I gave in.''

''Are you over him now?'' Gregory asked after a short silence. ''I mean...completely?''

She turned to find his gaze on her. ''Yes,'' she said quietly. ''I'm completely over him.''

Smiling, he wrapped an arm around her and pulled her close as he returned his attention to the boat race. ''I'm very glad to hear that.''

It was five o'clock by the time they reached the parking garage where Rachel had left her Jeep.

''Why don't you let me drive you home,'' Gregory said as they walked along a deserted aisle on the second level. ''I'd feel much better if you didn't have to make the trip back alone.''

Rachel gave a shake of her head. ''Absolutely not. I won't deny that the attack in the pool the other night frightened me, but I refuse to live my life in a state of constant fear. I'll be careful, Gregory, but that's all I'll concede to.''

He sighed but didn't press her.

''In the meantime,'' she said with a grateful smile, ''thanks for a lovely day. It was just what I needed.''

"I hope you'll come back often."

"Just say the word and I'll be there." They had reached the white Jeep and Rachel was already rummaging through her tote bag in search of her keys. "And maybe one Sunday, you could bring Willie to—"

She never had a chance to fully extend the invitation. Gripping her shoulders, Gregory pulled her to him and kissed her. This time it wasn't a quick peck and an even quicker dismissal, but a hot, passionate kiss that triggered yearnings she had sworn to never experience again.

It would have been easy enough to pull away from him, had she wanted to. And she should have wanted to. Her recent breakup with Preston had left her disillusioned and vulnerable, and in no condition to handle a new romance.

So why was she kissing him back? Why were her arms, obviously powered by a will of their own, coiling around his neck as her body leaned against his so shamelessly?

She never got around to answering her own questions. Overwhelmed by sensations and longings that made her head swim, she deepened the kiss as a delicious ache shifted deep within her.

His hands were all over her now, touching her face, skimming her throat, lingering on her breasts, heating her from head to toe. She had never been touched that way before, with such gentleness, such…restrained passion.

Deep down, an alarm rang. *It's too soon, you're not ready.* The warning was like a chant, impossible to ignore. Using every ounce of willpower she could summon, Rachel put her hands on Gregory's chest and gently pushed him away. "I'm sorry, I shouldn't have…"

"I started it." He stopped to take a deep breath. "But if you expect me to apologize, you could be waiting a very long time. I'm not one bit sorry I did that. In fact, if you don't leave right now, I might just do it again."

From the hot, lusty expression in his eyes she had no doubt he meant every word. Before he could see how badly she wanted him to kiss her again, she opened the driver's door. "In that case, I'd better go."

He held her hand while she jumped in. "Call me as soon as you get home so I'll know you made it there safely."

"I will."

With the taste of his lips on hers, she drove off.

Thirty

Ginnie had never been so happy. After more than three decades, the daughter she thought she had lost forever had been given back to her.

Following Saturday's absolutely perfect alfresco lunch, Hubert had excused himself and the two women had spent the afternoon catching up.

Ginnie had wanted to know everything about her daughter, where she had gone to school, the sports she had played, even the boys she had dated.

"Preston was a fool," she said when Rachel told her about the breakup. "But I agree with your friend Tina. You're better off without him. Gregory, on the other hand, seems like a wonderful man. Hubert is very fond of him."

Though Rachel had made no comment, Ginnie could tell the relationship between those two was a lot more than Rachel wanted to admit, but that was all right. There would be plenty of opportunities in the next few months for long mother/daughter talks. They had already made plans for Rachel to come and visit her in France. Ginnie would show her the Auvergne, climb the rugged mountains with her and swim in the crystal lake on the Laperousse property.

"A penny for your thoughts."

As Hubert, who had come from behind, bent to kiss the back of her neck, Ginnie smiled. "Oh, Hubert, I'm so happy. Now I truly have everything a woman could possibly want.''

"How can that be?" he said, his voice teasing. "You haven't had your jelly doughnut yet."

She laughed. "That's true. I'm beginning to feel very deprived."

He kissed her again. "In that case, I must hurry."

She watched him drive away in the cream-colored, nondescript sedan they had rented at the San Francisco airport. Dear Hubert. He had been so worried about the trip, so frightened she might be recognized, but now, finally, he was beginning to relax. She had been nervous, too, until she had realized there was nothing to fear. Though Alyssa Dassante and her daughter had elicited a great deal of interest throughout the valley, no one had made any connection between Rachel Spaulding and the woman in the rented cottage.

Even those two gunshots in the garden on Friday, which Hubert had reported to the rental agent, were forgotten. She was much too happy to burden herself with silly, unfounded fears.

She was still smiling when the phone rang. Wondering if it could be Rachel, she hurried to answer it. "Hello?"

There was a short silence then a voice she thought she'd never hear again said, *"Buon giorno, Alyssa."*

The breath went out of her as if she had been punched in the chest. Her legs suddenly weak, Ginnie gripped the arm of the chair beside her then slowly sank into it. "Sal?" Her voice sounded faraway, as though it belonged to someone else.

"You didn't forget my name. That's good, Alyssa, because I didn't forget yours."

"How...how did you find me?"

He laughed. "This is old Sal you're talking to, Alyssa. I find out everything—sooner or later."

"What do you want?" It took all her willpower to keep her voice on an even keel, not to let him sense she was terrified.

"To talk," he said, surprising her.

She gazed out the open window, toward the woods. "I have nothing to say to you, Sal."

"You know," he said, his voice remarkably calm, "for a long time that's what I thought, too. All I cared about was that you had killed my son and you had to pay."

Ginnie shivered and said nothing.

"Things are different now," Sal continued. "There's Rachel."

Rachel. Her stomach began to churn. Did he know she had come here? What a stupid question. Of course he knew. If he knew she was in Napa Valley, he had to know Rachel had been here. He may even be the one who had fired those shots. "What does Rachel have to do with anything?" she asked.

"Well, for starters, she's got this crazy idea you didn't kill Mario."

"I didn't."

"I'm not so sure about that, but like I said, Rachel does, and because of that, because of her, I'm willing to listen to what you have to say."

"Is she aware…"

"That I know you're here? Not yet. But she already knows I've dropped my vendetta against you."

"You will never do that."

"I already did. I fired my private detective and I canceled the reward."

She couldn't verify his claim about the private detective, but she knew he had canceled the reward. Rachel had showed her the article that had appeared in the *Winters Journal*.

In spite of Sal's apparent willingness to let bygones be bygones, Ginnie hadn't been as quick to accept his change of heart as Rachel seemed to be. The Sal she knew was crafty and as dangerous as a shark. He could say one thing and turn around and do another. "Why would you be interested in my side of the story all of a sudden?"

"Because that will make my granddaughter happy. She'll realize I'm a fair man, a man of my word. And who knows? If you convince me you didn't kill Mario, maybe I can convince the cops. That really would impress Rachel."

"You would do that?" she asked.

"Yes, I would. For Rachel. How much are you willing to do for your daughter, Alyssa?"

For a moment, Ginnie allowed herself to believe him. Wouldn't it be wonderful to no longer be a fugitive? To come and go between France and the U.S. as she pleased, to see Rachel walk around with her head held high.

But what if Sal's seemingly genuine offer was nothing but a trick? What if the police showed up instead of him? "How can I trust you, Sal?" she asked, desperately wanting to. "What if you show up with the police?"

"And risk never seeing my granddaughter again? You gotta be kidding. I love that kid. I'm not gonna lose her now that I found her."

"I don't know if I can trust you. You're an evil man, Sal Dassante."

"Not when it comes to my family. You, more than anyone, should know that."

She did. No man had been more devoted to his family than Sal. And he had adored Lillie, had doted on her like a proud grandpa during those first two weeks. The affection she heard in his voice now as he talked about Rachel was no act. It was genuine.

"What have you got to lose in talking to me, Alyssa?" he asked, as though he knew she needed a little more convincing. "I know where you are. One word to the Calistoga police and you'll be behind bars forever. At least this way you got a chance."

In the warm, cozy little cottage, she felt suddenly cold. Yet outside everything was the same, calm and peaceful with only the muted sound of traffic in the distance. Sal was right. Any moment now, her wonderful world could fall apart, her freedom taken away from her. She thought of the things she and Rachel had planned to do together, the simple joy of just looking at her daughter, holding her hand, being her confidante. All that would be gone the moment those prison cell doors closed behind her.

Unless she did as Sal asked.

"Did you come here the other day?" she asked abruptly. "Was that you who shot at me?"

There was a short silence, then a sarcastic laugh. "What the hell are you talking about, shooting? Are you crazy? You think I play games like that?"

"I wouldn't put it past you."

"Why would I shoot at you?"

"To frighten me. To let me know you're in control."

"That's stupid. I don't even own a gun. And even if I did, you think I'd risk being arrested just to scare you?" He laughed again. "Maybe the old Sal, but not Rachel's grandpa."

She thought about that for several seconds, torn. "Where do you want to meet?" she asked at last. Oh, God, was she serious? Was she really going to meet this man? This man, who for thirty-one years had wanted only one thing—to kill her. I'm doing it for Rachel, she thought resolutely. So she can never be labeled a murderer's daughter again.

"Well…" He seemed to ponder the question for a few seconds. "I don't suppose you would want to come here?"

"No!" What made him think she'd ever want to see that house again? "It's too far."

"Okay," Sal said in a conciliatory tone. "We can meet someplace close to you. You pick it. You know the area better than I do. Make it at night, though. I don't want my family to know about this and think I'm getting soft."

Ginnie thought for a while. Yes, nighttime would be best for her, too. And it had to be somewhere safe, quiet. "There's a small church on the outskirts of Calistoga," she said, remembering passing it the other night. "At the intersection of Route 128 and Petrified Forest Road. It's open all night."

"I'll be there. When?"

"Tonight? At about eleven?"

"Eleven it is. And don't do anything cute, Alyssa."

"Like what?"

"Like taking off again. I've got a man watching your house. One step out of it between now and eleven this evening and I'm calling the cops."

The anxiety in her gut wound even tighter. He had thought of everything. "I'll see you tonight," she said.

"*Arrivederci, Alyssa.*"

"What are you grinning about?" Nico asked Sal as the two men sat in the livingroom, having a late afternoon drink.

At the question, Sal leaned back in his chair and looked at his son, savoring the moment. "Alyssa is here," he said slowly. "In California. Napa Valley to be exact."

Nico stared at him in shock. "What are you talking about? What the hell would she be doing here?"

"She found out Lillie was alive and she came. Kelsey found her."

"Where has she been all this time?"

"I don't know and I don't care. She's here now. That's all that matters."

"The cops know?"

Sal shook his head and sipped his sherry. "No, and we're not gonna tell them."

"Why the hell not?"

"Because I want to hear what she has to say first."

"Since when you give a fuck what Alyssa has to say?"

"Since I realized it would make a difference to Rachel."

"Rachel!" Nico threw his hands up in the air. "I should have known. First it was Mario. Now it's Rachel. Rachel, Rachel, Rachel. That's all I fucking hear all day."

"Mind your language when you speak about my grand-daughter," Sal said sharply.

Nico didn't seem to have heard him. "You don't want to hear what Alyssa has to say, Pop. You want to kill her. You're using that as an excuse to get her to come to you."

Sal chuckled inwardly. The kid wasn't so thick, after all. "You're wrong," he lied. "I'm too old to keep carrying a grudge. If she's innocent, I want to know it."

"Bull. You're going to kill her. You're going to destroy this family."

"Oh, stop the *High Noon* garbage, Nico. I told you, all I want to do is talk to her. If she's lying, I'll call the cops."

Nico still wasn't convinced. "Where are you meeting her? When?"

"Don't know that yet," he lied again.

"You can't go alone, Pop. You'll lose your cool. I know you will. Let me come with you."

"You're starting to piss me off, Nico."

"Then I'm going to tell Erica. She'll put some sense into that thick skull of yours."

She could try, Sal thought as he took another sip of his sherry. She could try until she turned blue, for all he cared. It wouldn't change a damm thing.

He sat there for several minutes, ignoring Nico, who kept mouthing off, and thought about his phone call to Alyssa. He hadn't been sure at first if she would buy his story about a man watching her house, but he could tell by the sound of her voice that she had. She would stay put. Until tonight when she went to that church to meet him.

And the rest would soon be history.

Several cars were parked on Petrified Forest Road when Ginnie arrived a few minutes after eleven, but only one was in front of St. Mary's Church—an old Plymouth station wagon as big as a hearse. It had to be Sal's. Who else would drive such a relic?

The small overnight bag she had packed earlier while Hubert had been outside gardening sat on the floor on the passenger side. Inside her purse were her passport and a thousand dollars in traveler's checks. It would be enough for a one-way ticket back to Europe. Not France, where she might be found, but somewhere else, the Netherlands, perhaps, or Sweden.

She couldn't bear the thought of being on the run again, of leaving Hubert and everything she loved behind. But if something inside that church went wrong and she had enough time to escape, at least she had the means to do so.

Her body rigid with apprehension, she brought the car to a stop behind the station wagon and shone her high beams into it. No one was inside, and there was no sign of activity on the deserted road. She stepped out of her car.

Wrapping her arms around her midriff to ward off the sudden chill, she glanced toward the church. Behind a stained-glass window, a light, probably a candle, flickered.

The church door was closed but unlocked. As she pushed it open, the familiar smell of incense brought back vague memories. Moderately religious, she had stopped going to church after Lillie's death and had never stepped inside a place of worship again.

This particular church was small, with six rows of wooden pews on each side and a pulpit. High above it was a life-size statue of the Virgin Mary, her hands raised in a blessing. The only light came from a row of candles in various sizes, their flickering flames throwing oddly shaped shadows on the wall.

A man sat in the first pew, his head bowed. Sal, she thought. She began walking toward him, barely making a sound in her crepe-soled shoes. With each step, she cast quick furtive glances around her, half expecting to see a uniformed cop jump out, his gun pointed at her.

"What am I doing here?" she murmured, once again second guessing her decision. "I must be crazy."

She stopped, aware that her heart was beating erratically. Out of the corner of her eye, she caught a shadow. Stifling a cry, she glanced in that direction, only to realize the shadow came from a pillar candle.

She reached the pew where Sal was seated, obviously praying. Should she wait until he was finished? she wondered. Or should she let him know she was here? She longed to be back in the little cottage, in the warm bed with Hubert's body next to hers. That thought made the decision for her.

She lay a hand on her ex-father-in-law's shoulder. "Sal?"

He didn't reply or acknowledge her presence in any way.

"Sal," she said again, hoping she wasn't committing some sort of sacrilege. "I can't stay long...." She gripped his arm and shook it gently.

And choked back a cry.

Sal's head lolled back. His eyes, a glassy, lifeless hazel, stared at her.

A pair of scissors stuck out of his bloody chest.

Thirty-One

Ginnie's hand flew to her mouth. For a moment her feet seemed nailed to the floor as a voice inside her head screamed, Run, run.

"Sal," she said at last. "Oh, my God. Sal. Oh, my God." As her legs began functioning once again, she took a step back, then another. On the third step, she bumped into something solid.

With a gasp, she spun around. A young man, a priest, she realized as her frightened gaze took in the white collar, stood behind her.

"Are you all right?" he asked anxiously. "Someone just called to report a disturbance..." He glanced above her shoulder, toward the pew where Sal sat, and let the rest of his sentence go unfinished. "Excuse me for a minute."

As he started walking toward Sal, Ginnie ran out.

"What do you mean, we're through?" Ryan stood in Annie's office, his face white with shock, his eyes filled with anguish. "I love you. We're going to get married."

"That's just it, Ryan. We're *not* going to get married. Except in your fantasies."

Sitting at her desk, Annie watched Ryan with a mixture of pity and worry. He looked like a bomb about to go off. If she'd known he'd take it so badly, she wouldn't have been so blunt, but dammit, she was fed up with his jealousy, with his references to a marriage that would never happen. It was time to end this ridiculous relationship. And if bluntness was what it took for her message to get through, so be it.

"Fantasies?" His mouth pulled into something resembling more of a grimace than a smile. "Is that what you think? That I'm some dumb jock fantasizing about the girl of my dreams?"

"I never called you a dumb j—"

"You're the one who's fantasizing, Annie, if you think I'm going to let you go." He walked toward her slowly, until he stood only a couple of feet from her. "I'll never do that. I have risked too much for you."

"What are you talking about? What have you risked?"

"Everything—my job, my reputation, my future as a successful winemaker. And how do you thank me? By dumping me."

Annie nervously licked her lips. He was acting totally out of character, and his eyes burned with a strange intensity. Still, she refused to let him intimidate her. "I have no idea what you're talking about," she said calmly.

"You used me, Annie." His voice was thin and nasty, not cajoling as it had been a moment ago. "You got me to do your dirty little deed, and when it didn't turn out as you hoped, you decided to dump me."

"Dammit, Ryan, will you stop talking in riddles. What dirty little deed?"

"Getting rid of Rachel!"

Annie's mouth opened but no sound came out. It was her turn to experience cold, paralyzing shock as the horrible truth dawned on her. "What did you do, Ryan?" she asked in a whisper.

He laughed, a short, brittle laugh that sent a shiver down her back. "Oh, listen to you, innocent little Annie. If I didn't know any better, I'd almost buy the act. 'What did you do, Ryan?'" His mimicking of her voice was perfect, and frightening. "I almost killed for you, baby." This time he brought his face a scant three inches from hers. "How does that grab you? Yeah, that's right," he added as she stared at him. "I'm the guy who let those barrels loose on Rachel. And tried to run her off the road. And attempted to drown her in the Hughes's pool."

Stunned, Annie could only stare at him.

He laughed. "I see she didn't tell you about the pool fight, huh? I almost had her there," he boasted. "I remembered too late what a strong swimmer she was, still is."

"Why?" Annie cried. "Why would you want to kill Rachel?"

"So we could be together! I hated it when you said you couldn't marry me because of her. Why should she stand in the way of our happiness?" His eyes burned even brighter. "So I thought, with Rachel gone we could both have what we wanted. You would have Spaulding, which I know you want more than anything in the world, and I would have you."

Something about the way he said those last four words sent a chill along her spine. Annie leaned back in her chair, trying to put as much distance as possible between her and Ryan. Though her office was on the top floor and isolated from the rest of the winery, she knew that all she had to do was scream and people would come running. She didn't want to do that. At this point, she didn't want to do anything that would antagonize him further.

"I never asked you to kill her." She tried to speak in a soft, appeasing voice and was disgusted when her words came out in a trembling whisper.

"You wanted her out! Are you denying that?"

"I wanted her out but not killed!" Pushing up from her

chair and moving to stand in front of him, all thought of appeasing Ryan flew out the window. If there was one thing she hated, it was to be accused of something she didn't do. "Only a twisted mind like yours would interpret my words as a go-ahead to commit murder."

"Don't you dare try to back out of this, Annie. We're in this together."

"Like hell we are." She gave him a hard shove. "I'm calling the police right now. No way am I going to take the fall for—"

As she reached for the phone, he slapped his hand over hers, trapping it there. "You don't want to do that, Annie." He smiled. "You know why? Because no one will believe you. It's your word against mine. Who do you think they'll believe? The irreproachable, hardworking, trustworthy assistant or the devious, jealous sister who will stop at nothing to get what she wants?"

Every muscle in her body went taut. Oh, God, why hadn't she seen this coming?

"You told me not too long ago that you were on probation at Spaulding," he continued, his hand still on hers. "That you couldn't afford to make another mistake. Well, guess what, my love? You're about to make that mistake. You're about to lose everything."

"They'll never buy your story."

"Wrong, Annie. They *will* buy it. I'll tell them how you seduced me, how you begged me to kill Rachel so you could have Spaulding. They'll buy it," he repeated, "because they know how you operate."

Panic lodged in her stomach, making her feel ill. He was right. They would believe him—Rachel, Ambrose, Gregory, Sam. They all knew what she had done, how far she could go. Would it be such a stretch of the imagination for them to believe she'd get a man to kill for her?

He removed his hand. "Has it sunk in yet, Annie?" He was openly gloating now, totally sure of himself.

"How about you?" She tried to keep her tone challenging, her voice free of fear, but she knew her trembling once again gave her away. "Do you realize you could go to jail for attempted murder?"

"Of course I do, but I don't give a damn what happens to me if I can't have you. So you see, it's quite simple." He gave a careless shrug. "I go down, you go down with me." He ran the back of his finger along her cheek, a gesture she had come to loathe. "I wonder how much time one gets these days for co-conspiracy to commit murder? Five years? Ten?"

The cold knot in her stomach tightened. How could she have been attracted to this man? What was wrong with her?

"Of course, it doesn't have to be that way." Ryan pulled back a little and let his gaze move up and down her body in a way that made her cringe. "All you have to do is forget what you said earlier, about us being through, and I'll forget we ever had this discussion."

"What about Joe Brock? You let the police think he tried to kill Rachel, when all along it was you. And now Joe's a fugitive."

Another shrug. "Tough break."

"You're insane," she whispered.

"No, baby." He shook his head. "I'm just a man in love. And I do love you, Annie. Change your mind and I'll show you how much. If you want I'll even take another stab at Rachel. I won't miss this time—"

"No!" She grabbed him by his shirt collar and shook him. "Stay away from her, do you hear me?"

He raised his hands in surrender. "Okay, okay, I won't. Jesus," he added when she let him go, "you almost sound like you care."

"I…just don't want anything to happen to her."

"Okay, nothing will." His eyes bore into hers. "We have a deal, then?"

She gave a single blink. What choice did she have?

"Say it, Annie. Say we're staying together."

She swallowed. "We're staying together."

He kissed her, a hard, passionate kiss she didn't return. "I'll see you tonight, then. The usual time?"

She nodded and watched him walk out of her office. When he was gone, she ran to the ladies' room and threw up.

Rachel sat at her desk, trying hard not to think too much about the heated kiss she and Gregory had exchanged on Sunday afternoon. It hadn't meant anything, she kept telling herself. Both she and Gregory had simply given in to a moment of passion, and she would have to forget about it. Never mind that the kiss was the first thing she'd thought of upon awakening on Monday and again this morning, or that she had spent the past two hours feeling giddy and silly and hoping Gregory would call.

All right, Rachel, enough nonsense. Concentrate on your work.

She was trying to calculate how many barrels to order for next year's crop when the phone rang. Her fingers on the calculator on her desk, she picked it up. "Hello?"

"Rachel, thank God, you're there."

"Hubert," she said, immediately recognizing the Frenchman's voice. "What's wrong? You sound—"

"It's your mother!" he cried. "She has been arrested for the murder of Salvatore Dassante."

Thirty-Two

Rachel drove the short distance between Spaulding Vineyards and the Calistoga police station on Washington Avenue in record time. The brief, sketchy story Hubert had told her on the phone kept playing in her mind, each time sounding more terrifying. Two things were certain—Sal was dead and Ginnie had been arrested for his murder. A priest, who had arrived just as Ginnie was fleeing the church where he'd been killed, had taken down her license plate number as she'd sped away.

From the Jeep, Rachel had called Ambrose who had immediately given her the name of a criminal lawyer in Napa City. "Jake Lindquist is one of the best attorneys in the valley," he had assured her. "I'll call him and tell him to meet you at the police station."

Hubert was there when she arrived. He looked pale and was a far cry from the poised, polished gentleman she had first met at the winery.

"Did you find an attorney?" he asked when she walked in.

"Yes. Our family lawyer is sending someone right away, a local man who specializes in criminal cases. His name is Jake Lindquist." She had no idea how good he was, but for the time being, he would have to do. "Have you talked to Ginnie?"

He nodded and reclaimed his seat. "Briefly." He sat

with his head between his hands. "This is all my fault," he murmured. "If I hadn't been sleeping so soundly..."

Rachel frowned. "You didn't know she was gone?"

"No. She waited until I had fallen asleep, then got out of bed and drove to the church in Calistoga to meet Sal." He raised his head, a haggard look in his eyes. "They found a gun in his pocket, Rachel. He had come to kill her."

"Is that what the police are saying?"

He shook his head. "They're saying he was afraid of what she might do to him and brought the gun for protection."

"How did he know she was in California?"

Hubert just shook his head.

"Miss Spaulding?"

A uniformed guard stood in front of them. "You can have a few minutes with Mrs. Laperousse now."

"Wait for me here." Rachel lay a hand on Hubert's shoulder. "If Lindquist shows up, have someone call me." She followed the guard down a hall and into a windowless room with a wooden table in the center and four chairs.

Ginnie sat at the table. Her face was white, her eyes wide with panic, her hair in disarray. "Oh, Rachel." Pushing her chair back, she started to rise but the guard, positioned at the door, raised his hand. "No physical contact, please."

As Rachel took a seat, Ginnie did the same, placing her clasped hands on the table. "I didn't do it, Rachel. I swear I didn't kill Sal."

"Just tell me what happened," Rachel said gently.

"Earlier today—" Ginnie pressed two fingers to her eyes "—I mean yesterday, Sal called me."

"How did he find you?" Rachel asked, remembering the many precautions she and Gregory had taken.

"I don't know. He said something about a man watching me, probably the detective he claimed to have fired."

Rachel pinched the bridge of her nose. "I should have never believed him."

"This is not your fault," Ginnie said fiercely, leaning over the table. "I'm the one who believed him. I'm the one who went to that church." Ginnie took a deep breath before continuing. "Sal said he wanted to talk. He said he was willing to listen to my side of the story regarding Mario's death."

"Why would he want to do that?"

"He said he was doing it for you. At first I didn't want to believe him. I was afraid he was trying to trick me. Then he started talking about you and how you deserved to know the truth. I could understand that. I thought finally your life could return to normal and you wouldn't have to be ashamed of me anymore."

"I was never ashamed." Rachel started to take her mother's hand then remembered the guard's warning. "Go on."

"He swore to me he wouldn't bring the police, because if he did he would lose you and he couldn't bear it if that happened."

"You shouldn't have gone there."

Ginnie laughed. "He didn't leave me much of a choice, Rachel. He knew where I was. I could either meet him and try to convince him I was innocent, or he could call the police and tell them where I was. He even warned me not to step out of the house. If I did, his man would see me and call the police."

"Hubert said you took your passport with you, and...money."

She looked away. "I thought...if Sal didn't believe me, or if he tried to kill me, I could escape."

A smart D.A. would use that testimony as evidence of premeditation. "Did he choose the location?"

"No, that was my decision. I wanted to be close to home." She took a deep breath. "I waited until Hubert was asleep, then I got out of bed and drove to the church. It was empty, except for that one man in the front pew. He was praying. Or so I thought at the time." She ran her hands through her hair. "It was Sal. But he wasn't praying. He was dead and he had scissors sticking out of his chest."

Please, God, Rachel prayed silently. Don't let her have touched those scissors. "You didn't touch them, did you?"

"No. For a while, I couldn't even move, then I started backing away, not knowing a priest was right behind me."

"That's when you ran?"

Ginnie nodded. "I didn't think, Rachel. I had this awful sense of déjà vu, of blaring headlines and another state-wide search. All I could think of was to get away, so I ran. I never thought the priest would have the presence of mind to run out and take down the number on my license plate. If I had, I would have driven straight to the airport and taken my chances there. Instead, I drove back to the cottage, thinking I was safe."

"Why did they wait so long to arrest you?"

"They couldn't trace the license plate to our rental car until this morning."

"What about the scissors? Where did they come from?"

"I don't know, but they're not mine, Rachel. I've never seen them before."

Thank God for that. "Were you officially interrogated? Did you sign anything?"

She shook her head. "I didn't sign anything, but when a detective asked if I was willing to answer a few questions, even though my attorney wasn't here yet, I said yes. Why shouldn't I?" she asked as Rachel briefly closed her eyes. "I had nothing to hide. I didn't kill Sal."

Rachel let out a long sigh. She wasn't an expert in criminal law, but she had been around Preston long enough to know that talking to the police without an attorney present was tantamount to signing a confession.

She didn't share her depressing thoughts with Ginnie. More than ever now, her mother needed to keep her faith in the justice system. "All right," she said with more confidence than she felt. "It's not as bad as it sounds. Your fingerprints aren't on the murder weapon, and no one came forward claiming to be an eye witness. All the police have against you right now is circumstantial evidence."

"But they have me at the scene of the crime."

"Also circumstantial."

"And there's Mario's murder," Ginnie reminded her. "Don't forget that. If they don't hang me for one Dassante killing, they'll hang me for the other."

"Why don't we let your attorney worry about that? In fact—" Rachel glanced at her watch "—he should be here right about now." She stood. "Is there anything else you want to tell me?"

Ginnie attempted a smile, her first. "Get me out of here?"

"I'm going to try, Ginnie."

Back in the waiting room, Rachel stopped dead in her tracks. Nico sat on a wooden bench, his head in his hands. Beside him, Erica, her face a white mask, was trying to comfort him. Hubert was nowhere in sight.

At the sounds of footsteps against the tile floor, Erica looked up. Her eyes were red and swollen.

"Erica, I'm so sorry about Sal," Rachel began. "I know—"

Nico's head snapped up. There was pain in his eyes, but there was also hatred, and it was directed at her. "Are you happy?'' he asked, his voice thin and nasty. ''Was that what you wanted?''

''Of course not!'' Any other time she would have responded to the blatant attack with a sharp remark of her own, but she knew all about grief, knew what it could do to a person. ''I never wished Sal any harm.''

''But you're the reason Alyssa came back,'' Nico continued. ''If you had done the right thing and told her she wasn't welcome in your life she would have been on the next plane back to France. But no, you had to go and play the loving, forgiving daughter. And now my father is dead. That bitch killed him, just like she killed my brother.''

''Nico, stop it.'' Erica gave his arm a little shake. ''You're not being fair.''

''Fair?'' Nico swatted his wife's hand away. ''My father is dead, killed in cold blood, and you're talking to me about fair?''

''Rachel had nothing to do with Sal's death.''

''And neither had my mother.'' Rachel made a supreme effort not to snap at him. ''She went to that church because Sal asked her to.''

''What's going on here?'' a male voice asked from behind her. ''What's all the shouting about?''

Rachel turned around. A heavyset man with acne scars and a bulbous nose stood staring at them. Behind him, still looking distraught, was Hubert.

''I'm Detective Bob Green.'' The man looked at Rachel with a dispassionate expression. ''I'm in charge of this case.''

Rachel didn't offer her hand. ''I'm Rachel Spaulding. Virginia Laperousse is my mother.''

The detective nodded. ''Then I have a message for you. Your mother's attorney just called. He's been delayed in traffic but should be here in a few minutes.''

"Thank you, Detective. I wonder if I could have a word with you? I—"

Before Rachel could finish her sentence, the detective turned his back on her. "Mr. and Mrs. Dassante, you both have my sincere sympathy."

"I don't want your sympathy, Detective," Nico said in a tight, angry voice. "I want you to tell me what measures are being taken to charge Alyssa with murdering my father."

"Virginia Laperousse will be formally charged, Mr. Dassante. But not until her attorney arrives." Green motioned toward a door in the back. "Now, why don't you both come into my office where we can talk in private?"

Angry to have been brushed aside in such an uncivilized manner, Rachel stepped forward. "May I ask you a question before you go, Detective?" She kept just enough sharpness in her tone to make Green realize she wasn't going to be ignored, or pushed around.

"What do you want to know?"

"Why was my mother interrogated without an attorney in the room?"

"She waived her rights of her own free will, Miss Spaulding," he said, sounding annoyed. "No one held a gun to her head."

"Was she advised that waiving her rights gave *you* the right to later challenge her trial testimony?"

The detective's eyes narrowed. "Are you accusing this department of impropriety, Miss Spaulding?"

"You didn't answer my question, Detective."

He looked at her for a good three seconds, slowly reassessing her. "The arresting officer gave Mrs. Laperousse the Miranda warnings. That was enough."

Rachel didn't think it was, but would leave the interpretation of the law to Jake Lindquist.

Thirty-Three

Bail was denied. Prior to the ruling, Ginnie's attorney had repeatedly brought up the matter of circumstantial evidence, but the judge had remained steadfast in his convictions. No one in his courtroom ever made bail on a first-degree murder charge. The assistant D.A. had been equally adamant, claiming the murder was premeditated and that, in view of her previous record, Virginia Laperousse was a flight risk. A preliminary trial was set for October 21.

"Rachel!"

She turned around. Gregory stood in the courtroom gallery, impeccably dressed in a light gray business suit, white shirt and tie.

Relief shot through her. He looked so unwaveringly strong and solid. His presence alone seemed to bring a little sanity to today's crazy events.

"I came as soon as I heard," he said as she rushed into his arms.

"Thank you." She didn't ask how he'd heard. She was just glad he was there, with his arms around her, his mouth pressed against her cheek.

"Let's get out of here," he said. "Is the Jeep outside?"

She nodded.

"We'll leave it here and ask Sam or Ryan to bring it later." He glanced at Hubert, whose eyes were still riveted on the door through which Ginnie had disappeared. "Hubert, come on, let's go."

A mob of reporters was waiting outside the courthouse when the three of them stepped out. They immediately rushed forward, launching a series of rapid-fire questions that had Rachel's head spinning.

"Ignore them," Gregory instructed. "Hubert, you take your car. I'll take mine."

Perfectly synchronized, as though they had rehearsed the scene a hundred times, Hubert made a quick dash for his Buick, taking half the crowd with him.

His arm still firmly anchored around Rachel's waist, Gregory shouldered his way through the other half, until he reached the Jaguar, parked a few feet behind Hubert's car. He pushed Rachel inside and slammed the door shut.

She heard a brief, scathing exchange of words before the door on the driver's side opened and Gregory jumped in. An intrepid reporter grabbed the door handle, but when Gregory gunned the engine, he leaped out of the way.

"I called Willie earlier," Gregory said as he made a quick U-turn. "She'll be glad to have you stay with her until this blows over. Just say the word and I'll take you there right now."

Rachel pressed the back of her head against the seat. She would love nothing more than to escape to those quiet hills and forget, if only for a short time, the chaos of the last five hours. But fleeing from disaster had never been her style. She shook her head. "I'm not going to run, Gregory, and I'm not going to hide. Besides, I need to tell Annie and the others what happened."

He nodded. "All right." He looked both ways before turning onto Route 29. "Why don't you tell me what happened?"

Just sitting next to him and listening to the quiet sound

of his voice was enough to restore her mental balance. She told him what she knew, starting with Hubert's frantic phone call to the moment bail was denied.

"Sal lied to me," Rachel said when she was finished. "He told me he'd stop looking for my mother when all along he was planning to kill her." She looked out the window. "Maybe if I had been a little more suspicious of him, not so damned trusting, none of this would have happened."

"Don't blame yourself, Rachel. Sal was a shrewd old man. Deceiving people was his specialty."

They were silent for a while, each lost in their own thoughts. When Gregory glanced back at her, there was an odd expression on his face. "How much faith do you have in Jake Lindquist?" he asked.

She gave a tired shrug. "I'm not sure. Ambrose says he's the best criminal attorney in the valley, but this area isn't exactly a hotbed for high-profile murder cases. And since we've already seen the attention this particular case is getting, I doubt Jake will know how to effectively handle the press, not to mention the D.A."

"I don't know anything about that D.A. Do you?"

She laughed. "Enough to know he's coming up for re-election and needs a big win. At the bail hearing, he shot down every one of Lindquist's arguments as though he knew exactly what they were going to be. Poor Jake didn't have a chance."

Gregory reached for her hand and held it. "I know a couple of people in San Francisco. Let me see what I can do, okay?"

She pressed his hand in response and remained silent for the rest of the trip to Spaulding Vineyards.

Rather than ask Annie to let her use the main house, Rachel had chosen to hold the family meeting in the

Hughes's home where she felt more comfortable.

They were all assembled in the cozy living room—Annie, Sam, Tina and Courtney, who had just arrived from school. Amazingly calm, at least on the outside, Rachel stood by the brick fireplace and told them about the Laperousses's visit to the winery, Rachel's subsequent discovery that Ginnie was Alyssa Dassante, and ultimately about Sal's death and Ginnie's arrest.

"My God!" Looking stunned, Annie gaped at her. "Killing one Dassante wasn't enough for her? She had to kill another?"

"She didn't kill Sal," Rachel snapped. "And she didn't kill Mario, either. So if you can't be objective, or God forbid, supportive, shut the hell up."

"Wait a minute. You can't—"

"*You* wait just a minute, Annie." Rachel pointed a finger at her sister. "I included you in this discussion because we're family and the least you can do is return the favor by sparing me your caustic and unjustified comments."

The sharp rebuttal struck home. Her cheeks red, Annie folded her arms across her chest and sank into her chair, like a pouting child.

"What can we do?" Sam asked.

"Tell the staff. I'd do it myself," she added with a small sigh, "but frankly, I'm not up to it."

Sam nodded. "Consider it done."

Courtney came to her, tears in her eyes. "Oh, Aunt Rachel, I'm so sorry. I knew how badly you wanted to find your mother and now that you have..."

"She's going to be all right," Rachel replied, wishing she could believe her own words. "The case won't even go to trial. I have to believe that."

"Who's her attorney?" Tina asked.

"Jake Lindquist. He's a friend of Ambrose's."

"Is he any good?"

She wiped a tear that had escaped in spite of her valiant effort to keep her emotions under control. "I hope so. Ambrose says he is."

"So if he's so good, what is your mother doing still in jail?" The question had come from Annie, who could never stay silent for long.

Rachel gave her sister a long, troubled look. "I don't know, Annie. I honestly don't know."

After dropping Rachel off at Spaulding Vineyards, Gregory had driven straight to Pacific Heights where his father still lived. As he turned on Presidio Avenue, he was reminded once again that he hadn't set foot in this house since his last battle with Milton six months ago.

Thinking back, he couldn't remember how the argument had started, probably with some disparaging remarks on Milton's part. Within moments the quarrel had escalated into a virtual shouting match, and Gregory had stormed out, this time swearing to never set foot in the house again.

Coming here was a lousy idea, Gregory kept repeating to himself as he drove. A waste of time. Milton would never agree to represent Ginnie. Why should he? When was the last time he had done his son a favor? In the past hour, he had come up with a dozen reasons why he shouldn't have come. And only one why he should—Rachel.

In spite of the good front she had put up at the courthouse earlier, the despair in her eyes as her mother was led away had told the true story. And that defeated look from someone so strong had stirred something deep inside him in a way he hadn't expected.

How could he do nothing, knowing he had the power to help her?

And so he had come home, to do what he had sworn he'd never do. Ask his father for help. Now, standing at the front door of the imposing Colonial where he was raised, he waited for Niles, Milton's quiet, efficient house-keeper, to open the door. When he did, the Englishman's impassive face showed instant joy.

"Mr. Shaw. What a pleasant surprise."

"Good afternoon, Niles. My father in?"

"Yes, sir. He's in the game room. I'll—"

"Never mind." Gregory waved. "I don't need to be an-nounced." He probably did, but what the hell.

The game room, where his father liked to unwind after a trying case, hadn't changed. It was still dominated by a large antique pool table with a Tiffany chandelier hanging over it. Beyond the table, framed in the bay window, was a card table where Milton and his friends used to indulge in an occasional game of poker. Gregory had no idea if they still did or not.

Dressed in brown slacks, a white shirt and a brown car-digan he'd left unbuttoned, Milton Shaw stood at the pool table, cue stick in hand, carefully studying the position of the remaining seven balls.

He was a portly man with steel-gray hair, piercing eyes as blue as Gregory's, and a commanding presence. Seeing him there, planning his next move, Gregory was taken back to another time. When he was a boy, he'd come here often to play pool by himself or to watch his father in action, wishing the man would turn around, see him and wave him over.

Come here, son. Let's you and me shoot a game or two.

But those words never came. His father had never ac-knowledged Gregory's presence in the room.

Gregory continued to watch him. Milton was bent over the table, the fingers of his left hand splayed over the green felt. The cue stick rested loosely between his thumb and his index finger. Aligning his shot, he slowly pulled the stick back and shot the cue ball with a smooth, expert stroke that sent the six ball rolling into the far corner pocket. With hardly a pause, he walked around the table, assumed his position again, this time aiming at the ten ball. He sank that one, too.

Gregory smiled. The old man hadn't lost his touch.

Milton was coating the tip of his cue stick with a stubby piece of blue chalk when he suddenly looked up. Gregory waited for his father's expression to change, to register surprise or anger, anything but this level, neutral stare of his.

"Hello, Dad." The word, spoken so seldom, almost died in his throat.

"Gregory." The voice was cool, detached. He could have been greeting a stranger. No, that wasn't an accurate description, Gregory thought. A stranger would have elicited more warmth.

As if Gregory wasn't there, Milton eyed the table again, carefully selecting his next shot.

Gregory cleared his throat. "You got a minute to talk?"

"Sure." Milton aimed at the five ball and watched it make its way toward the left corner pocket and disappear.

It was now or never, Gregory thought. Taking his aunt Willie's advice—"When in doubt, dive in headfirst"—he did just that. "I need your help, Dad."

He thought—or did he imagine it?—that for a microsecond, the flawless concentration was lost. Then the moment passed and Milton sent another ball careening across the felt, heading straight for the side pocket.

Taking his silence as an invitation to continue, Gregory told him the details of Ginnie's arrest—which Milton probably already knew—the circumstances that had taken her to France thirty-one years ago, then back to the United

States. And he told him about Rachel, how much she loved her mother and how guilty he still felt for messing up her life.

"Guilt is a useless emotion," Milton remarked. And sank another ball.

You ought to know. Gregory didn't want to get into a philosophical discussion over the uselessness or benefits of guilt. He ignored the comment. "Ginnie's husband has retained a local attorney, a man by the name of Jake Lindquist." He took a deep breath. "I don't think he can get Ginnie off."

Their eyes met then and Gregory fought hard not to flinch. Flinching and backing away from this formidable man had been one of Gregory's most despised weaknesses. But those days were over now. Like it or not, his father would have to accept that.

"Your point?" Milton bent over the table again.

"I'd like you to take over her defense."

This time the ball hit the corner of the pocket and rolled back to the center of the table. Straightening slowly, Milton gave Gregory another stare. "Give me a reason why I should."

If Gregory hadn't been prepared for that reaction, the question alone, and the way it was asked, would have been enough to send him walking. "It's a high-profile case," he said calmly. "One that has already generated tons of publicity, not just locally but nationwide. By tomorrow morning, I expect every European newspaper will have the story."

"You think that's why I do what I do?" Milton asked coldly. "For the glory?"

"Yes, I do." Gregory held his gaze. "The glory and the money. At least, that's what was hammered into my head when I was a kid.'' He waited a beat. ''Although today, I was hoping you'd do it because I asked.''

''My caseload is full at the moment.'' Milton studied the table again where only two balls remained.

''Not that full. I checked.'' He had, by calling his father's very stoic and very sweet secretary.

The ball missed the pocket again, and this time Milton cursed under his breath. He had never been a gracious loser, in or out of the courtroom.

''She didn't do it, Dad.'' As Milton nonchalantly reached for the chalk again, Gregory grabbed the cue stick from him, ignoring his father's startled and angry glare. ''Somebody else killed Sal and let her take the fall. Maybe the killer is the same one who killed Mario and maybe he's not. What I do know is that Ginnie is innocent of both crimes, and unless she fires Lindquist and hires a top-notch attorney, she'll go to prison.''

''I can think of a half dozen lawyers in this city alone who fit that description.''

''None are as good as you.''

Milton's expression didn't soften at the compliment. ''Are you in love with Rachel Spaulding?''

The question took Gregory by surprise. To his recollection, he and Milton had never discussed women. One day, he had introduced Lindsay to his father, told him they were getting married and that was about it. Six years later, when he had announced he was divorcing Lindsay because the marriage wasn't working, Milton had replied, in his usual direct style, ''Never thought it would.''

It took him a moment to reply, not so much because he was caught off guard but because he had not yet admitted his true feelings about Rachel to himself, much less expressed them out loud. How odd he should have to express them now and to a man who knew so little about love.

"Yes," he said at last. "I'm in love with Rachel."

"That's what I thought."

Gregory was instantly on the defensive. "What the hell does that mean?"

"It means that you're acting impulsively again. You're letting a woman manipulate you into doing something you don't want to do. It happened with Lindsay and it's happening now."

In spite of his promise to keep calm, Gregory blew up. "Bullshit. Rachel is nothing like Lindsay. And no one is manipulating me to do anything."

"No?" Milton's tone turned sarcastic. "You think I'm stupid? You think I don't know you'd rather be chewing glass right now than be here asking me for a favor?"

"What difference does it make where I'd rather be? I'm here, aren't I? And I'm asking for your help. A woman's life is at stake. An innocent woman. I thought if you could defend a creep like Freddy Bloom, surely you could defend Ginnie Laperousse." He shook his head. "I thought you'd changed, Dad. I thought you could put your bitterness aside for one moment and do this for me." Disgusted, he threw the cue stick on the table. "I guess I was wrong."

He walked out of the game room and bumped into Niles, who had probably heard the shouts. "Don't bother to show me out," he said to the startled housekeeper. "You couldn't possibly walk me to the door fast enough."

His hand was on the Jaguar's door handle when he heard his father's voice again.

"Gregory!"

Gregory turned around, preparing for one last parting shot.

"Come back." Milton waved him in. "Let's talk some more."

Thirty-Four

They sat in Milton's study, Gregory in a deep leather chair and his father behind his desk, taking notes and looking up from time to time to ask a question. It felt odd being here, talking in a civilized manner for a change as they discussed, not their personal problems, but a criminal case.

Gregory had no illusion that his father's decision to represent Ginnie was in any way an indication he'd had a change of heart about his son. This was business, the kind of business Milton Shaw thrived on, and because of that, he had agreed to a temporary cease-fire.

"The first thing we need to find out," Milton said as he wrote on a yellow legal pad, "is, which case is going to be tried first."

"Isn't it customary to try the case that's ready for trial first?"

Milton looked up from his notes. "I see you learned a thing or two from the old man." Before Gregory could decide if the remark was an insult or a compliment, Milton tapped the point of his pencil against the pad. "Do you know if there's an outstanding warrant for Ginnie's arrest regarding Mario's murder?"

Gregory kicked himself for not having checked that out. "I don't know," he admitted. "Shouldn't there be?"

"Sometimes in old cases, warrants have a way of getting lost in the system."

"Can't a judge issue another warrant?"

"Sure, but that will take time. The police would have to practically reopen the case, question witnesses, some of whom may have moved away or even died. And then there's the evidence. Policies are very strict, as you know. A chain of supervision of evidence must be maintained to ensure against tampering. This means evidence has to be warehoused. If as much as one piece gets misplaced or is tampered with, the case won't stand up in court."

"So Ginnie will most likely be tried for Sal's murder first."

"I would think so. It's easier to line up witnesses and collect evidence in a recent case than it is in an old one."

"What about bail? You think you can get her out? Or is it too late to reverse the decision?"

Milton gave him a thin but confident smile. "It's never too late. All I have to do is convince the district attorney to reduce the charge to manslaughter."

"Can you do that?"

Milton looked at him above his rimless glasses. "Of course, I can do that."

Gregory smiled. "I guess they don't call you the silver-tongued fox for nothing."

"How do you know that's what they call me?"

Gregory shrugged. "Oh, I follow your cases occasionally."

Milton tilted back in his chair but his expression remained unreadable. "Do you really?"

Gregory nodded. "I came to the courthouse last week to hear your closing arguments on The Slasher's case."

The blue eyes didn't flinch. "What did you think?"

Gregory hesitated. To tell him what he truly thought would destroy what little progress they had made so far.

"It was a brilliant summation," he said truthfully. "You even had one juror fighting tears."

Milton nodded. "Juror number six. She kept the deliberations going for seventy-six hours, but in the end her compassion wasn't enough to save Freddy."

"Should he have been saved?" The question came before he could stop it. He cursed himself silently. He and his big mouth.

As expected, Milton bristled. "Are you still questioning the right of every man, even a criminal, to have a defense? And a fair trial?"

There it was, Gregory thought, "The Challenge," as he had called it in the good old days. All he had to do was take the bait and the civilized conversation would escalate into a full-blown battle, with scars to add upon other scars.

And this bait wasn't one that could easily be ignored. From the moment Gregory had thought of going to law school, he had never made it a secret that hard-core criminals should lose their rights the moment their victims were robbed of theirs. As a defense attorney, Milton had fiercely argued against that position.

His thoughts firmly centered on Rachel, Gregory summoned every ounce of diplomacy he had in him. "Not if justice is served. And I feel that in Freddy's case, it was."

Milton's eyes narrowed and there seemed to be the hint of a smile in those familiar baby blues. But the illusion was short-lived.

Milton flattened his palms on his desk. "I'll tell you what. Call Rachel, tell her I'll take the case, and then I'll go talk to Mr. and Mrs. Laperousse." He handed Gregory his cordless phone.

Sundays and holidays in the valley were a chaos no local could escape. Visitors from San Francisco and other surrounding areas came in droves, swarming into stores and wineries, picnicking by the side of the road and creating major traffic jams on Route 29. Valley Week, which had begun the weekend before and would continue through the next, was no exception.

Sitting on Rachel's hillside terrace where they had come to spend a few hours, Gregory watched the lengthening ribbon of cars below as it snaked its way south. On the glass-topped table were the remains of a celebration lunch he and Rachel had shared with Hubert and Ginnie, whom Milton, true to his promise, had bailed out of jail earlier this morning.

"Here."

Gregory took his gaze off the congestion below and glanced up at Rachel as she put a package wrapped in pretty blue foil on the table. "What's this?"

She piled the lunch dishes onto a tray. "A small token of my appreciation. I don't think I thanked you properly for all you've done so far."

"Thanks aren't necessary."

"Yes, they are. It couldn't have been easy for you to go to your father, but you did it. I'll never forget it."

Gregory toyed with the curled ribbon but didn't pull it. "It wasn't that big a deal. In fact, the whole thing was strangely painless."

She gave his shoulder a light tap. "I'm not taking the gift back, so stop being so bullheaded and open the damn package."

Grinning, he untied the ribbon and tore the wrapping paper, exposing a plain white box. Lifting the lid, he laughed. Inside was a radar detector. "Are you trying to tell me something?"

"Well, you did get a speeding ticket the other morning, and since a lot of your driving these days is done on account of me, I'd feel better if you had this little gadget with you. It's very effective.''

He looked up. "Oh yeah? And how would you know?''

She grinned and glanced at the Cherokee she had just gotten back from the body shop. "Because I have one, too.''

"I see." He returned the detector to the box. "Thank you, Rachel. That was very sweet of you.''

The roar of an engine made them both look up. One eyebrow cocked, Gregory watched a shiny red Corvette convertible come up the driveway and slide smoothly between Rachel's Jeep and Gregory's Jaguar.

Preston Farley stepped out of his car, every blond hair in place. In his pale linen jacket and impeccably cut trousers, he looked cool and polished and not at all bothered to see that Rachel had company.

Acting as though he had never stopped being a welcomed guest, he took the steps to the terrace two at a time. "Your assistant told me you had taken the afternoon off.'' He bent forward to kiss Rachel on the cheek and looked disappointed when she snapped her head back to avoid the contact.

"What the hell do you want?'' she asked.

Impervious to her sharp tone, Preston sat. "I need to talk to you." He glanced at Gregory then back at Rachel. "Alone.''

"You had your chance to talk to me three weeks ago.'' Her tone was cool and detached. "You weren't available, remember?''

"This isn't about us.''

She let out a short, derisive laugh. "Then we really have nothing to talk about, Preston.''

"It's about your mother.''

To Gregory's irritation, Rachel stiffened. The jerk had

managed to get her full attention. "What about my mother?" she asked.

Preston glanced at Gregory again, this time with the cold all-encompassing look of a man assessing another man he perceived as a lesser human being.

Gregory knew why. A few years ago when Preston was an assistant district attorney, he and Milton had faced each other in the courtroom often. And more times than Preston probably cared to count, the older attorney had beaten the pants off him. For reasons that escaped Gregory, Preston Farley's hate campaign against Milton Shaw had included his son, as well.

"Alone," Preston repeated.

"Gregory and I have no secrets." Still standing beside Gregory's chair, Rachel rested her hand on his shoulder. "Whatever you have to say, you can say in front of him." She smiled sweetly. "You do know Gregory Shaw, don't you?"

"We've met."

Having already guessed the reason for the impromptu visit, Gregory sat back in his chair and stretched his long legs in front of him, crossing them at the ankles. He was going to enjoy this.

"Very well, then." Preston cleared his throat. "I'll come straight to the point. I'd like to represent your mother."

Rachel's mouth twitched, which Gregory took as a sign that she, too, had guessed Preston's motive. "You would?" she asked, feigning mild surprise.

"Yes. And before you turn me down, hear me out."

"Oh, Preston, I'm afraid you're too late." Rachel did a masterful job of sounding truly regretful. "You see, my mother already has an attorney. I believe you know him—"

"Jake Lindquist, yes, I know him." Preston snorted with disdain. "He's a country lawyer, Rachel, and not a very good one at that. Your mother needs a strategist, someone skilled, aggressive and not easily intimidated.''

Gregory chuckled. Farley had always had an overinflated opinion of himself. ''And that someone would be you?'' he asked.

This time Preston's glare could have frozen the hot spring next door. ''Butt out, Shaw,'' he snapped. ''This doesn't concern you.''

''Au contraire, mon ami.'' Gregory wrapped one arm around Rachel's hips and gave her a deliberately intimate smile. ''What concerns Rachel concerns me. You see, I'm the case investigator. So even if Rachel did agree to let you represent her mother, I'm sure you wouldn't want to work with me.''

Preston turned to Rachel. ''Is that true?''

''If you mean, is Gregory the case investigator—'' she nodded ''—yes, it's true.''

''Have you asked him when was the last time he investigated a murder case?''

''That's not important to me, Preston. What is important is that he found my mother.''

Preston's mouth turned downward in a contemptuous smirk. ''He didn't find her. She came back to the States on her own.''

Farley hadn't changed, Gregory thought. He loved accolades but was stingy as hell when it came to returning them. ''Does your mother know you're here?'' he asked sarcastically.

''Fuck off, Shaw.'' The words spewed from between clenched teeth. Then, as if realizing anger would get him nowhere, he refocused his attention on Rachel and turned on the charm again. ''I know you're mad at me for the way I handled our breakup, and frankly, I'm not proud of it, either—''

"You're flattering yourself, Preston," Rachel said coolly. "I'm not mad, I'm not upset, I'm not anything." She gave a small shrug. "I just don't care."

Preston stared at her, a look of mild shock on his face, as if the thought that she was over him had never occurred to him. "Uh…well…all right. What I was trying to say is that…regardless of what happened between us, I still care about you. When I heard your mother was in trouble—"

"You came to the rescue," Gregory said. "How gallant of you. And, of course, your generosity has nothing to do with the fact that Virginia Laperousse is the wife of a famous concert pianist, does it, Counselor? And that defending her would give one hell of a boost to your flagging career."

"You know nothing about me," Preston snapped. "And my career is certainly not flagging, so kindly refrain from making rash statements."

Gregory laughed. "Rash? I don't think so, Farley. I can smell lawyers like you a mile away. You and ambulance chasers."

"Why, you—"

Incensed, Preston jumped out of his chair. Gregory rose lazily and was pleased to see he was a half head taller than Pretty Boy. "Don't do anything you can't finish, Farley," he warned.

The attorney looked him up and down, as if actually considering taking him on, then, with the look of one who didn't want to get his hands dirty, he turned to Rachel again. Gregory gave him credit. The guy knew how to go after what he wanted. Itching to see that smug smile disappear, he wondered when the real fun would start.

"Let me do this for you, Rachel, and for your mother. I promise you won't regret it."

"But, Preston…" she said sweetly. "You're not listening. I told you, my mother already has an attorney." She gave Gregory a slight nod.

Hands in his pockets, Gregory leaned forward and his best James Bond impression said, "The name is Shaw. Milton Shaw."

The shock on Farley's face was so damned satisfying, Gregory burst out laughing. "How does it feel, Farley? To know the old man's outfoxed you once again?"

Speechless, nearly choking with all the things he wanted to say and couldn't, Preston just stood there and glared at him. "Is this some kind of joke?" he asked, finally taking his eyes off Gregory and looking at Rachel.

Rachel shook her head.

"You're making a big mistake," he said, dropping the syrupy act. "Milton Shaw is not the right attorney for your mother. He's overbearing, arrogant and will totally destroy her self-confidence."

"Goodbye, Preston."

Shaking his head, he gave an exasperated sigh and strode away.

Thirty-Five

After the Corvette had disappeared, Rachel and Gregory sat on the terrace enjoying the last of the cherry pie Gregory had brought along with the chocolates. Both were Rachel's favorites, and she was touched that he had gone to the trouble of calling Tina to find out what she liked.

Before she could get too mushy about the man, she stood up. "More coffee?"

"Sounds good. Here, let me help you with these." Gregory stood, as well, took the dessert dishes from her hands and carried them into the kitchen. "That was an excellent lunch, Rachel," he said. "Thank you."

"You're welcome." Rachel busied herself with the coffeemaker, trying to keep her hands from shaking as she went through the familiar routine. Now that they were alone, in these close surroundings, she was keenly aware of the effect Gregory was having on her, and of the way her body reacted whenever he was near.

Feeling his eyes on her, she glanced over her shoulder and saw that he was watching her with bold, open admiration. It was a look she had noticed before, at Willie's house, but she had felt safe there, less vulnerable.

She laughed, a small, self-conscious laugh. "What's the matter? Why are you looking like that?"

He looked amused. "No reason except that you're beautiful to look at." He leaned a shoulder against the door-jamb. "I don't make you nervous, do I, Rachel?"

"Of course not." She snapped the carafe lid in place, hoping he wouldn't notice the sudden flush in her cheeks.

He moved away from the door and came to stand directly behind her, close enough for her to feel his body heat. "Then why are you so tense?"

"I wasn't aware...oh."

He put his hands on her shoulders and began to massage them. Eyes closed, Rachel slowly rotated her head. "I had no idea you had such hidden talents," she murmured.

"There's a lot you don't know about me."

When she didn't answer, he turned her around, very slowly, very gently. The humor was gone from his eyes, replaced by something more serious and much more intense. Rachel felt momentarily spellbound.

"You don't mind if we pick up where we left off the other afternoon, do you?" he asked.

"I..." But when he pulled her to him, she offered no resistance. How could she when a part of her wanted so desperately to be kissed again?

The moment his lips touched hers, desire flooded her veins. At the same time she was vaguely aware of those same warnings she'd had before, reminders of another time when she had been just as vulnerable. She ignored them this time and threw herself into the kiss.

"Yes, Rachel," he whispered, tightening his hold on her. "That's it, baby. Don't fight it. Let it go."

His hands went to her face, framing it as he looked into her eyes. It was that look, that gesture, that moment of absolute tenderness that won her in the end, for tenderness wasn't something she had known with Preston. As the last doubts melted away, she wrapped her arms around his neck. "Who's fighting?"

He swept her off her feet in one quick, fluid motion, his mouth never letting go of hers, and carried her to the bedroom, which he had no trouble finding.

He lowered her onto the bed, his movements as gentle, as if he were handling a china doll. All inhibition gone, she tugged the polo shirt over his head and laid her hands on his broad chest, marveling at the hardness of it, moving her fingers toward his heart, that heart that had beaten so fiercely for her a few days ago. It still did.

Expert hands worked the zipper on her jeans and pushed the rough denim over her hips. His movements as he undressed her were deliciously unhurried, as if he had all the time in the world. He was much quicker with his own clothes, though, tearing them off and tossing them behind him.

He sat beside her and looked at her naked body with a mixture of wonder and desire. "You're even more beautiful than I imagined," he murmured.

"I wasn't aware you were thinking of me that way."

He lowered his head and kissed her breast, drawing the hardening nipple into his mouth. "Liar. You've known all along how I felt about you." He took the other nipple and subjected it to the same exquisite torture.

A delicious heat pooled in her lower belly. Nothing had ever felt like this, no one had ever awakened such raw passion in her. As probing fingers teased and explored, making her gasp with pleasure, she doubted either one of them would be able to make this moment last as long as they hoped.

Determined to try, she pushed him away gently. "Lie down," she whispered. "Facing me."

A light danced in his eyes but he did as he was told.

"Now don't move."

He remained perfectly still, his chest barely touching her

breasts, his breathing not yet out of control but beginning to quicken. "Are we having a contest?" he asked.

She met his hot gaze. "Are you up to it?"

He laughed. "Can't you tell?"

"Mmm. Yes, indeed I can." If she had really tried, she might have stayed this way for a few moments more, but when he slid over her, covering her body with his, her senses, already inflamed, ran away from her.

"You cheated," she said against his mouth.

"That's another thing you don't know about me."

"That you're a cheater?"

"No. That your body drives me crazy."

The intensity in his voice made Rachel shudder. Her need exploding, she arched her back. "I want you, Gregory," she whispered against his open mouth. "I want you now."

As he slid into her, she moaned with pleasure and began to move, slowly at first, then with mounting speed, astonished that their bodies could meld so perfectly, could move with such synchronized rhythm.

The climax tore into her with such force, she thought she would faint. But even then, he was there for her, taking her hands, interlacing his fingers with hers, murmuring her name as his own passion was released.

He found her in the shower, the steam wrapping her luscious body in an erotic cloud.

She giggled as he stepped inside and closed the door. "What do you think you're doing?"

"Making certain I'm fulfilling my duties as the perfect guest." He took the bar of soap from her hands and was glad to see it wasn't one of those sweetly scented things. "Because perfect guests get invited back."

"I see." She let out a small groan as he began to soap

her back, moving slowly downward. "And that's your only motive? To be the perfect guest?"

"Well…" He let his hand run down her slick, sudsy thighs and was instantly aroused. "I also wanted to see you like this, hot, wet, slippery." He pressed himself against her. "Do you have any idea what you're doing to me?"

"Yes." She sighed deeply. "I had a sample of what I'm doing to you earlier."

When he turned her around to do her front, she threw her head back and closed her eyes. "Hmm. I could get used to that."

His lips covered hers. "I'm counting on it."

He took her standing up, the steaming water sliding off his back and her little whimpers of pleasure filling his senses.

"Erica, I don't care what Sal would have wanted," Rachel said over the phone. "He went to that church with the intention of killing my mother. Do you think I can forgive that?"

"God has forgiven him."

"Well, I'm not God," Rachel snapped. "And I'm not a hypocrite. I refuse to stand at his graveside, pretending to be mourning him when every fiber of my being hates him. If it weren't for him, Ginnie wouldn't be facing a murder trial right now."

Rachel took a deep breath. What was she doing? Erica was grieving for her father-in-law and here she was shouting at her. "I'm sorry, Erica," she said in a lower voice. "I know you loved him and in a way, I admire you for that. Maybe you saw something in him I didn't."

"I told you he wasn't perfect."

Rachel laughed. That had to be the understatement of the year. "I'm not coming to the funeral," she said again. "I hope that decision won't affect our friendship, but if it does..." She let it go at that.

There was a long silence before Erica spoke again. "It won't," she said softly. "I've become much too attached to you to lose you over a disagreement."

Rachel smiled. "I'm glad. I'll call you in a couple of days."

"I'd like that." She paused. "Rachel?"

"Yes?"

"I heard your mother was out on bail. I'm happy for you."

"So am I. She shouldn't have been arrested in the first place. She didn't kill Sal."

"I never thought she did."

It felt good, working with his father, exchanging ideas, discussing potential witnesses, comparing notes. At times, there was even an occasional hint of respect in the old man's eyes, as if he hadn't expected Gregory to be so thorough in his research.

As Milton had predicted, the thirty-one-year-old warrant had been lost in the system and it would take some time before another one could be issued. Consequently, Ginnie would be tried for Sal's murder first. What happened after that pretty much depended on the outcome of the preliminary hearing next week.

Gregory looked up from his own notes. "Have you given any more thought about Mario's suspicions that Nico was embezzling money from the farm? I know we're investigating Sal's murder, but...what if the two murders are connected? What if Sal, somehow, found out money was missing and was beginning to put two and two together?"

Milton gave him a speculative look. "He'd have a motive for killing his father, as well." He nodded. "I thought about that. Unfortunately, Ginnie's memories on that subject are vague. I could requisition tax records and try to compare them with the company's books, but that would take time, especially if the old books are hidden or were destroyed. Nico isn't as stupid as I first thought. If he's the killer, he's covered his tracks very well."

"There's got to be proof somewhere, Dad. Maybe I should—"

Milton raised a hand. "If you're thinking what I'm thinking, don't tell me about it. I don't want to know."

"How would you know what I was thinking?"

Once again a brief little smile flickered in his father's eyes. "I know you better than you think I do." He slid a printed sheet of paper across his desk.

"What's that?" Gregory asked.

"A copy of Sal's phone record the police requisitioned the other day. That highlighted number at the top is the Laperousse number. Sal made the call this past Sunday at 9:17 a.m."

"Does that help our case?"

Milton shrugged. "Not a whole lot. It just proves Ginnie was telling the truth about Sal calling her and not the other way around."

Milton wrote as he talked, and Gregory couldn't help but admire the old man's incredible ability to do more than one thing at the same time without ever missing a beat.

"I'd like you to talk to the priest who took down Ginnie's license plate number," Milton continued. "I know he already gave a statement and claims to have seen only Ginnie's and Sal's cars in front of the church, but see if you can tweak his memory a little."

Gregory wrote Father Genardi's name on his pad. "Anything else?" he asked. "You want me to talk to Harold Mertz again? Maybe he's the one who killed Mario."

"You still think the former Winters P.D. detective had the hots for Alyssa?"

"There's no doubt in my mind he had the hots for Alyssa."

"She doesn't even remember him, Gregory."

"So what? It's possible Mario caught him ogling her and he got pissed off. It's worth pursuing, isn't it? Considering how little we've got to work with?"

Milton pursed his lips and then nodded. "You're right. It is worth pursuing. But let me do it this time, okay? A different approach might throw Mertz off a little. You concentrate on the padre."

He leaned back in his chair. "Anything new about the person who tried to kill Rachel?" he asked.

Gregory shook his head. He had been pestering Detective Crowley about that until the man actually hissed at him, but Gregory's persistence hadn't done much good. The case was at a standstill.

"The number one suspect is still Joe Brock," Gregory said. "Spaulding's ex-employee, and the last I heard, he was still at large."

Milton studied Gregory for a moment. "But you don't have to worry about Rachel, right? She's staying with her friends."

"For now," he said grimly, remembering how often she had hinted that the danger was past and she longed to return to her house.

"Can't you convince her that staying at the Hughes's is in her best interest?"

Gregory laughed. "I forgot to tell you a little detail about Rachel Spaulding. She's stubborn as a mule."

"Ah." Milton let out a rare chuckle. "Beautiful and stubborn. A lethal combination when it comes to a woman."

Thirty-Six

"**M**om, I need to talk to you."

Annie stood in front of her mirror, weaving a narrow belt through the loops of her jeans. "Sure, baby. What is it?"

Courtney gave her a quick, reproachful look. "Are you going out again?"

Annie laughed. "What do you mean, again? Have you been keeping tabs on your old mom?"

"No, but I know you've been out every night this week."

Annie buckled her belt and let out a small sigh. What could she say to that? The girl was right. Since that confrontation with Ryan the other day, he had asked to see her every night, even when she tried to beg off, claiming to be too tired.

Today had been a particularly busy day at Spaulding, interrupted by dozens of phone calls as RSVPs for the Harvest Ball arrived from all over the country. She would have given anything to spend a quiet evening at home with her daughter and a bowl of Ming's wonderful wonton soup.

But Ryan had left yet another message on her machine, and until she figured out a way to get out of the mess she had made for herself, she had to do as he said.

"What did you want to talk to me about?" she asked, searching through her closet for a jacket.

"I was wondering if you'd take me shopping tomorrow?"

"Oh, darling, is that all? Of course, I can take you shopping. What do you need? A new purse? Shoes?"

"A ball gown."

Annie turned around. "A gown?"

"For the Harvest Ball on Saturday night."

"But, darling, you have lots of pretty dresses you can wear. What about that pink one with the—"

"I'm too old for that dress, Mom. I want something a little more sophisticated." Courtney's cheeks turned deep red. "I want something…special."

Annie was quick to grasp the meaning of that statement. "Special, huh?" She smiled. "Who's your date?"

"No one," Courtney said a shade too quickly. "It's just that it's an important event for Spaulding and I want to…make a good impression." She shrugged. "That's all."

Annie took Courtney's hand and pulled her to a settee, forcing her to sit. Ryan would wait, she thought, feeling a sudden surge of motherly guilt. For so many years she had ignored her daughter, letting others, Grams, Rachel, and even Tina, provide the emotional support the child needed. She wasn't going to do that anymore. She wasn't going to shirk her responsibility as a parent and let someone else fill in for her. If there was one thing she had learned from this crazy affair with Ryan it was that family should come first. And from now on, it would.

"You have a new boyfriend, don't you?" she asked gently. "That's why you want to look special."

"He's not my boyfriend."

"All right, he's not your boyfriend. Tell me his name, anyway. Do I know him?"

Courtney started picking at a cuticle. "Sort of."

"Sort of?" Annie laughed. "What kind of answer is that? Either I know him or I don't."

"All right," her daughter said reluctantly. "You do know him." She pushed harder on the cuticle. "It's...Ryan."

The shock almost sent Annie reeling. "Ryan Cummings?" she asked in a strangled voice.

Courtney, thank God, didn't notice her reaction. "He doesn't seem to be involved with anyone, so I was hoping maybe we could go to the ball together."

A chill settled in Annie's stomach. "Did he ask you to go?"

"No," Courtney said sadly. "Not yet."

"Does he know how you feel about him?"

Courtney shook her head.

Annie almost cried with relief. Knowing Ryan's manipulative tendencies, she wouldn't put it past him to use Courtney to hold on to Annie. But how could she warn her daughter against this man without giving herself away?

"Darling," she said, taking Courtney's hand and speaking softly, "I know you have your heart set on going to the ball with Ryan, but...I don't think it's a good idea."

Courtney yanked her hand away. "Why not?"

"Because he's much older than you are."

"So was Daddy, but that didn't stop you."

"I was twenty-three years old when I met your father. You're a child. Ryan is a man, with a man's needs—"

In a clearly defiant gesture, Courtney flipped her long blond hair behind one shoulder. "I am not a child, Mom. I wish you'd stop calling me that."

With tears in her eyes, Annie remembered the pigtailed little girl who, only a few years ago, had been trying on Annie's high heels and playing grown-up. That little girl was a young woman now, and Annie had missed the entire transitional period.

"I know you're not a child, darling. That was a poor choice of words on my part." She took a long strand of hair and draped it back where it belonged. "But you have to trust me on this. I have a lot more experience in matters of the heart than you do."

"What does experience have to do with anything? I'm not going to marry Ryan, or have sex with him, if that's what you're afraid of. I just want to go to the Harvest Ball with him."

Annie decided to try a new tactic. "Have you wondered why he hasn't asked you yet?"

"He doesn't know I'm alive," Courtney said with a sad pout.

"Or maybe," Annie said in her sweetest, most diplomatic tone, "it's because he has a girlfriend and he's planning to take *her* to the ball."

"No, he doesn't have a girlfriend. Aunt Rachel never sees him with anyone. In fact, she was going to ask him about that, but I guess with all that's happened to her lately, she forgot."

Annie almost choked. "Rachel has been helping you get a date with Ryan?"

"What's wrong with that? She likes Ryan a lot. She even thinks I should just go and ask him to the ball. And that's exactly what I'm going to do."

Annie sat seething for several seconds. How typical of Rachel to butt in at a time like this and screw things up.

Fingers drumming rapidly on her lap, Annie took a few deep breaths. Once her breathing was back to normal, she forced herself to examine the situation calmly and rationally, something else she hadn't been doing a lot of lately. Rachel probably wasn't entirely to blame. Courtney could be relentless at times, and since her mother hadn't been available, what better person to turn to than the aunt she loved? And how could Rachel have known that Ryan was a snake in disguise?

"Look, darling, I'm truly sorry I wasn't there for you before, when you needed me. I can see now what a terrible mistake that was on my part, and as much as I'd love to make you happy right now and restore your trust in me..." She shook her head. "I can't do it. I can't allow you to go out with Ryan Cummings."

Anger sparked in the teenager's eyes. "You can't stop me! You have no right."

"I have every right," Annie snapped. "I'm your mother."

"Since when?" Courtney's expression was openly challenging. "You've never cared what I did before, who I dated, or even where I went. Why are you so interested all of a sudden?"

The words stung, but she probably deserved them, Annie thought. "Because I don't want you to be hurt, and you would be if you went out with this man."

"How can you say that about Ryan?" Courtney cried. "You know nothing about him."

Before Annie could stop her, Courtney ran out of the room.

"You see, Daddy, it's like this." In the busy downtown snack bar where Gregory and Noelle always stopped after gymnastic class, the twelve-year-old moved her straw through the thick strawberry shake. "Mom needs me right now."

While he had pretty much guessed the direction this conversation was taking, Gregory felt vaguely disappointed. Since his last conversation with Noelle, he had been seriously thinking about asking for full custody of his daughter, not through a nasty court battle, but through an amicable arrangement with Lindsay.

He picked up his coffee cup. "She needs you?"

"Uh-huh. That accident I had really freaked her out."

Gregory smiled. "Is she still cooking up a storm?"

Noelle pulled hard on her straw, sucking in her cheeks. "And coming home at five, sometimes earlier. The other evening she even rented a video and watched it with me."

"I see."

"She's really trying, Dad. And I'm afraid if I told her I wanted to live with you, she'd go to pieces."

He wondered if Lindsay had any idea that her twelve-year-old daughter had her figured out so well. "Yes," he said, looking at Noelle with a thoughtful expression. "I guess she would."

"So, Zoe and I were talking," she went on in that same serious tone. "And we decided that what you need is a girlfriend."

Gregory choked on his coffee. "You're discussing my private life *with Zoe?*"

Noelle gave him a sweet smile. "Only because I love you, Daddy, and I'm concerned about you."

"There's no need for you to be concerned. I'm doing just fine."

"I know you are. I just don't want you to spend the rest of your life alone."

"I don't intend to."

"Oh?" Two blond eyebrows went up immediately. "Is there something you want to tell me, Daddy?"

He laughed. "No, absolutely not."

But it was obvious Noelle wasn't buying it. "You met someone, didn't you?" The sparkle in her eyes could have started a Fourth of July fireworks. "Zoe was right. She said you're too good-looking not to have a girlfriend."

"I need to have a serious talk with Zoe."

But Noelle wasn't about to be sidetracked. She pushed her shake aside and propped her elbows on the table. "You might as well come clean, Daddy. We're not leaving here until you do."

"Are you sure you know what you're doing?" Rachel whispered.

As she talked, she threw another worried glance around her. The Dassante production plant was in darkness and, thank God, far enough from the house for their nocturnal visit not to be noticed. Unless, of course, someone happened to be standing at a window, watching.

"Of course, I do," Gregory whispered back. "I'm a private investigator, remember?"

"When was the last time you picked a lock?"

He kept his head lowered over his task. "Don't worry about it. And keep that light still, will you? You're all over the place."

Maybe the fact that she was shaking with terror had something to do with it, but she didn't tell him that. He hadn't been too keen on taking her along in the first place, and one word from her now would bring a well-deserved "I told you so."

His decision to search Nico's office had sent her into fits of anxiety. "Why you?" she had demanded. "Why can't you send one of your operatives?"

"Because this is a private matter," he had replied, kissing the tip of her nose in dismissal. "And I prefer to handle it myself."

A soft click as the lock sprung back made her sigh with

relief. Gregory's hand was already on the knob when she stopped him. "What if there's an alarm?"

"Why don't you stop being so negative?"

"Why don't you answer the question?"

"There's no alarm," he said, pushing the door open. "These people are too damned cheap. Besides, I already checked the place. It's clean."

"What do you mean, you've checked the place? When did you do that?"

"This morning. I pretended to be a walnut distributor from back east and got the plant manager to give me a tour of the place."

"My God!" Rachel gasped. "Are you crazy? Did Nico see you?"

"He wasn't there."

"But what if he had been?"

Instead of answering, Gregory took the flashlight from her hand and led the way into a cavernous warehouse in the center of which were twin conveyor belts with various pieces of machinery attached to them. Against the walls, stacks upon stacks of wooden crates filled with walnuts waited to be shipped.

"The executive offices are up on the loft," Gregory said, pointing toward a metal catwalk similar to the one at Spaulding.

"Which one is Nico's office?"

"The last one. The first one was Sal's and is now used for storage, at least from what I could see, and the middle one belongs to the plant manager."

With the flashlight lighting their way, they moved up the stairs quickly. "What are we looking for exactly?" Rachel asked.

"Old books, bank records, deposit slips, anything that

would show large money transfers from one place to another."

"Aren't money transfers done electronically?"

"Nowadays, yes, but not in the sixties."

Nico's door was locked and Gregory had to pull out his little tool kit again. Either this lock was easier to work or Gregory was getting better because the mechanism clicked open in a few seconds.

Nico's office was neat as a pin, with several file cabinets against the far wall, a desk with a computer, a telephone and a photo of Erica. On the walls were color prints of Dassante walnuts in various forms of packaging. The large window gave them an unobstructed view of the entire production floor.

"Okay, let's get to work," Gregory said. "You take the desk, I'll take the file cabinets."

"The drawers are locked."

Gregory cursed under his breath. "Locked office door, locked desk, locked file cabinets. Don't tell me this guy doesn't have something to hide."

"Maybe he's not the trusting type."

But after thirty-five minutes they had found nothing to suggest Nico had embezzled money from Dassante Farms, and when Gregory tried to access the computer, attempting a half dozen possible passwords, he struck out each time and had to give up.

"Damn," he said, hitting the exit key. "He must have the stuff at the house."

"Or maybe Mario was wrong and Nico never embezzled money."

"He stole money from the army. Once a thief always a thief."

"So what do we do now?" The question she really wanted to ask was, When do we get out of here?

"We go home and regroup."

She didn't like the sound of that. "You're not thinking of searching Nico's house, are you?"

"I'm not sure yet." He was closing Nico's door when he stopped abruptly. "Did you hear that?"

Rachel froze. "Heard what?" she asked in a whisper.

He flicked off the light. "Footsteps. I think they came from Sal's office."

Rachel strained to pick up the sounds, then shook her head. "I don't hear a thing."

"Shh." As he flattened himself against the wall, one hand held protectively across her body, a shadow lunged out of Sal's office and made a run for the stairs.

"Stay here!"

Gregory took off after the intruder, his rubber soles pounding on the catwalk so hard, Rachel could feel every vibration. Before the fleeing man could reach the first step, Gregory leaped, arms extended. She heard a loud grunt as both men went down in a tangle of limbs and curses.

The struggle lasted only a few seconds. Breathing hard, Gregory flipped the man over and straddled him.

Praying he hadn't attacked a security guard or worse, a police officer, Rachel took a couple of steps forward. She heard Gregory's exclamation as he shone the light on the man's face.

"Luis!"

Thirty-Seven

Gregory pulled himself to his feet and waited for Luis to do the same. "What's going on, *amigo?* What are you doing here?"

Luis stuck his chin out. "I could ask you the same thing."

"True." Gregory's gaze fell on the folded sheet of paper the grocer clutched in his hand. "Is this something that could clear Alyssa Dassante?"

"No." In the indirect beam of the flashlight, Gregory saw him glancing uneasily at Rachel. "I heard about...your mother's arrest, Miss Spaulding. I'm sorry."

"Look, Luis," Gregory said, cutting off any possible reply from Rachel, whom he knew had a soft heart. "I want to believe you, but I'm having a hard time doing that. The other day you told me you didn't kill Mario—"

"I didn't!"

"But here you are now, coming out of Sal's office, with something in your hand you obviously don't want anyone else to see. Do you blame me for being a little suspicious?"

"I told you this has nothing to do with Mario's death."

"Does it have something to do with Sal's death?" Gregory asked quietly.

"No."

Gregory didn't know why, but he believed him. He also had a pretty good idea why Luis had come to the plant in the middle of the night, so soon after Sal's death. "Was Sal blackmailing you, Luis?"

Like a punctured balloon, Luis seemed to deflate. His shoulders sagged and his chin dropped as he looked down at the piece of paper but didn't unfold it. "You going to call the cops?"

"Not if you level with me."

Luis nodded as though he knew a confession was inevitable. "When I was seventeen," he began in a low voice, "I got into a brawl at one of the local cantinas." He paused. "I killed a man, another migrant worker. It was an accident, but instead of waiting for the police and explaining what happened, I ran to Sal. I was working for him at the time and I knew he was happy with me. I was cheap and I was fast and I kept to myself."

"What did he do?"

"He paid one of the local cops to hush up the incident."

Gregory nodded toward the paper in Luis's hand. "What's that?"

"Before he bailed me out, he made me sign a confession. He said it was for his own protection, just in case I later decided to implicate him. I told him I'd be crazy to do that, but he insisted that those were his conditions. So I wrote down everything and signed my name."

"And afterward, did he hold that confession over your head?"

"All the time. First he asked me to spy on my fellow workers. He wanted to know who was slacking off the job and who was stealing from the factory." He shrugged. "I didn't mind. I told him only what I wanted to, anyway.

"Two weeks later, a friend of mine who worked in the fields got sick. I didn't want Sal to dock him so I sneaked out of the production plant and went out to do my friend's work. Somebody must have ratted on me because a few minutes later, there is Mario, yelling at me and calling me names. Before I could do anything, he was all over me, beating me to a pulp. It took two men to pull him off.''

''I hope you went to the authorities,'' Rachel said, her voice trembling with outrage.

Luis laughed. ''No, Miss Spaulding, I didn't go to the authorities. Sal warned me that if I breathed a word of the incident to anyone, including the police, he'd give them my confession.''

''He could have gone to jail, too,'' Rachel insisted. ''For aiding and abetting.''

''I never even thought about that. I was too scared of going to prison.''

''What about that statement you made to the police after Mario's death?'' Gregory asked.

Obviously distraught, Luis looked at Rachel. ''I wasn't going to tell them anything about Mrs. Dassante, I swear, but Sal made me. He told me what to say and wouldn't let me out of his house until I had rehearsed it half a dozen times.''

Gregory heard Rachel expel a breath.

''How long did you continue to work for Sal after that?'' Gregory asked.

''Close to twenty years, until I had enough money to buy the store, but even then, he always found a way of reminding me how much I owed him. He used to come into the store and tell me he was proud of me, of the way I had turned out, but he made sure I remembered that I was where I was because of him.''

Gregory glanced toward Sal's office. ''And when you heard Sal died, you figured this was your chance to get that confession back.''

Luis nodded. ''I had a duplicate key made a long time ago, just for that reason, but I never had the guts to come and search his office. Just the thought that Sal was in that house, maybe watching, scared the hell out of me.''

"Didn't Nico know about the confession?"

"I don't think anyone knew, but tonight, I was willing to take a chance. I figured, even if Nico knew, with the note destroyed, it would be his word against mine." He glanced toward Nico's office. "I was already here when you and Miss Spaulding came in."

"So you know what we're looking for."

Luis nodded. "Did you find it?"

"No."

Luis sighed. "I wish I could help you, Mr. Shaw, but I told you the truth. I don't know anything about Nico embezzling money, honest."

Rachel extended a hand and squeezed Luis's arm. "Thank you, Luis. And don't worry about your secret. It's safe with us."

"Thank you, Miss Spaulding." Luis threw a worried look at Gregory.

Rachel gave his ribs a nudge. "Gregory?"

"The same goes for me, Luis." He made a motion with his flashlight. "And now what do you say we get the hell out of here?"

As Dassante Farms disappeared from sight, Gregory glanced at Rachel, sitting beside him in the Jaguar. "That was a nice thing you did back there," he said. "Not getting mad at Luis for lying to the police."

He saw her wipe a tear with her finger. "That poor man. I can't believe what Sal put him through all these years. What a despicable man. And to think I was almost beginning to like him."

"You've got a good heart, Spaulding. Nothing wrong with that."

She still looked worried. "What are we going to do?"

"About what?"

"Luis, of course," she said impatiently. "What he told us could help my mother, but if he admits to the police that he lied thirty-one years ago, they'll want to know why. And Luis would tell them. He's one of those people who can't tell a lie. I saw that tonight." She stared into the darkness. "I can't bear the thought of him going to prison."

"He won't have to. His earlier statement wasn't instrumental in building the case against your mother. It's just another piece of circumstantial evidence the police accumulated. Dismissing that statement wouldn't help her any. Luis is safe."

She let out a sigh of relief.

"Come here," he said when he saw her rub her eyes. He wrapped an arm around her shoulders and brought her close. "Don't think about Sal anymore. Or Luis. Or anyone else. Just close your eyes."

He smiled when she snuggled against him and made little contented sounds. Then, taking advantage of the deserted road and the silent radar detector on his dashboard, he pressed the gas pedal and sped away.

Once again, Milton had been right. After a little prying, Father Genardi, the young priest Ginnie had bumped into as she'd fled Saint Mary's church, had remembered one vital detail. There had been a few other cars parked on Petrified Forest Road the night of Sal's murder, but one in particular emerged from his memory—a dark-colored sports utility vehicle. He had barely noticed it because it was parked more than a hundred feet from the church.

Father Genardi had been returning from a parishioner's house, and in the dim light, he hadn't been able to distinguish the truck's exact color or the make, but he was certain it was an SUV. He was equally certain he'd seen some kind of rack on the roof.

"What kind of car does Nico drive?" Gregory asked Rachel when he called her a few moments later.

"I don't know. Erica drives a BMW, but I don't believe I've ever seen Nico's car. Why?"

He told her about the SUV the priest had seen the night of Sal's murder.

"I suppose I could ask Erica," Rachel offered. "But I'd be tipping her off that Nico is under some kind of suspicion."

"That's all right, I'll ask Luis to check it out for me. He's bound to have a friend or two who work at the farm."

Three hours later, Luis had come through for him. With good news. Nico Dassante owned a dark green Pathfinder—with a ski rack on top.

"Look, Mr. Shaw." Detective Bob Green slowly unwrapped a stick of gum, rolled it neatly and popped it into his mouth. "I know you're a hot-shot lawyer and you're used to having things your way," he said, chewing noisily. "But your strong-arm tactics won't work in my department." He glanced at Gregory, who was perfectly content to lean back and watch the show. "So if the two of you think you can come in here and tell me how to do my job, you're not as bright as you think you are."

Gregory glanced at his father and was surprised to see him smile. And even more surprised to see that it was having a calming effect on the policeman.

"I would never presume to tell one of Napa Valley's finest how to do his job," Milton said mildly. "But a woman's life is at stake here, Detective. And I wouldn't be doing *my* job if I didn't explore every possibility."

Before Detective Green could reply, Milton leaned forward. "Believe me, Detective, I wouldn't be bugging you right now if I thought Nico Dassante's Pathfinder was a non-issue. But the fact is, Father Genardi saw a dark-colored SUV with a roof rack parked at the end of the street the night of Sal's murder. My son and I went door to door and talked to everyone in that neighborhood. We didn't find a single person who owned a car fitting that description. But we found out that Nico owns a dark green Pathfinder equipped with a ski rack."

He leaned back in his chair. "Now, you tell me I don't have a damn good reason for wanting that Pathfinder searched for possible bloodstains."

"What motive could Nico Dassante possibly have for killing his father?" the detective asked, but Gregory could see Milton had already turned him around.

"Money. According to the Dassante family attorney, Sal was in the process of writing a new will. He was going to leave half of everything he owned, including the business, to his granddaughter, Rachel Spaulding."

"Did Nico know that?"

Milton's smile was sweet as syrup. "I don't know, Detective. Like I said, I wouldn't presume to tell you what to do, but if I were you, I'd sure as hell would want that question answered."

The two men stared at each other for a good half minute until Green finally nodded. "All right," he said. "I'll humor you and talk to the judge about a search warrant." He pointed a finger at Milton. "But don't be surprised if he turns you down. Your interpretation of probable cause and his could be two different things."

"I'll take my chances." Milton stood up and put out his hand. "Thank you, Detective. Let me know if I can do you a favor sometime."

Green had no choice but to shake the offered hand. He even managed a smile. "I'll do that."

"And you will let me know if you find any blood?"

"Unless you want to come along," Green said sarcastically, "and inspect the vehicle yourself."

An amused smile flickered in Milton's eyes. "I'll leave that part to the experts."

Gregory, who had enjoyed the little exchange immensely, waited until they were outside and out of earshot before speaking. "Good work, Dad. For a moment there, I thought Green was going to throw us out. Then he made a complete turnaround."

"Logic has that effect on people."

But it was more than that, Gregory thought admiringly. It was Milton's patience, his diplomacy, and his extensive knowledge of human behavior that had given him his advantage. Maybe someday the two of them could sit down and discuss that subject in length. Maybe.

They had reached the end of Washington Street where Milton's white Eldorado was parked. "How long do you think it'll be before the lab results come in?" Gregory asked.

Milton glanced back at the two-story stucco building. "Probably not until tomorrow. I thought about asking, but I didn't want to sound pushy."

Gregory laughed. "Perish the thought."

Milton opened his car door. "Are you going back to San Francisco?"

"I have to. Ed scheduled a meeting with a prospective client and I have to be there. After that I'll be heading back here for the Harvest Ball, but I'll have my cell phone with me, so you know how to reach me."

Milton slid behind the wheel. "Have a good time, then."

Gregory waited until the Caddy had turned the corner before heading for his Jaguar.

Annie couldn't remember ever being in a worse mood. And today of all days when she was expected to be charming while playing host to a dozen important distributors from all over the country.

With the Harvest Ball only hours away, problems were piling up, testing her at every turn. Under normal circumstances she would have been able to meet the challenge with a cool head, but not today. Her conversation with Courtney the other night had shaken her badly, but when she had tried to talk to her daughter again, Courtney had refused to come out of her room.

Sighing, Annie walked over to her bedroom window. A huge white tent had been erected on the south lawn and caterers were already setting up tables of twelve. To her left, three men were putting the last nails into a stage, while an electrician checked the sound system.

She watched the frantic pace with a disinterested eye. Her little girl, she thought, feeling emotional again. Her sweet, wonderful Courtney, the best thing that ever happened to her, in love with Ryan Cummings.

She wouldn't let it happen. She would put an end to this insane, mismatched relationship right now, then she would tell Rachel the truth, which is what she should have done in the first place.

She glanced at her watch. Three o'clock. Except for Ryan, who was working on a new blend, everyone was outside, helping out with the preparations for tonight's ball. Now was the perfect time to catch her soon-to-be-ex-lover alone.

Thirty-Eight

This time when Annie told Ryan their affair was over, there was no violent reaction on his part, no sign of shock, or even surprise. He steepled his fingers and pressed them against his mouth, his expression strangely calm, and simply waited for Annie to finish.

In spite of her earlier burst of courage, the long, intense silence that followed her announcement, and the way he kept looking at her, made her break into a cold sweat.

When he finally spoke, his voice was cool, almost detached. "I don't think you've given this decision a lot of thought, Annie."

She squared her shoulders, determined not to be intimidated. "On the contrary, Ryan, I've given it a lot of thought. I can't live like this anymore. Our relationship was meant to be fun, easy and free of stress. You've turned it into a nightmare."

Nonchalantly, he leaned back in his chair and propped his feet up on his desk. "You realize that if you leave me, I'll go to the police and tell them you asked me to kill Rachel."

"Be my guest."

He quirked a brow. "You don't care what happens to you? You don't care that you'll be tried for co-conspiracy in attempted murder? That you'll lose your job, your daughter, everything that's dear to you?"

He was so sure of himself, so certain she would cave in. She might have if it hadn't been for Courtney. "I do care, Ryan, and I'd be lying if I said I wasn't scared, but I'm more scared of what this relationship will do to me if I don't get out of it."

"You'll be disgraced, Annie. Everything you've worked for all these years will be gone. You'll rot in prison."

She could almost hear those cell doors clanging shut behind her.

"You don't think I'll do it, is that it?" He laughed. "You're underestimating me, baby. And you've underestimated my love for you."

"You don't love me, Ryan. You're obsessed with me. There's a huge difference—"

A crashing sound outside the office made them both spin around. Annie let out a cry. "What was that?"

Ryan shot out of his chair and made a run for the door, which Annie had left ajar. Ryan's clipboard, which he always left on a barrel outside his office, had fallen to the floor. The sounds of running footsteps echoed through the empty cellars, then silence. Ryan hit the door with his fist. "Damm."

Annie closed her eyes. Someone had heard them.

Gregory had almost reached Spaulding Vineyards and could already hear the orchestra playing a familiar Broadway tune when his father called him on his cell phone. He had spent enough time in the old man's company in the last few days to recognize the restrained excitement in Milton's voice.

"You sound like a man with good news," he said.

Milton chuckled. "Maybe that's because I *have* good news. Detective Green called. Nico Dassante was just taken into custody."

"What?" Gregory almost drove the Jaguar into a ditch.

"They found traces of blood on the Pathfinder's seat belt, not a lot of it but enough to get a decent sample."

"Whose blood is it?"

"They're testing it right now, but my guess is it belongs to Sal, and if it does, Nico will most likely be charged with murder one."

"What does Nico say?"

"He's screaming it's a setup. And so is his wife. She swears he was home that night, in bed."

Another protective wife, Gregory thought as he pulled up in front of the Hughes's house. "Does Ginnie know?"

"I'm going to wait for the lab report before I tell her anything."

"Good idea."

Gregory folded his phone and tucked it inside his tuxedo jacket. Then, grinning from ear to ear, he got out of the car and headed for the house.

Rachel stood in front of a full-length mirror in the Hughes's guest room, smoothed down her gown, a narrow, off-the-shoulder column of black silk, and wondered if anyone would realize she was wearing last year's dress.

With all that had happened in the past three weeks, shopping for a gown had been the last thing on her mind. Otherwise she might have tried to squeeze in a trip to Jan's boutique in Napa City where all the Spaulding women shopped.

She wasn't in a party mood, anyway. Partly because of Grams's absence this year and partly because after her and Gregory's unsuccessful search of Nico's office, Ginnie's fate seemed more uncertain than ever.

With a sigh, she turned away from the mirror and rummaged through the jewelry box she had brought from her bungalow earlier, wishing Courtney was here to advise her. Accessorizing, as her niece knew only too well, was another of her shortcomings.

"Ah," she said, pulling out a pair of small black pearls from the box. These would do just fine.

As she secured one stud to her ear, her thoughts went back to Courtney. The fact that her niece hadn't asked any more questions about Ryan was encouraging. Maybe the crush wasn't as serious as Rachel had thought, after all, in which case Courtney would probably go to the ball with Peter, her on-again off-again boyfriend. But where *was* her niece? She hadn't seen her in at least two days.

"Rachel," Tina called from behind the closed door. "Your date is here."

"Coming."

She was fastening the other stud to her earlobe when she walked into Tina's living room.

Gregory's admiring gaze moved up and down her body. "You do clean up nicely, Spaulding."

She felt a twinge of pleasure. "Thank you, Sherlock. You don't look so bad yourself." Familiar with his mood shifts, she looked at him a little more closely. "Something happened I should know about?"

"Maybe, maybe not."

She loved that playful side of him. "Tell me."

"No."

She batted her eyelashes. "What if I offered you an incentive?"

He seemed to give the thought some consideration. "What kind of incentive?"

"I don't know. I'm open to suggestions."

"How about this kind." He kissed her deeply until they heard a discreet cough behind them.

Tina, wearing a black sequined pantsuit, held a camera to her eye. "Say cheese, you two."

Rachel and Gregory smiled as Tina snapped the picture. "A little something for the grandchildren," she said with a teasing smile.

"Very good, Tina," Sam said, rolling his eyes as he approached. "Very subtle."

His wife shrugged. "Subtlety is overrated."

"Gregory has something to tell us," Rachel said, giving his arm a little shake. "And he's playing hardball."

Sam chuckled. "Better 'fess up, Gregory. Or you'll be sorry. Take it from an old married man who knows." He raised his eyebrows in rapid succession a few times.

"All right. I guess I made you guys wait long enough." Gregory looked at Rachel. "The police have arrested Nico."

Rachel's hands flew to her mouth. "They found blood in the Pathfinder?"

He nodded. "Milton is waiting for the lab results before he tells Ginnie, but chances are the blood is Sal's, and Nico will be formally charged with first-degree murder."

"When will they know?" Sam asked.

"No idea. My father will call as soon as he hears."

Rachel was in a much better mood when she and Gregory left for the ball a few minutes later.

More than four hundred people had come to attend this year's Harvest Ball, all of them dressed to the nines.

In the night sky, the stars shone bright and on the south lawn, the champagne flowed as people walked around, admiring the lavish displays of hors d'oeuvres, the exotic flower arrangements and the ice sculptures in the shape of grape clusters.

Under the white tent, the tables glowed with candlelight

and sparkling silver, and on a stage, a six-piece orchestra played Gershwin, setting the mood for this year's theme: The Best of Broadway.

Scanning the crowd, Annie tried to relax. It had been hours since she and Ryan had realized someone had overheard their conversation. She had been on pins and needles ever since, wondering who that person was and how long until he or she came forward.

One thing was certain. It wasn't Rachel. Her sister would have already read her the riot act by now. Then who? One of the cellar workers? Someone from the lab? The uncertainty was killing her. Maybe, instead of telling Rachel everything after the ball, she should do it now and get this whole nightmare over with.

She was about to take her own suggestion when she saw Courtney sitting on the edge of an oversize terra-cotta pot. Annie smiled, admiring her daughter's lovely dress, a cloud of blue chiffon that made her look like a princess.

"Courtney! Here you are."

Courtney kept her head down as Annie bent to kiss her cheek.

"What a lovely dress, darling," she said, forgetting her anxiety for a moment. "Jan told me you had bought something wonderful and she was right. You look dreamy." She laughed. "You should be out dancing instead of sitting on a flowerpot."

Courtney continued to stare into the glass in her hand. "I don't feel like dancing."

"Are you still mad at me?"

"No."

"You are, too," Annie said, stroking Courtney's hair. "You're still upset because I wouldn't let you go out with Ryan."

"No, I'm not!" Courtney's head snapped up. "So why don't you leave me alone, all right?"

"Courtney!" Annie took a step back. She had never seen Courtney acting so rude and irrational. "What in the world has gotten into you?"

"Nothing got into me." Courtney stood and started to walk away. "I just want to be left alone."

Annie quickly caught up with her. "I will not leave you alone. Something is bothering you and I want to know what it is." Then as Courtney hiccuped, Annie's gaze shot to the empty glass in her hand. "My God, have you been drinking?"

Before Courtney could deny it, Annie snatched the glass from her hand and sniffed it. "Gin." She looked crestfallen. "Oh, Courtney, how could you?"

"What's the big deal?" Courtney met Annie's gaze head-on.

"The big deal is that you're drunk." Annie slammed the glass down on a nearby table and looked around her. "Where's Peter? I'm going to tell him to take you home."

"Peter isn't here. Poor little Courtney doesn't have a date." She hiccuped again. "What about you, Mommy dearest?" she asked with a nasty snear. "Where is *your* date?"

"Courtney, for God's sake, you're making a scene."

"I don't care."

Suddenly, Courtney glanced beyond Annie's shoulder and turned pale. Puzzled, Annie followed her gaze, and had a little shock herself. Ryan stood only a few feet from her, looking fabulous in his tuxedo. With that enigmatic smile on his lips and a champagne glass in his hand, for a second he reminded her of Jay, the handsome hero in *The Great Gatsby*. But she could see that under that calculated nonchalance he, too, was all wound up.

Courtney let out a sarcastic chuckle. "Well, what do you know," she said, slurring her words a little. "Look who's here, Mom. Your lover, in all his splendor."

Feeling the blood drain from her face, Annie gripped the hors d'oeuvres table. Dear God. It was Courtney who had stood outside Ryan's office.

"Well, Mom?" Courtney said with a laugh. "Aren't you going to say something? Or give your handsome man a hug? Oh, I know, why don't you two dance? You make such a lovely couple."

Annie was aware that people had stopped talking and were looking at them with puzzled expressions. "Please, darling," Annie whispered. "Don't. Not now."

"Why? Are you afraid I'll ruin your precious party? Well, why shouldn't I?" Her tone turned brittle. "You ruined mine."

A deadly silence fell on the crowd. Someone must have signaled the band to stop playing because suddenly the music stopped. Small groups gathered together in hushed shock and watched in morbid fascination as the drama unfolded in front of their very eyes.

In her peripheral vision, Annie caught sight of Rachel and Gregory as they made their way through the crowd. Ryan, apparently recovered from the shock, quickly took Courtney's arm. "Come on, Courtney," he said between clenched teeth but loud enough for Annie to hear. "Let me take you home."

"Why?" She pulled her arm free. "So you can try to kill me, too? Like you tried to kill my aunt Rachel?"

A horrified gasp rippled through the crowd.

Annie saw Rachel stop dead in her tracks. Her face, too, had turned pale as she stared from Courtney to Ryan. "Is this true?" she asked her assistant.

"Of course it's not true," Ryan cried, outraged. "It's all

a bunch of lies. Why would I want to kill you? I love you like a sister.'' He threw a condescending look at Courtney. ''Can't you see the girl is drunk out of her mind and making all this up?''

At those words, Annie was filled with sudden rage. This was her daughter he was talking about with such contempt, her baby.

Wrapping a protective arm around Courtney's shoulders, she met her sister's angry gaze. ''Ryan is lying,'' Annie said, holding her head high. ''Courtney isn't making anything up. Everything she said is true.''

Thirty-Nine

Ryan took off like a shot, knocking down a waiter carrying a platter of salmon canapés.

Racing after him, Gregory caught him easily. "You son of a bitch," he said, grabbing the younger man's jacket and whipping him around. "You think I'm going to let you get away?" He rammed his fist into the younger man's face with enough force to send Ryan flying into the rhododendrons. He would have gone back for an encore if Sam hadn't stopped him.

"That's enough, Gregory. Let the authorities do the rest." He held up his cell phone. "I just called them. Crowley's on his way."

Gregory tugged at his jacket. "Spineless little bastard."

Sam laid a hand on his shoulder. "How do you think I feel? I'm the one who brought him to Spaulding."

Someone must have signaled the band to start playing again because the night was suddenly filled with the lively sounds of "Hello, Dolly." The few bystanders who had lingered to watch the brief struggle were coaxed away by savvy waiters offering fresh glasses of champagne. Rachel, too upset to talk, kept staring at Ryan, who chose to cower in the bushes until Crowley and two uniformed officers arrived.

"I didn't do it alone," he shouted, glaring at Annie as

one of the officers pulled him up to his feet. "That bitch over there forced me to do it."

"I did no such thing!" Annie cried. "He's lying."

"She's the one who's lying." He struggled as the officer cuffed him. "Dammit, Crowley, you've got to believe me."

Crowley gave him a shove. "Tell it to the judge."

After they were gone, Gregory gathered Rachel in his arms. She stayed there for a moment, her body trembling, her hands fisted against his chest, wondering how much more she could take.

Then, remembering Courtney, she blew out a breath and pulled away from the comfort of Gregory's arms. "I have to take Courtney to her room," she said quietly. "Then I need to talk to Annie." She looked up. "Will you stay?"

"As long as you need me."

Except for the sound of the music drifting in from outside, the house was quiet when Rachel entered the living room after putting Courtney to bed.

Annie stood in front of the fireplace where a bright fire crackled, an incongruous contrast to the somber mood inside the room.

Two sisters facing another moment of truth, Rachel thought, as she observed her sibling for a moment. When was it all going to end? How many more lives had to be destroyed and reputations tarnished before this nonsense between them could finally come to rest?

She wanted to lash out at Annie, not only for conspiring to kill her and for embarrassing Spaulding, but especially for hurting Courtney.

She couldn't bring herself to do it. Something about the way Annie held herself, shoulders hunched, touched a cord deep in Rachel's heart she couldn't ignore.

As she took a few steps farther inside the room, Annie turned her head part way, avoiding eye contact. "Is Courtney all right?"

"She's fine. She'll have one hell of a hangover in the morning, but for now, she's asleep."

"Did she say anything?"

"I wouldn't let her. I just put her to bed." Rachel came to stand beside Annie. "You, on the other hand, have some explaining to do."

"I don't even know where to start," Annie replied.

"The beginning is usually a good place."

"You won't believe me."

"Oh, I don't know. You've told me some pretty incredible tales over the years and I've often—not always, but often—given you the benefit of the doubt."

Annie turned around at last and studied Rachel as if she was seeing her for the first time. Then, moving slowly, she walked over to Grams's rocker, started to sit then changed her mind and sat in the easy chair next to it. "You take Grams's rocker," she said.

"All right." Rachel sat and waited for Annie to speak.

Annie kept her gaze on the shifting flames. "I don't expect you to understand how I could have an affair with a man fourteen years my junior, but I'll try to explain it, anyway, because…you deserve the truth."

"I appreciate that."

She took a deep breath. "I was devastated after Grams's death. I know…" she said after a quick glance in Rachel's direction. "We all were, but me especially because I felt as if my last ally had been taken from me. Grams was the one person who would stand by me no matter what, the one person who loved me in spite of all my flaws."

Though angry, Rachel had to fight the emotions that threatened to fracture her composure. Hadn't the woman learned anything in the past thirty-one years? "I love you, too, Annie. So does Courtney."

"Not like Grams. Her love was unconditional." She reached for a gold-beaded purse on the table beside her chair and took out a lacy white handkerchief. She pressed it delicately to the corner of one eye. "When she left the winery to you, I was convinced she hadn't loved me at all."

"That couldn't be further from the truth!"

"But that's how I felt—betrayed and alone."

"That's why you went to Gregory."

Annie nodded. "I thought if I uncovered a scandal in your life, I might be able to have the contents of the will reversed."

So she had lied that morning in Ambrose's office, Rachel mused. She had been plotting to take Spaulding from her all along. "Go on."

"The night of Grams's funeral, I was alone in the gazebo. It was late and I felt particularly sorry for myself. For some reason, a sixth sense, perhaps, Ryan chose that moment to stop by and see if I was all right. He found me in the gazebo, in tears."

She leaned back against the chair and stared at a portrait of Grams above the mantel. "He was wonderful—tender, understanding, comforting. We became lovers that night.

"At first our relationship was everything I expected it to be—fun, exciting and without any strings. You know how I hate strings."

It was all Rachel could do to contain a smile. "I know."

"Then all of a sudden, everything changed. Ryan's feelings for me turned from attraction to obsession. He wanted to know where I went when I wasn't with him, what I did, who I saw. He even started talking about getting married. That totally freaked me out. After four failed marriages I wasn't about to plunge into a fifth. Besides, I didn't love him.''

"Did you tell him that?"

"Not right away. I didn't want to lose him, so I told him marriage was out of the question because if you found out the two of us were involved you'd have a fit. I didn't realize until later what an awful mistake that was."

Getting up abruptly, Annie walked over to the liquor cart and poured herself a cognac. She turned, holding the bottle. "Care for one?"

Rachel shook her head. "Is that when he decided to kill me?"

"I suppose. He didn't tell me anything about it until a few days ago when I decided he was becoming far too controlling and told him the affair was over."

"How did he take it?"

"He turned into a madman. He told me about his attempts to kill you, how he had done it for us, so we could be together. When I tried to call the police, he told me he would tell them *I* had asked him to kill you so I could have Spaulding, but I didn't, Rachel. I swear to you I had no idea he would do something so crazy. I couldn't even believe it when he told me."

Believing her sister was even crazier than Ryan's actions, yet for some strange reason, Rachel did. "You should have come to me," she said. "We would have figured a way out of this mess."

Annie sighed. "I was afraid you wouldn't believe me, especially after the stunt I had pulled a while back, so I agreed to stay with him. I was too damned scared to do otherwise."

"How did Courtney find out?"

Annie took another sip of her brandy. "Three nights ago, she told me she was in love with Ryan and was going to ask him to the dance. You can imagine what that did to me. My little girl, in love with a madman. We had a terrible fight. I told her she couldn't go out with him and she stormed out of my room.''

"That must be why I haven't seen her. She was hiding."

"She was hiding from me, Rachel, not you. That's when I realized what a bad mother I had been, but before I could even try to redeem myself, I had to protect her from that maniac. And to do that, I had to break up with him and tell you and Courtney the truth.

"At three o'clock this afternoon, I went down to the cellars to talk to Ryan, never imagining that Courtney would come down a few minutes later and hear every word we said.''

Remembering the part she had played in Courtney's crush on Ryan, Rachel took her head between her hands. "I'm just as much to blame," she murmured. "I knew how she felt and I encouraged her, perhaps because she reminded me of myself at her age. I even went and asked Ryan if he had a girlfriend.''

"You always were a busybody." The remark held only a slight trace of contempt.

"And this time it backfired on me.'' Watching the flames curl around the logs, Rachel told Annie about Ryan's reaction when she had questioned him and how she had suspected her assistant was involved with a married woman. "I kept quiet, hoping Courtney would forget about him. Apparently she didn't.''

Annie gazed into her drink and said nothing.

"She's going to need you in the morning, Annie."

"Are you kidding? She'll never want to lay her eyes on me again.''

Rachel stood and walked over to Annie. With a compassion she hadn't felt in a very long time, she draped an arm around her sister's shoulders. "Courtney is an intelligent, forgiving young woman, Annie. And she loves you, whether you believe it or not. Just be honest with her, the way you were with me, and everything will be all right."

Annie's eyes were filled with tears. "What about us, Rachel? Are we going to be all right?"

Rachel smiled. "I think so. It may have taken us a while to get there, but we're finally on the right track. You agree?"

Annie nodded.

"Good." Rachel glanced at her watch. "Now, what do you say you go back to the party, do one of your famous grand entrances and tell our guests something that will satisfy their curiosity without alarming them too much."

Annie let out a dry chuckle. "Why don't you just ask me to jump out of a plane? Without a parachute?"

Rachel yanked her close. "You screw up out there," she whispered in her ear, "and I might just push you out of that plane myself."

Forty

Thanks to Annie, who had charmed the crowd with her quick wit, the ball had been a huge success. None of the VIPs present had seemed upset over the impromptu side-show. The truth was, most of them had missed it, and by the time they'd heard about it, it was old news.

On Sunday morning, as Gregory and Rachel were enjoying a lazy breakfast at the bungalow, Milton called to say the blood found in the Pathfinder was Sal's. Nico had remained in custody and the charges against Ginnie had been dropped. However, in view of her pending arrest regarding Mario's murder, she had been asked not to leave town.

Now, as a new week was beginning and Rachel prepared for work on Monday morning, she caught the last minute of a local newscast from the TV set in her kitchen. On the screen, Erica, visibly shaken, was waving the cameras away as she walked out of the Calistoga police station.

"Oh, Erica," Rachel murmured. "I completely forgot about you." Hesitating for only a second, she picked up the phone and dialed the Dassante house. At the busy signal, Rachel let out a small sigh of disappointment. Was Erica talking to someone? she wondered. Or had she taken the phone off the hook?

Rather than speculate, she yanked her London Fog rain-coat from the closet and walked out. She would stop to check briefly on Courtney, then she would drive to Winters to spend an hour or so with Erica.

Moments later, she was on the road, driving through the rain at a slow but steady speed as the wipers worked furiously to keep the Cherokee's windshield clean. A storm front had come through during the night, bringing with it torrential rains and high winds, both of which made driving hazardous and visibility difficult.

When Rachel finally reached the Winters city limits, she quickly located a McDonald's and bought two Egg McMuffins, hoping she could persuade Erica to eat something.

Because of the dark skies, the old stone house was brilliantly lit when Rachel parked the Jeep next to Erica's BMW. The McDonald's take-out bag in her hand, she opened the car door, flipped her hood over her head and ran up the half dozen steps.

All things considered, Rachel thought when Erica opened the door, she didn't look too bad, just tired.

Rachel gave her a tentative smile. "I thought you could use a little company." She shook the bag. "Hope you like Egg McMuffins."

Erica smiled, a tired little smile that betrayed her exhaustion. "I'm not hungry, but that was sweet of you, Rachel." She moved aside. "Come in before you get washed away."

She took Rachel's drenched raincoat and draped it over a chair in the foyer. "Why don't we go into the kitchen? I'll make some coffee."

Rachel followed her down the hallway and into a large gleaming kitchen. "Where is Maria?" she asked.

Erica opened the freezer of a stainless-steel refrigerator and took out a bag of coffee. "Sal's death affected her badly, so I gave her a few days off."

"I called earlier, but your line was busy." Rachel took

a seat at the kitchen table. "I thought you had taken your phone off the hook."

"I was talking to Nico's attorney."

"How is Nico?"

"Angry." She sighed. "Josh, that's his attorney, wants me to convince Nico to confess to killing Sal so he can work out a deal with the D.A."

"And you don't want to do that?"

Erica turned stricken eyes at Rachel. "How can I ask my husband to confess to a crime he didn't commit?"

"Erica," Rachel said gently. "They found blood in the Pathfinder."

"I don't care! He didn't do it." With the back of her hand, she took a swipe at a tear. "You didn't believe your mother was guilty, why shouldn't I believe the same of my husband?"

A twinge of guilt speared through Rachel. Erica had a point. "I'm sorry. I didn't mean to sound so callous."

"And I didn't mean to shout at you." She joined Rachel at the kitchen table. "My nerves are shot."

"Maybe this will help." Rachel opened the McDonald's bag and took out the egg and sausage sandwiches. "And don't worry about me. I've got thick skin." She smiled. "I've had to, growing up with Annie."

Erica slowly dragged her hands down her face. "I've been so wrapped up in my own problems, I completely forgot about yours. They arrested your assistant, didn't they? For that attempt on your life a couple of weeks ago, and two others I knew nothing about."

"I didn't tell anyone. I thought it was better that way." Rachel set one of the muffins on a paper napkin in front of Erica and picked up hers with both hands. "The good side of this little Greek melodrama is that Joe Brock, the police's prime suspect, heard about Ryan's arrest and came back home to his wife and children.''

Erica nodded absently. Rachel couldn't blame her for not being very interested. This chatter had been meant to take her mind off her problems, but apparently the ploy hadn't worked.

She was about to take a bite of her muffin when the phone rang. ''Would you like me to get that?'' she offered when her aunt didn't move.

Erica shook her head and stood. ''I'd better get it. It could be Nico.''

From the sound of the conversation, it wasn't Nico but his attorney.

''All right, Josh,'' Erica said listlessly. ''I'll meet you at the house instead. Yes, four o'clock will be fine.

''That was Nico's attorney,'' she said, returning to her chair. ''He wants to talk to me in private before we meet Nico.''

Rachel covered Erica's hand in a brief, encouraging squeeze. ''It's going to be all right, Erica.''

''I don't know, Rachel.'' She looked at her sandwich but didn't touch it. ''What am I going to do without Nico? What am I going to do with this house? The business? All the things he always took care of?''

''I'll be glad to help if you think—''

''Oh, no!'' Erica suddenly exclaimed, glancing out the window.

Rachel followed her gaze but saw nothing. ''What is it?''

''The sprinklers. They've just come on.''

Through the downpour, Rachel could barely see them.

''They come on automatically,'' Erica explained as she rose from her chair. ''I'll have to go shut them off.''

''Can I help?''

Erica shook her head. ''No. I'll just be a minute. The

controls are in the basement. Maria showed me how they worked once, so I should be all right. I'll holler if I need help.'' She motioned toward the counter. ''Coffee's ready. Help yourself.''

When she was gone, Rachel got up, filled one of the mugs Erica had set on the counter and stared into her coffee. Poor Erica. Only a week ago she had everything—a husband and a father-in-law who loved her, an active social life—and practically overnight, it had all been taken away from her.

She was sipping her coffee when the cordless phone Erica had used a moment earlier rang again. ''Erica!'' she called. ''Telephone!''

When no one answered, Rachel shrugged and picked up the receiver. ''Hello?''

''Oh, Mrs. Dassante,'' a female voice said at the other end before Rachel had a chance to correct the error. ''I was afraid you had already left for the airport. This is Charlene at United Airlines. The departure of your flight to Zurich has been changed from 1:10 p.m. to 3:15 p.m.. You'll land in Zurich at approximately two o'clock tomorrow afternoon. Have a nice trip, Mrs. Dassante, and once again, thank you for choosing United Airlines.''

Stunned, Rachel stared at the phone in her hand as the significance of what she had just heard dawned on her. Erica was leaving for Zurich. No, she wasn't just leaving, she realized, remembering Erica's telephone conversation with Nico's attorney. She was fleeing.

''Who was that?''

Rachel spun around. Erica stood in the doorway, her head tilted to the side as she waited for an answer.

''Charlene at United Airlines,'' Rachel said dully. She saw the brief flare of panic in Erica's eyes. ''Your flight to Zurich has been delayed until three-fifteen.''

"Flight to Zurich?" Erica shook her head. "She must have had the wrong number."

"She didn't. She called you Mrs. Dassante. Would you like me to call her back?" Rachel set the phone on the counter. "You're leaving the country, aren't you? You have no intention of meeting with Nico and his attorney at four o'clock. You'll be on a plane to Switzerland by then."

Erica let out a long sigh. "Oh, Rachel, you shouldn't have answered that call." She moved nonchalantly toward the kitchen counter, opened a drawer and retrieved something from it. "Now I'll have to kill you."

Forty-One

Without taking his eyes from the drenched road, Gregory turned off his cell phone and cursed softly. He had been trying to track Rachel down for the past ten minutes to no avail. She wasn't at the winery, or at the Hughes's, or at the Laperousses's. She wasn't even answering her cell phone.

He didn't like it. It wasn't like Rachel to be completely out of reach.

"I wouldn't worry, Gregory. She's probably having breakfast with one of our distributors," Sam had told Gregory. "A few of them decided to spend one more day in the valley. She could be showing them around and just forgot to call."

Sam was right, Gregory kept telling himself as he headed north. With Ryan and Nico both behind bars, Rachel was in no immediate danger. So why did he have this creepy feeling that all was not right?

On the off chance she had gone to the police station to confront Ryan, he picked up his cell phone again. "Detective Crowley, please," he said.

The detective answered within seconds, in his same abrupt manner. "Crowley."

"Detective, this is Gregory Shaw. I'm looking for Rachel Spaulding. Have you seen her?"

"Should I have?"

"I can't find her anywhere," he replied, peeved at the man's shortness. "I thought she might have stopped by to talk to Ryan Cummings."

"She didn't." He paused. "I take it you called the usual suspects."

"Yes. No one has seen her. Even her cell phone doesn't answer."

The detective's tone softened a notch. "Maybe the lady needs to be alone. She's got a lot on her plate right now."

"You don't know her like I do. If she knew she was going to be delayed, she would have called in."

Crowley sighed and Gregory could tell by that sigh that the brief moment of compassion had passed. "I can't help you. Call me if she's still missing twenty-four hours from now."

"Thanks a lot." Gregory snapped the phone shut.

He had just reached the valley's boundaries when he thought of calling Courtney. She and Rachel were as close as sisters. It was possible her niece would know something no one else knew.

From the sound of the teenager's voice, Courtney was feeling much better than she had the last time he'd seen her.

"She stopped in early this morning to see how I was doing," Courtney said. "But I assumed she was on her way to work." Her voice sounded worried when she asked, "Isn't she at the winery?"

"No."

"Oh." There was another pause, then, "Wait a minute. She did say something about checking on Erica when she was here earlier. I'm not sure if that meant by phone or in person, but I know she was concerned about her."

Finally, someone who used her brains. "Thanks, Courtney. I'll try her."

But all he got when he called the Dassantes's number was the answering machine. With the barrage of publicity Erica would be facing now that Nico was in jail, she probably wasn't answering her phone.

He turned the car around and headed for Winters.

Rachel stared in horror at the gun in Erica's hand. "Erica, please, put that gun down. You won't solve anything by—"

"Shut up." Erica's face was white but her hand was steady as she aimed the gun at Rachel's midriff. "Nico was right. You should have told your mother to go back to France. She brought you nothing but grief."

Rachel tried to affect a calm she was far from feeling. "Nico didn't kill Sal, did he?" she said more as a statement than a question. Her gaze finally managed to detach itself from the revolver and rest on Erica's face. "You did."

"Bingo." Erica smiled.

"Did you kill Mario, too?"

Erica shrugged. "I guess there's no harm in admitting it, now. You're going to die, anyway. Yes, I killed Mario."

Rachel gripped the kitchen counter behind her with both hands. "I never suspected you. How could you have been so…"

"Deceitful?" Erica gave another shrug. "I've had lots of practice. Why the look of surprise?" she asked as Rachel shot her another quick glance. "You don't think I married that big ugly ape for love, do you? I hate him almost as much as I've hated living in this mausoleum for thirty-three years."

Rachel edged back a step. "Then why did you?" Maybe if she encouraged her to talk, she would have time to come up with a plan of escape, though from the look of things, that was a very remote possibility. To one side, Erica blocked the kitchen doorway and to the other, the French doors that lead to the walnut grove were shut tight. One move in that direction and Erica would shoot her.

"Money, Rachel," Erica replied. "It's probably hard for you to understand because you've always had it, but I grew up in the slums where girls like me would do practically anything for a chance at the good life." She laughed. "And I did. I prostituted myself by marrying a man I despised, and moving into a house that gave me the creeps."

Her eyes softened. "I wouldn't have lasted a year if it hadn't been for Mario."

Rachel's brow furrowed for a moment before the truth hit her like a rock. "You were in love with Mario?"

Erica's smile turned dreamy. "I was crazy about him. He was the most gorgeous man I had ever seen. I tried to let him know how I felt in dozens of subtle ways. I might as well have flirted with a brick wall." Her eyes hardened again. "And then one day, to add insult to injury, he brought your mother home and announced he was marrying her."

Her cold gaze fastened on Rachel. "The man I loved was about to be lost to me forever because of a slut."

That remark gave Rachel another jolt. "I thought you liked Alyssa. You told me—"

"I hated her! She had everything I didn't have—beauty, charm, passion. And above all, she had Mario's love." She took a step forward, waving the gun as she spoke. "She's the one I should have killed. I might have, too, if…" Erica's gaze drifted toward the window as though she was suddenly lost in her thoughts.

Taking advantage of Erica's momentary distraction, Rachel looked desperately around her. There were no weapons within her reach, nothing she could use to defend herself.

Her purse with her cell phone was on the table and so was her coffee mug.

Erica's gaze snapped back to her. "But Mario had to be noble."

"What do you mean?"

"He told me he knew what I was up to and he was going to tell Nico. And you know what that meant, don't you?"

Rachel shook her head.

"Nico would have thrown me out of the house. I would have been left with nothing, as penniless as the day I married him.

"That's why I couldn't sleep the night your mother left," she continued. "My insomnia had nothing to do with the storm. I was trying to come up with some kind of defense, a way of making Nico believe me over his brother. That's when I heard Alyssa and Mario arguing. I went down to check it out, alone, but by the time I got there, the argument was over, Alyssa was gone and Mario was sitting on the ground, the back of his head a bloody mess."

She laughed again. "Don't look at me like that. I did what I had to do. You would have, too, if your future had been at stake."

Rachel stared at her. "What exactly *did* you do?"

"I put the son of a bitch out of his misery. He wasn't in much of a position to fight back so I grabbed him by the shoulders and banged his head on that tractor one more time, hard. He died instantly."

"You killed the man you loved?"

"He was going to destroy me! Have me thrown out of here like a dirty rag. Those were his exact words."

The coffeepot, Rachel thought. It was there, just behind her. If she could only get to it without attracting Erica's attention.... "And after killing him," she said, holding her aunt's gaze. "You went back upstairs to get Sal and Nico?"

Erica's expression turned smug. "Pretty clever, huh?"

"It's sickening. I can't believe I liked you and trusted you, while all the time you…" She shook her head. "How could you let an innocent woman be blamed for something you did? Let her be hunted down like an animal."

"It was her or me, Rachel."

"What about Sal? Why did you kill him?"

When she took another step forward, Rachel took one back. "He was going to rewrite his will, leave half of what he owned to you." She shrugged. "I didn't mind that. Half of Sal's fortune is still a lot of money. But Nico was furious. He saw that as the ultimate slap in the face and this time he wasn't going to take it. He was going to leave Dassante Farms and start his own business. He said we had enough money saved to buy a small grove somewhere."

She laughed. "Of course we would have to be frugal for a few years, give up the designer clothes, the trips to Europe, the country club membership.

"And you know what else? He expected me to help out with the business, answer the phone, take orders, keep the books."

"Would that have been so bad?"

"Yes, Rachel." Erica's voice was suddenly infused with rage. "That would have been very bad. I spent thirty-three years in this godforsaken place. You think I was going to give up what was coming to me because of an old man's sudden decision to change his will? Besides," she added, "I knew Nico didn't have it in him to succeed in business, not without his father behind him. He's too damned stupid."

"How did you know Sal was going to meet my

mother?'' As she talked, Rachel's hand crept along the counter behind her, praying Erica wouldn't notice.

"Sal told Nico about his meeting with Alyssa, but he wouldn't tell him where or when it was going to take place. So I just waited until the old man made his move, which was that very same night, and I followed him.''

The phone rang and they both jumped. Rachel's hand shot toward the cordless phone she'd used earlier, but Erica was faster. In one quick motion she snatched the receiver from the counter. "Good way to get yourself shot, Rachel.''

"You're going to shoot me, anyway." Rachel's hand began its slow search again.

"True.'' The phone rang four times and then stopped abruptly as a machine somewhere in the house picked up the call.

"Did you know Sal was going to kill my mother?''

Erica laughed. "Of course I did. That's all he thought about for thirty-one long years and nothing was going to detract him from that. Not even you," she added with a condescending look at Rachel.

"So why didn't you let him go ahead with his plan?'' Rachel asked. "Since you hated my mother so much.''

"I thought about it. I thought I'd let him kill her and then I would kill him. But if I did that, the police wouldn't have a prime suspect and their investigation might lead them to me.''

"So you set my mother up by letting her discover the body and then calling the rectory to report a disturbance.''

Erica's hand tightened on the gun. "She set herself up by agreeing to meet Sal,'' she snapped. "I merely took advantage of her stupidity.''

"Why did you drive Nico's Pathfinder?''

A look of irritation flashed in her eyes. "I hadn't meant to, but my car was in the shop for a tune-up, and that was my downfall. If I had driven the BMW, the priest might not have noticed it.''

Rachel gave a slow, mystified shake of her head. ''And you were so overwrought on TV this morning. When I saw you, sobbing as you ran to your car, it broke my heart.''

Erica smiled. ''Thank you, Rachel. I'm rather proud of that performance.''

''You're a monster. I don't know how you can look at your face in the mirror each morning, go to church every Sunday. You killed a man in a house of worship, Erica. Doesn't that mean anything to you?''

''As I said before, I did what I had to do. Survival is a formidable motivator.''

''You mean greed, don't you?''

Erica pushed the safety. ''Say your prayers, Rachel.''

Forty-Two

With a grunt of frustration, Gregory threw the cell phone onto the seat next to him. Where the hell was Erica? He had already called her house three times and all he kept getting was an answering machine.

And where was Rachel in this weather? Why wasn't she checking in with the winery? Was she out of her mind scaring him like that?

Leaning forward in his seat, he peered through the Jaguar's windshield. Although it was only 9:00 a.m., the skies were almost black from the storm and the roads slick and dangerous. This trip was probably a total waste of time, but then again, maybe Erica was home and didn't want to answer the phone. Who could blame her?

The visibility was so bad, he almost missed the sign for the Dassante Farms turnoff.

But he didn't miss Erica's black BMW parked in front of the stone house when he arrived there.

Or Rachel's red Cherokee.

Rachel knew she wouldn't get a second chance. She had to be fast and she had to be accurate.

Her fingers made contact with the glass carafe. She would have to pull the pot out, without being noticed, and throw it, all in one quick motion.

"Look, Erica," she said, hoping to distract her. "This is

silly. You can't kill me here, in this house. The police will know you did it.''

"By the time they find you, I'll be long gone."

"They'll trace you through the airline."

Erica's smile was smug. "No, they won't, because I won't be staying in Zurich. I have it all planned, Rachel." She smiled. "Just like your mother did."

"And you're going to leave all that money behind?" she asked, trying to sound incredulous.

Erica's body quivered with silent laughter. "Don't worry about me. Sal had a lot of hidden cash, money he had syphoned from the business over the years. Nico and I didn't know exactly how much until we opened Sal's safe after his death. And you know what's really funny? Years ago, Mario had suspected Nico of embezzling, when all along it was Sal who was stealing money and hiding it from the IRS."

Her eyes shone with greed. "Three million dollars, Rachel. I suppose I could have waited for Sal's will to be probated so I could collect the rest, but frankly, I'm afraid to stick around. Nico is already beginning to act peculiar, almost as if he suspects me. He hasn't said anything yet, but I can tell something's going on in his head. That's why I had to book a flight today.

"Three million is a tidy little sum. The interest alone will keep me in designer clothes for the rest of my life."

Rachel yanked the pot out and hurled it at her aunt's face.

With a scream, Erica stumbled back and went crashing into the hutch.

Rachel didn't waste a moment. Springing into action, she unlocked the French doors and ran out into the pouring rain. If she could make it to the Cherokee before—

The sound of a gunshot made her jump a foot. She had no choice now but to head for the walnut grove.

Gregory was about to ring the doorbell a second time when he heard the shot. "What the hell!" He took off toward the grove where the shot had come from and cursed himself for not having had the presence of mind to bring a gun.

Through the downpour he saw Erica, a gun in her hand, running after Rachel, who was darting in and out between the trees. He didn't stop to ask himself why or how. He just cupped his hands around his mouth and called out. "Erica, stop!"

The woman kept on running. Either she hadn't heard him or she wasn't about to be distracted.

Another shot rang out.

He heard Rachel's cry but was fairly sure it wasn't a cry of pain, even though she had suddenly disappeared from sight.

He'd never reach Erica in time to stop her from firing again. He had to do something—now.

Frantically, he looked around him. His gaze fell on a rock that lay at his feet. It was roughly the shape, if not the size, of a football. Bending to pick it up, he wrapped the fingers of his right hand around the rough surface as he would a football. Not the best fit in the world, he thought, but it would have to do.

Using the form that had served him so well during his four years at U.C.L.A., he brought his arm back, kept his eyes on the target, now standing still, and gave it all he had.

The rock hit Erica just below the shoulder. She fell like a rag doll, her legs folding underneath her.

Gregory reached her in an instant, saw that she was only

unconscious, and called Rachel's name again. "Rachel, it's me, Gregory," he shouted, trying to be heard above the raging storm. "It's all right, darling. You can come out."

She stepped from behind a tree. She was soaked through and her hair was pasted to her head, but she was unharmed. With a small cry, she took off at a dead run and collapsed into his arms, sobbing.

By the time Gregory and Rachel arrived at Spaulding Vineyards, the place was mobbed. Braving the rain, the media, along with about a hundred onlookers, had descended on the winery and were pushing and shoving for a glimpse at the two people a radio station had dubbed "Napa Valley's Mighty Duo."

Wearing loose-fitting clothes a female officer at Winters P.D. had given her, Rachel faced the glare of cameras as she held on to Gregory's arm.

Her voice was relatively calm as she told reporters what most of them already knew. Erica Dassante had been formally charged with the murders of Sal and Mario Dassante. Nico had been released, and Ginnie Laperousse was cleared of all charges.

A reporter in a back row raised his hand. "Did you suspect your aunt might be the killer when you went to see her, Miss Spaulding?"

"I'm not that brave," Rachel replied with a smile. "Or that foolish. If I had known, I wouldn't have gone there alone."

Another reporter, one Rachel knew, pointed his pen at Gregory. "Nothing wrong with your throwing arm," he commented with a grin. "Any chance you could give us a replay?" He reached into a bag at his feet and retrieved a football. "I brought the real thing with me."

Gregory laughed and shook his head. "I'm afraid my

football days are over." He took Rachel's hand. "Now if you'll excuse us..."

"One more question, please," someone else said. "Miss Spaulding?"

Rachel turned around. "Yes?"

"Are you aware that Mrs. Dassante just hired a new attorney?"

Rachel glanced at Gregory, who had stiffened. Oh, no, she thought, not Milton. "No," she said, her hand firmly wrapped around Gregory's. "I didn't know. Who is it?"

"Your former fiancé—Preston Farley."

She choked back a laugh and heard Gregory do the same. "I'm sure that's an excellent match," she deadpanned as she pulled Gregory inside.

They were all assembled around the large dining room table where Ming had just finished serving a feast that almost rivaled the one at the Harvest Ball.

Ginnie and Hubert were there, as were Tina and Sam, along with Annie and Courtney. Turning down Annie's offer of a second slice of pumpkin pie, Gregory watched her as she signaled Ming to pour more coffee.

The tension that had developed the night of the ball was gone, and it was obvious from Annie and Courtney's behavior toward each other that the situation between mother and daughter had changed considerably. It wasn't perfect, but those two were definitely headed for better days.

The big surprise of the evening, however, had been Annie herself. Shortly before dinner, she had taken Gregory aside and had apologized, quite humbly, for dragging him into her sordid plan.

He was still smiling at the thought when Ming approached him and told him he had a call.

Excusing himself, he walked into the foyer and picked up the extension. "Hello?"

"How are you, son?"

That last word brought a lump to his throat. He couldn't remember the last time Milton had called him son. "I'm fine, Dad. Glad it's all over."

"I caught that newscast at Spaulding Vineyards earlier. I half expected you to take that reporter's challenge and make that pass."

Gregory laughed. "I was never big on theatrics."

"No, you weren't." He paused. "I was wondering…"

Gregory tried not to let his hopes rise unnecessarily. "Yes?"

"A couple of my friends have challenged me to a game of pool next Sunday. How would you like to be my partner?" Before Gregory could recover from the shock, he added, "And afterward we could talk. I figure we're way overdue in that department. Is that all right with you?"

"It's just fine with me, Dad." Gregory's voice was thick with emotion.

As if he sensed the heavy moment needed a little lightening, Milton let out a chuckle. "Good. Until then, practice a little, will you? I feel like kicking ass."

It was a long time until they were alone, at the bungalow, snuggled in front of a crackling fire.

His arms wrapped around Rachel as if he would never let her go, Gregory bent his head until his lips touched her ear. "Willie called while you were making coffee. She says when you're through basking in all the fame, you'll have to come down for another visit."

Rachel laughed. "Did you tell her I'm not the basking type?"

"Yes." He was silent for a moment. "My daughter also called."

Rachel heard the contentment in his voice and pressed the back of her head against his chest. "She must be very proud of you."

"Hmm, I don't know. She seemed more interested in you than in my prowess."

Rachel bolted to a sitting position and turned to face him. "In me?"

"Uh-huh. She saw you on TV and, being Noelle, she grilled me with a thousand questions. She wanted to know how old you were, if you like teenage girls, if I was in love with you...."

Her heart was beating so fast, Rachel wondered if he heard it. Gregory had never mentioned the word love before and neither had she. She wasn't sure why. Lord knew she loved him. She had loved him since she had first laid eyes on him the night of Annie's rehearsal dinner. Through the next sixteen years and through her relationship with Preston, those feelings had remained carefully buried, and forgotten.

Until he had walked back into her life.

"What...did you say to that?" she asked, trembling.

He raised a brow. "To what?"

She slapped his hand. "To that last question, about...you loving me."

"Oh, *that* question." When she threatened to hit him again, he caught her hand. "I told her the truth," he said. "I told her I was madly, hopelessly, irrevocably in love with you."

She beamed. "Did you tell her I felt the same way about her father?"

"No. I thought I'd let you tell her that." He kissed the

tip of her nose. "So what do you say, Spaulding? Are you up to the challenge of meeting Noelle Shaw?"

She remembered that frightening first meeting with the Farleys and felt suddenly terrified. "Oh, Gregory, I don't know. What if she hates me?"

"How can she hate you? You're the most—"

"What if I do something stupid? What if I start talking too much, or too fast? What if I ramble about nothing at all and bore her to death? I do that all the time, you know. I do it when I'm nervous, or when I'm—"

He cut her off with a passionate kiss.

"Well," she said when he finally let her go. "If you put it that way…"

Grabbing him by the collar, she pulled him back for another kiss.

* * * * *

She's stolen his heart, but should she be trusted?

CANDACE CAMP

Lord Thorpe's new American business partner, Alexandra Ward, is beautiful, outspoken *and* the perfect image of a woman long thought dead. Her appearance on Thorpe's arm sends shock rippling through society, arouses hushed whispers in the night. Is she a schemer in search of a dead woman's fortune, or an innocent caught up in circumstances she doesn't understand?

Someone knows the truth, someone who doesn't want Alexandra to learn too much. Only Lord Thorpe can help her—if he can overcome his own suspicions. But even if he does, at what price?

A STOLEN HEART

"Oddball characters and misadventures are plentiful in this delightful romp, making it one of Camp's best."
—*Publishers Weekly* on *Indiscreet*

On sale mid-March 2000
wherever paperbacks are sold!

If you enjoyed what you just read,
then we've got an offer you can't resist!

Take 2 bestselling love stories FREE!

Plus get a FREE surprise gift!

Clip this page and mail it to The Best of the Best™

IN U.S.A.
3010 Walden Ave.
P.O. Box 1867
Buffalo, N.Y. 14240-1867

IN CANADA
P.O. Box 609
Fort Erie, Ontario
L2A 5X3

YES! Please send me 2 free Best of the Best™ novels and my free surprise gift. Then send me 3 brand-new novels every month, which I will receive months before they're available in stores. In the U.S.A., bill me at the bargain price of $4.24 plus 25¢ delivery per book and applicable sales tax, if any*. In Canada, bill me at the bargain price of $4.74 plus 25¢ delivery per book and applicable taxes**. That's the complete price and a savings of over 10% off the cover prices—what a great deal! I understand that accepting the 2 free books and gift places me under no obligation ever to buy any books. I can always return a shipment and cancel at any time. Even if I never buy another book from The Best of the Best™, the 2 free books and gift are mine to keep forever. So why not take us up on our invitation. You'll be glad you did!

183 MEN CNFK
383 MEN CNFL

Name _____ (PLEASE PRINT)

Address _____ Apt.#

City _____ State/Prov. _____ Zip/Postal Code

* Terms and prices subject to change without notice. Sales tax applicable in N.Y.
** Canadian residents will be charged applicable provincial taxes and GST.
  All orders subject to approval. Offer limited to one per household.
  ® are registered trademarks of Harlequin Enterprises Limited.

BOB99   ©1998 Harlequin Enterprises Limited